the First Ancestor

RANGER OF THE TITAN WILDS

BOOK TWO

J.D.L. ROSELL

This is a work of fiction. Names, characters, places, and incidents either are the product of the author's imagination or are used fictitiously. Any resemblance to actual persons, living or dead, events, or locales is entirely coincidental.

Copyright © 2023 by J.D.L. Rosell

All rights reserved.

Cover illustration © 2022 by Félix Ortiz
Cover design by Shawn T. King
Interior illustrations © 2022 & 2023 by Félix Ortiz
Book design by J.D.L. Rosell
Map by Keir Scott-Schrueder

ISBN # 978-1-952868-35-1 (hardcover with dust jacket)
ISBN # 978-1-952868-34-4 (IngramSpark paperback)
ISBN # 979-8-385545-22-3 (KDP Print paperback)
ISBN # 978-1-952868-33-7 (ebook)

Published by Rune & Requiem Press
jdlrosell.com

A NOTE ON APPENDICES

You can find appendices on the characters, creatures, and world of Ranger of the Titan Wilds located near the end of the book.

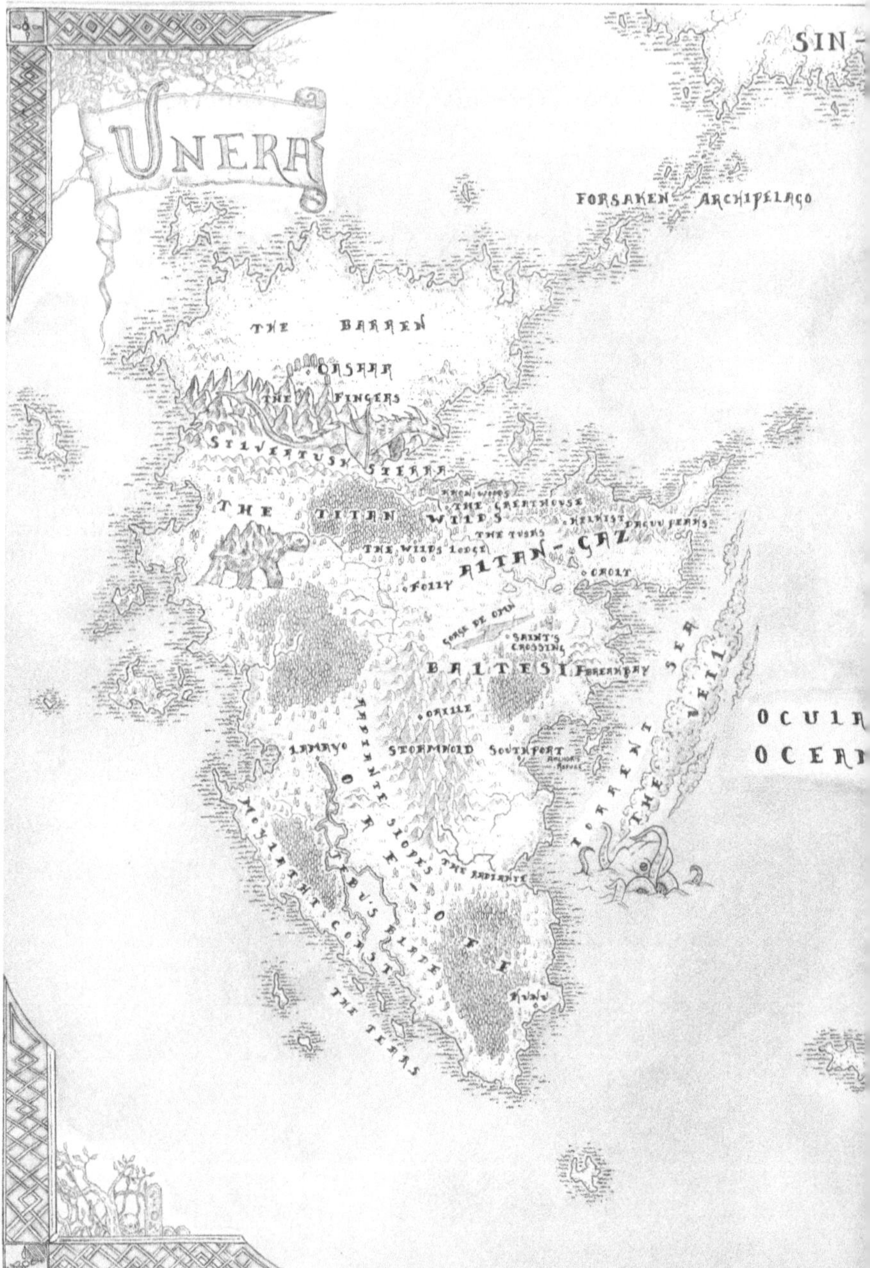

UNERA

SIN-

FORSAKEN ARCHIPELAGO

THE BARREN

ORSHAR

THE FINGERS

SILVERTUSK SIERRA

THE TITAN WILDS

IRON WILDS
THE GREATHOUSE
HELMIST
DROUU PEAKS
THE TUSKS
THE WILDS LODGE
ALTAN-GAZ
FOLLY
CROLT

GORGE DE OMN
SAINT'S CROSSING
BALTESI
BREAKBAY

ORILLE

LAMAYO
RADIANTE SLOPES
STORMHOLD
SOUTHFORT
THE RADIANTE

TORRENT SEA
THE VEIL

OCULR
OCERA

MOSIARTHI COAST
EBU'S RIDGE
THE TERAS

KEIR b.5

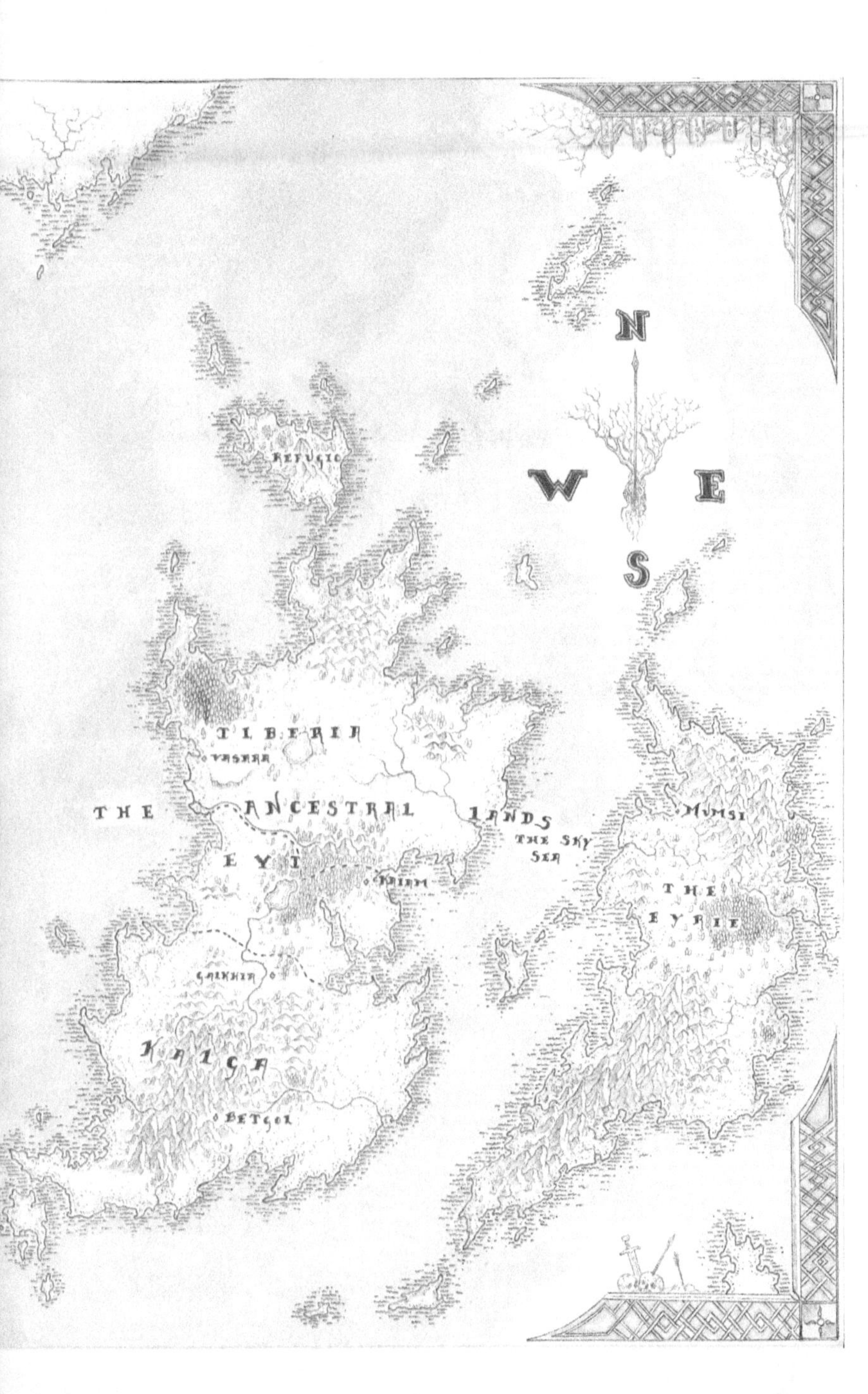
N
W
E
S
REFUGIO
TIBERIA
VASERA
THE ANCESTRAL LANDS
THE SKY SEA
MUMSI
EYI
KRIAM
THE EYRIE
GALKHIR
KAIGA
BETGOL

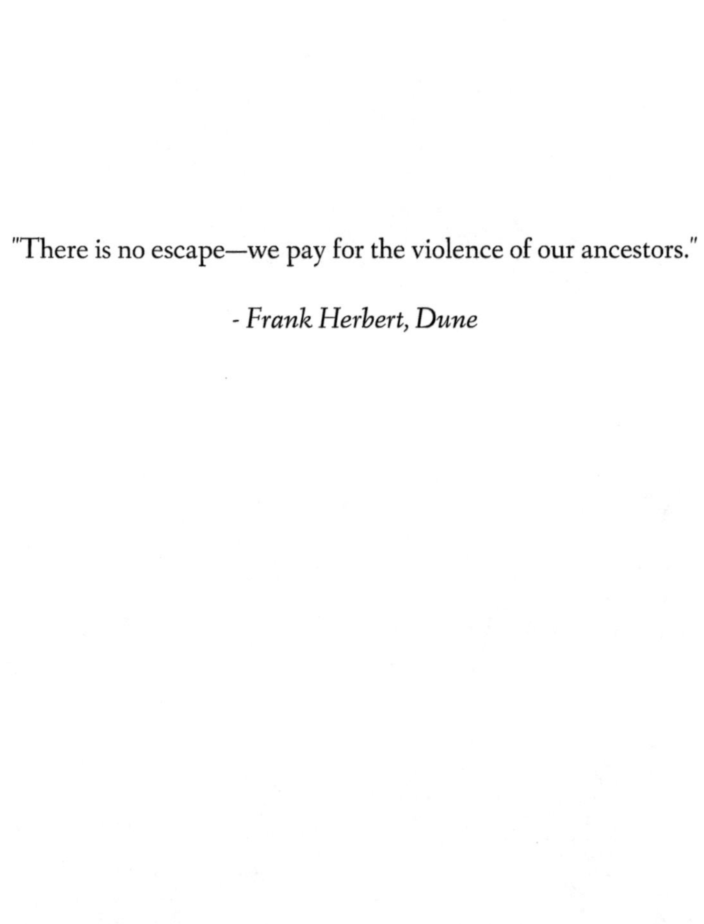

"There is no escape—we pay for the violence of our ancestors."

- Frank Herbert, Dune

PROLOGUE

Man'nah's Shadow stared into the wall of swirling dust.

Dust. What we have built. What we have let ourselves become.

He had only to look at his hands to know it. Even stone worn by time and wind would disappear. The Shadow had seen cities rise and fall, civilizations fade to memory, then legend, then carvings on cave walls. He'd become less than a story himself.

Except to a few.

He smiled, thinking of his games and his plans. In the end, amusement was all that remained. Once, he had loved and been loved in return. But like the wind across this desolation, feelings were far too fickle for a life's foundation.

He built his future on the tides of fear and power. To these, mortals moved ever predictably. By these, he would achieve his aims.

The Shadow looked now beyond the dust, to the city that lay uncounted leagues afar. Like fireflies in a field, humans flitted about the cliffs, living in houses that once belonged to an ancient people of which they knew little and cared less.

His lips curled. Amusing as mortals could be, they were too often short-sighted and dull-witted. They had no concept of the trajectory of an age. They lived at the feet of mountains, but never thought to look up.

But in his hands, time was the sharpest blade, and perspective the eye that guided it.

The Shadow looked to the ruined city behind him, back to the one who had cast his name into oblivion. Even eternity would end. No empire had yet risen that did not fall.

And perhaps, he thought, *a thousand years spent in the shadows means less than a moment in the light.*

Shaking his head, the Shadow drifted to his place at the foot of the stairs. The time had not yet come. His schemes still unfurled. But soon, at last, he would have his due.

Man'nah's Shadow reached the stairs, glanced up at his master, then faced the dust bank again. Stiffening his flesh, he set to waiting once more.

But only a little while longer.

PART I

BEYOND THE MOUNTAINS

1

PREY

As the evening light died behind the snow-capped Silvertusks, the beast finally caught up.

Leiyn raised her head to look at the incline by which it approached. She'd felt the creature at the edges of her lifesense for a league now and hoped it wouldn't come closer.

That hope soon frayed. A gentler being might have stayed away, but this one only drew nearer.

She didn't recognize the shape of its esse. Few beings burned as brightly as it did, only titans and dryvans. Whatever it was, it wouldn't easily fall.

Leiyn turned in Feral's saddle to the rider atop the draconion next to her. "We're being stalked."

Acalan followed her gaze. "From there?"

She nodded.

The Gast chieftain's dark eyes took in the lay of the land. His experience was carved into his skin, scars interwoven into the moss-green tattoos of the Tekuan tribe.

Leiyn looked with him. They were in a shallow pass, inclines to either side. Snow scattered among the stones and shrubs and mounded at the roots of the few scraggly trees capable of surviving this high into the mountains. The first snowfall had already come, a sign that autumn was on the decline. It wasn't a landscape in which prey could easily hide, nor could a predator approach unnoticed.

After several moments of observation, Acalan turned and nodded back the way they'd come. "The mating doves ought to be told."

Leiyn grimaced. "I'll do it. Keep an eye out."

It was an unnecessary request. Rare was the moment she'd caught Acalan unaware. Almost, he seemed to possess a lifesense of his own, if to a lesser degree. Still, he nodded as she turned away.

Feral bore her back toward the final two members of their company. Batu and Isla had been laughing, but they quieted as Leiyn wheeled Feral around to trot beside them. *Like I'm a thorn in their cocoon,* she thought with a wry smile.

"Leiyn," Isla greeted her. "Something wrong?"

Leiyn pretended affront. "Does something need to be wrong? Maybe I just fancied a chat with my friends."

Batu raised an eyebrow. Isla's expression echoed his skepticism, though she tried to hide it.

"What would you like to chat about, then? The weather? Seems bitter headed toward miserable, by the ache in my leg."

Leiyn only sighed. "Fine. There is something. A beast has been stalking us through the Silvertusks."

Their reactions were slow, wariness muddled by infatuation. To their credit, however, both reached for their bows within moments.

"How far?" Isla queried.

Leiyn arrowed her mahia toward the bright spot among the mountain slopes. "Half a league, maybe. Distance is always difficult to tell."

Isla nodded and followed Leiyn's line of sight. "We could try to outpace it."

"I doubt that'd work. It's kept up with us this long, and it's big, telling by its esse. Guessing it's a snow ape."

"A snow ape?" Batu frowned as he stared back. "I haven't heard of that before."

"It's a myth." Isla gave Leiyn a long-suffering look. "Even Tadeo had never seen one, only the lodgemaster before him. It could be anything, Leiyn—a thorned lion, maybe."

"I've met one of those, remember? This is different."

Isla sighed, but she nodded. Leiyn summoned a small smile, which her friend returned.

Leiyn gazed in the direction of their pursuer once more and gnawed her lip. "Nothing for it but to wait."

"And then?" Batu asked.

She only raised her eyebrows and dug her heels into Feral's flanks, eliciting whinnies of protest from the mare. By his expression, Batu knew the answer as well as she.

Whatever the hunter, they would meet it with arrows and steel—and, if necessary, magic.

⁓⁓

The beast had nearly crested the ridge to their left when Leiyn called for their party to form up.

As her companions galloped toward her, Leiyn dismounted and gave Feral a quick pat. "Be brave, old girl."

The mare stared at her as if planning mutiny, yet she stayed put as Leiyn extracted her bow.

The others followed suit, then looked to her. Even Acalan seemed content with Leiyn directing the defense, though with a watchful gaze, as if waiting for her to fail. She ignored him. She'd had enough men doubt her abilities to remain steady now.

"Batu, keep hold of our horses. Isla, Acalan, keep your bows at the ready. We'll take it down at a distance, if we can. If not, have other weapons close at hand."

Everyone nodded. Likely, the same plan had occurred to them. Yet someone had to lead, and Leiyn had never been one to follow.

Batu took the horses and led them back several paces. Though she'd chosen him for the task because of his unfailing obedience, his strength would be a boon if any tried to bolt.

From this creature's esse, bolting seemed a distinct possibility. Its spirit burned across the landscape so that she felt she should be able to see its life's glow with her eyes. But their first glimpse would come soon enough.

Leiyn and the other two lined up, Isla on her left, Acalan taking her right. Each had readied a bow and loosened the straps on their close-range weapons. Her fellow ranger bore a spear, obtained in Folly, slung with a strap over her back. The chieftain had his knife and *macua* on his belt. Her own long knives hung in their scabbards from her left hip.

No sooner had Leiyn set an arrow to her longbow than their guest appeared on the ridge.

Even across the distance, it took but a glance to know her guess had been correct: a snow ape lumbered toward them. It was large, perhaps half and again as tall as she was, though with it being hunched over, it was difficult to tell. Its coat was white and shaggy and rimed with frost, while its snout was a startling red. A patch of deep blue curled around its black eyes.

As the snow ape came closer, she detected yellowed fangs jutting from its mouth. It moved in a curious fashion, propelling itself forward on long, powerful arms, though its speed was no less for the odd stride.

Leiyn felt her shoulders tighten and consciously loosened them. The beast wouldn't die easily. They'd be lucky if their arrows penetrated its coat deep enough to be effective. Only one to an eye or the heart would put it down for good.

Her hidden sense gave graver warnings. Its lifeforce churned like a blizzard in full blush. More than a predator's determination to make the kill filled the snow ape.

Hunger. Fear.

It had been a lean hunting season, and it wouldn't survive the winter without another feast. Without killing Leiyn and her companions.

She pushed aside her guilt and lifted her bow. To either side, her friends mirrored her, knowing the stakes as well as she did.

The world, so often mired in shades of gray, had resolved into black and white.

Either they survived, or the ape would. There was no room for compromise in the Titan Wilds.

"Loose!" she called, and three bows thrummed.

2

MERCY

Their arrows whispered through the air.

Leiyn watched hers arc, judging where the arrow fell even as she reached for a second. Leiyn's and Isla's missed the mark, but Acalan's found the beast's shoulder. Even a hundred paces away, its pained roar thundered through the vale.

But the arrow didn't slow it; if anything, its stride lengthened.

Each archer began to loose at their own rhythm. Drawing, Leiyn adjusted her aim to compensate for the closing distance, then released. This one flew true, knocking against the creature's brow above its eye before ricocheting away. Isla still missed, while Acalan hit again, this time in the same arm as its injured shoulder.

Once more, they loosed, but all the while, the snow ape neared. Leiyn's stomach knotted as she drew what would be her last arrow. They'd marked it half a dozen times, yet the Wilds beast refused to fall. Even a thorned lion wasn't so resilient. Its lifeforce showed only the slightest signs of faltering.

Unless an arrow hit its eye, it would reach them. And she doubted they could survive that.

The battle thrill coursed through her veins, making her limbs tremble, yet Leiyn knew she must be steady. A shot could be thrown off even by the beat of her heart.

The others shouted around her, but she blocked them out. As she drew and took aim, the world narrowed to her and her target, coming quickly closer with every lumbering stride. The ape's malice seemed to radiate toward her as their eyes met.

She loosed.

The arrow flew, but a gust whipped up out of nowhere. Even before the missile landed, Leiyn was cursing and throwing down her bow to draw her knives.

The ape's head rocked back with a shriek.

She paused, baffled. The errant arrow hadn't hit its mark—it had hit the other eye instead.

The snow ape thrashed, shaking its head. Leiyn retreated, aware of Acalan and Isla doing the same. She gripped her knives, waiting for the beast to fall.

But it didn't. Impossibly, she felt its esse burn stubbornly on. The snow ape seemed to master its agony, for its movements slowed and its gaze leveled.

It roared as it once again charged.

"Isla!" Batu yelled from behind. Leiyn didn't turn to see why. From the beast's trajectory, it was headed toward Leiyn like it meant to repay her for the grievous wound she'd dealt it. Her knives suddenly felt little sharper than nails, her body frail as sticks.

Yet she stood her ground, even as the ape barreled toward her, and reached into her mahia. Pulling at her reserves of strength, she invigorated her muscles with a surplus of energy, then screamed in defiance.

The beast struck faster than she could hope to dodge.

Leiyn dove to one side, slashing wildly as she did, but its hand caught her ribs. Fire exploded through her as she crashed to the ground. Air was knocked from her lungs. Leiyn gasped even as she found her feet again. Without her mahia, such a blow might have killed her. As it was, she'd be lucky if she only suffered a few broken ribs.

The ape had turned from its assault, distracted by her companions. On one side, Isla stabbed at its joints with her spear, its length allowing her to remain out of reach. Acalan came in closer, the Gast chieftain a blur as he chopped with *macua* and knife at the beast's flank.

The ape was faster. It caught Acalan in the shoulder with its elbow, then spun to lunge at Isla. Before it could reach her, Isla anchored her spear against the ground, and the ape impaled itself upon it.

But still, it raged on. Isla tried moving out of reach, but the ape seized hold of her. Even then, its hands possessed the power to tear her apart.

Leiyn charged. Fear and fury crowded out her pain as she threw herself onto the snow ape's back. Her knives flashed, burying into the sides of its neck. Though the beast's movements faltered, Leiyn didn't relent.

She struck at it with weapons unseen.

Its esse leaked with encroaching death, creating an opening for her magic. She seized it, pulling its lifeforce into herself. Fire blossomed within, knitting her bones together and revitalizing her strength.

The ape sagged beneath her, but she didn't stop. Isla wasn't safe; none of her companions were. She stabbed it, again and again, searching for arteries and the spine. Hot liquid sprayed over her arms and hands, and she drank at the life spilling with them.

Abruptly, she halted. The body beneath had grown dark, its esse dissipated.

At last, the snow ape was dead.

"Leiyn."

Leiyn withdrew her knives from the blood-soaked fur and leaped off. After a fight, she usually felt dizzy and tired, but with the ape's esse filling her, she could run the night through. She practically twitched with the energy coursing through her veins and found it hard to meet Isla's eyes.

What she saw in them finally snapped her back to reality.

Leiyn looked down at herself. Blood soaked her coat, her

pants, her boots. Her gloves were saturated, her face sticky with it. Its stench hung thick in her nostrils.

As she looked up and saw Isla's worry again, she knew how it must appear. And though her fellow ranger had never condemned her magic, Leiyn always feared a day might come that it would push past even her tolerance.

She pried herself free of her roiling thoughts. "You alright?" she asked Isla, looking her up and down. Her clothes were smeared with mud, but she showed no sign of injury.

"I'm fine. Acalan, too." Her friend's expression didn't soften as her eyes flickered to the fallen ape. "You?"

Leiyn touched a hand to her side. The pain had faded to an ache. In the rush of magic, she'd once more healed herself. But her mind flitted to a different thought.

"It was starving, Isla. It wouldn't have lasted the winter." She didn't look at the slain creature, with its blood-soaked fur and mangled neck. The damage she'd done to it. "It didn't have a choice."

Her friend drew near, but she didn't reach out. Isla knew from their years together Leiyn didn't like being touched after violence.

"Neither did we," Isla murmured. "It wasn't anyone's fault, Leiyn. Just the circumstances."

Leiyn nodded, averting her gaze. It had been a majestic animal in its peculiar, harsh way. She wondered how many remained. Had she killed the last of their kind?

"Your spirit touches mine," she muttered. But just then, the Ranger's Lament rang hollow in her ears.

Leiyn shook her head, rallying herself. "I hope there's a stream nearby. I could use a wash."

Isla gave her a small smile, while Acalan answered. "A creek lies not far ahead. We can reach it before nightfall."

"That'll have to do." Leiyn glanced at the chieftain before looking away. Even Acalan's gaze was hard to meet, though the Gast had no qualms with mahia that she knew of.

Batu still stood at a distance, his hands full keeping hold of the horses. Feral in particular fought to win free of him, her head whipping back and forth, her eyes wide as she stared at the ape. Leiyn had to smile at that. As likely as not, the mare had been itching to get into the fight herself.

The former plainsrider met her eyes for a moment. She looked away first. Leiyn wondered if her friends could see beneath the blood, or if she seemed a monster to them as well.

Acalan kneeled next to the snow ape's corpse. "The pelt is salvageable. Rinse the blood, and we can leave the rest to my people. They will pass by within a day or two. The meat may be preserved by the cold. For us, we cannot afford further delay."

Leiyn swallowed her revulsion at the task, then chided herself for her weakness. How many times had she skinned a deer or hare? Yet the reawakening of her mahia seemed to have softened her in ways she hadn't anticipated.

She couldn't be soft. Not for her sake, nor for any of them. Mercy was a luxury she couldn't afford.

Leiyn touched the pouch that held Tadeo's fox figurine, then went to Feral to retrieve her waterskins. She would honor the lodgemaster's philosophy. She would do what she must.

She only wondered how deeply duty would cut this time.

3

FIRESIDE

They'd traveled for weeks to reach the Silvertusks. The journey had taken up the rest of the summer, and the aspen leaves had long turned gold. Acalan had chosen to venture ahead with Leiyn, Isla, and Batu, while the rest of his tribe trailed behind.

Irritating as Isla and Batu's romance was at times, Leiyn had begun to enjoy the easy companionship among their foursome. Their pace was quick, but not the forbidding march it had been during their journey south.

Yet with war ahead and rising around them, she could never be completely at ease.

Little trouble found them before the snow ape, yet signs of the Suncoats and their supporters abounded along the Frontier Road. Burned farmhouses. Bodies swinging from trees and crucified at crossroads. Baltesian patrols—sometimes from the Southport militia, but mostly locals protecting their own—often passed, telling tales of their encounters with their Ilberian counterparts.

Conflicts had even come to Folly's stoop. When they stopped for a couple of days in the bordertown, Mayor Itzel had told them of all the local woes. A small company of Suncoats had briefly sieged the town but had been driven away when a Baltesian company came to the fight.

"The cowards ran," Itzel grated, "but they're still out there, somewhere. My soldiers will find them; they've sworn to it."

Leiyn nodded, understanding her fervor. Tadeo, the man they'd each loved in their own way, had died at Suncoat hands. Until every last one of them was rooted out of the Tricolonies, there could be no peace in their hearts.

In Folly, she also realized her firstdawn had come and gone, leaving her twenty-six years old. It recalled to mind past celebrations at the Wilds Lodge: sugarcakes and honeywine brought up from the local villages and passed among the rangers, apprentices, and staff; Yolant's music, more raucous than ever; Isla and her clumsy dancing, Old Nathan's scowling, Gan's outrageous flirting... Even as the memories made Leiyn smile, they cut deep. At night, cloistered in her room, she ran them through her mind and let the tears flow until they dried.

But once they left Folly, Leiyn hardened her heart again. Beyond the town lay the heart of the Titan Wilds. Always dangerous in their own right, they'd only grown more so with Suncoats on the loose. And there was also the Gasts' mysterious war awaiting them, and whatever enemy lay behind it.

She was ready even before the snow ape found them in the mountains. Ready to hunt, to kill. But the rage that had fueled her had dulled. She remembered now all the blood she'd spilled and how it had only left her emptier.

She would touch her auburn tress, the legacy of her mother. Touch Tadeo's fox figurine, his final gift. Feel for Zuma's spark deep within.

She knew the cost of war. Yet the battles had only just begun.

～

They made camp that night at the base of a cliff. Sheltered from the wind and with a merrily blazing campfire, Leiyn was almost comfortable.

Yet the encounter with the snow ape had stained her, body

and soul. Its excess of lifeforce burned within, and the stink of blood lingered on her clothes, despite a thorough washing in an icy river.

She forced the thoughts away, instead focusing on their surroundings. The tundra below had looked bare to the eye before darkness fell, but her mahia felt it to be otherwise. Shrubs defied winds so cold they froze Leiyn's breath, rooting in the stony ground with stubborn glows. Marmots and pikas hid among boulder fields, invisible to all but her. When they had first arrived, their squeaking cries had sounded warning and provoked Leiyn and her party to smiles. Now, the creatures had quieted and burrowed deep within their tunnels to wait out the frigid night.

Leiyn shifted her gaze upward. She had only just begun drawing constellations when Acalan broke the silence.

"Do you know the story of Leaping Stars?"

Lowering her gaze, she saw the chieftain was looking at Batu. When the former plainsrider shook his head, Acalan frowned.

"All should know of the Night Cloud. He is not of the stars, but the gentle light between them." He pointed at the pale mist that backed a portion of the night sky. "His tale is of finding his own story, as we all must."

Leiyn held her tongue, though she wondered what had provoked this bout of loquacity. Once, she had rejected Gast stories when Tadeo tried passing them on to her and Isla. Now, she was as eager as the others to hear it, if not more so. She had come north on a promise to aid Zuma's people, after a lifetime of hatred. Learning their myths seemed one small step toward absolution.

And Saints know I have much to atone for.

Acalan puffed on his pipe for a long moment. "Leaping Stars is a curious spirit. He is often drawn to show his mischievous nature. Long ago, when he was young and newly formed, he traveled to each constellation, wondering at what stories they held. Touching upon them, Leaping Stars witnessed great deeds. He learned of my people's legends: of Chimalli of the Hill, the first to leash a *kainox*, a titan; of Ehetia of the Birch, who first brought the Many Tribes together; of Iuit of the Dam, the foremost ancestor of my tribe, whose friendship with the Copper Beaver saved us Tekuan from a great flood."

Leiyn stared at the chieftain, thoughts churning. *A copper beaver...* As Acalan raised an eyebrow at her, she looked aside. The words prodded at part of her past that seemed too private to share.

"Leaping Stars," the chieftain continued, "also entered the fables of his fellow spirits. He witnessed *Tlalli's* birthing of herself and her creation of titans and humankind. He swam through the oceans with the first fish and rode draconions before any man or woman thought to tame one. The beginnings of all things were his fireside stories, and he rested full of their threads."

"To see all that." Isla wore a small smile, her eyes bright with reflected firelight like coals catching flame.

Acalan nodded. "Every wonder upon this world, Leaping Stars visited. Every story worth knowing, and some that were not, he took as his own. Perhaps mortals such as us would have long before tired of bearing witness and never acting, but not he. His appetite is insatiable, even now. So though he knows all that has been, Leaping Stars looks eagerly upon *Tlalli*, waiting for new tales to weave into constellations. So must we all strive to be worthy of his gaze."

"A beautiful story," Isla said, and Batu echoed the sentiment. Their eyes turned to Leiyn and she shifted uncomfortably.

"It was nice," Leiyn managed. "But it seems unlikely, doesn't it? A god just sitting around, watching humans stumble through life?"

Isla shook her head in disbelief, while Acalan drew on his pipe and almost smiled. "Leaping Stars is not a god," he said, smoke leaking from between his lips. "He is not like your Omn, all-knowing and all-powerful. Beings such as he are beyond our understanding, the same as the *kainox* and other spirits. Perhaps it is the shortness of our lives that sparks his curiosity, and how much we still accomplish. What else should draw his interest?"

Leiyn shrugged. Having seen so many things she couldn't understand, how could she question his beliefs? Yet the tale seemed too large to accept as true.

The high pitch of Isla's voice betrayed her discomfort as she intervened. "Batu, tell us a Kalgan story." The young man's brow creased, and Isla laughed. "Oh, don't get tongue-tied! It's just us."

Batu sighed and huddled closer to the fire. "I can think of one, though the details..." He shook his head, but with all their gazes upon him, he soldiered on. "It's about how Kalga first came to the Veiled Lands. Do you know it?"

Leiyn shook her head with the others. It was common knowledge that the Kalgan Dominion had been the first of the Ancestral Lands to visit this half of the world, but she had never heard the particulars.

Clearing his throat, Batu began in a low voice, "For many years, ships sailed from Dominion across the western sea, wishing to see what lay on the other side. Each time, the Veil repelled them. A wall of fog reaching as high as the eye can see, it is said to be a living thing. Ships that sailed into its depths never returned, and those that came near it spoke of horrors reaching out to claim their souls. Most believed it couldn't be crossed, and some thought it shouldn't be—that demons lived on the other side, and this was the gods' protection against them."

Leiyn hid a smile. The more he spoke, the more confident Batu's words became. He wasn't as ineloquent as his timidity made him seem.

"Then came Gerel Chiru. A wisewoman of great renown, she requested the reigning Hesh Jin give her a boat so she could open a way through the Veil. The Hesh Jin was hesitant at first, but his respect for Gerel was great, so he relented to her wishes."

"Was it respect, or greed for possible riches?" Leiyn muttered, only to be shushed by Isla.

Batu smiled and continued. "Soon, the wisewoman sailed with the finest crew upon the Hesh Jin's personal ship. Reaching the Veil, Gerel commanded them to anchor before it, refusing to believe the tales warning against it. With the Hesh Jin's authority behind her, the crew obeyed. Gerel sat at the bow, legs crossed and eyes closed, and for twelve days and nights, she communed with the spirits in the mists."

Having gone half that amount of time without sustenance, Leiyn again found her protests rising. Seeing Isla's warning look, however, she stifled them.

"On the thirteenth day, the wisewoman finally rose. The captain had believed her already dead, and with the crew suffering terrible dreams each night spent near the Veil, he had been about to turn back for shore. But upon seeing Gerel not only awake, but alive and standing, he bowed before her, and all the men and women followed suit.

"Gerel paid them no heed. Facing the Veil, she raised her hands and said, 'Demons, begone! I banish you from this world! Return to the hells from which you arose!'

"At once, the spirits obeyed, and the fog parted. For the first time, a passage through the Veil formed. So it was that Kalga became the first to land upon the Veiled Lands' shores, and so was Altan Gaz established."

Batu blinked and raised his gaze from the fire, having stared at it all the while he spoke. Isla squeezed his shoulder, while Acalan frowned.

"And so began the Titan War," the chieftain said in a low rumble.

Leiyn had her own doubts about the story's truth, but she hid them behind a smile. "Still, a tale well told."

"Yes, it was," Isla added.

Batu gave Leiyn a small smile, then glanced at Isla. "And now it's your turn."

"Oh, I see. You must have your revenge." Despite her words, Isla appeared far from dismayed as she met each of their gazes. "I have one suited to this dark, chill night. Leiyn, you'll know it, but perhaps you two won't: how Legion came to be."

"Ah, Isla," Leiyn said with a grin, "but you'll scare them so they'll never sleep!"

At Acalan's quizzical look, Isla explained. "Legion was used as a story to keep children in their beds. Now, it begins with Blinding Omn's creation of Unera. If you can accept the Catedrál's version of events," she added with a glance the chieftain's way.

Acalan nodded and puffed on his pipe.

"Once, there was only Omn Almighty, and light filled every corner of existence. In Its unknowable wisdom, the First sought to create something not entirely of Itself, and so Omn retracted Itself to the orb we know as the sun. But while this act allowed room for creation, it also gave birth to darkness.

"Omn formed our world and cast Its glow upon it, gifting us with the warmth and light we need to live. Though we cannot know Its intentions, it is believed Omn sought to make Unera a place of good and bounty. But beneath the surface, darkness had established deep roots. And when Omn gifted us with life, so, too, did demons take form.

"In tunnels and caves, in shade and shadows, these devils came together, seeking to become strong enough to challenge the light above. But despite their intentions, they could never truly merge, their natures being too chaotic. Thus, they became a many-minded creature, one that hated all that could tread the light it could not. It was called Legion.

"To this day, it lives on. In the places Omn does not shine, there Legion walks. Beware dark paths, for these are Legion's ways. All who remain in the light, however, will be beyond his reach."

Leiyn had kept the cold away through a gentle burning of her esse, but now it crept back in. She wrapped her arms around herself and repressed a shiver. It was all she could do not to stare fearfully into the surrounding darkness. Even held at bay by her lifesense, she couldn't kill the instinctive fear of it. Yet it wasn't enemies conjured from the night that disturbed her. Something lingered beneath the surface of her thoughts, an uneasiness she couldn't place, that the stories had only distracted her from.

"So this is why the darkness frightens you," Acalan rumbled.

Looking up, Leiyn found him giving her a small smile. She barked a false laugh and rose. "That's right. Which is why I'm eager to hide in my bedroll."

"And just when it's her turn," Batu murmured. "Perhaps she is scared of something."

"Oh, terrified."

"Don't you want a go, Leiyn?" Among their party, Isla alone frowned.

"Another night." Leiyn gave a chagrined shrug. "Not feeling up to it just now."

"If that's how you feel..."

She looked aside, disliking to disappoint Isla, but unable to scrounge up any enthusiasm for the task. A heaviness had been growing within her since earlier that day, but now it settled in deep. She wanted nothing more than to sit alone and think.

Soon, the others had dispersed and settled down for the night. Leiyn volunteered for the first watch, partly by way of apology, partly because she doubted she could sleep. Sitting back before the banked fire, she stared into the red embers with her mind muddled, keeping watch all the while through her lifesense.

But solitude wasn't to be hers. Isla sat next to her, facing out from the fire instead of in. Willowy as she was, she still shivered beneath her bundled furs.

"You'd be warmer huddled next to Batu," Leiyn observed with a slight smile.

"I'm more worried about you." Isla's teeth chattered with every word. "Everything alright?"

Leiyn scooted closer to lend her body's warmth. "Nothing time won't mend."

"Is this about the snow ape?"

She looked over to find Isla's eye on her. "What do you mean?"

Isla stared out across the dark tundra. "After the attack, you seemed... sad, I suppose. I know you don't like killing, even creatures that would kill you. Just know you couldn't have done anything else. We fought to survive."

"I know." Her pulse quickened as she remembered the melee. Remembered sucking out the beast's life. "I don't doubt it. Though... It hurts worse than it did before, killing. Because of my mahia."

Isla extracted an arm from her wrappings to pull Leiyn into a side hug. "You'll adapt. We rangers always do."

Leiyn leaned into her for a moment before pulling away. She was about to insist that Isla return to her bedroll when a thought at the back of her mind crystallized.

"Do you still believe in the Saints? The stories of the Catedrál, of Omn and Legion—is any of it real?"

Isla was quiet for a long moment. "I don't know, really. I haven't known what to believe for most of my life." She gave her a lopsided smile. "Though having heretic parents makes you used to doubting."

Leiyn nodded. Over the years, they had spoken often of Isla's upbringing. Her parents' denunciation of the Eyin religion—and, consequently, the authority of the Empire and its Sky Queen— had been a foundational part of it. Yet their personal beliefs had entered into the conversation less often. For Leiyn's part, she'd always had doubts, but never known enough to feel convicted in them.

"In a lot of ways, though," her friend continued, "it doesn't matter if gods or spirits or demons exist. What counts is what we do with our lives, don't you think? That we're doing what we know to be good."

"Sounds about right."

Leiyn had thought solitude was what she sought, but Isla's words lifted the malaise. Perhaps she couldn't parse the truth from falsities in myth and religion, but it didn't change all she knew.

She had friends by her side and a war to win. For now, questions of faith could wait.

"Thanks," Leiyn murmured, squeezing Isla's hand through the furs. "Now, you should try to get some sleep."

"I'm going, I'm going."

Her friend rose and went to lie beside Batu. By Leiyn's life-sense, she felt the former plainsrider turn over and wrap his arms around her.

She only smiled. Their relationship, and how it naturally excluded her, no longer bothered her.

The mountains were cold and dark, but Leiyn didn't feel alone anymore.

4

WARM WELCOME

*L*eiyn hadn't known what to expect upon emerging from the other side of the Silvertusks, but it wasn't the sight that greeted her.

They were at the top of the last descent when they gained their first proper view of the Barren. They'd made good time through the rest of the Silvertusks over the next several days, though the mountains' majesty tempted them to slow. Tipped with ice and snow, the peaks towered around them, shimmering when sunlight caught them. At dawn and dusk, they glowed pink in the dying light, and the sight awakened Leiyn's smile. Unpleasant and difficult as diplomacy would likely prove to be, she was glad she could roam the range she still called her own. A ranger of the Titan Wilds didn't belong in cities and among civilization—the wilderness was her home.

The Silvertusks evoked fresh awe in her with her lifesense open. Now, she felt the fire of life, down to the smallest sparks. The ice worms in the snow, impossibly alive. The blue-tailed hawks circling overhead, and the pikas and marmots evading them among the boulders. Every resilient plant that still grew or waited across the cold tundra for spring to come again.

And underneath it all, the thrumming pulses of the titans.

Her mahia had grown more acute with use and practice. Now, she didn't have to strain to detect where a titan lay dormant. She felt them all around, slumbering in the land, water, and sky, be they lake crabs, river serpents, hill tortoises, or one of the many others. As they passed under Nesilfo, the Clouded Fang, she expected to sense the ash dragon dwelling within it, resting for another decade or so. That titan, at least, had departed, perhaps straying to the next mountain that would erupt. Still, she couldn't take a step without traveling over a stone claimed by one of the spirit beasts.

Now, she truly understood in a way she never had before: this wilderness belonged to the titans. Humans were the ants allowed to walk its surface.

There were other sensations that she understood less. As they neared the end of the mountain range, Leiyn sensed pulsations coming from either side that belonged to neither titan nor animal. Frowning, she sought it out with her mahia, but it was a long while before she set eyes upon it.

What she saw made little sense: the source was a pillar of stone. Wondering if it was simply a different kind of titan, she compelled her companions to tarry so she could stare at it a little longer. The stone was striated with black, orange, yellow, and red, scarcely matching the surrounding terrain. The pulses of mahia came at regular intervals. Stranger still, beyond the pillar on the far side of the mountains, Leiyn sensed no titans.

"It is a wardstone," was all Acalan said of it. When Leiyn pressed for more, the chieftain only shook his head and led them onward.

Knowing they shouldn't delay, Leiyn moved on with the others. As they approached the last stretch of their journey, her perplexity was smothered by the sight that appeared.

Beyond the Silvertusks lay a wasteland as desolate as she'd ever seen.

Acalan grimaced at their expressions. "It is as I said. Only death reigns here."

It could hardly be called an exaggeration. Though the land was golden and brown, wilted grasses and stubborn shrubs its primary inhabitants, there were some signs of life there. Mesas rose from the foothills of the Silvertusks, canyons yawning between, and though lakes and rivers were absent from view, Leiyn knew there must be some nearby. The Gasts had made their home here, after all.

Yet her lifesense confirmed the truth of the chieftain's words. Titans didn't slumber in the lands below; titans didn't exist there at all. Unease trembled through her as she wondered if even they feared the Gasts' enemies.

She still didn't know who or what they faced. Upon their arrival, she and Isla, as envoys of Baltesia, were obligated to send word as to what forces were necessary to secure the Gasts as allies. She'd asked Acalan about the enemy's identity on countless occasions. Each time, his answer had been the same as the first: *death.*

Yet she'd faced death before, nestled in its embrace. This was something else entirely.

"Like the Gazian plains," Batu murmured. "But even more lifeless."

"Hard to imagine anyone lives down there." Isla glanced at Acalan with a wince. Leiyn wondered if she also thought of how the Gasts and other natives had been driven to such desperation by their ancestors. She wondered if Isla also bore the guilt heavy in her heart.

If the chieftain noticed their reactions, he gave no sign of it. Leiyn shrugged at her fellow ranger, then followed Acalan down the trail.

They were nearly upon the first of the mesas when the dust cloud appeared.

Leiyn saw the danger before her lifesense could feel it. Their view extended for dozens of leagues, as high on the mountains as they were. Those approaching were positioned at the bottom of the slope and seemed to be emerging from the largest of the canyons.

"A Gast patrol?" she asked Acalan.

"Most likely."

Though it seemed welcome news, the chieftain wore a frown. Still, there was no other choice but to continue down the path. Leiyn made sure her warbow, already strung, was ready to take in hand.

The slope they descended soon leveled off, though it continued steadily downward. Leiyn trusted her mare to step true, but only so long as she kept a tight grip on the reins; a spill from Feral's back could mean a broken neck. The temperature grew milder the further they went. Though winter was nearly upon them, the far side of the Silvertusks seemed untouched by it. She wondered if it would be as warm as a summer's day when they reached the bottom.

Before long, her mahia could distinguish between the riders. There were four of them, all atop draconions. *Natives, then.* She knew little of the relations between the Gasts and other indigenous tribes, only that the Gasts were the most numerous and powerful among them. Oftentimes, colonists referred to them one and all as Gasts, though Leiyn had learned enough from Tadeo to know that to be a conflation. "The Many Tribes," the native peoples called themselves. Once, they'd united against the colonists from the Ancestral Lands, but it had been many long decades since then, and nothing promoted fractures between groups like privation. She could only hope they would be able to unify once more.

Across a span of hours, they closed the gap between them and the party below until Leiyn could make out individual silhouettes. A little longer, and they approached each other along a stretch of stony path. Leiyn, second in their caravan, reached to take up her warbow, then hesitated. Acalan still went unarmed, and a glance back showed that though Isla and Batu frowned with worry, they'd taken a similar approach. Gritting her teeth, Leiyn withdrew her hand and instead delved inward, readying her mahia, though she scarcely knew how to use it as a weapon.

The best she could do was suck the life from them, but only if she held them in her grasp.

Seek peace before war, Tadeo whispered in her mind. She hoped that, for once, she could follow his advice.

A hail came in the Gast tongue, and Acalan bellowed back a greeting. Their approach continued, slow and measured; not the approach of two friendly parties. Her hands tightened on Feral's reins, but she kept her expression impassive. Aggression had betrayed her too often in the past for her to lead with it now.

She peered at the opposing party as they stopped twenty paces short. Like themselves, they traveled single-file, so she could only observe the one leading. It was a woman, not much older than Leiyn, judging by the smoothness of her face. Her hair was shaved to stubble on either side of her head, while from the top hung many dark braids falling to her chin. Over a sleeveless tunic and fringed vest hung a turquoise stone on a leather cord, the color rich and deep as the sunlit ocean. Subtle red tattoos adorned her skin, differing from the leaf-green hue of Acalan's. A pair of spirals graced her cheeks, and three vertical lines were inked across her forehead.

The woman's esse felt even more potent than her appearance. Each person's lifeforce manifested in subtle ways entirely unique to them. Acalan's ran deep and hot and hinted of red all the way through. Batu's was banked and tinged green. Isla's expanded from her in gold, like spread arms inviting the world in.

This woman burned as hot as Acalan and expanded like Isla. Her spirit was the pure blue of water from freshly melted glaciers. She was like a rare bloom found in an unexpected place.

Leiyn had rarely beheld anything so beautiful.

The woman's dark eyes flickered over to alight on hers. Leiyn quickly looked away, cursing silently as she tried mastering her spreading flush. Perhaps she'd been too long without intimacy, or her jealousy of Isla and Batu had seeped in deeper than she realized. She didn't even know if this Gast was an ally or enemy.

The woman didn't seem to share her feelings. Her face was

carved of granite as she turned her gaze back to Acalan. After a brief silence, she spoke in the Gast tongue to him.

"Well, you returned after all, Toa Acalan Tikau. Many will be poorer for it."

"And many richer," Acalan countered. "Were you one of those to bet for or against me, Spear Teya?"

Teya. Leiyn repeated the name in her mind. She guessed "spear" to be a title for a warrior of some kind, and not just from her choice of weapon.

A sudden grin claimed Teya's face. "Don't you already know? Though you came, it was not with the army you promised. Without the outlanders, how will you claim your cherished title, *Toa'Yao?*"

There were hidden depths between these two, dynamics of which Leiyn hadn't been apprised. She stared at the back of Acalan's bald head, wondering just how much the chieftain had held back from them.

He jerked his head back. "They are rangers, Teya, and emissaries for their people. They will bring my army when they see the enemy we face."

The scout laughed, scornful. "If they have any sense, they will flee back to their stolen lands."

Leiyn found animosity replacing attraction with every word the woman spoke. Clearly, she was at odds with Acalan. Despite the rocky beginning to their relationship, Leiyn and the chieftain were friends now. Even if she scarcely understood the conflict, she knew whose side she must take.

Pressing her heels lightly into Feral's flanks, she edged forward and brought the scout's attention to her. "Baltesians are true allies," Leiyn said, speaking in the Gast tongue. "We do not run from shadows."

Teya's hard gaze turned on her, and she found it again difficult to bear. Leiyn tapped on her growing resentment and coaxed it to burn higher, searing away any fledgling feelings.

"You wish to be brave," the scout said flatly, "but only fools do not fear what we face. Leave us; return across the mountains. We do not need outlander aid in our war."

"But we do, Teya," Acalan broke in. Rare had been the moment she witnessed his implacable control breaking, but he seemed hard-pressed to keep hold of it now. "We do. The outlanders have shaman-killers. Enough of them, and perhaps we stand a chance."

Shaman-killers. Leiyn's shoulders tightened. She suspected he referenced odiosas. But surely, after his time in Baltesia, he knew them to be the bloodhounds of the World King, not the governor.

"They will not give them to you, Acalan," Teya sneered. "And even if they came, who is to say they would not kill off the last of our shamans? No, Chieftain of the Tekuan, your hope is as fruitless as ever." She seemed to think of something, for she peered around him to look at the rest of their party. "Where is Taht Zuma? And the rest of your people?"

"They follow." Acalan didn't elaborate. Leiyn's misgivings multiplied as she felt for the shaman's spark resting in her and found it. Not for the first time, she wished Zuma could offer the counsel he had in life. But whatever was left of him remained silent.

The scout's gaze burned the chieftain for a moment longer, then she jerked her head and turned her draconion, a dusky orange brute, back around.

"Come. If you've lost him, you can explain it to the Tetrad yourself."

Teya cast one last glance at Leiyn. The scout's smile only made her own scowl deepen. Then she whistled, and her fellow scouts turned back down the path, swaying with their giant lizards' steps. After a moment, Acalan whistled low to his own mount, urging it after them.

Leiyn stared hard at her companion's back, channeling her embarrassment into fresh fury. Hidden currents moved here, far deeper than Acalan had let on. She'd known he withheld information about the enemies they faced; she hadn't realized he also held back on their allies. If a common scout spoke to him in such a way, how much respect did he truly command? He was chieftain of the Jaguar tribe, but did his influence extend beyond it? Did he have the authority to make the alliance he had forged with the governor? From what she'd heard, he was beholden to this "Tetrad"—a council of chieftains, perhaps. She suspected these were the people she had to sway to their cause, not Acalan alone.

"Got our work cut out for us, old girl," Leiyn muttered into Feral's mane.

She would have confronted Acalan about it all and conferred with Isla and Batu, but the narrowness of the path confined them to single file. As soon as they reached the bottom of the slope where the path widened, Leiyn coaxed Feral into riding beside the chieftain. She pitched her voice low, her words just audible above the movements of their mounts.

"*Fesht*, Acalan—what in Legion's hells was that?"

The muscles in his face tightened, wrinkling the tattoos spiraling over his skull. After a moment, his dark eyes darted toward her.

"I will explain," he said. "But not now. First, we must reach Qasaar."

Qasaar. The Gast city beyond the mountains had been mentioned many times on their journey north, yet she still knew little of it. Her temper made her want to lash out at the mention of it again. Instead, she drew in a steadying breath.

"So you'll have us ride in blind?"

His impatience wasn't only for Teya now. "I have trusted you, Huntress. You must trust me now."

Trust a Gast. Once, she would have laughed at the suggestion. But though it annoyed her, she couldn't deny that she did trust him.

"You better have a good reason for this," she warned, then fell behind him and his black draconion. Some of the tension eased out of Feral as the giant lizard drew away. No matter how much time they spent together, the horses would never grow used to the oversized reptiles.

Leiyn fell in step beside Isla. Batu flanked her fellow ranger's other side.

"What's happening?" Isla muttered. "I can barely hear back here."

"Nothing good. Acalan wouldn't explain anything, though he says he will when we reach Qasaar."

"Hope it's not too late by then."

"We come as allies," Batu spoke up. Unlike the rangers, he seemed to accept their situation. "They won't harm us."

Leiyn looked at Isla, expecting her to share her reservations. Faith, she'd long ago learned, was a frail raft for hope. But Isla only looked over at Batu and smiled.

Leiyn set her face in stone and rode forward without another word. If she was the only one who entered the city warily, so be it. She would keep watch for them all.

Her eyes strayed to the backs of the Gast scouts, while her lifesense reached forward. Before she realized it, her mahia brushed against Teya, drawn to her lifeforce like a moth to a flame. As if she sensed it, the warrior turned and stared back with a flinty gaze.

Leiyn looked aside, wishing her cheeks didn't warm. She would watch the scout closest of all.

5

CITY OF CLIFFS

Feral approached the edge of the cliff. The mare seemed to share her rider's hesitancy. The stone crumbled into a slope and a long fall to the canyon below. Yet as the Gasts stared back at her and her companions, disdain plain on their faces, Leiyn refused to submit to fear. Setting her jaw, she led them forward.

"Qasaar," Teya announced flatly. "What do you make of it, Ranger?"

Leiyn hadn't expected much. The lands beyond the Silver-tusks were dry and foreboding, and she'd been skeptical they would hold much cause for interest.

Yet wonder touched her as she stared down at the Gast city.

Qasaar was like nothing she'd seen before. The canyon, a deep gash among the mesas, didn't hold the city; it *was* the city. Buildings carved from the ocher stone lined the sheer faces. Once, it had been meticulously and lovingly built, and signs of that grandeur remained in the elegant arches and faded colors.

The clearest sign of its ancient origins was invisible to the eyes. The buildings weren't dark to her mahia as rock should have been but felt alive like the wardstone they'd passed, or the bridge at Saints' Crossing. Wordless whispers edged into her thoughts, unsettlingly human in their feel. Leiyn was tempted to throw up her walls against them but resisted the urge. She couldn't afford to blind her lifesense now, nor did she truly wish to repress her magic anymore.

The paths to the canyon's bottom were mostly intact, but where they'd eroded, they were shored up by wooden walkways and plank bridges. Those who trod upon them seemed not to fear their haphazard roads. Up and down the canyon, Leiyn saw hundreds of people at a glance and sensed many more within the buildings. Qasaar wasn't near as large as Southport, but it was far more expansive than either Folly or Saints' Crossing. Calling it a city proved no exaggeration.

Teya's gaze lingered on Leiyn, perhaps evaluating her reaction. Leiyn ignored the scout and turned to Acalan.

"You must have found this place. Your people have only been here, what, six decades? This took centuries to build."

The chieftain's eyes flickered toward his fellow Gasts. "No. We did not carve Qasaar."

She'd hoped for answers, but once more, Acalan held back, turning toward the winding, narrow path down the canyon wall to the city below. Leiyn pretended not to see the scouts' shared amusement as they followed. She looked back at Isla and Batu, who stayed farther from the edge.

"Gasts," she muttered, to their fleeting smiles. Then she turned Feral down after the chieftain and scouts.

Her vexation was soon replaced by apprehension. The path clearly wasn't made for horses, and Feral knew it. Though wide enough for a cart, the edges had eroded enough that a misstep would cause both rider and mount to tumble to their deaths. Draconions had their claws to maintain a steady grip. Horses had no such advantage.

The whites of Feral's eyes showed as she tossed her head, backing up instead of moving forward. In the end, Leiyn had to dismount and haul at her reins. Her jaw clenched tighter at the amused look from the scouts, Teya's smarting worst of all. She cursed at Feral as she dragged the mare forward.

Despite the plodding pace, they made progress down the path, and soon it widened. Feral settled, but Leiyn kept walking, still uneasy at the great height. This high on the cliffs, only a few people milled about, but all of them watched as they approached.

The path widened further, becoming large enough that traffic could proceed in both directions. Holes appeared in the side of the cliff. These seemed roughly hewn as caves at first glance. Yet the entrances rounded into archways, and images had been carved around the openings in intricate detail. Paint in aqua, scarlet, and gold freshened up the old art. To her surprise, Leiyn found the decorations cheery and attractive. They were so unlike anything she'd seen in Southport or Orille, and not in a bad way. From the doorways issued forth scents stranger still, some less pleasant. The aroma of food both sour and spicy made her nose itch and her eyes water.

The populace was less welcoming. While most stared blankly, the children seemed amazed by the strangers. Others wore their hostility openly. More than once, Leiyn heard muttered curses and identified gestures as offensive.

Her ire flared, but she kept it locked behind a stony mask. She was an envoy of Baltesia. She could not go around challenging Gasts to honor bouts at the slightest offense, much as she might feel tempted. She wondered how it must feel to be in their place, to have three of their old enemies enter their refuge.

Sympathizing with Gasts now, are we? she mocked herself. *Tadeo would be proud.*

By reflex, Leiyn touched the pouch with the fox figurine he'd carved. A smile flitted across her lips.

Acalan and the scouts led them past one section of the cliff city, which gently sloped downward, and followed a switchback to the next. At the curves, fences had been erected, likely to stop any runaway carts or clumsy children. Down the next slope, they arrived at an opening more generous than the others. Leiyn guessed it to be a stable by the reptilian stink wafting from it.

Acalan slid off his mount, and the others followed suit. Feral danced, eyeing the cave with wide-eyed distrust. A glance inside showed the *axolto* were placed four to a gated section, all surprisingly complacent in the shared space.

Leiyn ran a hand down the mare's snout, avoiding the snap of her teeth. "Don't take it out on me," she muttered. "Wouldn't be my first choice of accommodations, either."

After stripping Feral of her saddlebags, Leiyn was almost relieved to hand the reins over to the nearest groom, a girl no older than fourteen who wore her hair in twin braids like Zuma had. The girl seemed as leery of the horse as Leiyn was around the giant lizards. She hid a smile as the girl jumped at Feral's sudden stamp.

"Good luck," Leiyn said in the Gast tongue before turning away.

Acalan, unburdened by his packs, waited for their companions. Next to him stood a man shorter and slighter than the chieftain, and with an eye that wandered with a will of its own. His tattoos were green, marking him as one of Acalan's tribesmen.

"This is Tozi," Acalan said. "He will show you to your rooms."

"And you won't?" Leiyn, already on edge, found her temper flaring.

As usual, the chieftain appeared unaffected. "I have other business. The Tetrad summons me, and I must go."

That he went running at the first call from this "Tetrad" was further proof of his lack of authority. Still, he remained their best link to an alliance. She had to trust he knew what he was doing—for the moment, at least.

"Fine," she relented.

Isla was already stepping forward, even as she trembled under the weight of her own saddlebags. "May the sky lift your spirit," she said to Tozi.

The man seemed delighted by the ritualistic greeting. "And the hills bury your fears." He switched to Ilberian. "You do not come to Qasaar unprepared. I am impressed!"

"As you too often are." Acalan crossed his arms and glanced back at Leiyn. "Wait in your rooms. I will come for you soon."

Sending us to our rooms like children. But she only gave a stiff nod. Isla was more gracious in her reply.

"Thank you, Acalan. We will be eager to meet the Tetrad ourselves."

The chieftain only gave a grunted farewell, then strode down the path.

"You will want to set those down, I am sure," Tozi said brightly. "Please, follow me. The grooms can carry your bags. We will not go far."

Leiyn glanced at Acalan's receding figure, then shook her head. "If it's not far, we'll carry our packs."

Tozi's smile faltered, but he only bobbed his head and turned down the path.

She watched Acalan descend into the valley, while they continued along the ledge. Leiyn's back soon screamed with the weight of the saddlebags, but she stubbornly kept it from showing. Isla had more trouble with that. The limp in her half-mended leg grew more pronounced, but she refused Batu each time he offered to carry her luggage. Leiyn faced forward, smiling. No matter how much her friend had changed, Isla still had a ranger's pride.

After passing several more cavernous shops, Tozi led them out from the overhanging and into the sunshine. "You may stay here. I hope you find the rooms to your liking..."

Leiyn craned back her neck to look at their accommodations. Holes were the best she could say for them; they rose three stories high and spread a dozen in each direction. Spacious, perhaps, but seeming to lack comfort.

Like sleeping in a bear's den.

Still, she'd stayed in worse. She spared their host a smile, not wishing his good humor to slip away. "They'll be fine. Good, even," she added as Tozi's brow crinkled.

Isla chuckled as she hobbled up next to her. "I believe my fellow envoy is trying to thank you, Tozi."

The Gast's grin widened. He dipped a bow before gesturing to the open doorway. "Please, allow me to show you to your chambers."

With bracing enthusiasm, Leiyn led her small company inside. She found her initial judgments too harsh, though not by much. The building seemed to have been just as carefully carved out as the rest of Qasaar, though time had worn away some of the efforts. Still, ornate murals decorated the walls, telling stories of which Leiyn could only guess. Even worn, they were beautiful to behold, and though painted in a foreign style, she found them oddly comforting.

Tozi showed them to rooms on the second floor. Isla and Batu took the first two, so Leiyn approached the third doorway. A curtain hung open before it, and there was no evidence a door had ever existed. Grimacing, Leiyn stepped inside and slumped off her bags. She hoped any activities her companions got up to wouldn't be too loud. Saints knew she'd endured enough of their antics already.

She looked around the room. More murals decorated the walls, but they were otherwise bare. A single, arched window was set into the wall facing out toward Qasaar, devoid of glass, its curtains billowing from the constant winds. Other than a chair, there was no more furniture but the bed, if it could even be called that. The cot boasted a single blanket, and when she peered under it, she was surprised to find no mattress, but only what appeared to be a solid wooden block, gray and smooth with age.

Some envoy I am, she thought with a twisted smile. Even a ranger would struggle to sleep with such scant comforts. Still, all she wanted was to lie down, close her eyes, and try to rest. But that was a dream that would have to wait until nightfall.

Repressing a sigh, Leiyn stepped back into the corridor to find Tozi standing there. He looked as if he wanted to leave but wasn't sure how to broach the subject. She smiled at him, and he looked at her as if she were a lioness and he a doe, his lazy eye wandering away.

She spoke her question. "Do you know where Acalan went?"

Tozi hesitated, then nodded. "The Tetrad meets in the Whisperspire."

"Good. Bring me there."

"Please, Envoy Leiyn, I do not think—"

"Just call me Leiyn," she interrupted. "Or 'ranger,' if you must."

Isla stepped out into the hallway then, Batu emerging behind her. "Might as well relent now," her fellow ranger advised the caretaker. "She'll get her way in the end."

The poor man looked between them, then flashed another of his long-suffering smiles. "Very well. Follow me, Envoy Isla, Envoy Batu and, ah, Ranger Leiyn—that is, if you are not too weary."

Leiyn only sighed and trailed Tozi as he led her and her companions from the old barracks.

6

WHISPERS

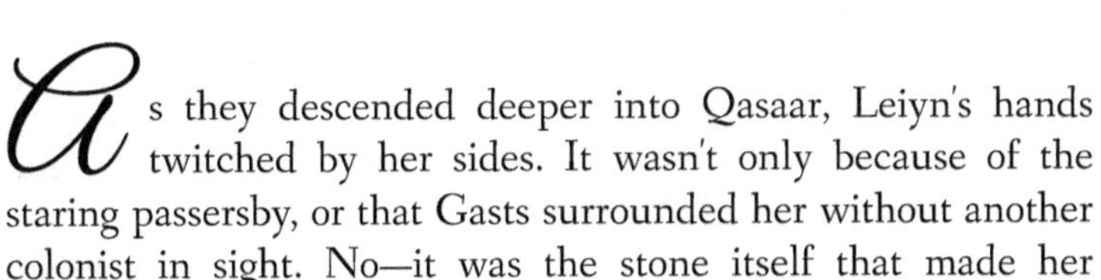

As they descended deeper into Qasaar, Leiyn's hands twitched by her sides. It wasn't only because of the staring passersby, or that Gasts surrounded her without another colonist in sight. No—it was the stone itself that made her uneasy, teasing her lifesense, muddling her mind. The mass of humanity had already made her want to retreat into her own body; the phantoms almost forced it.

She'd never been fond of cities. This one was quickly becoming her most hated of all.

She exhaled a long-held breath when Tozi finally gestured up. "There it is: the *Tepe'laka*, or the Whisperspire, in your tongue."

Little seemed to whisper about the sight. Rising from the surrounding plaza, it was the most prominent feature around. Its stone was striated in the same way as the wardstone Leiyn had glimpsed at a distance, though it didn't pulse esse as the monolith had. Still, her lifesense felt something stirring within the stone. Not quite alive, yet neither dead.

Leiyn frowned. The idea of entering was even less appealing than traveling through the city. Still, she only said, "Lead, and we'll follow."

Their guide smiled and did as she bade. Leiyn's eyes lingered on the archway as she passed beneath it, observing the carvings worn down by the years. The whispers grew louder as she stepped inside, and not in her ears. Like a multitude of tiny breezes against her lifefire, they seemed, tossing it this way and that. Her temper, thus far tightly reined in, began to fray.

She saw only one solution. Though she'd resolved not to close herself off any longer and to embrace the magic she'd once seen as a curse, Leiyn put up her mahia's walls. The murmurs dulled at once, and her lifeforce stood tall. She sucked in a deep breath, then let it out slowly.

Tozi glanced back, then away. *Wondering if I'm mad, no doubt.* She fought down a smile.

The Whisperspire only went one direction: up. There were no offshooting chambers, no landings to rest on, no windows to provide relief from the stifling heat, which amassed in the stair-well despite the chill outside. The stairs curled around and around, too narrow and high for comfortable strides.

Other voices sounded from above, and these not in her head. Leiyn braced herself as they reached the top, wiped the sweat from her brow, and stepped through the low archway.

The chamber resembled a rotunda, circular with a high, domed roof, all made of seamless stone. A brilliant fresco was painted upon it. By the depictions, Leiyn guessed the Gasts couldn't take credit for it. The style was wrong for them, far more delicate and finicky than the indigenous art she'd seen; it was more like something she'd expect in a Catedrál temple. There was an additional spark to the drawings, almost like the characters upon it might come alive at any moment. She didn't lower her mahia's walls to test the theory.

Lowering her gaze, she saw similar paintings down the walls between the many windows, open from floor to ceiling to the air outside. Though a breeze crept in, it lacked the chill Leiyn would have expected at that height.

The people in the center of the chamber drew her attention. They sat around a table, almost circular but with many straight edges like a cut gem. A faded map was brushed upon its face, though the land it portrayed was very different from the one surrounding them, green and blue instead of orange and yellow.

Three women and one man sat, most grayed and weathered with age. The other chieftains of the Tetrad, she presumed them to be. The women looked to be Gast, while the man was from a different tribe. Many tribes had gone north after the Titan War, and though Gasts made up the largest portion of them, other peoples had also forged a home here on the peripheries of Unera.

These others she distinguished by their accoutrements. When the man smiled, she quickly saw he was Uman, for only their people glued precious stones and metal to their teeth. She had heard it was done not only to signal personal power, but also because it was thought to be beneficial to one's health.

Acalan stood on the opposite end of the chamber. He'd been speaking passionately before Leiyn had entered, though she hadn't caught much of his words. As he stared at her, she found not the anger she'd expected, but heavy resignation. That, more than anything else, unsettled Leiyn.

But she hardened herself to him. She'd come north for a purpose, and she would accomplish it as soon as possible.

If only to escape this damned city.

"Who are they?" the older of the chieftainesses spoke from her seat at the table. She had a score of thin braids, all of which were decorated with thick blue beads, and a wrinkled, round face. "The outlander rangers?"

Her tone pricked at Leiyn. Before she could shoot off a biting retort, Acalan intervened.

"Yes. These were my companions for the journey north: Isla Ogbi and Leiyn of Orille, formerly rangers of Baltesia, and now its envoys."

"We're still rangers," Leiyn interrupted. "Though it's true we're presently acting as Lord Mauricio's diplomats."

Both Acalan and Isla gave her long-suffering looks, but neither contradicted her.

"So you are sent by that scrawny governor." The Uman chieftain spoke now, gold and turquoise flashing on his teeth.

Leiyn had always shot straight and true; she saw no reason to change that now. "Yes. We come to forge an alliance between our peoples, so we may face our enemies together."

Whispers and louder remarks sounded at once. Leiyn kept her face impassive, but her mind raced. If she hadn't known better, she would have thought them surprised by her pronouncement. Her gaze traveled back to Acalan, realizing just how little she knew of what she'd entered into.

Saints above, you've stepped in it now, Firebrand.

"Toa Acalan," the blue-beaded chieftainess spoke, "you have not told us everything. An alliance with the southern invaders? Are we so desperate as to rest our hopes on them?"

Invaders. Leiyn's smile slipped away. It didn't matter that she'd been born to this land, or that she knew the Titan Wilds better than any of them after so long away. She and her people would always be considered outsiders to them, and no number of years would change that.

But that topic was a hornet's nest, so she held her tongue and looked to Acalan. Maybe it was too late, but she had no choice but to follow his lead now.

His dark eyes alighted on hers and his familiar scowl appeared. "What Ranger Leiyn said, blunt though it was, is true." He swept his gaze over the gathered men and women. "They seek the alliance not for our war, but theirs. Their originland attacks its own people. The governor fears they cannot stand against them without our aid. Ilberia has their shamans, and Baltesia none."

A younger woman stood, her face a set of hard planes. A prominent red tattoo painted wings over her eyes, the white beak of a bird stretching down her nose.

"And why should we die for them? They, whose ancestors killed ours? They, who killed my grandmother and grandfather?"

Leiyn's temper was rising, but that revelation cooled it. She looked around at the gathered elders and wondered how many remembered the Titan War. *Too many, I'll warrant.* Conflict with the colonists was no event of history for them; it was a bloody memory never forgotten. Old enemies rarely were.

She wondered how they'd ever hoped to find allies in Gasts.

The others gathered were nodding and many affirmed her words. Acalan, however, remained unmoved.

"They are not the only ones at war, Toa Ilaoti," he said, the words quiet but firm. "The Devils of the Barren pick us off, one by one by one. Can we afford to fight them any longer without aid?"

Devils of the Barren. Was this the enemy the chieftain had named "death" before? She wondered what manner of being they were, beast or human.

Or something else.

The whisper-winds nudging against her mahia's walls were evidence that the likelihood existed. Dryvans, after all, walked Unera's surface; perhaps other such powerful beings, and with worse intent, also lingered in the far corners of the world.

Acalan paused, letting his words sink in before continuing.

"Leiyn is not only a ranger. She is a shaman or could be. Zuma rested his hopes on her."

"Taht Zuma." The blue-beaded woman, Zyanya, went back on the offensive. "Where has your shaman gone, Acalan?"

The others looked to Acalan. His frown deepened further still.

"Zuma did not return," he said quietly. "He fell in a battle at Southport."

His eyes flickered to Leiyn, and she suffered the damning weight of his gaze. Her thoughts went back to the old shaman, how frail he'd looked on his death bed. A hand went to her chest, as if to feel the last spark of his life that lodged there.

She stopped herself at the last moment. Now was not the time to remember.

Harden your walls, Firebrand. Keep your head on straight.

"He died saving me," she said. All the chieftains stared at her again. Leiyn met Acalan's eyes, and when he didn't speak against her, she continued. "I summoned a titan of the sea, a kraken, to strike my enemy, but I gave more of myself than I should have. Zuma... he pulled me back, but the strain proved too great."

Her eyes burned, but she blinked rapidly and drew her thoughts away from his sacrifice. She wouldn't cry. Now, she needed to be strong.

Zyanya watched her with pursed lips. It was the Uman chieftain who spoke now.

"You tell a funny tale, Ranger Leiyn! You summoned a titan, did you? What, are we to believe you to be one of your people's shamans as well as a ranger?" He looked to his peers with a grin, putting his shiny teeth on display. When he found no reciprocation, his smile slowly slipped.

"You cannot be," the younger chieftainess, Ilaoti, all but snapped. "Your people hunt shamans and kill them at birth."

Leiyn met her gaze. She was barely older than Leiyn and robust in size, curvaceous without excess. Her dress was dyed a deep scarlet to match her facial tattoos, and red jewelry dangled from her neck and ears. Leiyn suspected the color to be of importance. It couldn't be a coincidence that her tattoos matched the scout Teya's. Likely, this was the leader of Teya's tribe.

Before Leiyn could speak, Acalan intervened. "She is as she says. You would sense the strength of her magic if you had the touch, Toa Ilaoti. As Taht Xepi no doubt does."

His gaze went to the last woman in the room, and Leiyn looked at her for the first time. She had a wide face that was somewhat like a toad's: splayed cheekbones, a heavy brow, and a plate-like jaw. In contrast, her lips and eyebrows were thin and spare. Pale blue tattoos spiderwebbed across her face and into her shortly cropped hair. Her girth was generous as well beneath undyed doeskin robes. A thick necklace of bones and beads rattled with her every movement.

It was the feather-tipped staff leaning on the window behind her that alerted Leiyn to what she was as much as Acalan's address to her. Zuma had borne a similar staff. Leiyn tried not to feel uneasy as she awaited her answer.

Mother Xepi twisted her lips to one side before she spoke.

Her voice was more melodious than her appearance had led Leiyn to expect. "I do, though she tries to hide it."

Leiyn almost released her walls by a sudden guilty impulse. That had sounded like an accusation. Excuses came up, but fear swallowed them. Zuma had heard the whispers back in the ancient ruins they'd stayed in, but she wouldn't risk being thought mad before these strangers.

"I don't mean to hide from you," Leiyn said carefully. "It's an old habit that has been hard to kill."

The shaman only twisted her lips to the other side and said nothing.

"She swore an oath to Zuma," Acalan spoke into the silence. "That she would aid us. Teach her, Mother, so she might fight against our enemies. It is what he would have wanted."

Leiyn opened her mouth to speak against this, but hesitated. She had promised Zuma, true enough. But to be volunteered instead of choosing for herself... Still, though apprehension roiled inside her, she sealed her lips shut again. She was supposed to be an envoy now.

Past time I started acting like it.

"That's correct," she said aloud. "In exchange for your assistance in the coming war, I intend to provide my own." Though she had her doubts on how much that would be worth.

"Trained as a shaman?" Zyanya glared first at Acalan, then Xepi. "Surely, you cannot mean to—"

She never finished her sentence. Where nothing had been a moment before, a being stepped into the Whisperspire.

Leiyn felt the ripple of magic signaling their arrival even through her walls. As the chieftains stood, shouting in alarm, she drew the knife tucked into the small of her back and held it before her. Only then did she pause to look at the newcomer.

A dryvan?

That she was a skin-walker was immediately apparent by her appearance, too strange to be human. She had a female body, with the semblance of breasts and hips, though they were so covered in silver fur as to almost be obscured. Yet other features seemed more familiar: the taloned feet and clawed hands, the acorn quality of her skin, the green vines that acted as both hair and clothes...

"Rowan?" Leiyn blurted.

The dryvan grinned and tilted her head to one side. "Hello, Awakener. How wonderful to see you again."

"*Sach'aan*," Zyanya said sharply. "You are from south of the mountains?"

Rowan slowly looked over at her, and Leiyn hastily sheathed her knife. Something in her stare made Leiyn's skin crawl. It seemed even sharper than her teeth, which had only elongated since the last time she'd seen her.

"If I were not, your shaman would have attacked me on sight." The dryvan's head fell to the other side as she looked back to Leiyn. "And how else would she know me? Our enemies do not dare venture into my territory."

Our enemies. Leiyn narrowed her eyes as she pondered the implications in the words. *Do the dryvans and the Gasts share foes?* She couldn't see how that would be. The skin-walkers had never seemed much concerned with human affairs before Leiyn and her friends had stumbled upon them.

"What's going on, Rowan? Why are you here?"

"Rowan..." The dryvan pursed her lips, inasmuch as she had any in that woody face of hers. "I don't quite think that name suits me any longer, do you? Not with my present companion." She gestured down her body and grinned. "How about... Foxfur? Call me Foxfur, Awakener."

"Foxfur," Leiyn complied.

Rowan—or Foxfur, now—grinned wider. "Ah, yes! He likes it as well. Foxfur it is!"

Acalan looked over his fellow chieftains, his eyes full of warning. His hand had come away from his *macua's* hilt to hang limp at his side.

"*Sach'aan*," he rumbled, "you do not often visit. Why do you come now?"

Leiyn wondered at the wariness in Acalan's tone. If they

shared enemies, didn't that make them allies? Yet their interactions seemed more like those of adversaries.

Foxfur raised a gnarled hand to point at Leiyn, though her eyes remained on Acalan. "Her. There is something she must see if she is to do what she must."

See? Do what I must? Her irritation was beginning to fan into anger. Each one of these people had their own agendas for her, and she was getting damned tired of it.

"Why don't we start with a few explanations?" she said, biting off each word.

Foxfur loosed a laugh, her body trembling with it. "Words. They are always so... insufficient, do you not think? No, Awakener—I have a much more effective way of helping you learn all you must."

Before Leiyn could react, the dryvan lunged across the room and seized her arm. Leiyn tried pulling away, but her grip was as strong and implacable as a tree's roots.

"What are you—?"

She never finished the sentence. Foxfur dragged her toward a window, then flashed a sharp-toothed grin.

The dryvan stepped through and pulled Leiyn down after her.

7

DEATH'S OWN

The scream welling in Leiyn's throat died as soon as it rose.

She stumbled, barely keeping her feet. Somehow, she wasn't falling, but standing on solid ground: dry dirt and stone, orange and red in hue.

"Legion's hells," she gasped. "What is this?"

Leiyn looked around her in a daze. A moment before, she'd been falling to her death from the top of the Whisperspire. Now, she stood on cracked earth, neither the tower nor the rest of Qasaar anywhere to be seen.

Foxfur stepped into view from behind her, still wearing an infuriating grin. "Humans are always so amusing. Must the grottos make you unsettled?"

Leiyn only shook her head. "Where are we, Foxfur? Where did you take me, and for the Saints' sakes, why?"

"Time tells all, Awakener. Come. Let us leave behind that dead city for a time. And what are you closed off for? I thought I told you not to hide!"

Leiyn hastily lowered her mahia's walls before the dryvan took it upon herself to break them down, then tried to orient herself to the situation. It seemed the dryvan had taken her to that *other* place, the same existence occupied by the dryvans' home, Glade. Though there was little esse populating the world around them, what there was had an undefinable quality nonexistent in her own world, a sense of being fully and entirely alive. Almost like life's essence lay exposed here, where in Leiyn's world, it remained hidden.

"Grotto." Leiyn repeated the word, moving it about her mouth, then squinted at Foxfur, as the sun was directly behind the skin-walker. "Is that what this place is called?"

"It is one name for them." Foxfur strolled ahead, adopting the same rolling gait as she'd had before. "But you wanted answers. Come, Awakener—you will not find them there!"

The dryvan swiftly drew away, yet Leiyn hesitated and glanced back behind. With her panic subsided, she saw that Qasaar wasn't entirely gone, but lay nestled among ocher cliffs in the distance. Still, her stomach churned. Once again, she was at the mercy of the forest witch, and she found she had little appetite for it.

But what other choice do I have?

Lips twisted in a smile, Leiyn followed.

With the mesas left behind, dun stone and dusty dirt stretched before them in all directions, interrupted by streaks of gray stone and short pillars of black rock, none taller than herself. The distance was obscured, sand permeating the air like mist. *More sand.* As if she'd needed more of the blasted stuff.

Leiyn had almost caught up with Foxfur when something materialized from the haze. Its profile was tall and dark, a giant specter looming overhead. She eyed it distrustfully until it came more fully into view. It wasn't a strange, new titan as she'd feared, but a wardstone, looking much the same as the other she'd encountered. Drawing closer, she saw it rose hundreds of feet in the air, as tall as the cliffs they'd left behind. The same striped pattern as before ran down its sides: orange and red, black and gold.

The dryvan headed straight for the pillar, stopping and turning around once she reached its base. Leiyn hurried to join her. The dryvan had her head cocked to the side, though it seemed less like a bird's mannerism now that she wore a fox's skin. Ignoring her, Leiyn scanned the spire. It had a smoother surface than she'd anticipated, almost glassy. She reached to touch it, then hesitated as a pulse emanated from it, falling over her like a shimmer of water.

Leiyn repressed a shiver and took a step back. "So this is a wardstone."

The dryvan's head twisted toward her with a grin. Sharp teeth glimmered from behind her wooden lips. "So your hosts call it."

"Why does it do... that?"

The pillar had pulsed again, and a thin wash of esse brushed over her. Leiyn shuddered. Something about it wasn't warm as life should be, but cold and uninviting.

"Because it was made to."

Leiyn flashed her a look. "I mean, what does it do it for?"

"Ah! Why not ask what you mean?" The dryvan stepped forward and reached a hand to the striped stone. Her claw touched lightly along its smooth edge. "It keeps away the Vast Ones."

Leiyn stared at it with fresh awe. *Stone that turns back titans.* It explained the curious lack of them surrounding Qasaar. How valuable would these stones be to the Tricolonies? To anywhere the titans roamed? Entire towns and villages had been destroyed by idle awakenings. Breakbay, once a mighty fortress, had been trampled into ruins. If titans could be kept away, Baltesians could fully inhabit the Titan Wilds. What was more, they would no longer need to fear the Gasts who had driven the spirits beasts against their cities. Perhaps their peoples could establish a permanent peace.

Or colonists could hunt Gasts down more ruthlessly than before.

She shook her head, not wanting to think on the matter. She was free of her own prejudices, or at least strove to be, but she wasn't so naive as to believe other frontierfolk would reverse their beliefs so quickly. Only with time and hard work could that happen. Until then, she doubted the power these stones conferred would be put to good use.

Leiyn turned back to Foxfur. "How did it come to be here? And what does this have to do with the Gasts' enemies? If they're protected from titans—"

"The Vast Ones are not the enemy," the dryvan interrupted. "True, they might bring ruin if allowed near the city, but they can also be allies if trouble comes. No—these wardstones have been here long before the Gasts. Before death came to this land and claimed it for its own. They mark the borders of a long-departed civilization."

Leiyn studied Foxfur. Dryvan expressions were difficult to read at the best of times, and whatever claimed her features now was far from a simple emotion. *Regret? Sorrow? Irony?* She wondered at all she didn't know of her companion. Of her life. Of what she even was.

"Beyond the wardstones," the skin-walker continued, "awaits the true enemy. *My* enemy. Those who could break apart mortal society if even one crack appears."

Leiyn's impatience, already simmering, boiled over. "Enough! Everyone talks around these things like they're specters of death. Who are these enemies? *What* are they?"

Foxfur flashed her a smile, but her eyes burned with a different feeling. "Your haste has always been charming. Will a name suffice? We call them lyshans now. They are like my kind, and not."

She hadn't known what she expected, but it wasn't this. Cold dread robbed Leiyn of her rashness. Almost, she wished she hadn't asked.

"Like dryvans?" she echoed, hoping she'd misunderstood.

"Yes, Awakener. Just as powerful, with similar capabilities. Yet they are... corrupted." Foxfur strolled around the edge of the wardstone. Leiyn followed at her side.

"Corrupted?" She feared to know more, yet she'd never been one to balk at something unpleasant.

"Long ago, you could have called us the same, lyshans and

dryvans. We were one people. But what we do changes who we are. Those of us in Glade chose to rectify the wrongs of the past, to shed our hubris. Moths emerge from the darkness of their cocoons changed for the better, do they not? So we longed to be. But those who remained behind, these lyshans, did not see our shortcomings as errors, but a sign we had grown complacent and weak. Though our legacy has faded and all we have built has fallen to dust, still, they have tried to reclaim the world."

For the first time, Foxfur sounded as old as Eld, the tree dryvan who had healed Isla, and less like the mischievous imp she had acted like before. That unsettled Leiyn as much as her words.

"What is broken can be mended," Leiyn said. "It has to be, Foxfur. Or else all of us, humans and dryvans alike, would've died out long ago."

She thought of the Lodge as she'd last seen it, blackened and fallen to ash. Could that, too, be rebuilt?

It's not the same. It will never be the same. It couldn't be, without Tadeo to lead them.

Yet she had to believe it could return. She and Isla were the last of the rangers, but as long as even one of them remained, the Wilds Lodge would rise again.

The dryvan glanced at her, then snorted a laugh. "Mortals. The shorter your life, the greater your need for hope." She shrugged, the fur on her shoulders rippling with silver light. "We should return. They will wonder where I have taken you." A cruel smile curled her lips. "And if I have killed you."

"Would they believe that of you?" Leiyn's uneasiness returned. Gasts believed dryvans to have the capacity for malevolence. She wondered if she should consider it as well. Without knowing their reasons for aiding her and her companions, she couldn't say they were truly allies.

"They would." Foxfur strode away from the wardstone, then halted and tensed. Suddenly wary, Leiyn stretched out her senses and reached for a dagger. Her eyes saw nothing, nor did her ears detect any sound amiss, but her mahia felt something glimmering from the other side of the monolith. A presence reaching for her, inviting...

Foxfur's hand clasped her arm painfully tight, and the sensation receded.

"We go," the dryvan said. As she tugged Leiyn forward, the world rippled away.

8

CLOSED IN

Leiyn stumbled to a halt as the world steadied around her. When she gathered her bearings, she spun around, barbed words on her tongue, but there was no one to aim them at. Foxfur was gone. Even more startling, the blighted landscape had been replaced by the walls of a shadowed alley and the rank stench of urine.

She was back in Qasaar.

She'd scarcely come to terms with this when an indistinct shout brought her whirling back around. Leiyn stared at the four men sauntering toward her from either direction. Judging by their red tattoos, they were from the same tribe. The same as the younger chieftainess, Ilaoti, and the scout, Teya.

Leiyn hardened herself to her fear and tensed, readying for what would come next.

She'd encountered enough men intent on spilling blood to know their look. Reinforcing her assumption was the state of their lifeforce, all burning in their bodies. Their motivations were obvious: just as with the colonists, many of the natives had never forgotten the old grudges.

Leiyn drew her second knife and let both blades hang at her sides, as sure a warning as a hound's growl. She waited for them to near, keeping her body turned sideways so neither pair was to her back.

"So," one of the men sneered in the Gast tongue, the one approaching from the direction of what looked like a main street. His hair hung about his head in many small braids like the leaves of a willow. "The outlander has claws. But can she use them?"

"Come a little closer." She bared her teeth in a smile. "I'll show you."

The men laughed. Leiyn tensed further. Her knives rose of their own volition. The rogues had drawn weapons of their own: a hatchet and a knife on one side, two clubs on the other. Hardly warriors' weapons; these were filth that existed in the shadows. She'd met their kind in every city she'd had the misfortune of visiting. But though they might be untrained, men didn't survive long in a city's underbelly without being able to survive a scrap.

She was outnumbered and in a poor position. Negotiation was her best route now.

If only I hadn't run my mouth as usual.

"Before you do," she said, "I should warn you: your chieftain won't be happy if you harm me. Toa Ilaoti recognizes me as an envoy of Baltesia."

"Baltesia!" A second man, this one large and brutish, spat on the dirt. "That is our land, not yours!"

"Hold, you great oaf." Willowhair raised a hand and narrowed his eyes at her. "It is a bluff. All know of the envoys' arrival. A diplomat would not be so stupid as to be here, nor be so rude."

Leiyn tried for a casual shrug. "That's not what you should be concerned about. Ask yourself: is it worth risking a noose from the Whisperspire for a chance at me?"

Willowhair's lips curled. The other men muttered their discontent.

"Ignore her, Yant," Great Oaf grated. "Can't talk if she's dead."

The first man, Yant, rounded on his companion. "I won't *ignore* her. Use that thick skull of yours, Goti. If she is the envoy, think the chieftainess will let that lie? She will find out, one way or another."

"'Toa Ilaoti hates the invaders!" Goti protested. "She would not execute us for this!"

Strike now, a part of her urged. *While they fight among themselves.* But though her fists tightened over her knives' hilts, Leiyn held back. In the past, she might have acted before thinking, but she'd learned from her rashness. Killing Gasts would do her mission for Mauricio no favors. And she had no desire to have more blood on her hands. To snuff out more lifefires.

As they continued to argue, she cycled through her options. *Yell for help?* That would likely provoke them into action, and not the kind she'd like.

Try to run? But she'd have to fight free first, and that didn't seem likely to prove fruitful.

Use your magic?

She wondered how it had taken her so long to come up with it. How she could use her mahia, she scarcely knew. But at this point, it stood as good a chance of working as anything else.

Diving into her hidden sense, Leiyn reached forward with invisible hands for the esses of the quarreling men. It was the same way she had reached for her companions in the temple dungeon, the same as searching for the kraken in Southport's bay. The tips of their flames bent toward her touch, yielding to it. Almost, she could taste the power they would give her.

Power enough to overcome them? That remained to be seen.

A sudden jolt brought her back to her body. Pain flooded her skull. The Gasts had closed in around her, within arm's reach. Great Oaf had apparently shoved her into the wall, his arm still raised, a cruel smile on his lips.

"She has the blessing," Willowhair said softly. "Good thing she doesn't know how to use it."

"I do," Leiyn said, but the words came out thick. Her mind was muddled, her tongue clumsy. Silently, she cursed herself as she thought of a way out of this. She had been a fool to believe she could wield her mahia as Zuma had, to confound the senses of men who stared directly at him.

Now, her rashness might have gotten her killed.

The rogues raised their weapons, sharp tips pointing at her. "Now, Yant," Great Oaf breathed. "We do her in now."

Leiyn heaved in a breath and held up her knives. "Don't even think about trying—"

She barely noticed the other person's approach before they struck.

Willowhair went down howling, clutching at his leg even as he spun toward his assailant. Great Oaf was quicker on the uptake, but he'd no sooner raised his club before he went still. Leiyn saw the reason a moment later: the tip of a spear nudged against the bruised skin just below his left eye.

"Do not try me, Goti," the scout Teya said. "All of you will leave her be."

"Dead ancestors, we will!" Willowhair, who had suffered a hit from the newcomer to the leg, sprang back to his feet, though he favored his injured leg. "You don't command us, *egreshti* bitch!"

The scout stared down the man, no hesitation in her eyes.

"I do not," Teya said calmly. "But I can have each one of you strung up for assaulting a Baltesian envoy."

Leiyn watched the truth settle into the men. Their eyes flickered toward Leiyn, then back to Teya. Great Oaf grimaced, and Willowhair backed away, hands raised.

"Only scared her a bit, that's all," he muttered. "Shouldn't be here, besides. We were warning her off."

"Of course you were." With a grim smile, the scout lifted her spear from the bigger man's eye. He swiftly followed his companion, though not without a surly grunt. The last two, who had remained silent throughout the affair, kept their peace a little longer as they sidled around Leiyn and her protector and followed their comrades out of the alley.

Only once they'd gone did the scout turn back. With Teya's expression blank, Leiyn struggled to guess at her thoughts.

"Thank you," she offered, trying to sound sincere despite the woman's earlier hostility.

Teya snorted a laugh and turned away. "Come. I will walk

you back to your room, since you cannot be trusted to go on your own."

Without waiting for a reply, the scout turned and walked away, her spear thudding on the ground with each step.

Leiyn bristled, but there was nothing for it. With a final glance behind, she followed the scout out into the street.

9

CHALLENGE

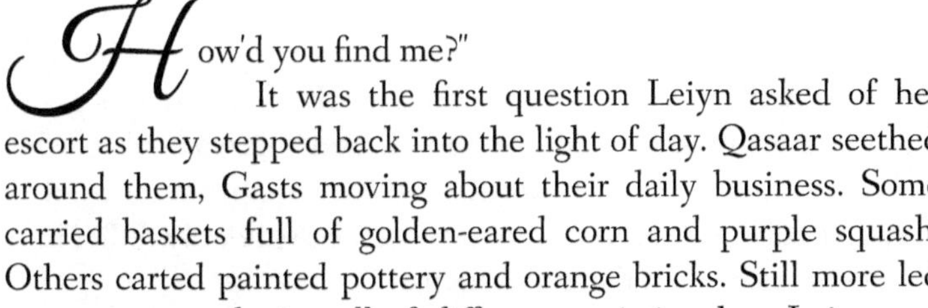

*H*ow'd you find me?"

It was the first question Leiyn asked of her escort as they stepped back into the light of day. Qasaar seethed around them, Gasts moving about their daily business. Some carried baskets full of golden-eared corn and purple squash. Others carted painted pottery and orange bricks. Still more led oxen, goats, and pigs, all of different varieties than Leiyn was used to, along the uneven cobblestones. The cliff-carved dwellings rose in layer after layer around them, like she stood at the bottom of a vast quarry.

After the incident in the alley, whatever charm Qasaar had had was lost. She needed answers, and unpleasant as Teya was, the scout was her best chance for them.

Teya glanced over at her, not bothering to hide her amusement. "We were searching for you. Apparently, you disappeared out the window of the Whisperspire with a *sach'aan* and needed fetching. And saving, it seems."

"I could have handled it." Even as the words left her mouth, Leiyn wished she could take them back. It was a foolish boast, and both of them knew it telling by the glint in the scout's eye.

"Of course, Redlock."

Leiyn hid a frown. From a friend's mouth, it might have been a term of endearment. From Teya's, it rang with mockery.

"Call me 'ranger' or Leiyn," she said stiffly. "Not envoy; that's best saved for Isla."

As Teya turned another smile on her, Leiyn cursed herself again. She couldn't say anything right around the damned woman. Turning away, she hoped she hid the flush rising up her neck as she pretended to study their surroundings.

Teya led them through the city. Foxfur had dumped her off deeper within the canyon, so they had to walk back toward the Whisperspire before they could start taking the path up the eastern cliff to the old barracks where she, Isla, and Batu had been put up. She hoped her companions weren't worrying about her. Next time the dryvan appeared, Leiyn vowed to have a few stern words ready.

If she deigns to show up again.

They reached the bottom of the upward path as the light began to fade. Leiyn had recovered enough of her composure to look back at Teya. A gust of wind carried the woman's earthy, coffee-and-honey scent to her nose. Swallowing, Leiyn tried to keep her voice hard, though the task seemed suddenly difficult.

"What can you tell me of lyshans?"

The scout jerked around to stare at her with narrowed eyes, lips pressed into a tight line. "The *sach'aan* told you."

"She did."

Teya faced forward again and quickened their pace. "For all they affect our lives, we know little of our enemy. They keep to the shadows until they strike and elude any efforts at tracking."

Leiyn couldn't resist a smirk. "Not much of a scout if you cannot find them."

To her surprise, the scout found a smile of her own. "I suppose you outlander rangers are better trained?"

"I have little doubt of it."

"Good." Teya jerked her head toward the far end of the cliff they ascended. "Meet me at the Spear Circle atop Lualli at dawn tomorrow. We shall test who is fiercer."

Leiyn followed her gaze. She could see nothing of the "Spear Circle" the scout referenced. What did this contest entail? A sparring bout? She'd won her fair share of duels back at the Lodge, though she'd always been a stronger shot than a brawler.

Still, before that snide look of Teya's, how could she refuse?

"I look forward to it."

"As do I."

Teya stopped. Belatedly, Leiyn realized they'd reached the barracks. "Thanks for the escort," she said wryly.

"Wouldn't want you to get lost again, Redlock."

With that, the scout turned on her heel and set back down the path.

Leiyn watched her until she grew small, only turning away when Teya glanced over her shoulder. Cheeks flushed again, she wondered at the unfamiliar feeling that had stolen over her, and what it meant for the future.

"Nothing good," she muttered under her breath as she turned inside.

* * *

Leiyn had only just beat the dust from her shoes when pattering footsteps warned of her friends' return. She peeked outside her room just as Isla and Batu burst from the stairwell. Her fellow ranger strode toward her, panting and sheened with exertion.

"There you are! Saints, where did you go, Leiyn? Rowan— that is, Foxfur—she dragged you out the window and then you just... disappeared!"

"Sounds about right." Leiyn pulled her friend into a tight embrace, then looked at Batu. "Did you worry about me?"

The young man shrugged. "No."

As Leiyn grinned, Isla slapped Batu's chest lightly. "We both did, whatever he says. Those dryvans helped us before, and I'm grateful for it. But who knows what they really want? We had no idea where or when you'd come back if you would at all."

"Don't worry, Isla. I wouldn't leave you to be the last ranger of the Lodge." She patted her cheek before her friend jerked away with a grimace.

"Honestly, Leiyn. Tell us what happened."

Leiyn's smile slipped as she complied. By the time she finished, they were all sitting, she and Isla on the bed, Batu on the wooden chair in the corner. Having let her mahia's walls fall after a time, she was surprised to find the wood was surprisingly comfortable. Raising them made the wood hard once more.

Clearly, it was an enchanted artifact. But, absorbed as she was with telling her story, Leiyn soon ignored the fact. Stranger things had happened that day.

"Lyshans," Isla murmured. "Like dryvans, but corrupted? I don't fancy the sound of that."

"How can we fight them?" Batu shook his head. "They can take us to other worlds. And they move so swiftly..."

"There must be a way." Leiyn spoke firmly, despite harboring the same doubts. "Besides, dryvans and lyshans are mortal enemies from the sound of it. If it comes to it, we can set them on each other."

Batu nodded, but Isla looked far from convinced. "What does any of this have to do with you, Leiyn? Why would Zuma think you could make a difference in this war? Is it something with your magic?"

"I don't know. But if that shaman, Mother Xepi, means to train me, I suppose we'll find out soon enough." The thought of the coming days reminded her of one thing she'd forgotten to mention. "Ah, and I suppose I should say... I agreed to meet that scout Teya at the Spear Circle tomorrow morning. To spar, I think."

"She saved you, then challenged you?" Batu's brow crinkled.

Leiyn shrugged. It was strange, now that he pointed it out. "Guess so."

Isla gave her a hard look. "Leiyn, why did you agree to that?"

Leiyn turned to Batu, preferring his bemusement to Isla's scorn. "She challenged me. I couldn't refuse without losing face. Besides," she added as inspiration struck, "if I win, I might gain us respect. We're sorely lacking it here, and it could help win our alliance."

"Or it could get you killed. Or you could kill her. Or maybe it's not sparring at all, but a dance. How could you know when you agreed to it without even asking? Honestly, Leiyn, do you always have to act first and think later?"

Leiyn frowned. It took no small feat to keep her temper reined in. "You worry too much, Isla. Come tomorrow; it'll turn out fine, you'll see."

"I only hope it will."

With that, her fellow ranger rose and left the room. Batu followed a moment after, flashing an apologetic smile before disappearing through the doorway.

Leiyn went to close the room's curtains, then collapsed back onto the bed. She suddenly felt weary. And hungry. Tozi had shown them the kitchens and the mess hall, but the larder had been stocked with uncooked and unfamiliar foods. She'd eaten some of the maize bread, but it had been dry and crumbly with age.

Settling onto the strange wooden mattress, she chewed on some of their remaining road jerky, the city pressing gently against her mahia. For the moment, its whispers were tolerable, enough to leave her walls down.

Leiyn closed her eyes and lay back, wishing for sleep to come and carry away her cares.

PART II

CITY OF ANCIENTS

10

NINE YEARS BEFORE

ome on, Firebrand!" Gan called across the sparring yard. "Sweep her legs!"

Leiyn ground her hands into the quarterstaff, unable to close her ears to the older ranger's goading. She kept her eyes on Isla, her opponent for the moment, who stalked the stretch of trampled grass opposite her. Isla appeared much calmer, her steps measured and light.

For good reason.

Though Isla was a year older, Leiyn had eclipsed her in size and weight, and it had provided enough of an edge to help her win when grappling. But now that Isla had a quarterstaff in hand, nothing Leiyn did was able to cinch her a victory.

Gan wasn't the only ranger to watch them spar. Marina sat on a stool next to him fletching arrows, always necessary for the Wilds Lodge, and Tadeo, as usual, oversaw his pupils. He offered the occasional correction or word of encouragement, letting the apprentices figure out the various weapons they'd tried for themselves. Often, it was a methodology Leiyn preferred.

But not when Isla was trouncing her.

Isla feinted a move, then jabbed forward. Leiyn wasn't so green as to fall for it, yet she barely turned aside the follow up. Skirting back, Leiyn didn't go far, but launched an attack of her own.

Even as her staff sailed forward, Isla's dove for her legs. Next that she knew, Leiyn lay flat on her back, the breath knocked out of her.

She rolled to her feet before she'd caught her breath, quarterstaff raised and ready. Leiyn tried not to show her frustration, though she suspected she did a poor job of it. The length of wood felt unwieldy in her hands, and it made her somehow clumsy as well. No matter how hard she tried to move it around, she always trailed a step behind Isla.

"Your front leg." Tadeo's call was quiet but firm. "Keep it beneath your body so you don't overextend."

"I am," Leiyn muttered under her breath. By Isla's grin, she hadn't spoken as quietly as she thought.

I'll wipe off that smile.

Dashing forward, she drove a furious attack, stabbing and slashing, working against her friend's defenses. Isla never faltered. No matter how hard or how fast Leiyn struck, she rebuffed every effort.

Then Isla took to the offensive. Leiyn found herself backtracking, desperately warding off the onslaught and failing half the time. Had they not fought with quarterstaffs, she would have bled a dozen times over. As it was, welts covered her like a rosy bouquet.

Isla's staff dipped. Too late, Leiyn saw she'd overextended her front leg again and tried drawing it back. Not quickly enough —as her foot was scooped out from under her, Leiyn went tumbling to the ground.

This time, she didn't rise, but only sprawled out. "Do it," she spoke to the sky. "Put me out of my misery."

Isla's grin appeared above her. "Can't beat me at everything."

"Apparently."

After moping a moment longer, Leiyn grasped Isla's offered hand and tottered to her feet. As her eyes flickered toward her audience, Gan began to slowly clap, his smile even wider than Isla's.

"Marvelous!" the Gazian ranger called. "Never have I seen such prowess."

Marina slapped his arm while Isla muttered in her ear, "Ignore him."

Instead, Leiyn shouted back, "Heard I beat your long-shot record on the range. Care to see if you can beat mine?"

The ranger stopped clapping, but his smile remained. "Maybe I'll take you up on that later. Just now, I'm having too much fun."

Tadeo turned toward him. "The stall could use mucking," he said quietly.

Leiyn knew a suggestion from the lodgemaster could easily be a threat. It was sufficient to quell Gan's amusement.

"She'll face tougher things than me out there," he said, jerking his head toward the Lodge's outer walls. "Harden her up now or she'll never stand a chance."

"It's fine, Tadeo." Leiyn turned toward the weapon rack, hefting her quarterstaff to put it away. Her shoulders were raised like the hackles of a spooked cat, resisting her efforts to relax them. She hated others fighting her battles even more than being mocked.

She fitted the staff on the rack with the others and paused to stare across the other weapons. Swords—bastard, broad, and several other varieties—hung in wooden sheaths. Axes, both single and double-headed, were stored next to them. Knives, maces, hammers, whips—she had a dozen options, yet none so far had suited her.

Maybe nothing will, she thought morosely. She could handle herself with a bow, but if she couldn't fight close quarters, she would never earn her cloak. For the rest of her days, she'd be stuck at the Wilds Lodge, cleaning and cooking while Isla and the older rangers patrolled. If Tadeo didn't kick her out altogether.

She sensed someone approaching, though the footsteps only whispered across the dirt. With a start, Leiyn realized she'd let her walls drop around her mahia. She slammed them back up, catching her breath as she did. Her cursed magic always worked its way out when she was most vulnerable.

"We'll find it," Tadeo spoke from behind her. "Or it will find you."

"Think so?"

His hand settled on her shoulder and squeezed it. "I know. Turn around. I have an idea."

Leiyn did as the lodgemaster asked. She saw Isla had settled into practicing the exercises Tadeo had shown them before setting them against each other. She made the movements look effortless, though Leiyn knew well they were far from easy.

"Guess she's found her weapon."

"Yes. So let's concentrate on you." Tadeo raised his hands in fists. "Put up your hands and block."

Leiyn raised an eyebrow but complied. The lodgemaster kept the blows easy and slow enough that it was simple for her to knock them aside. She'd never struggled in hand-to-hand combat, where her reflexes and strength came to bear.

After a few minutes, Tadeo stopped and lowered his arms. The frown of concentration had been replaced by a smile. "You block with both hands equally."

Leiyn still scowled. "So?"

Instead of answering, the lodgemaster stepped around her to the weapon rack. She watched as his hand glided over the hilts of the knives, then halted on one. Reaching forward, he drew two of them.

Leiyn stared at the bright steel. They were a similar type and clearly forged by the same smith. Both edges were sharp, though one side was favored with the curve. The blades ended in deadly tips. They were long for knives, longer than her forearm.

"Anelaces," Tadeo said. "Forged specifically for a ranger's purposes." He flourished the long knives, spinning them in his hands. With a raise of his eyebrows, he balanced them against his palms, leaving the hilts open.

A tickle in her throat, Leiyn stepped forward, twisted her hands around, then took them in hand.

Awkwardly, she raised the anelaces, crossing them before holding them upright. They were lighter than she'd anticipated, and the balance weighted toward the tip, unlike other blades she'd tried. The grips were single-handed, though fitted for larger hands than hers, and made of fresh cow leather. The hilts were made of ash and stained a deep russet, with plain crossguards a hand wide and rounded pommels. In the middle of the cross guards was carved the symbol for the Wilds Lodge, the drawn bow-and-arrow.

As she became aware of Isla and the other rangers watching, she dropped the knives to her sides and looked at Tadeo. "You think I should have two of them?"

He nodded. "Most people have a dominant hand. Yours are equally matched. You fight with instinct, speed, and precision, but also... ferocity." The lodgemaster gave her a wan smile. "You want to be close to your opponent. To control the fight. To strike when and where you wish, and for each blow to count. That requires a particular weapon, or two."

Leiyn backed up a step and raised the blades again. She slowly drew them through the air one way, then the other, keeping them parallel in their movements. As she started to get the feel for them, she moved them more quickly and in opposite directions. Though having two weapons seemed a strange idea, she found herself imagining the applications in the fight she'd just had against Isla and her mock spear. *One to block, one to strike.* With enough training, her friend's reach would be no match for Leiyn's adaptability and speed.

She lowered the anelaces. "Thanks, Tadeo."

He smiled. "I'll carve some wasters for you to practice with. And, if you don't mind, I'll add something to the pommels."

"Of course, I don't mind." Leiyn raised the knives again and crossed them before her. The sun made the steel candle-bright and difficult to look at. Yet she saw her face in them, her mussed hair free of its braid, the faint layer of dust on her tanned skin. But it was her eyes that caught her, as bright as the sky above.

She would become a cloaked ranger after all. With her bow

and her knives, there wouldn't be a threat in this wilderness she couldn't handle, be it beast, Gast, or titan.

"They suit you!" Isla called from the yard.

Leiyn smiled and raised one above her head. "Just wait till you have to face me with them!"

"A fearsome sight you'll be!" Gan wore a broad smile, and for once, it seemed devoid of mockery.

Even still, Leiyn stuck out her tongue at him before looking back at Tadeo. "Best get carving. I have some fights ahead of me."

The lodgemaster inclined his head, then eyed her for a long moment. "Just remember," he said, his voice dropping low. "What is most important is not how well you wield them, but when and where you draw them."

That sobered her mood. Though she wanted to tease him, Leiyn instead nodded.

"I'll remember," she murmured, hoping she would.

11

THE SPEAR CIRCLE

$\mathscr{L}$eiyn was up and dressed before the sun rose on Qasaar.

Though she'd slept soundly the night before, her hands shook as she shrugged on her jerkin. The more she thought on it, the more ominous a bout in this "Spear Circle" sounded. *Don't be rash,* Tadeo had told her, and Isla often repeated the advice. Yet Leiyn persisted in ignoring them both.

Not knowing what she might need, she took all her equipment with her. Her anelaces hung from her left hip, her quiver of broadhead arrows from the right. Her longbow was strung and a comforting weight in her hand. It was probably too much; if she was supposed to fight Teya to the death, she'd already resolved to bow out. Slaying a Gast would win Baltesia no friends, and she doubted she could force herself to it anyway. Teya was far too intriguing to kill.

Once dressed, Leiyn felt more herself. Though she was in a foreign land, now that she wore her greens, she returned to being a ranger and less the awkward envoy she had been thus far.

She exited into the hallway to see Tozi coming toward her. "May the spirits of hill and heather bless you this day, Ranger Leiyn!" their caretaker called merrily as he approached. "You did have an exciting day yesterday, no?"

"Unexpected, at least." Leiyn returned his smile, glad at least one Gast seemed to like her. "And I could use a few blessings. I'm to meet the scout Teya at the Spear Circle at dawn."

Tozi's smile slipped away. "The Spear Circle? Against Teya of the Hunt? Please tell me this is strange southern humor!"

Isla emerged from her room and spoke before Leiyn could. "It's not, unfortunately. My friend is skilled at getting herself into tangles."

"Thanks for that." Leiyn grinned at her friend.

Isla only arched an eyebrow in return.

Batu stepped out of Isla's room a moment after. Leiyn fought down a sigh. It seemed their romance hadn't ended with the road.

Best accept and get over it, Firebrand, she lectured herself. It wasn't like she had much ground to stand on for being irritated about it.

"Dawn is coming." Batu's voice was gravelly from having just risen.

"Yes. We should go." Leiyn pushed down her inner tumult as she turned to Tozi. "Can you lead us to the Spear Circle?"

The thin man wrung his hands before bobbing his head. "If I must. The Spear Circle... How did this come to be, Envoy?"

"Call me Leiyn, remember? I'll tell you on the way."

He gave no further protests but escorted them out of the barracks. Leiyn looked over Qasaar and found it a different sort of enchanting amid the gloom. Either the whispers from the city had quieted, or she was growing used to them, for even with her mahia open, they were little more than a breeze against her life-sense. Occasional lights appeared through the cliffside dwellings and stony buildings below. Most were open flames, but not all. She stared at these others, which didn't glow orange or red, but green. What their origins were remained a mystery, for they were too far away, and her mahia detected no more than a glimmer from them.

No sooner had they exited than did another familiar face emerge around the lower bend of the path. Acalan looked weary but strode with his usual vigor. His inner fire blazed with resolve, a comforting sight when she faced an unknown bout.

Waiting for him, the Jaguar chieftain stopped in front of Leiyn and looked her up and down before grunting something. A sound of approval, she hoped.

"At least you dressed for a fight," he grated. "If a little too much."

He turned and set up the path. With no other recourse, Leiyn fell in step with him. She was used to his attitude, so it only slightly annoyed her. Crunching footsteps indicated the others followed behind.

"How did you hear about this?" she asked.

"Teya told Ilaoti. No avoiding it then. She gloated until past dusk." Acalan gave no outward show of disapproval, yet it seemed almost to radiate from him.

"Go on, then. Say your piece."

His dark eyes flashed toward her. "You do not know what you face, do you?"

"I can hazard a guess."

"You are supposed to be negotiating an alliance and winning a war, Huntress. Not provoking a fight with my people."

His words snapped out, hard-edged. She struggled to tamp down her own temper.

"I know that. But she challenged me, Acalan. Should I have refused and lost respect when we can ill afford to? I would have shown your people that Baltesians are cowards who cannot hold their own."

"You should never have let yourself be cornered into it. Teya is a spear, a leader of our scouts, and the best among them. She is not a shaman but is blessed enough to be deadly in many respects."

Leiyn frowned. "She possesses mahia?"

"A limited strand, yes, but enough for her purposes. Keep up your walls. Remain wary. And do not let her touch you."

She couldn't remain in ignorance any longer. "But what are

we doing in the Spear Circle? Is this a sparring match or some-thing worse?"

The chieftain looked over sharply. "That is why you bring your weapons," he muttered. "You agreed and did not even know what you agreed to."

Leiyn keenly hoped Isla hadn't overheard that. "Fine—I was a *feshtado* fool. Now help me survive this."

Acalan stared at her a moment longer, then looked up the rise again as they followed another switchback. "There are strict rules to the Spear Circle. Only blunted spears are used. Three killing blows wins the bout, or three stumbles outside the ring."

"Killing blows?"

"When your opponent is at your mercy. I do not think you could kill Teya even if you tried. But do not attempt it."

That, at least, was good news, though the rest of it fell short. *Only spears.* Isla might prefer the weapon, but it was the one Leiyn was least capable at. Hatchets, swords, and even maces would have been preferred.

It's what you deserve, putting your foot in the fire. Maybe next time you'll think twice before being rash.

Somehow, she doubted it.

Their journey took them to the top of the cliff where they'd entered Qasaar the day before. The sky had turned a lighter blue; the sun would break the horizon soon. People had begun to poke their heads outside their doors, and many stared openly at their strange party. Leiyn wondered how many knew of her misstep and already anticipated her failure.

You haven't lost yet, she told herself sternly. *It's like Tadeo always said, don't beat yourself before your opponent gets the chance.*

"How much farther?" Isla asked from behind.

When Acalan didn't immediately respond, Tozi spoke up. "Oh, it is not far now. Just at the end of the cliff."

Leiyn squinted toward where he indicated. She could just make out a dark ring against an outcropping that jutted from the cliff. Her stomach churned. A slip would lead to a long fall.

More disconcerting were the people congregated around the ring. By her mahia, she counted at least a dozen.

"No one mentioned an audience," she muttered.

Acalan only glanced at her.

With each fresh revelation, apprehension was swallowed by a growing anger. Teya had set her up. *She saw how you looked at her. What did you think would happen?* That her attraction was being exploited was insult upon injury. She vowed to pay it back in full.

They traveled over several more hills before reaching the Spear Circle. Leiyn saw Teya waiting next to whatever marked its perimeter. She knew her esse's blue hues and mesmerizing patterns, distinct as they were. As she drew nearer, her eyes detected the hard set of the scout's face. Leiyn found a grim smile and clung to it as she sauntered up to her.

She kept her gaze on the scout, showing no fear, like she faced down a lion or tusked jackal. In her peripherals, she scanned the crowd for familiar faces. The other chieftains had come: Ilaoti, the chieftainess of Teya's tribe, scowling as much as her scout. Zyanya, the same blue beads adorning her braids as before, her piercing eyes betraying nothing of what she thought of this spectacle. Tinoch was more transparent, a smile twitching on his lips as his eyes darted from Teya to Leiyn and back.

Leiyn stopped before the scout and waited. She was dressed the same as the day before in a simple tunic, trousers, and fringed vest, but had added to it two short spears, both just shy of her height. Her scent, the same as the day before, was but a hint on the steady winds that coursed over the cliff from the Barren.

Teya gave no greeting beyond an arched eyebrow. "You will not need those."

No need to ask what she meant. Leiyn did a small flourish with her bow. "Thought you might want to lose at other contests once we finished here."

The scout smiled, and to Leiyn's surprise, it wasn't unkind. "We shall see. Toa Acalan has told you how it works?"

"Dulled spears. Three kills. Don't leave the ring."

A grin claimed Teya's face. "I'm beginning to like you, Redlock. Don't let me gut you."

That dulled the moment a bit. Leiyn tried not to let her own smile slip. "The same goes for you."

The scout extended one spear, and Leiyn took it. Hefting it, she felt its balance and weight. She'd trained in the spear, but only in a cursory manner. The anelaces had always been her preferred weapons.

Leiyn turned back to her companions to find them several paces back. Advancing toward them, she held out her bow to Isla.

"Guess you were right. Maybe I was a bit rash."

Isla rolled her eyes, but relieved Leiyn of the longbow all the same. "Just try to keep your distance. And remember your legs— you always overextended one."

Leiyn repressed an eye roll of her own. "I remembered that much, thanks."

She handed the blunted spear to Batu while she undid her quiver and knives. When her companions were burdened with all her weapons, she took the spear back with a thankful nod.

"Wish me luck," she muttered before turning away.

"How about blessings from all the Saints?" Isla said to her back, louder than Leiyn preferred.

"I'll ask my gods as well," Batu added, and she heard the smile in his voice.

Shaking her head, Leiyn gripped her spear in both hands and advanced toward the Circle.

While Leiyn readied for the bout, Teya had entered the ring to stand against the far side. Only then did Leiyn notice what made up the Spear Circle: two dozen spears, broken so their jagged shafts jutted up toward the sky several feet from the ground. She sidled between two to enter the patch of sandy dirt. Wind-swept and sun-packed, it was flat and hard. Good for planting her feet, but it would hurt to fall.

Then best not let her knock you down.

Leiyn spared a glance for their audience, but no more. Her

focus sharpened as her body grew warm and ready. She held Teya's gaze and smiled as she fell into a wide, balanced stance. Then she waited, muscles taut but relaxed, prepared to react to the slightest provocation.

Teya, on the other hand, remained upright, her spear held loosely in both hands before her. Leiyn looked for openings in the casual stance and was surprised to find none. Though she appeared unprepared, it was the best defensive posture she could have adopted.

It was then that she began to wonder if she was in trouble.

Only one way to find out.

Teeth gritted, Leiyn shuffled forward and struck.

12

CONTROL

*D*on't rush. Don't overcommit. Know where to strike, then strike without hesitation.

Tadeo's counsel murmured in the back of Leiyn's mind as she jabbed forward. She didn't expect to hit the scout, only to test the soundness of her defenses. It was a cautious approach, but one that, with time, she hoped would claim her victory.

Yet her spear had only just extended when Teya whipped into motion. Striking Leiyn's spear to the side, she lunged forward and swept her own weapon around, lightning-quick. Leiyn tried to dodge the blur of wood, but only managed an awkward skip before fire raced up her front leg and she went down on her side.

Teya's spearpoint rested against Leiyn's throat.

"A kill to me," the scout said as she withdrew her weapon. She retreated a few steps and resumed the same relaxed position as before.

Leiyn scrambled back to her feet. *That damned leg.* As usual, Isla had been right; she still overextended it with a spear. Her cheeks burned and her side ached, but she couldn't let herself be distracted. She had to keep her head level and a watchful eye for any attack. She suspected they would be allowed to reset their positions before the duel commenced, but she couldn't rely on any assumption now.

As Leiyn waited for the next strike, she thought through her mistakes. *Too cautious.* She'd probed for information and paid for it. She had learned one thing, though: just how outmatched she was.

A weakness. She must have a weakness.

It was a vain hope. A scout wouldn't last long in the Barren if they made mistakes, the same as for rangers in the Titan Wilds. Teya looked to have trained with the spear all her life. There was no trick she hadn't seen, especially from amateurs such as Leiyn.

Unless...

Double-checking that the scout kept her distance, Leiyn focused on her mahia. Teya's esse was easy to touch; even with the distance between them, it flowed around and encircled her body in a way that most did not. Reaching for it, Leiyn grasped at her lifefire, then drew it toward herself.

A flash of flames was her only warning.

Focusing on her vision, Leiyn snapped her spear around and narrowly knocked aside Teya's thrust. Had she not, the blow likely would have impaled her, even with its blunted point.

Teya rolled into the next attack, the butt of her spear whacking against Leiyn's thigh. Pain burned up her leg, but she ignored it to slash at her opponent. The scout was lithe as an otter, somehow melting out of the way.

They broke apart, but Leiyn had barely caught her breath before Teya skirted in again. She jabbed twice, and only by luck did Leiyn manage to avoid them. Her jaw ached from how hard she clenched it. Breath whistled in her throat.

But a savage smile had appeared. No contest was as thrilling as the impossible one.

Leiyn was starting to get the feel for her spear: its balance, its weight, its length. But Teya had levels of mastery above her. Through a series of quick blows, the scout cornered her against the edge of the ring of broken spears. Leiyn tried everything she could think of to gain room, but all her efforts achieved were fresh welts.

Her smile fled, and her anger surged.

My mahia. It was her only advantage. She had failed to draw out Teya's lifeforce at a distance, but if she could close the gap and make contact with her, she could weaken the scout and strengthen herself.

But how to get there?

Leiyn threw it all in a desperate bid. As she knocked aside Teya's spear, Leiyn released her weapon and lunged. The scout's eyes widened, but she kept calm, evading and bringing her weapon back around.

Not quick enough. Leiyn was on her, hands grappling for anywhere she could touch her opponent. Teya had worked the spear between them, but she couldn't protect her arms.

Leiyn grasped the scout's forearms and almost lost herself. With her mahia open, she and the scout's esse leaped toward each other like eager puppies. It took a colossal effort to stay on her task, an effort almost beyond her.

The hard wood pressing against her sternum and the pain screaming along her body helped return her focus. Baring her teeth, Leiyn separated herself from Teya and dragged the scout's lifeforce into herself

Teya fought like a cornered badger, both in body and spirit. As if with claw and nail, she thrashed and scored rents through Leiyn's mind. But here, Leiyn was the more powerful. Flame by reluctant flame, she pulled the life out of Teya. A grin pulled at the corners of her mouth. With each bit she gained from her adversary, she became that much stronger. She had flailed before with a spear, but here, the scout couldn't hope to match her.

Teya's resistance faded. Leiyn didn't relent. Only then did she realize she couldn't stop herself. A touch of horror threaded through her, but it wasn't enough to break the connection. Her mahia hungered for the esse, and like a wolf with its jaw set, it wouldn't relinquish its hold.

Hands touched her shoulders; a third life joined the fray. Before Leiyn could grasp who it was, a sensation like someone grabbing her hair came over her.

Leiyn was yanked away from Teya, and her mahia finally released its hold.

As her senses reassured themselves, she became aware of shouting around her. Blinking through the fog over her mind, she stared down at the figure huddled before her. Teya had crumpled upon the desiccated dirt, barely having the energy to lift her head. Her golden skin had lost its haleness, and she seemed thinner somehow.

Leiyn blanched, the last of the thrill fading. By her look, Leiyn had come close to killing her.

Isla and Batu hurried toward her. Acalan remained on the sidelines, silent and scowling with arms crossed. She'd thought one of them had interrupted the bout, but it appeared otherwise.

Then who...?

She twisted around to see a vaguely familiar face. *The shaman at the Whisperspire—Mother Xepi.* The woman's heavy features were weighed further down by a frown, but her eyes remained dark and distant.

"Enough," she murmured, her mouth close enough to Leiyn's ear to be audible. "Close yourself off. You have taken too much from her."

In that moment, Leiyn wanted nothing more. She put up her walls, and Mother Xepi's lifeforce lost its scalding touch.

"Good," the shaman said. "Come with me. We cannot afford to delay."

With her hands still on Leiyn's shoulders, Mother Xepi tried directing her out of the Spear Circle. But with her mahia's closure, a presence of mind returned to her. Leiyn shrugged off the shaman and stepped toward Teya, a hand outstretched as if to help her up, though the scout didn't look as if she'd stand anytime soon.

"Teya—Spear Teya, I mean—I'm sorry. I didn't mean to—"

Before she could reach her, others stood in her way.

"Away from her, invader!" Chief Ilaoti shouted, the veins in her face bulging. "You are devoid of honor!"

As if appearing from nowhere, Acalan stood before Leiyn,

facing down the Red Hawk chieftainess. "Enough, Ilaoti. They fought in the Circle. She did nothing shameful."

Ilaoti flashed him a wild smile. "We will see, Acalan. Soon, we will see."

Leiyn's head spun. She'd made a mess of things, worse than she'd believed possible. *If only I'd lost.* Even disgrace would have been preferable to the guilt wracking her.

"Sorry," she muttered to Teya once more, though in the clamor, the scout probably couldn't hear it. Teya's eyes were no longer open; she'd fully collapsed, limbs gone limp. Leiyn hoped it was only from exhaustion and not something worse.

"*Osat,* come. You cannot help here."

Mother Xepi's quiet voice again broke through the din. Though Leiyn didn't understand why she would call her "fox," she still turned away from the scout to follow. Shame was all she had to offer Teya, and that would do her no good.

As she sidled between the broken shafts to leave the Spear Circle, Isla and Batu waited for her. Shoving Leiyn's longbow at the former plainsrider, her fellow ranger stepped up to grip her by the shoulders.

"Leiyn, what happened? Was it your magic?"

Leiyn nodded, then looked at Batu. His stare was easier to meet, for though he looked worried, no horror touched his expression.

"I have to go with the shaman," she muttered, jerking her head toward Mother Xepi, who waited an arm's length away. "Can you look after my gear?"

"Of course. Should we come?"

Leiyn glanced at the waiting woman, then shook her head. "I'll be fine. Though," she added, remembering the incident in the alley the day before, "give me my knives just in case."

Isla stepped back so she could accept the weapons from Batu. As Leiyn undid her belt to slip the double sheath back on, he bent toward her.

"Be careful. They have the eyes of tigers."

She looked over her shoulder to see the hostile gazes of many of the Gasts upon her, then shrugged. "At least we know our standing."

Outfitted once more, Leiyn glanced back again at Teya to see her sitting upright and conscious. Her chest loosened, and she breathed a quiet sigh of relief.

"She will survive." Mother Xepi spoke again, her voice barely louder than before. "Come, *Osat*. Do not delay."

Leiyn shared one last look with her companions, then followed the shaman away from the crowd.

13

THREE SPARKS

She walked after Mother Xepi through nearly all of Qasaar.

The shaman led her down the winding path along the eastern cliff—Lualli, Teya had named it—until they reached the bottom of the valley. Leiyn thought they might be headed for the Whisperspire, but their path went past it to the road that led up the western cliff face. She hadn't questioned the shaman to that point, wracked by guilty thoughts. She spoke as they ascended.

"Where are we going?"

The shaman remained facing forward, her expression placid and steady as a mule.

And as dull as one.

"My hut," Mother Xepi answered after several strides.

Where her hut lay, the shaman didn't deign to say. Leiyn kept her silence as she walked beside her, supposing she'd find out soon enough.

As they went up one switchback after another, Leiyn thought over all that had occurred. She'd lost control. Again. For all her training at the Lodge, for all the discipline she'd tried so hard to acquire, she was still the same Firebrand that had first arrived at the Lodge. She smiled ruefully.

At least that much hasn't changed.

But though the instinct for action had saved her before, in

this mission, it was a liability. She was no envoy. She'd never been one to reason calmly or placate others like Isla could. Whatever Mauricio had seen that compelled him to deem her a representative of Baltesia was beyond her sight. The best thing she could do was stay away from politics. Isla would fare far better alone.

Leiyn observed the cliff they traveled along now. While Lualli boasted many markets and shops, the western cliff seemed dedicated to homes. People hung up their wash, tended to goats, pigs, and gardens. Elders chatted with one another over fences. They seemed ordinary lives, if odd for taking place off the side of a cliff. They didn't seem like a people beset by war.

Yet they are. She remembered what Foxfur had shown and told her. Remembered the look on Acalan's face whenever their enemy came up.

Corrupted dryvans. Leiyn wondered how she could ever fight them.

As they passed the last of the houses and proceeded toward the top of the cliff, she asked, "Where did you say this hut was?"

Xepi frowned at her, but only briefly. "Where I may keep watch."

Suspecting she'd receive no more satisfactory answer, Leiyn held her tongue. They walked along the cliff, where cacti and yucca stubbornly clung to existence. She'd expected the edge to be slowly eroding, but it instead cut a sharp line toward the Barren. She wondered if this had to do with the ancient whispers that emanated from Qasaar, if magic reinforced it from the valley floor all the way to the tops of the cliffs. It was yet another question for Foxfur, or perhaps Xepi, if the shaman proved more talkative than she had been thus far.

After traveling nearly the length of the cliff, Leiyn finally saw their destination. "Hut" was an accurate description, for the small, squat structure could be called nothing else. As they neared, she took in more details. Single-storied, it was round and made of the same ocher stone as the rest of the city. No windows appeared on its sides, though there were rectangular indentations where they seemed to have been filled in. A plot of soil marked a garden, but it had long ago been baked over by the sun, unrelenting with its heat even in late autumn.

Signs of life appeared as Leiyn followed Xepi around to the front door. Flowered vines draped along the head and jambs. Leiyn knew them at once: everscent blossoms, which mysteriously changed their aroma. She detected a hint of rain from them just then, a comforting smell in the arid surroundings. She longed to lean closer and smell deeper of them, but resisted, conscious of the shaman at her shoulder. A sidelong glance showed Xepi wasn't immune to the flowers; the ghost of a smile curled up one corner of her perpetual frown.

The shaman led the way into the hut, then closed the door after Leiyn entered. For a moment, the hut was cast in darkness. Leiyn instinctively lowered her mahia's walls as a hand fell to an anelace. She could no longer see the shaman, and while she didn't think Xepi meant her harm, she didn't know her well enough to fully trust that.

The shaman's esse was unique in its own way, and much the opposite of Teya's. Where the scout's was all movement and color, Xepi's barely moved beyond a stir. She was like a pool of light with a breeze running over its surface, depthless and colorless.

Xepi reached toward the wall and laid a hand upon it. A breath after, light touched Leiyn's eyes again. She stared at the growing rectangle of light—sunlight, impossible as it was. Almost, the slab of stone seemed to glow with esse as it unveiled the light. It whispered against Leiyn's mahia like a voice muffled by a pillow. And it wasn't alone; as Xepi moved around the hut, her hand touched the wall at regular intervals, and more slabs came alive and raised.

Leiyn shifted to the center of the hut, wary. Ancient magic— it had to be. She didn't understand how stone could come alive at a touch. Only living things were supposed to possess esse, yet the magic she'd witnessed in Qasaar, and the ruins she'd encountered before, kept defying that belief.

As the shaman opened a dozen windows, Leiyn could see inside the hut clearly. The space was cramped, but tidy. Furniture was scarce, consisting largely of a round table with two chairs at one end and a bed at the other. There was no fireplace, and Leiyn wondered how Xepi kept warm on winter nights, if winter even touched this place.

Cabinets and shelves dominated the space, occupying every free inch. Each object seemed to have its place, though Leiyn understood the purpose of few of them. Pebbles of amber sat in a bowl. Drying herbs hung from the rafters, some familiar—oregano, echinacea, lavender—while others were foreign. Pots, both small and large, were lidded and interred upon the shelves. Some of these held the glow of life as well, enough that Leiyn wondered if the shaman kept insects of some kind within them, though they didn't move that she could feel. The green glass orb hanging from the middle of the hut's conical ceiling did little to settle her. Was it the green light she'd seen atop the cliff that morning? Though there seemed no way for it to glow, what did she know of this witchery?

Leiyn lowered her gaze to find Xepi watching her. She tried disguising her unease, and only then noticed she still had a hand on her knife. Slowly, she removed it and gestured at one of the windows.

"How did you open them?"

It was the least of her questions, but it was a start. Xepi stared at her for a long while before indicating the table and chairs.

"Sit. It will not be a short answer."

Though she should have been exhausted from the day, Leiyn didn't want to sit. Teya's lifeforce had mended her wounds and filled her to brimming with energy. Yet she'd already done too much to offend her hosts as things stood, so she forced herself to comply.

Almost as soon as she sat, Leiyn jerked back up. With her mahia open, she'd felt something from the chair, like it had briefly come alive. A moment later, she recognized it as the same sensation as emanated from her bed. She sighed and relented to it. Magic abounded around her; better to get used to it now.

Xepi's gaze never shifted. It felt like an eagle watched her, unblinking and predatory. Leiyn wondered just what the shaman wanted from her.

"You felt it. The magic."

Leiyn struggled to keep her twitching hands still. "What of it?"

"That sorcery was put here by the ancients who built this place."

"And who were they?" Leiyn swallowed, struggling for a moment to give voice to her suspicions. "Gast ancestors? Dryvans?"

Lyshans, she wanted to ask, but couldn't eke the word out.

Xepi smiled, lightening her blunt features. "We believe them to be our ancestors, but we do not know. Perhaps the *sach'aan* were behind it; perhaps a different people lost from memory. But Qasaar has sheltered us for too long to believe it did not once belong to our people."

Leiyn nodded and tucked away the information, resolving to pry more from Foxfur whenever the dryvan next appeared.

"That didn't answer my question," she said aloud. "I've felt this ancestral magic before, but it makes no sense. Stone shouldn't be able to come alive."

"The stone is not alive, *Osat*."

Though Leiyn wanted to know why she kept calling her that name, she kept quiet, her other question demanding precedence.

Xepi's gaze wandered the hut. Without explanation, she rose and removed the lid from a ewer, then poured its contents into a cup. Leiyn crossed her arms tightly about her middle as the shaman brought both the ewer and cup back to the table. Water, she saw it to be. A thirst awoke in her. It had been some time since she'd drank anything, and while her stolen esse helped to sustain her, hydration was also welcome.

Yet Xepi didn't offer it, but only leaned back in her chair once more. "Your people believe each individual possesses a spirit separate from your body. A force behind your thoughts, your feelings, your greatest self. 'Soul,' you call it?"

Leiyn shrugged. "That's how the Catedrál puts it."

"That is not how spirit exists. It does not live separate from the body but is born of it and sustains it. It does not belong only to humanity, but all that lives. Plants. Beasts. *Kainox*—titans."

Leiyn struggled to stifle her skepticism. She was no devout believer, but to say the soul didn't exist? That was a hard draught to swallow. All the same, she thought she understood.

"You speak of esse. Lifeforce."

The shaman's eyes narrowed slightly. "Yes. What you stole from Teya of the Hunt in the Spear Circle."

Leiyn winced. Guilt surged in her, acid in its touch.

"I didn't mean to. Not that much."

"Yet you did."

Her anger caught flame. Preferring it to the guilt, Leiyn seized hold. "That doesn't answer my question, Xepi."

If the shaman noticed the lack of the honorific, she didn't acknowledge it. After a long pause, she spoke in measured words.

"You must understand *ilis*, essence, to understand how ancestral magic works. Knowledge comes with listening, *Osat*. When you speak, you only share your ignorance."

The reprimand further inflamed her. Yet Leiyn had faced enough provocation to be ready for it. She put on a smile, determined to outlast the shaman. She needed these answers, no matter how it bruised her pride to get them.

"Though it is born of the body," Xepi continued, "*ilis* is not restricted to it, as you have experienced. For those blessed by the land, it can be used like a liquid."

The shaman lifted the cup. Leiyn's dry throat throbbed at the reminder.

"*Ilis* takes the shape of the vessel in which it rests. It is malleable and can be preserved beyond the place from which it came. Pour it into another vessel"—she tilted the cup so water trickled back into the ewer—"and it takes on a new shape." She righted the cup and set it back on the table, now half-full. "Just as there are many different liquids, so there are many types of *ilis*, as varied as the species that populate *Tlalli's* surface. Oil and water will not mix well, while honey and hot water can."

Leiyn found her temper dissipating as she absorbed the lesson. It resonated at once; she remembered all too well how she'd nearly killed Isla by imbuing her with lifeforce taken from trees. The dryvans of Glade had told her things in the same vein.

She raised her gaze from the cup to look at Xepi. "What of esse and stone?"

The shaman glanced at the window next to where they sat, then reached for the ewer and lifted it. In further torment, she poured a trickle onto the stone floor.

"That which is not alive cannot give or take *ilis*."

"Then what about the windows? The city's whispers? The wardstones?"

Xepi's gaze sharpened. "The wardstones. The *sach'aan* told you of them?"

Leiyn shrugged, glad to have the advantage in at least one thing. "Saw one on the way in, but yes, Foxfur also showed me one. Told me their use, too. I felt the life pulsing." She paused, remembering the strangeness of the sensation. "Do they really keep away titans?"

"Yes." The shaman's mouth screwed up to one side as she studied her. "There is too much you do not know, too much you must learn. We must use a swifter method."

Leiyn's guard raised again, but she kept her tone light. "Let me guess—you'll brew everything in a potion that I'll drink down. That would be easiest."

If Xepi caught her mockery, she didn't show it. "Zuma lives within you," she stated baldly.

She'd been ready for pivots, but this one caught Leiyn by surprise. "How do you know? Can you... feel him?"

"Yes. His spark is faint, but distinct. I know his mark."

"His mark?"

Xepi sighed, her shoulders slumping. Leiyn finally saw

through her mask and glimpsed the weariness that assailed her. The sight of it lowered her own defenses, if slightly.

"Lifemark," the shaman explained, her voice soft. "Each person has them. Those blessed by *Tlalli* possess more distinct and vibrant ones. Perhaps you have noticed them as smell, taste, touch."

Leiyn thought at once of Teya and her intoxicating esse. "I think I know what you mean."

The shaman had grown alert again, her momentary lapse gone. "But there is another within you. You have taken the last rites for a second shaman?"

It took a measure of will not to falter. The implications in her words rang loudly in Leiyn's ears.

"I didn't kill one, if that's what you're thinking," she said drily. "You must mean my mother. She traded her life for mine when I was a babe. Zuma gave her lifeforce to me."

Xepi was silent for a long while. At last, she shook her head.

"Convergence," she murmured, as if to herself. Then she seemed to remember where she was. "But that is not our present concern. Sparks such as those, *Osat*, hold more than the last glimmer of life. Esse is not just an energy. It is the essence, the core of a person, both in body and in spirit."

"I don't understand."

"The *sach'aan*. You have seen how they change?"

"Yes. Once. At least, I saw the change afterward."

"They do so by gathering sparks into themselves—such as the silver fox the *sach'aan* in the Whisperspire wore. Within the essence lies that power and more, especially for such a creature as that fox. The shape and form of a body. The memories of their life."

"Memories." Leiyn sprinted down the line of reasoning. "Could I witness Zuma's life? And... my mother's?" She didn't dare hope, yet it filled her all the same.

Xepi nodded.

Leiyn barely saw it through the wash of emotion. *It cannot be.* To see through her mother's eyes... It was something she'd dreamed of doing all her life. A childhood wish made real. A hand rose to touch her auburn tress.

Mother.

The older woman spoke softly into the silence. "That is why Zuma gave of himself to you, why every shaman must pass on their *ilis*. Why the loss of even one shaman is a grave wound to the world."

Leiyn lowered her hand. Only then did she realize how the news of Zuma's death might affect her. "Was he your friend?"

Xepi nodded and looked out the window. Leiyn didn't think she imagined the shimmer in her eyes, yet her voice was hard as she spoke again.

"We have lost too many. In the war against your people, most of the blessed fell before they passed on their sparks. Much knowledge was lost along with those lives."

She paused. Leiyn tried hard not to fidget. Though she hadn't been the one to kill the Gasts in the Titan War, she felt an inherited guilt. Considering how she'd treated Gasts since, it wasn't entirely undeserved.

"Then we came north of the mountains and suffered further tragedy. The lyshans have never relented, not in the decades since we settled here. Slowly, they have whittled away our shamans, culling magic from our lines. Precious few are born with the blessing now. Yet we have nowhere else to flee."

"Why? Why do they hunt and kill you?"

The shaman's eyes smoldered like coals. "Not hunt, *Osat*. Harvest. Reap. That is the reason for the wardstones. Not to keep out the lyshans, but the *kainox* they might command."

She worked through the puzzle. "Why do they need shamans? To bypass the wardstones?"

"No. Not for the wardstones. Those can be overcome by any titan if they are determined. But only one called would make the effort, and only a shaman can command the titans."

Leiyn clenched her hands into fists. There was the critical piece of information she'd been missing. The question she hadn't thought to ask yet filled in so many gaps.

"Dryvans and lyshans—they cannot call titans?"

Xepi shook their head. "No. That, *Tlalli* be thanked, is a blessing only humanity holds."

It seemed strange, that such powerful beings couldn't do what she herself had accidentally done. Foxfur could change her skin at will yet couldn't have commanded the kraken at Southport.

The thought summoned another. "The titans... I've always thought of them as adversaries, beings that must be defied whenever possible. But they're our guardians. They're how humanity has survived."

"So I suspect." The shaman bowed her head. "But the knowledge of how they were once wielded has been lost."

Leiyn opened her mouth to ask another burning question, but paused, realizing it might have a painful answer. *I have to know.* She couldn't stumble blindly into this war, not as she had the Spear Circle.

"Xepi, how many shamans are left?"

As if a bag of sand weighed upon her neck, the shaman slowly looked up. "Too few."

"How many?"

Xepi's sigh whistled between her teeth. "Two."

Two. Leiyn tried to draw a breath and failed. *Only two.*

"Including you?"

A damning nod.

Irrationally, Leiyn found a smile tugging at her lips. This wasn't a war; it was a slow bleeding out years in the making. Their magic was almost evaporated.

And she'd let one of their last shamans die.

You expected too much of me, she thought to Zuma. Instinctively, she reached for his spark. Just as Xepi was able to distinguish his esse from hers, sometimes Leiyn could feel his ember of life if she honed her focus to a fine point.

I cannot fight this war. I cannot save your people.

Yet the old shaman had saved her; not once, but many times

over. He'd been banished for resurrecting her as a babe and acceding to her mother's wishes. He'd died for her.

She wouldn't betray her promise to him.

Purpose. Leiyn hadn't recognized the lack of it until that moment. Now, she grasped it again. Even when she didn't have the first idea of how she would aid Zuma's people, she knew she would try to her last breath. Just as she'd owed Tadeo and the fallen rangers justice, she owed Zuma her life. She would give it if it came to that.

I will win this war. No matter the cost.

Amid the reverie, her gaze had fallen to the table. Leiyn raised it to see Xepi watching her.

"What can I do?"

A small smile broke across the shaman's face. "You must learn to access Zuma's *ilis*. Only then can his lifetime of experience and knowledge be yours."

Once, learning more of her mahia would have scared Leiyn to her core. Now, she leaned forward with barely repressed eagerness.

"Where do we begin?"

14

FIRST LESSON

By the time Leiyn left the clifftop cottage, her head was pounding. She made her way down the path to Qasaar alone, Xepi remaining behind. The sun mocked her with blinding ambivalence.

Yet for all her suffering, she wore a smile. It had been a long time since she'd set her mind to mastering a new skill.

Accessing Zuma's *ilis* promised to be a long and difficult affair. First, she had to learn to control her mahia as precisely and adroitly as she could a bow and arrow, or she risked extinguishing the spark for good. So the shaman had begun with basic exercises suitable to an initiate, as Xepi called her. Leiyn surprised her new teacher with the force of her mahia's walls but was confounded in turn that she left gaps that could be exploited.

"Secure your walls," Xepi had said, "and no lyshan nor titan will penetrate your protections."

Leiyn proved less adept in questing with her mahia, or "seeking," as the shaman named it. Xepi set her to using her mahia to explore various lifeforms, first with touch, then from a distance. She'd started learning the distinct lifemarks for the plants scattered about the shaman's house with the promise that she would apply this knowledge to later manipulate esse. Zuma had demonstrated this trick on Suncoats during their journey south, as had the odiosa during Leiyn's brief captivity.

First, Xepi had set her to understanding her own lifemark. The lesson began with a bald question. "What is your lifemark?"

Leiyn was taken aback. Until then, she hadn't considered that she even had one. "Don't know. How can I tell?"

Xepi twisted her mouth to one side, as she often seemed to do when thinking. "Some are marked by experiences early in life. Others, by a strong disposition. Still others bear resemblances to natural things—animals, plants, weather."

Part of Leiyn didn't want to ask the question, but her mouth had different plans. "What are mine?"

The shaman flashed her a rare smile. "That, *Osat*, is something you must discover for yourself."

Xepi wouldn't budge on this point, and though Leiyn tried to apply the same techniques on herself as she had the plants and insects, she left the hut with no more insight on the matter. Her lifefire was just that: herself. She didn't see how she was supposed to differentiate anything more.

Those tasks took the rest of the morning. Though her progress was slight, it was worth every pain it took to gain it. The magic she'd once considered a curse had begun to seem much more like the blessing Gasts claimed it was.

It was also a weapon. A weapon she would need in the coming days.

As she descended into the city, Leiyn pressed her palm to her brow and looked about her. The Gasts milling about their daily routines again stared at her, but there seemed something different to their whispering now. Some remained hostile, but most looked curious. A few verged on what she could only call awe. Leiyn smiled queasily at a few open-mouthed children until their mother shooed them back inside with a scowl. She wondered what tales had spread from the Spear Circle to provoke such a reaction. It took all her remaining willpower not to bow her head and stay to the center of the lane. She refused to flinch before their attention, but would hold her head high, no matter how badly it ached.

When she reached the main square—the Spire Plaza, as Xepi called it—a familiar face appeared from the crowd. Acalan was smoking his pipe and leaning against the side of the Whisperspire, eyes downcast as if in thought. As she approached, his head lifted, and he surprised her with a smile.

"So," he said in his gravelly bass, "you did not ruin everything."

Leiyn rested a hand on one hip. "And after I tried so hard. I'm guessing this has something to do with why everyone is staring at me?"

The chieftain puffed on his pipe, then turned his head aside to blow out the smoke. "You are an outlander. They will always wonder at you."

"This was different than before."

His insufferable smile appeared again. "'Truth crawls, rumors fly,' as my people say. Though most of what spreads is not far from true."

It seemed her suspicions were justified. A hard pit formed in her gut. "They heard I used magic against Teya."

"Better still. They believe you an outlander shaman. And that you won in the Spear Circle."

"And did I win?"

Acalan let out a deep-throated chuckle. "That depends on who you ask. Ilaoti would not see it that way."

"Does Teya?" Only then did she realize what she'd neglected to ask. "Saints, tell me she's alright."

The laughter faded from the chieftain's eyes, replaced by a shrewd look. Leiyn turned away, pretending to observe the people around them, most headed to or from the wells.

"She is," he answered at length. "Patli has ordered her to remain in bed. She has not taken to it well. I am sure she will be upright tomorrow morning."

The tightness in Leiyn's chest loosened. "Good."

His silence drew her into looking at him again. "She believes you won as well."

The emotion that rose before that surprised her. *Elation?* It made no sense. What should she care for Teya's opinion?

Yet you do.

She quickly pressed on. "Looks like it pays to be rash."

"This time." Acalan drew on his pipe once more. "But though most respect you, Ilaoti will turn the Red Hawks against you. Keep your ears open, Huntress, and your blessing as well."

Leiyn wondered if Teya would be among those to retaliate. "When am I not careful?"

He didn't rise to the goad, his expression stony. "I will come by the barracks later. There is much to discuss if we are to move forward."

"Ah, missing our company already?" She flashed him a smirk. "Don't worry—I'll keep you close. You still have a lot of explaining to do."

With a parting wave, she made her way up the cliff to the old barracks.

She'd barely entered before she heard the clatter of footsteps. Having kept her mahia open, she knew it to be Isla and Batu even before they burst into the hallway, the differing qualities of their esse betraying them even when their lifemarks remained obscured.

Isla brought her out of her musings. "I'm beginning to think you'll never be around."

Leiyn flashed a belated smile. "Sorry. Xepi wants to train me as a shaman."

Into their stunned silence, she explained all she'd learned. A growl from her belly moved them into the mess hall midway through, where Batu had already manifested his newfound skills in cooking to produce a savory soup from what they'd scrounged from the larder. Leiyn devoured two bowls and eyed a third by the time she'd rounded out her revelations.

Isla shook her head. "I hope you'll tap into Zuma's spark soon. Even so, when facing corrupted dryvans... I don't see how it will be enough to fight them."

"With the titans."

At this quiet assertion from Batu, Leiyn turned with Isla to stare at the former plainsrider. He only shrugged his broad shoulders.

"Mother Xepi said lyshans cannot command them. You can. Perhaps they can do what we cannot."

Isla pressed the young man's arm. Leiyn spoke to head off any further displays of affection.

"You know, you're smarter than you look."

Batu gave her a rueful smile, while Isla raised an eyebrow.

"A man can be handsome as well as intelligent," her fellow ranger said.

Leiyn rolled her eyes. "A third bowl isn't worth enduring this."

She stood, pretending to leave, when her mahia detected someone strolling toward the barracks. Only as she recognized Acalan's esse did she relax.

"Couldn't stay away for long, could you?" she called as he entered the building.

Isla and Batu shared a confused glance until the Jaguar chieftain turned the corner. "Acalan!" Isla greeted him cheerily. "We wondered when you would be by. Judging by your expression, the council went well?"

"It did." His dark eyes slid to Leiyn. "It seems 'Firebrand' is not as much of a liability as I feared."

Isla and Batu chuckled, while Leiyn pretended to scowl. "Where did you hear that name?" she demanded. "Did Isla tell you?"

The chieftain only smiled. "But there is still much work to do. Taht Xepi has explained what she intends for you?"

"Yes." Leiyn crossed her arms and leaned back in her chair.

Nodding, he looked at Isla. "I want you to attend Tetrad meetings while Leiyn trains as an initiate. Soon, they will become accustomed to your presence. Then we will win them over to your cause."

Isla nodded, though Leiyn could see the worry in her eyes. "I intend to listen at first. In time, I hope to know what to say and when to say it."

Leiyn reached back to grip her friend's hand. "You'll find the words. Always been better with them than me."

"That's not difficult." Isla pressed her hand back with a small smile.

"And me?" Batu asked. He sounded a bit morose to Leiyn's ear, though he kept his expression carefully blank.

Acalan studied the former plainsrider. "Train as a *situal*. Teya should be willing to show you the ways of our scouts. It is a great honor and would be good for my people to see you taking an active role in the city's defense."

Batu's placidity eroded into relief. He bobbed a quick bow. "I will ask her. Thank you, Toa Acalan."

While the chieftain gazed at the former plainsrider with open bemusement, Leiyn found herself speaking. "I'll go with him. Xepi cannot keep me tied up all the time, and it'd be good to stretch my legs."

Only as the others turned to her with matching expressions did she recognize why she might have truly volunteered. Her cheeks burned, but she kept her stare defiant.

"Well?" she challenged them. "If one of us going is good, two is better."

"It is." Acalan sounded on the verge of laughter. She was grateful he repressed it. "Teya would be amenable to that."

Leiyn wondered if there were hidden currents to his words as Isla spoke. "I'm glad we know what to do next, but what comes after? Your people, Acalan, cannot be our allies until your war is finished. If Leiyn means to fight them with titans—"

"With the *kainox*?" Acalan interrupted, then stared down at Leiyn. "Xepi did not tell you to do this."

"No, she didn't." Leiyn matched his stare. "Batu had the idea, and it's a good one, as far as I can see."

The chieftain's expression darkened further still. "It would fail if you tried it."

Batu hunched his shoulders. Isla glanced at him, then leaned against the table. "Why? How else can Leiyn, or any shaman, challenge these lyshans?"

The muscles in Acalan's jaw tightened as he swiveled his gaze over them. After a few moments, he loosened it and spoke.

"Titans cannot fight the *sach'aan*, for they cannot catch them. You are not the first to think of it; many shamans have tried before and failed. Lyshans and dryvans were the first masters of this world, and though they have faded, they still command powers of which humans can only dream."

Leiyn found her temper rising. "Then why am I here? What use am I in this war of yours?"

Acalan's eyes smoldered as they settled on her. "I thought," he said in a low rumble, "you had understood by now that this is not my people's war, Huntress. It is a war that will engulf all people, from every land and every tribe. No matter how large or small the kingdom, they will feel the ripples of what happens here. For if we fail, these devils will take back what they believe still belongs to them."

She didn't lower her gaze, though she wanted to. *And here, I just resolved to die for this war.* So swiftly, she'd shied away from the task, pushing it away as if it weren't her concern.

No longer.

"I understand, Acalan. It is my war as well. I could honor Zuma no other way. But I want to know there's hope in our fight."

The chieftain stared at her a moment longer before softening. "There is. I once told you Zuma's reason for going south with me was to serve as a scribe for our negotiations with Baltesia. That was true, but only in part. You know now how valuable and scarce our shamans are. Though he was still hale for his age, I would not have risked Zuma had he not insisted."

He paused and Leiyn couldn't help herself. "Well? What was it?"

Acalan ran a hand over his bare scalp, the green tattoos distorting as the skin pulled. "He searched for those blessed by

Tlalli so he might bring them back and train them as shamans. He was looking for you, Leiyn, and those like you."

Convergences. Leiyn remembered Xepi muttering the word before. Now, she understood what she'd meant. How unlikely that Zuma should save her as a child, then later find her as an adult. That their fates would become so intertwined that she bore a fragment of his soul inside her. That his war would become hers.

Almost as if this was the way it was always meant to be.

She shook her head. *Saints, am I starting to believe in destiny?* She'd started out with little faith and lost it amidst childhood tragedies. These were coincidences, yes, and great ones at that. But it was a far stretch to destiny.

Especially since they could still lose the war.

Leiyn raised her eyes to find the others watching her. She gave them a weak smile. "I'm starting to think you're avoiding the question. How can we fight the lyshans, Acalan?"

He returned her smile with a grim one of his own. "I dance around the answer because I do not have it."

She felt as if she were back in the Spear Circle, knocked flat on her back. Isla failed to repress her gasp. Before either of them could find the breath for words, Acalan spoke on.

"But though I do not understand, I know the solution exists. Zuma discovered something of titans before he went south. Perhaps he shared this with the other shamans. I do know it was his purpose to find more initiates to pass on this knowledge, to train shamans who would take the fight to the lyshans. Shamans such as you will become."

It was a poor comfort, but enough that Leiyn could breathe again. "I suppose Xepi will tell me in due course."

The chieftain glanced back toward the door. "I must go. The Tetrad will convene again soon. Not today," he said as Isla opened her mouth to speak. "Tomorrow, you may come. Ilaoti is still too angry to make progress."

"Tomorrow will do," Isla said, her relief evident.

Acalan almost smiled, his features lightening. "Rest tonight. Eat and recover. It may be your last opportunity."

With that, the chieftain turned and strode out of the mess hall.

Leiyn turned in her chair to exchange glances with the others, her eyebrows raised. "If the chieftain commands it, so we must do. Found any liquor in that larder?"

Batu suddenly wore a boyish grin. "One jug had the right smell."

"Then what are you waiting for? Fetch it, man!"

With a laugh, she shooed her two companions toward the pantry.

15

BEYOND THE WALL

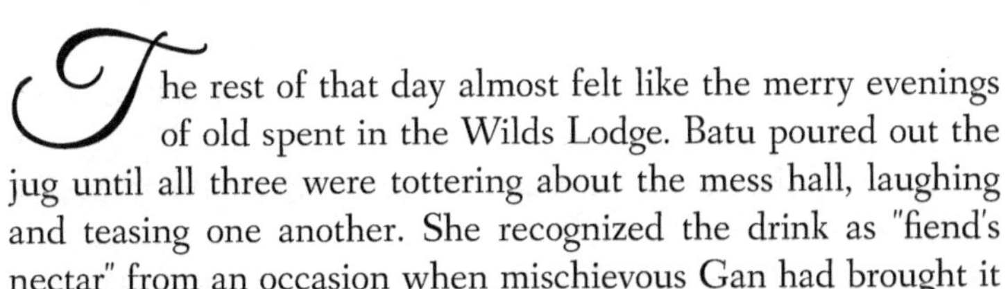

The rest of that day almost felt like the merry evenings of old spent in the Wilds Lodge. Batu poured out the jug until all three were tottering about the mess hall, laughing and teasing one another. She recognized the drink as "fiend's nectar" from an occasion when mischievous Gan had brought it to the Lodge. As it had been then, the alcohol was strong and burned as Leiyn swallowed it. Though there was a slimy feel to it, its agreeable sweetness made it easy to refill her glass again and again.

As the pitcher emptied, their entertainment grew more outrageous. They began with stories from their past, both amusing and otherwise. Isla reminded Leiyn of how thoroughly she'd beaten her at quarterstaffs. Batu admitted to pulling a prank on a few of the nastier older pupils, lacing their drinks with a laxative that kept them in the outhouses all night. Leiyn told of how she'd received the scars around her neck, a story she'd never before told in full, considering how intertwined it was with her magic. Now, she added only slight embellishments, for in a fight involving half a dozen trappers, an odiosa, and a titan, little else was needed.

Long after they'd devolved to singing bawdy songs and twirling in wild dances, the three stumbled up the stairs to their beds. Her companions entered the same room, but just then,

Leiyn couldn't have cared less. The room spun around as she pulled off her clothes and weaved her way across the floor to collapse on her wooden bed. She couldn't recall the last time she'd drank so much.

"Fiend's nectar lives up to its name," she mumbled to the room.

Ordinarily, the lack of control would have bothered her, but for once, she didn't fight it. She sucked in the cool air with easy breaths, her chest loose for the first time in what felt like months.

Her mahia open, the bed cradled her body in perfect comfort. Yet she could also sense the other two through the walls, their lifeforce pressed together and intertwining. Leiyn groaned and put her hands over her eyes, for all the good it would do. Only putting up her walls could shut out sensing their coupling, and she had no desire to wake up bruised and aching from sleeping on unyielding wood.

Instead, she sought distraction, questing for other nearby esse. To her surprise, she didn't have to go far. Something glowed in the walls, faint but persistent. Leiyn sat up and pressed a hand to the spot.

"What in Omn's bloody name..."

It wasn't the drink crossing her senses; *something* was alive in the wall. She even felt a slight warmth pulsating from it, similar to the bed under her, though different in its presentation.

For a moment, she only stared at it, wondering at what it could be. Then she remembered the windows in Xepi's hut and how they'd opened with a touch.

"A door...?"

A distant part of her rang with alarm, but it was only a murmur amid her buzzing mind. Leiyn stretched her mahia toward the esse, touching it through the stone like she'd grasped at Teya during their bout.

Only instead of Leiyn seizing hold of it, the esse grabbed and dragged her in.

The world pitched even more violently than before. She felt

her limbs sprawl, but it was her mahia that stretched furthest, taut as a sail in high wind.

Stone appeared beneath her hands and knees, somehow soft, just as the bed had been. Only, she was no longer in her room.

There was no light, yet her surroundings were alive to her lifesense. Wherever she'd arrived was teeming with life. It glimmered in the floor, in the walls; it radiated from down the corridor ahead, where she guessed other rooms lay. They didn't have the feel of humans or animals, but something else, something... unmoving.

She stifled a groan. *What have you done now, Firebrand?*

Reawakened caution kept her from speaking aloud. She still reeled from the nectar and was devoid of even her undergarments. Her position was sorely vulnerable. About her drunkenness, at least, she had an idea of what to do.

Leiyn reached for her lifefire and pulled at it in a similar way as she had when healing herself in the past. But now, instead of directing it toward a wound, Leiyn let it spread throughout her body, filling the streams of blood in her limbs. With her hidden sense opened, she felt the alcohol working on her body, tiny flecks of black corruption dotting her lifefire.

The esse burned them away. Within minutes, Unera settled below her. She was back in control—of herself, at least.

Leiyn leaned against the wall, panting from the effort. Drawing on her own lifeforce was especially draining.

At least I can string two thoughts together again.

She only rested for a few moments before the situation struck her in all its oddity. For all she knew, she was stuck in this dark corridor. There was a lack of scent to it that spoke of disuse despite the life filtering through it. She heard whispers from the wall, gently touching against her mahia.

Ruins, she realized. She'd heard Qasaar was built atop ancient ruins. She just hadn't known how deep those ruins went.

Leiyn quested out with her lifesense. Though Qasaar should have been around her, the city seemed to have disappeared. She sensed no people nor any other signs of life beyond the wall.

Only the strange ruins shone, and nameless objects littered the rooms farther down the corridors.

A brighter patch of esse emanated from the wall at her back. Leiyn turned, feeling the need to face it, and only as she focused on it did she realize the circle of esse felt familiar. It was similar to the one she'd touched in her room.

Perhaps the opposite side of the same panel.

She had to hope. Nothing else in this strange place held a better promise of returning her to the barracks. Whether this corridor belonged to Gast ancestors, the *sach'aan,* or some other unknown race, she assumed they'd have a way to leave as well as arrive. Like a door, it only made sense for it to be where she'd appeared.

Leiyn sucked in a breath, then exhaled. Once more, she reached into the wall.

Upon contact with the slab of esse, the stone again tried to suck her into it. This time, she was ready for it and resisted. Its pull was strong, but not so much she couldn't stop it. Leiyn hovered, suspended between the lightless corridor and wherever the wall wished to whisk her away to. She felt her spirit wandering from the boundaries of her body, as if it were no longer sufficient to contain it. The entire ruins seemed somehow brighter, like she had become more aware of just how much life remained in it.

But she would get nowhere if she resisted forever. With a muttered prayer, Leiyn relented to the current.

The transition lasted only a moment. With her head clear, the disorientation wasn't nearly as bad. As Leiyn became aware of her body again, she blinked and held up her hands before her eyes.

Hands. Eyes.

She could see again, feel the bed beneath her, sense Isla and Batu mingling in the room next to her. Seeking farther, she sensed Qasaar and its populace splayed out along the cliffs opposite her and in the canyon below.

She heaved a sigh and flopped back onto the wooden mattress.

Though she no longer had a head stuffed full of the Gast drink to distract her, the bizarre exploit proved sufficient to occupy her mind and help her ignore her companions' activities in the adjoining room. Drawing up the blankets, Leiyn soon drifted to sleep and down strange corridors.

16

ROUTINE

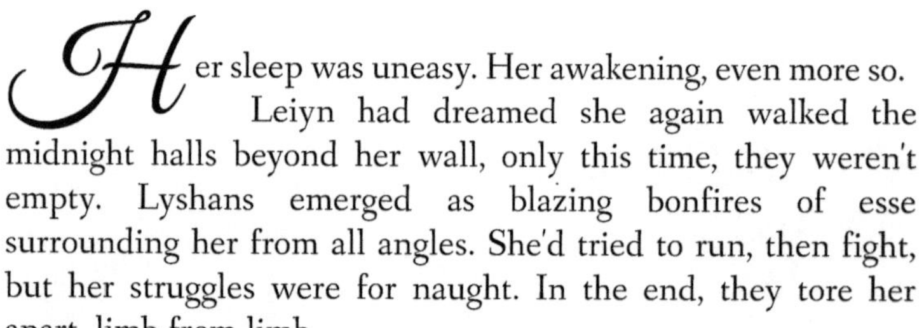

Her sleep was uneasy. Her awakening, even more so.

Leiyn had dreamed she again walked the midnight halls beyond her wall, only this time, they weren't empty. Lyshans emerged as blazing bonfires of esse surrounding her from all angles. She'd tried to run, then fight, but her struggles were for naught. In the end, they tore her apart, limb from limb.

As her head twisted free in their hands, Leiyn bolted upright, panting. Her skull pulsed, but not as badly as suffering from a hangover. Slowly, she breathed through the panic, grounding herself in her senses.

And froze. With her mahia, she sensed someone standing in the doorway.

Leiyn whipped her head around, body tensed for a fight, even as she drew her blankets over her bared chest. "What're you doing here?"

Teya gave her a wide grin. "Fair morning, Redlock. You look ready to train."

Leiyn rubbed her eyes free of dreamdust, hoping to hide her embarrassment. Her mouth sour, her hair an eagle's nest, covers bunched about her, she knew she made for quite the sight.

"Mind if I dress first?"

"If you insist." The scout's teasing smile was the last thing Leiyn saw before Teya pulled the curtain closed.

Shooting out of bed, Leiyn muttered curses under her breath as she gathered her clothes, strewn across the floor during her drunken disrobing. Dressed once more in her ranger greens with her long knives hanging from her belt, she braided her hair, hoping she looked halfway presentable.

Satisfied, Leiyn pulled aside the curtain and stepped out. Teya was absent, but Batu stood just outside, his eyes scrunched and his shoulders hunched. He'd managed to drag on his clothes, though sloppily.

She grinned and slapped him on the back. "Thought you'd be hardier than this! Surely, a few drinks don't put you down."

Batu grunted something in reply and shuffled toward the stairs. Leiyn shook her head and followed. A glance inside Isla's room showed her fellow ranger still lying in bed, face turned away.

"Being an envoy's not so bad, after all," Leiyn called in as she passed.

"I don't see you signing up to attend the Tetrad," came Isla's muffled reply.

Leiyn only laughed.

Her head had ceased aching by the time she descended to the first floor, though her stomach rumbled like a rising hill tortoise. Teya waited by the door, one hand propped on a hip, the other holding the short spear she'd carried when they first met. It was slightly shorter than Teya, making it roughly Leiyn's height, its blade a foot long and curvy at the end like a snake. *For deeper cuts,* Tadeo had once explained of similar blades in the Lodge's weapon stock. Having contended with her in the Spear Circle, Leiyn didn't envy the enemy who fought the scout when she wielded such a weapon.

"Come," Teya said as they reached her. "You have many things to learn and little time to do it."

"Enough time to break our fast." Leiyn adjusted course and made for the kitchens.

"If you outlanders need it," the scout called at her back.

A short while later, with her and Batu's bellies settled by a meal of old maize bread and wrinkled apples, they followed Teya out. A dusty haze had settled over Qasaar. Noticing the scout had pulled up some sort of kerchief from around her neck up over her nose, Leiyn covered her face with the edge of her cloak. Batu had neglected a cloak and seemed the more miserable for it. He pressed his nose into his upraised arm and bent his head before the winds.

The dust lessened as they ascended Lualli, enough to drop their face coverings. They came around the switchback and headed toward the Spear Circle but stopped short of it. Fields Leiyn had only noticed peripherally before now had their uses become apparent. Farther out were those that grew the Gasts' crops, of which maize, squash, and potatoes were predominant. Closer at hand were training yards, judging by the warriors and the pells, notched wooden posts used for weapons practice, erected every dozen paces. A score of men and women already toiled away at the posts, most using blunted spears such as Leiyn and Teya had wielded in their bout. As Leiyn's party passed, they called out greetings to Teya, and she shouted them back, often accompanied by a quip.

The scout stopped in front of an unoccupied practice post. "I will fetch us spears, then show you how a Red Hawk fights."

"Wait." Leiyn pulled back her cloak to reveal the long knives at her hip. "I have all the weapons I need right here."

Teya raised an eyebrow. "If you insist. We have wooden swords that mimic *macuas*, if that would suit you?"

Leiyn nodded, and the scout fetched the faux weapons. While they waited, she glanced at her friend. "Holding up alright?"

Batu gave her a sullen look. "The maize didn't settle well."

She barked a laugh. "Hold down your meal, Batu. If my guess is right, you're in for a long morning."

Teya returned moments later. Setting aside her anelaces and cloak, Leiyn hefted the wooden wasters in both hands. They weren't balanced the same as her blades and were at least twice as heavy. But as she didn't want to dull her blades by chopping at pells, these were her best option.

Leiyn set to practicing her forms while the scout showed Batu her tribe's way of fighting with a spear. At first, she watched the pair from the corner of her eye. She longed to be the one working with Teya, if only to be near her, but not so much as to be embarrassed again at the end of the scout's spear.

At length, she settled into a rhythm. Leiyn let her body recall the sequences she'd spent hours rehearsing under Tadeo's tutelage and many more hours perfecting since. Though her shoulders ached, her legs trembled, and her breath came quick, she imagined the pell to be an attacking Suncoat and pressed on.

When she completed the last of the forms, Leiyn took a step back and wiped the sweat from her forehead. Sensing someone's stare, she looked over to find Teya watching her. Batu was stumbling through a spear routine that looked familiar. Leiyn had always suspected Tadeo had borrowed the fighting style from the Gasts; now, she had proof.

"You are slow," the scout called to her.

From another Gast, it might have been insulting, but Leiyn found herself smiling. "I'll get faster."

Teya grinned back. Batu paused to glance her way, and Leiyn quickly turned aside. Judging by that look, the coquetry hadn't been lost on him.

Thus did the morning pass until Leiyn had to depart. Tozi had passed along a message from Xepi the previous day to meet the shaman at noon, so Leiyn put the practice swords back in the storage wagon, waved farewell to Teya and Batu, who remained the scout's unfortunate pupil, and made the long trek over to the shaman's hut on the opposite cliff.

"If only there were a bridge," she muttered under her cloak as she headed down the slope into the dusty canyon below.

She made good time, reaching the hut as the sun burned directly overhead. The hut's windows were already open. She sensed the shaman within, her esse bright. Leiyn's pace increased as she neared. On the walk over, the events of the night before, forgotten in the rush of the morning, had flooded back in. If anyone could promise answers to what had occurred, it was Xepi.

No sooner had she entered and set aside her cloak and weapons did she speak. "What's beyond the barracks' walls?"

Xepi eyed her from where she sat by the table. "How do you know about that?"

Leiyn only hesitated a moment before confessing. She told all except for her inebriated state; she didn't need Xepi to think her rasher than she must already, considering her exploits in the Spear Circle.

The shaman listened, not speaking or reacting until she'd finished. Only then did she sag forward, eyes set on the table, looking wearied to Leiyn's eye. Leiyn had remained standing and only then sat, fidgeting with nervous energy despite the morning's exercise.

Finally, Xepi raised her gaze to hold Leiyn's. "*Osat*, you must listen to me. Do not visit this place again."

Leiyn narrowed her eyes. "What? Why?"

The shaman's lips pressed into a thin line. Leiyn could almost see her deciding how much to reveal behind those placid eyes of hers.

"It is an ancestral place," she said finally. "Ruins remain across much of Qasaar. They are dangerous places, unprotected and full of things unknown and mystifying. Many shamans have entered in the time since we made this place our home, curious as you are. Some were injured; some were driven mad by visions and voices. A few died. Still others vanished, their bodies never recovered."

Leiyn leaned back in her chair. "What killed them?"

Xepi shook her head. "Much of what we think we know is mere suspicion. Artifacts, imbued with ancestral magic, remain in those halls. Some, like the windows of this hut, or the panel through which you moved, appear to be harmless. Others have been less so."

Leiyn frowned toward the ceiling. "So shamans died because they tried using these objects?"

"Yes. Three have passed that way."

"And the ones who vanished? Were they also using these artifacts?"

Again, the shaman hesitated. "We do not know. But I suspect not."

"And why's that?"

Xepi stared at her again, iron returning to her dark gaze. "They entered alone. And after each disappearance, the lyshans attacked Qasaar with titans."

Leiyn abruptly righted her chair and leaned forward. "They took them," she guessed. "The lyshans can find us beyond the wall."

"So we suspect."

That gave her earlier dream a deadly new meaning. Leiyn studied the whorls in the wood of the table as she thought it through. Something didn't add up, and only then did she realize what it was.

"Why wait until someone is in the ruins? If they want shamans, why don't the lyshans take them anytime they like? Foxfur entered Qasaar at will." Leiyn looked around the hut as if their enemy might be lurking in the shadowed corners even then.

Xepi gave her a tight smile. "Because they cannot. Long ago, before we Gasts came here, the dryvans cast a spell upon Qasaar. It allows them, but not lyshans, to enter the city. Do not ask me how it works," she added at Leiyn's look. "Such is not within my understanding. But it seems to protect only the outlying world. Any who enter the inner ruins are at risk."

Leiyn clenched her fists. *Nothing happened to me. Dreams are dreams. I will not fear them.* Yet a shiver ran through her at what might have occurred the previous night.

Xepi seemed to see it. "*Osat,*" she spoke softly, "you must swear to me you will not enter the ancestral ruins again. We cannot risk you, not when so few of us remain."

Leiyn had always been curious. But just then, her fear was stronger.

"I swear it."

The shaman watched her a moment longer, then nodded. "Good. We will practice seeking first."

With their mysterious enemy in mind, Leiyn set to the exercise with abandon. Though the identification of lifemarks still evaded her, she found her seeking had already improved. Her mahia's walls were even better, for Xepi no longer found weaknesses to exploit. After a half hour attempting to break through, the shaman reluctantly acknowledged Leiyn had a certain mastery in that respect.

"But we will continue to test them," she warned.

With one hand rubbing her temples, Xepi set forth a fresh task. "One of our best defenses against lyshans is to hide. How would you hide?"

"Let me guess—putting up my walls won't help."

"That would be the surest way to guarantee your death." Xepi let her hand drop, her gaze intensifying once more. "Only those blessed by *Tlalli* can guard themselves so. No, it is not behind walls that you will survive, but through disguise."

"Disguise? Isn't that the same thing?" Even as she spoke, Leiyn remembered the things Zuma had done on their journey south. He'd confounded the senses of Suncoats on multiple occasions so that they stared directly at their party and never saw them.

The shaman shook her head. "I will demonstrate."

Leiyn braced herself, her walls ready to raise at the first sign of attack. She didn't know what it would feel like, this blurring of the senses. Only because she was paying attention did she notice Xepi's touch. It was like a warm breeze against her lifefire, almost imperceptible in the way it danced with her flames.

She blinked and stared across the table. The shaman had disappeared.

Leiyn stood abruptly. Even as she moved, Xepi reappeared. Her teacher wore a grim smile.

"You could no longer see me."

"No." Her cheeks felt warm as Leiyn sat again. "I felt something against my esse, then you were just... gone. How did you do it?"

"It is well that you could sense it. As for how, it is not so different from walling yourself off. Subtler, yes, but a similar act."

In fits and starts, the shaman showed her how it was done, demonstrating it again, then allowing Leiyn to try to emulate it. As Xepi said, it was similar to building her barriers, only she had to do it around another person's esse. It proved more challenging than she expected, yet as the sun sailed toward the horizon, Xepi claimed Leiyn was almost hidden from view.

"A few more days," she said with rare approval, "and you shall succeed."

Leiyn left the hut, weary and satisfied by the day. She'd barely eaten since that morning, only the little that Xepi had offered, yet she found a different sort of satisfaction filling her. Almost, she felt like a ranger again, though half of what occupied her was the magic she'd always denied at the Lodge. Yet being a ranger was more than a certain set of activities. It was learning, observing, and adapting in the name of protecting those who needed it.

The Lodge lives on. She touched Tadeo's fox figurine, always secure in the pouch at her hip. *I'll make sure it doesn't die.*

She hoped it wasn't a lie. Remembering the enemies lurking behind Qasaar's walls, it was hard to hold to hope. Yet resilience was a ranger's first weapon. She'd survived death too many times to submit to it now.

Leiyn kept her chin high and carried on.

DUTY

*H*er days fell into a routine.

Each morning, Leiyn went with Batu and Teya to the practice yards. Sometimes, she worked on her fighting forms, a necessity after too long without them. She'd been slack in her training since the Suncoats' attack on the Lodge, and though her skills had kept her alive, they were showing their rust. But as the days and weeks passed, her speed, precision, and sequencing almost returned to their peak.

Her bow saw fresh use as well. At last, she gave it the care she'd been neglecting. She inspected each arrow for flaws and discarded any that didn't meet a ranger's standards. She missed the arrows she'd fletched herself or, better still, those crafted by Tadeo. She oiled the arrows and waxed the fletching, replaced the bowstrings for both her longbow and warbow, then checked them over for cracks.

Maintenance complete, she visited the range, drawing and loosing until her shoulders and back ached in that familiar way. Her precision, at least, hadn't suffered for her laxness. The other Gasts on the range took notice, and on the second day, they approached her with friendly bets. Leiyn was happy to accept them and won more often than lost. Her coin purse had flattened over the journey, even with the governor's stipend. She looked forward to not entirely living off Acalan's charity.

Better still, Teya often checked in with her. Since the scout's change of heart at the Spear Circle, she'd only grown warmer toward Leiyn and her friends. Each day, Leiyn tried not to sneak glances as Teya tutored Batu in spear techniques. Her enchantment hadn't waned with familiarity, but waxed, and Leiyn most looked forward to the hours spent near her.

The afternoons held a different allure. Under Xepi's instruction, Leiyn advanced in her mahia by long strides. She continued to seek until she could clearly identify human lifeforce on the other side of Qasaar without strain. Her mastery of putting up walls around herself proved a boon in obscuring others' senses, and soon, Xepi struggled to fight her off.

After growing frustrated with lifemarks after three days without progress, the shaman found another way to explain the process. "You must look through the *ilis*, not at it. You are telling me what the qualities of the *ilis* is, but I want to know what you see beyond it. Have you not imagined scenes in campfires before, Osat?"

It was the key that turned the lock. Leiyn had stared into many bonfires in her time, between all the patrols as a ranger and journeys to and from Southport. She understood how the mind could play tricks on the eyes when looking at flames. Only as she remembered those instances did she know what Xepi meant.

Leiyn sensed Xepi's esse again, but instead of observing the lifefire itself, she stared past it, as if she unfocused her eyes. The specific qualities of the lifeforce faded, and faint images beyond it came into view.

"A draconion," Leiyn murmured. "It's dead, its entrails pulled out." She'd seen butchery, but the sight of it still made her instinctively draw away.

Leiyn looked up and met Xepi's eyes to find the shaman had gone very still. "This is part of your lifemark?" she asked softly. "An eviscerated draconion?"

Xepi's throat quivered. Her answer came out in a whisper. "Yes."

Leiyn waited for an explanation. When none came, she

shrugged and set back to practicing. If there was a story there, she wouldn't learn it by twisting Xepi's arm.

Finding the lifemark proved easier the second time. Within a minute, she muttered, "There's a hearth, lit with flames, but the fuel is exhausted, the fire sputtering out." Leiyn didn't stop this time but pressed on for the third part. "And beyond that, a spear broken in two." Smaller images hovered beyond, but she stopped, blinking to reassert her vision. She startled at the black expression on the shaman's face.

"That's what I saw," Leiyn said, slightly miffed. Even a misreading of her lifemark shouldn't have spawned such scorn.

Xepi shook her head, and the intensity lessened as she lowered her gaze. "It is not that."

Silence reigned for several minutes. Leiyn welcomed it, for her efforts that day were beginning to exhaust her. She was surprised when the shaman abruptly stood.

"That is all," she said, then opened the door. Perplexed, Leiyn left without question, though she didn't stop wondering just what those images meant.

She wasn't content to only see Xepi's lifemark. That night, she fought off sleep a little longer to try to detect her own. But peering into one's own esse proved more challenging than looking through another's, and after a dozen unsuccessful attempts, she conceded defeat for the night.

In the days following her advancement, Leiyn read the lifemarks of those around her. Isla's wasn't entirely surprising, though they did give her pause. First emerged the everscent blossom; then, a copse of golden-leafed aspens; and finally, a female thorned lion, who appeared to be crouched before a litter of cubs. The images fit her, though Leiyn couldn't say why. She tucked it away, just another of the many questions for her teacher.

Batu's proved easier to understand. At dinner, she stared through his lifefire until a cistern emerged from the flames. It was familiar, similar to the one at the Greathouse of the plain-sriders, yet looked to have once been cracked, but was now mended. Behind it, she saw several blades of autumn grass waving in a gentle breeze. Last of all, and most difficult to see, was a large animal, curled in slumber. *A bear*, she realized upon closer inspection. Gentle as the former plainsrider was, the beast suited him.

Much as she wished to see Teya's lifemark, Leiyn couldn't find the opportunity. Getting caught staring at the scout was the last thing she wished to happen; she could already picture the smirk she would earn for it. Yet though she snuck glances at her in the training yard, she never looked long enough to peer through her bright esse.

She hesitated to mention Batu and Isla's lifemarks to Xepi at their next lesson. It seemed too private a thing to reveal. Only when she realized the shaman could examine them herself anytime she wished did she divulge what she'd learned. To her revelations, Xepi only nodded, then sat in silence.

"So?" Leiyn prompted. "What do they mean?"

"Do you not know? The meanings are before you."

Leiyn crossed her arms. "Enlighten me."

The shaman wore a small smile as she spoke. "We will begin with the envoy. An 'everscent' flower, as you call it... what are its qualities?"

This line of questioning had always irritated Leiyn, yet she bridled her impatience and played along. "Its aroma shifts over time, usually to pleasant things. It's beautiful to look at." She paused, mulling over the plant. "I think it's resilient, too. And it's certainly rare."

Xepi nodded. "In all these respects and more, this is who Isla is. The aspens?"

Leiyn had to think hard on that. "Aspens have a flaky bark exterior, and a smooth inner one." She shook her head. "No, that's nothing."

"Perhaps," the shaman answered. "Perhaps not."

"Very helpful. Maybe it's because they're not just one, but many..." Her head shot up as it struck her. "Connected. Aspens grow with one another. They share a common root structure."

"Good." The shaman's smile widened ever so slightly. "And the lion?"

"Protective. Fierce. Loyal. Maternal?" Leiyn thought for a moment, then nodded with a grin. "I guess she is, in a way."

Xepi waved a hand before her. "I will leave you to think on your other companion. The lesson remains: you know what they mean. You must only draw the meanings out."

Leiyn thought again of the shaman's lifemark and how little she understood it. But considering Xepi's previous reaction, she thought it best not to resurrect that mystery.

Their lesson moved on to more practical applications of mahia. Xepi had Leiyn fetch a potted aloe vera from the corner of her hut and drag it next to the table. When she sat again, the shaman laid a hand on the thick, spiny leaves.

"Plants may hold great reserves of *ilis*." She spoke softly, as if afraid of awakening the aloe vera. "Trees, most of all, but medicinal plants such as *anxel*, what you know as aloe vera, do as well. For one who knows how to wield its force, many grave wounds can be mended."

Leiyn grimaced, the memory of her killing a grove rising to the surface. "You'll show me how?"

"Yes. Place your hand on its leaves..."

Over the next several hours, they practiced drawing in lifeforce from the plant, then giving it back. Leiyn knew intuitively how to absorb esse; she'd used it enough by now. But a slow, measured approach confounded her. After almost killing the aloe vera twice in a row, she stood and paced around the hut before returning to her chair. As much as it infuriated her, she knew she needed to control her mahia, or it would control her. She couldn't risk almost killing someone else by accident.

In the following days, she slowly began to master this technique as well, then employ it. Instead of giving back the esse, Xepi had her absorb it, again in a controlled and efficient manner.

"You suck at it like a woman dying of thirst," Xepi chastised when Leiyn again failed at her task. "Sips are all you need take. Anything else will be wasted."

She tried, but even over three days, she failed as often as she succeeded. At least from this, she left the hut feeling energized and alert. Absorbing esse was better than chewing tea leaves or coffee beans, as many rangers had done to stay awake during long watches. Even her hunger and thirst were dulled, though not entirely dissipated.

Remember these, Leiyn commanded herself when leaving Xepi's hut each day. *Remember and use them.* The lessons would only be as useful as she was able to implement them. She didn't need to merely understand them; she needed mastery.

At the end of the fifth day, however, she received a sharp reminder of a different goal. No sooner had she entered the barracks than Isla appeared from the mess hall. Leiyn halted midstep, sensing something was amiss even before Batu shuffled contritely into the hall.

"What's wrong?" Leiyn checked over her friends for injuries and saw only Batu's usual bruises and cuts gained during his training. "Did something happen?"

"Yes. Something has happened while you were playing with spears." Isla's pixie features were pinched, her brow drawn. "But you wouldn't know that, would you?"

As Leiyn stared at her friend, baffled, she noticed Batu mouth a word behind Isla's back. *Apologize.*

"I'm sorry?" she ventured.

Isla blew out a sigh. "Come in, then. Have your dinner."

Exchanging another look with Batu, Leiyn followed her fellow ranger into the mess hall. She didn't dare speak until she had the day's meal heaped onto her plate: charred mutton, roasted root vegetables, and maize bread, courtesy once again of Batu. With a nod of thanks, she turned back to her friend and waited.

Isla sucked in a breath before speaking. "Lord Governor Mauricio didn't just make me Baltesia's envoy, Leiyn. He named you one as well."

Leiyn swallowed a tough piece of meat. "Saints only know why."

A ghost of a smile touched her friend's lips, but it was gone as soon as it came. "You cannot just train. You have to help forge an alliance with the tribes. I cannot do this on my own."

Only then did Leiyn understand. Wiping the grease from her fingers on a rag, she pushed her plate aside and held Isla's gaze. "You're not on your own. We're in this together, I swear it. But we decided to lean into our strengths and each do what we're best at, remember? You're more diplomatic, so you're handling the Tetrad. I'm more a ranger than an envoy, so I'm handling this war."

Isla looked placated, yet still weary. "You're right. I wouldn't want you in the Whisperspire, anyway. It's just... Legion take me, they're insufferable!"

Leiyn listened with Batu as Isla aired her grievances, nodding along sympathetically as she finished her meal. Ilaoti was proving the greatest trouble, to no one's surprise, but even Acalan received his fair share of reprimands.

When she'd exhausted her complaints, Isla leaned back in her chair with a laugh. "Guess I just needed to vent. Sorry."

Leiyn waved a hand. "I left you out to dry."

"On that... if there is anything you could do to lighten the load, I'd appreciate it."

What more she could do was beyond her, but Leiyn sensed her fellow ranger needed this. "I'll do what I can."

Batu, who had been gently kneading Isla's shoulders with a hand, rose then. "I think there's some fiend's nectar left..."

They shared a look.

"Just a little," Leiyn conceded, and all three laughed as they scampered for the pantry.

PART III

DEVILS OF THE BARREN

THIRTEEN YEARS BEFORE

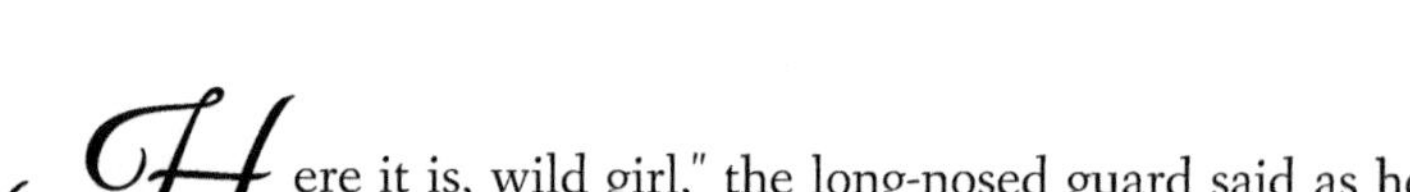

*H*ere it is, wild girl," the long-nosed guard said as he stopped in the middle of the road. "San Hugo's Sanctuary."

Leiyn raised her gaze and stared at the building before them. She'd barely looked up since arriving at Southport and being stopped by the guards, but the city still wormed into her senses. The stench of sewers filled her nose as they walked down the streets, at least where smoke and ash from the old burn piles didn't reign. The Blush seemed to be receding, but it left signs of its passage everywhere around her. She wondered how long the bones would remain.

Yet she didn't fear the dead, nor the plague that had stolen their lives; it was the people left behind that terrified her. Something in their eyes put a dread in her that had never been there before. Like they might see what she strained so hard to repress.

Her walls were raised around her magic, but with the presence of the crowds thronging every road battering against them, Leiyn felt others must know her secret. Mindful of her father's warnings, she'd feared the guards would bring her to the odiosas for her Gast curse. She'd tried to stay away from the city for this very reason.

But winter couldn't be denied for long. Nor could the memories.

They surfaced then, summoned by her thoughts. *Father. Licky. Hazel.* She tasted ash, blood, vomit, and felt the heat of stolen lives swell in her chest.

With an effort, Leiyn shut out the names and bolstered her barriers. To feel all she'd lost would drown her, and she had to swim for her father's sake.

And my own.

When she first reached Southport, the guards at the gate had fetched someone in the guardhouse to take her into custody. Leiyn had followed him, this man with a nose that put many birds' beaks to shame, wary yet resigned.

Now she studied the building he had taken her to. It was drab, white walls so badly weather-stained they'd become a mottled gray. Rising three stories high, it was taller than any home in Orille, though far from the greatest in the city. Precipitous towers ascended from either end, and half the windows were boarded up while the other half had glass so clouded light barely penetrated it.

From the corner of her eye, she saw Beak-Nose kneel. "Hear me, wild girl? This is your new home."

"Home." The word stuck in her throat, a stone she couldn't swallow. Home was a place gone. Home was cinder and bone. This wasn't home.

But shelter—that, she could accept.

Leiyn nodded, then sucked in a deep breath and walked toward the double doors.

"A 'thank you' seems in order!" the guard called at her back.

She stiffened, then glanced over her shoulder. "Thanks," she muttered, though probably too softly for him to hear. Conversation had become difficult after the months alone.

By his snort of laughter, he'd caught her mumble. "Hope you find your tongue soon, wild girl. Might be the Watch could use you when you grow. Tough enough to survive the journey south on your own, wherever you're from... Aye, we could find a place for you."

Not knowing how to respond, Leiyn only turned back to the

sanctuary. Drawing herself up, though not quite straight, she walked up the steps to the doors, then knocked.

And waited.

Minutes passed. Leiyn looked around to see Beak-Nose had left. She turned back to the entrance. Somehow, she was reluctant to knock again, as if the building were a monster she might awaken.

Just as she mastered her fear and raised her fist, one door opened. A girl stood there. She was around Leiyn's age, pretty but for her pinched nose. Grain-gold curls hung about her face, and her narrowed eyes, the green of sunlit leaves, gazed with an intensity Leiyn found hard to meet.

Leiyn's cheeks burned as she realized how she must look. *And smell.* She hadn't bathed since the weather's turning, and grime had become a second skin.

"Matron!" shouted the girl—Curly, she decided to name her—without taking her eyes off Leiyn. "Got another stray here!"

Footsteps clacked from within the sanctuary. Leiyn felt a sudden urge to bolt, to hide back in her burrow. But the silver fox had led her away when the snows would have buried her. There was no going back.

Curly stepped aside, and a tall woman took her place. Leiyn craned back her neck to stare up at her. She had high cheekbones and a severe, narrow look. *Like a bird in winter,* she thought. A plain habit the color of withered daisies billowed about her spare frame, swallowing her, and washing out her pale skin. Even her eyes showed little sign of life, the irises so dark her pupils were almost lost in them.

By Curly's address, Leiyn guessed her to be the priestess in charge of the sanctuary. Her sense of foreboding only grew.

"I see," the priestess said. "Fetch water, Isebel, and fill a tub."

The blonde girl scowled at Leiyn but left without another word.

The birdlike woman stared at Leiyn a moment longer before speaking again. "San Hugo smiles on you, child. Only four days ago, Amada passed into San Inhoa's arms and freed a bed. Saints be thanked the Blush is almost through." She half-turned away, then paused. "Do not let any more cold in. Come—we will find you an old smock."

Leiyn obeyed, stepping inside and shutting the door behind her with a resounding rumble. The room had tall ceilings and was grander than any she'd seen in Orille, town hall included. The windows admitted little light, as she'd suspected would be the case, but enough to lift the gloom. The walls and floor were made of a dark-stained wood, one whose grain she couldn't identify without more light. The house was old judging by its smell, the wood mildewy and far from fresh.

The priestess began striding down one narrow hall, and Leiyn followed. "I am Sister Alma," she said briskly. "I have been blessed with the charge of San Hugo's Sanctuary."

She didn't look like she felt blessed, but Leiyn kept the thought to herself and nodded. Sister Alma didn't see her nod, still facing forward.

"What is your name, girl?"

She had to work herself up to answering. "Leiyn."

"Leiyn of?"

Leiyn hesitated, her throat tightening. She couldn't say Orille, lest it connect her to what had happened there. Her curse might be discovered. Yet her mind was blank for other places.

She blurted the first one that came to mind. "Of Folly."

"Folly?" The priestess halted and frowned down at her. "A town for rangers, I have heard. Are you one of their foundlings?"

Leiyn thought for a moment, then shook her head. *If I had been,* she mused, *I never would have come here.* All knew the rangers could take care of themselves.

"A long way." Sister Alma pursed her thin lips so they almost disappeared. "A very long way for so young a girl."

Leiyn held her breath as she waited for the priestess to declare it a lie. But after a moment, she continued. Leiyn hissed out the air as quietly as she could and followed.

"Twenty-three other girls are sheltered by San Hugo's just

hands," she continued. "There are four rooms, and six sleep to a room. You have already met one of your bunkmates, Isebel."

Leiyn touched a hand to her auburn tress before she could stop herself. Though there was something entrancing about the girl, she filled her with too many conflicting emotions to want to be around her. Besides, Isebel had seemed disgusted by the very sight of Leiyn. Now, they'd be sharing a room.

But Leiyn only lowered her hand to her side and remained silent. What other choice did she have?

The priestess took an abrupt turn. Other voices sounded ahead. Leiyn passed by open doors and saw more girls, some older and some younger, all staring back at her, slate boards and chalk in their hands as they sat in creaky chairs. As soon as they laid eyes on her, they bent together, covering their mouths as they whispered. Leiyn couldn't help hunching her shoulders. She faced forward, trying not to hear their giggles following her.

"You will have daily chores," Sister Alma continued, acting as if she hadn't noticed the other girls' behavior. "If you fail to do them, you will be punished. You will also be reprimanded for failing to wash"—her nose wrinkled, and Leiyn wished again she could disappear—"ignoring my orders or those from other sisters, or being lax in learning your letters."

They entered a long room occupied by three tubs so close together they almost touched. Leiyn's cheeks colored as she imagined how bathing must proceed. She'd run the streets of Orille naked when she was much younger, as all children did, but exposing herself to these girls who didn't like her, seeing their bared bodies in turn... She quickly banished the thoughts from her mind and tried to ignore the warmth creeping through her.

Curly's presence—*Isebel,* she corrected herself—made this difficult to accomplish. The blonde girl's ruthless gaze caught her as she poured a bucket into the tub. By how quickly she had filled it, Leiyn guessed the water hadn't been warmed.

"Enough, Isebel. Leiyn will pour the rest."

Again, the blonde girl was silent as she obeyed, while her eyes were anything but. She stared at Leiyn sidelong until she slipped past and out the door. It did little to dissipate Leiyn's nerves.

Leiyn, taking her cues from Isebel, moved to start filling the tub without being asked, but halted as the priestess spoke.

"Unera is a harsh world, Leiyn, especially for the Virtuous. Since you are here, I trust you know that. But you have shelter and food now. All you need." Sister Alma nodded as if to herself, for she didn't look at Leiyn but at the far wall, her gaze distant. "Do as you are told, speak your prayers and remain faithful to the Sacred Saints, and you will have a good life."

Leiyn froze. *A good life.* She hadn't dreamed of a good life since the Blush caught her father. Those thoughts had died when her curse killed Licky and Hazel.

She didn't hope for a good life, only to live. To survive.

So do what you must. A part of her awoke from the numbness. *Survive as you survived out in the hills. You must, for your father. Or what did he die for?*

She couldn't begin to answer that question, so she pushed it from her mind. Without waiting for Sister Alma to dismiss her, Leiyn bent over, picked up the bucket, and turned back. She summoned her courage and spoke, the words directed at the floor.

"Which way is the well?"

19

BEFORE THE STORM

So went Leiyn's days in Qasaar. Training in one way in the mornings, training in another in afternoons, evenings together with her companions. Leiyn found a certain satisfaction in the routine. She saw progress each day, and though the work had her dropping onto her bed exhausted each night, she treasured those moments of respite with her friends.

But she'd never been long content with normalcy.

Even as she advanced, a restlessness began to grow. Each day they spent in Qasaar was another day for their enemies to marshal against them. Had Ilberia sent a fleet west? Had it already made landfall? She didn't know and had no way of finding out. The seed of worry found fertile soil among the uncertainty.

Yet her agitation spawned from more than that. She longed for action, to do something that would make a difference in this quiet war between the Gasts and lyshans. They couldn't win without battle, and she was ready to fight.

Still, the opportunity caught her by surprise.

Leiyn woke to someone striding into the ancient barracks. *Teya*—she recognized her esse at once. With the last time the scout had caught her unaware burned into her mind, she scrambled to dress, only just avoiding a second embarrassment as a whistle sounded from outside the curtain.

Opening it, she found Teya leaning against the doorframe, decked out in her full scout's regalia. Her smile, however, was just as bemused as ever, and her earthy scent seemed to fill the hall. Leiyn was getting better at hiding the woman's effect on her, though, and only raised an eyebrow.

"We going somewhere?"

"Only if you are up for it."

"I might be, if you tell me more."

Teya's smile widened. "Out."

"That's specific." Leiyn fought to suppress a smile of her own. "Count me in."

A laugh burst from the scout as she straightened. "You will have to dress better than that. We embark on a five-day patrol to the wardstones. An ordinary task, but with plenty of danger. Supplies are packed, but you must provide your own gear."

Wardstones. A thrill shivered through Leiyn. She'd thought occasionally of the monoliths since her visit with Foxfur. That she would soon see one again made her both uneasy and excited.

"My kind of trip." Relenting to a grin, Leiyn bowed back into her room.

Packing was a simple ordeal; she and her companions had agreed to keep ready bags in case they needed to make a quick getaway, even as the need for it seemed to fade. Minutes later, she hefted her saddlebags and gear and stepped into the hallway. With her mahia open, she sensed Isla standing next to Teya even before she saw them. Batu was still in his room, his hurried movements betraying less preparedness.

"You're getting soft," Leiyn called after him as she plodded over to the others, weighed down by her burdens. "Spending too much time in other beds," she added with a grin.

Teya raised an eyebrow, then followed Leiyn's gaze to Isla. Her fellow ranger looked away, cheeks darkening. Only then did Leiyn realize something was off. She stared at her friend, taking in her state of dress. Their wardrobes being limited by travel, Isla had slowly begun supplementing hers with Gast attire. Today's aqua-and-gold robe showed her intentions plain as a deer's tracks through mud.

"You're not coming," Leiyn said slowly, "are you?"

Isla turned back, her blush lingering. "Someone has to wrangle the Tetrad." Her eyes slid over to Teya, as if wondering how the scout would take the gibe.

Teya shrugged. "Chieftains are the most stubborn to guide, and yet need the most guidance."

All three women chuckled at that, though Leiyn's amusement didn't last long. She looked sidelong at her friend, wishing she had chosen otherwise. A ranger didn't belong in a tower politicking day after day. An edge not honed lost its sharpness, and it went doubly so for their hard-won skills.

How long can you play at being Baltesia's envoy? How long before you forget who you are?

But though she lamented the cost, Leiyn knew Isla was right; one of them did have to stay. Far better it be Isla than Leiyn, for all of their sakes.

Batu emerged at last, garbed in his assortment of old plain-srider attire and the pieces he'd supplemented it with along the way. The long tunics favored by Gazians had been replaced with one cut in the shorter Baltesian style, but he still wore baggy brown trousers tucked into his boots. That day, he'd donned his leather lamellar armor, which he'd neglected to wear during their days of training.

"Finally," Leiyn said with a lazy smile, pushing down her internal conflict. "Are we ready, then?"

Batu nodded.

Teya eyed Isla, then met Leiyn's gaze. "The others wait at the gates," she said. "We should not keep them waiting."

Isla stepped toward Leiyn. "Here. I'll help with your bags."

Teya was quicker and moved between them. "I will carry hers. You can help your... friend."

Isla frowned but complied. Leiyn, baffled yet pleased, decided to focus on something clearer cut.

"Yes, Isla," she said with twitching lips. "Go help your *friend*."

Isla's look was withering, while Batu wrinkled his brow. Leiyn shook her head and handed over her panniers at Teya's offered hand. The scout, taller and stockier than Leiyn, hefted them onto one shoulder with ease. Leiyn averted her gaze. Even having faced Teya's strength and speed, the woman never failed to impress her.

Together, they made for the stables. Though they weren't far, they had to travel uphill to reach them, yet Leiyn found the walk easy with only her weapons and belt pouches to bear. The morning was cool, though the cloudless sky and bright sun promised another warm afternoon.

Her reception at the stables was as lukewarm as she'd expected. As Leiyn entered the cavernous structure, a reptilian stink washed over her, and she grimaced as she stalked forward. She searched the stalls until she saw those that held her and her companions' mounts. Feral glowered as only the mare could, staring with one reproachful dark eye and baring her teeth. Leiyn leaned her bows next to the stall door and held up her hands.

"I know, I know, I've entirely abandoned you. But we're going for a ride now; you'll get over it soon."

She reached forward, hoping to make amends, but had to withdraw when Feral snapped at her. Leiyn bared her teeth back, though she kept her distance.

"And outlanders call *axolto* monsters," Teya noted as she set down the saddlebags next to Leiyn's bows, then passed on to a different stall.

Leiyn glanced at the draconion that ambled from the enclosure. "Just now, I'd prefer one of those oversized lizards."

The scout grinned, stroking her mount's head between the horns along its crown. "Might be you will need one if that beast does not settle. What do you call it?"

"Feral."

Teya laughed. "A fitting name!"

Leiyn smiled as she turned back to Feral and set to placating the quarrelsome mare. It took several near misses of snapping teeth and colorful curses, but Leiyn managed to enter the pen and fit her tack, the saddlebags, and her bows to her horse's back. Feral bumped her against the walls as often as she could. Leiyn had no choice but to endure her punishment.

"You better not be like this the entire expedition," she warned as she led her from the stable. "Or I'll find a different mount."

They were the last to emerge, the others wearing smiles as they waited. Leiyn ignored them and looked at Teya.

"To the gate, then?"

The scout nodded, then clicked her tongue and tugged lightly on her draconion's reins, a creature as orange as the city's cliffs. "On now, Bane. Feral is finally ready."

They led their mounts down the switchbacks toward the heart of Qasaar. It had been weeks since Leiyn had been in the city at this early hour, and she was surprised at how its residents were already embroiled in their daily tasks. The crowds parted for them, however, most acknowledging Teya with regard, calling her "brave one" and touching a hand to their lips. The scout nodded gravely in turn, seeming to act out a ritualistic departure. The Gasts also afforded a measure of respect to Leiyn and her friends, though they remained aloof.

As they passed the Whisperspire, the throng thinned, and Leiyn saw the rest of their scouting party ahead. Eight more waited for them. Seven were outfitted similarly to Teya, so Leiyn assumed them to be fellow scouts. At the sight of the last member, however, she drew up short.

"Is that man Baltesian?"

Teya grinned. "Did you think you were the first outlander shaman?"

Leiyn shared a bewildered look with her friends. The man was certainly dressed the part of the shaman, bearing a striking resemblance in garb to what Zuma had worn: a long, tasseled robe, two black braids falling to either side of his head, a staff topped with feathers. He wasn't nearly as old as Zuma nor Xepi, yet he leaned on his staff as if weary to his core.

She turned back to Teya. "I'll wager there's a tale behind how he came to be here."

"Yet it is Taht Patli's story to tell." The scout shrugged. "Come—we have made them wait too long."

As Teya strode ahead, Leiyn fell in step with Batu and Isla. Her fellow ranger drew in close and muttered, "An outlander shaman?"

"So it seems."

They quieted as they came within earshot of the scouting party, though there was scarce chance of being overheard. Like the rangers had once been among their own at the Wilds Lodge, they were boisterous in their banter. Leiyn recognized a few from the training yards. Two were so gregarious she couldn't have avoided them if she'd tried: Nahui, a short woman whose size didn't match her volume, and Taqel, a colossus that did. Their voices surged over the others, as did their laughter.

The last scout she knew lingered at the periphery of the group, though for different reasons. Coyoti stared up at the sky in his usual perplexing behavior. He'd spoken at length to Leiyn of the various birds populating the Barren while she practiced at the archery range. With no other choice but to be rude, she'd listened, irritated and baffled at the flood of knowledge pouring from his mouth. She'd thought to ask him why he was telling her this, then decided against it. Odd folks seemed to find her no matter where she went, and she knew the best ways to deal with their idiosyncrasies.

Perhaps because I never fit in.

The Baltesian shaman, Patli, also stood to the side, frowning toward the northern gate. Leiyn studied him a moment longer before turning to Isla and Batu.

"Well. Suppose we're off."

Isla surprised her with a tight hug. "Don't be rash," she murmured before pulling away.

Leiyn smiled weakly and nodded. "I'll try."

She turned away to give the other two privacy for their own farewell and led—or rather, dragged—Feral over to the shaman.

Nodding to the scouts she knew, she stopped next to the man and waited.

At length, he turned toward her. His expression lightened, but only slightly. "Leiyn the ranger, I trust."

She felt tendrils of his esse reaching toward her and had to restrain from slamming up her walls. *Perhaps this is how shamans greet each other.* She doubted it was a practice she could grow used to.

"And you're Father Patli."

He smiled, though the corners of his eyes still drooped. "I know. You must have questions."

"Just a few."

"Never fear, Ranger Leiyn. I will answer them. My past is no secret or shame. But we had best be on our way, for a delay could prove perilous."

The back of her neck prickled. "Lyshans?"

Patli's gaze sharpened, as if he'd only been halfway paying attention to their conversation until then. "Yes. They do not bother us in the city. But beyond its gates, we are vulnerable."

She knew the extent of that vulnerability. *If we fail, he will be taken. As might I.* But that was a worry for another time.

"Lead on, Shaman."

It only took a minute to round up the scouts. As soon as Teya gave the order—as the spear, she appeared to be in charge of the mission—the *situali* mounted their draconions and set off for the nearby gate. Leiyn waited until the others had their backs to her before attempting to get atop Feral. Though the mare tried sidestepping, her efforts proved futile, and soon the ornery horse was hoofing it after the others. With Batu mounted by her side, Leiyn turned in the saddle and waved to Isla, who held up a hand in response.

When she and the former plainsrider reached the rest of the scouting party, Patli had already dismounted and stood before the gate. Four guards stood to either side, clad in a similar manner as the scouts but with heavier armor and longer spears. Two others also waited, approaching as Leiyn neared.

"Mother Xepi. Acalan," she greeted them. "You two miss me already?"

Neither smiled, though the chieftain came close to it. "We came to caution you, Huntress," he said, "and hope you will listen."

"Not likely," Batu said from over her shoulder.

Leiyn flashed him a scowl. The young man only smiled.

Xepi's words brought Leiyn's gaze back around. "You know the dangers you face. This is a necessary risk. But if you are attacked, your first priority must be to return to Qasaar. Do not fight. Flee."

All amusement drained from her. *Flee instead of fight?* Rare was the time she ran from conflict. More often than not, she sought it out. And to abandon Batu and the scouts to death... It didn't comply with the oath she'd long ago sworn, to perceive, preserve, and protect.

She started to shake her head when Acalan spoke again, the grating in his voice more pronounced. "Please, Leiyn. Heed her words. We cannot lose any more with *Tlalli's* blessing to the Devils of the Barren. My people cannot survive it."

Leiyn looked between Acalan's clenched jaw and Xepi's hand tight on her staff. A sigh escaped her lips.

"I'll come back. That's all I can promise."

Neither looked pleased, but the chieftain nodded and looked at Batu. "Stay safe, Young Bear."

Young Bear. It couldn't be a coincidence that the title echoed Batu's lifemark. Leiyn wondered how Acalan knew of it. Still, Batu seemed gratified by the name, murmuring something in return as he bowed to the chieftain.

Distracted by the conversation, Leiyn almost missed what happened at the gate. Just as she glanced back toward Patli, he pressed his hand to a raised square of stone. Only as the gate began to glow to her lifesense did she realize how it was meant to open.

Ancestral magic.

She caught herself gaping as the two massive slabs of stone, groaning and grinding, began to slide apart. Batu suffered a similar reaction. Leiyn was so absorbed in the sight she didn't mind Teya grinning outright at them both.

When the doors had parted enough, Patli mounted his draconion and passed through. The rest of the scouts followed, and Leiyn and Batu brought up the rear. As she advanced between the massive stone blocks, she looked up again and marveled, then turned back one last time to Xepi and Acalan. Her teacher waited by one of the towers outside the gate, while the chieftain stood behind, as unmoving and solid as a statue. Leiyn sensed the brief moment of magic from Xepi, then the doors rumbled closed, hiding them from view.

Leiyn turned back to look over the landscape before them. The Barren was bright with sunlight now, though the sun was still low on the horizon to their right. Orange and rust-brown, sparsely littered with signs of life, were all the wasteland offered.

Teya gave her a look, then jerked her head forward. "Come, outlanders. Let me show you this land's bounty."

As the scouts laughed, Leiyn shared a look with Batu before prompting Feral to follow.

20

VIGILANCE

"Five days," Teya said as she swayed atop Bane. "Fourteen wardstones. Fifty leagues."

"Is that all?" Leiyn moistened her throat with a swig from her waterskin. Already, the Barren and the sun had conspired to dry her out.

Dry as venison cooked by Old Nathan, she thought with a wry smile.

"Not quite." The scout pointed toward the western side of the Barren. "After we determine which stones must be reinforced from the Mammoth ward, we proceed in a random order rather than sequentially. If we are predictable, our enemies will find us."

"How often do they? Find you, that is."

"Not often." Teya gave her a lazy smile. "Never when I lead the patrol."

"Because of your cloaking?"

The scout nodded. She'd told Leiyn and Batu of her use of magic to conceal their party's esse at the onset, with an added warning to Leiyn that she must obscure her own. *You shine like the sun,* she told her, and though Leiyn knew she didn't mean it as flattery, she couldn't help but flush with pride.

She raised her walls. It was surprising how blind she now felt without her lifesense open. Since Southport, she'd grown accustomed to relying upon it, especially in hostile territory.

Went years without it before, she reminded herself. *I can do it again.*

Batu spoke from Leiyn's other flank. "If these lyshans do find us, what then?"

Teya's smile turned grim. "Pray to your Saints, or gods, or whatever it is you believe in. Whether you fight or flee, few survive such attacks, shamans rarest of all."

Leiyn faced forward. She should have felt fear, but it was determination that filled her instead.

Let them try.

Still, she didn't tempt fate by uttering the challenge aloud.

Leiyn made careful note of their surroundings. The Barren had initially appeared featureless and unchanging, yet as their journey continued, Leiyn noticed subtle shifts. The land was composed of various shades of burnt oranges and dun reds, alternating between stone and sand. It rose and fell in gentle waves, only a few spots rising into minor plateaus. Short outcroppings of black rock shot up from the ground at regular intervals. Most were shorter than Leiyn, but a few towered twice as high as Feral. According to Teya, these structures were what gave this part of the Barren within the boundaries of the wardstones its name: the Fingers.

Though the wasteland seemed devoid of life without her lifesense telling her otherwise, her eyes picked up small signs of it. Here, a trail by a small creature; a lizard or rat, she guessed without closer inspection. A few plants, too, had managed to take root in the forbidding ground. Most were cacti, spiny and bulbous, and taking a variety of startling hues from basil green to cherry red to indigo. During one of their brief breaks, Teya showed how one rotund variety, the wellspring cactus, could be cut open to drink its milk in case of an emergency. Leiyn tried her hand at it and only succeeded after pricking her fingers a dozen times. The milk tasted bitter and sour, and Teya laughed at her expression as she swallowed it.

Slowly, the sun crossed the sky, and shapes appeared from the sandy haze. Leiyn squinted at them. "Are those what I think they are?"

"Yes. The wardstones."

They towered as high as the others she'd seen. She wondered if she would feel their pulse even with her walls up. She thought she'd detected something tickling against her hidden sense, but never enough to distinguish what it was. But she knew someone who could tell her.

Parting from Batu and Teya, Leiyn rode Feral up next to Patli, who led the procession. The shaman glanced over as she came astride but gave no other greeting.

"You had a story to tell," Leiyn prompted him.

"I suppose I do." Patli's gaze slid over to her again. He swayed atop his draconion as if he'd ridden them since he was a child. "You wonder how a Baltesian became a shaman."

Leiyn shrugged. "It's the obvious place to start."

"Very well. I was born to outlander parents, in a town called Lake's Edge."

"I knew someone from there." Her eyes pricked at the reminder. Tadeo had grown up in Lake's Edge before leaving to become a ranger, then later the lodgemaster.

The shaman studied her, but if he noticed anything amiss, he didn't comment on it. "It was a good childhood, but one cut short. I was born with *Tlalli's* blessing, the same as you. From infancy, I was taught this was a curse—as were you, I'd guess."

She winced. "For longer than I care to admit."

"It was the spirits' will I be spared most of that pain. My parents received report from the village elders that odiosas and Ilberian soldiers were coming to round up any children with an affinity for magic. Fearing I would be discovered, my father took me north to the only place he could think that would accept a child such as me." Patli gestured around at their party. "To the Many Tribes beyond the mountains."

Leiyn marveled at the father's dedication. Lake's Edge was as far away from Qasaar as Orille, if not farther. To make that journey and back must have taken the better part of a year and come with its fair share of risks.

"Your father loved you deeply," she murmured.

"Both my parents did." The man wore a pained smile, his eyes filled with memories. "Difficult as our journey was, my mother had the harder burden to bear. She had to make do without either of us, and had to give excuses for our absence as well."

Leiyn inclined her head. She hadn't even thought of the mother's part. *To give up her child...* Her mother had gone to even further extremes to save Leiyn's life.

"What then?" she asked. "You have lived here ever since?"

"Yes. The Many Tribes took me in and adopted me as their own. Now, I see myself as Gast in all but blood. I earned a place of honor among them, an unprecedented achievement for an outlander. Mother Xepi showed me all I know of magic, though I could never hope to match her ability."

"There's much I still don't know. Much she can teach me."

He nodded. "You would do well to listen. But it is I who must teach you what comes next."

The wardstone now loomed above them. Just beyond it, a wall of whipping sand rose, obscuring the landscape. Dust billowed out from the sandstorm, so Leiyn drew up the edge of her cloak and held it before her face, squinting as it found her eyes. Patli and the other Gasts covered their faces with thick wrappings, while Batu made do with his cloak the same as Leiyn. As the noise rose with it, conversations ceased, for it became impossible to hear one another.

The monolith drew ever closer, until finally, they reached its base. At Patli's indication, Leiyn dismounted Feral and handed her reins to Batu. Most of the scouting party remained a score of paces away, but the shaman beckoned Leiyn to follow him to the wardstone.

Leiyn stopped next to him and wiped the sand from her eyelashes. Patli, dismounted and freed from his draconion as well, had chosen the leeward side of the spire, for which she was grateful. It almost felt she could breathe without dust lining the inside of her throat.

She stared at the tall rock. Now, she could definitively sense the pulsations emanating from it as they washed against her mahia's walls. Even stronger, she felt the titans lingering just beyond the ward. Either a titan had awakened, or there were so many slumbering nearby that they asserted their esse just as strongly. She was eager to be done with their task, and swiftly.

"What now?" she shouted over the gale.

Patli answered by pressing his palms against the stone and nodding toward it. Leiyn followed suit, but with her mahia closed, she felt nothing coming from it. It seemed no more than warm rock.

"When I say," the shaman called, "unveil your magic!"

She nodded and watched as he closed his eyes and leaned against the wardstone. Time passed, so long she wondered if she'd missed a subtle signal. She glanced back at their companions to see they'd been reduced to silhouettes by the dust.

"Now, Leiyn!"

Turning back, Leiyn dropped her walls. Sensations flooded through her. Each member of the scouting party was a bright spot in the desert, Patli glowing brightest among them. But compared to the wardstone, they were sparks next to a pyre. She beheld the wardstone and the towering esse coursing through it with open-mouthed awe. It hadn't shone so brightly when she experienced it with Foxfur. Then, it had been sedated; now, it blazed like a second sun.

She mastered herself enough to focus on what the shaman was doing. Though the monolith didn't seem to need more energy, Patli's fire stretched toward it, seeming to feed it lifeforce. Leiyn watched the transference taking place and fought the temptation to join in. She didn't know what exactly he was doing, but she knew meddling with ancestral artifacts came with significant risks.

Patli moved, and his connection to the wardstone lessened as one hand pulled away. Leiyn opened her eyes and saw him reach toward her. Her throat parched, she took his hand.

The connection burned like forge-heated chains tugged through her. All of Patli's life lay exposed. The images of his life-mark leaped out first: a boy submerged in a deep pond, barely staying afloat; a skillful painting of a strong-jawed man burning at the edges; a shadow rising from a deeper darkness, swallowing all light. She didn't linger on them but brushed past to the depths below.

Memories surrounded her. Patli's father clutching his young son tightly, then rising and leaving without a backward glance. The boy Patli curled up in a bed, weeping himself to sleep. Then, Patli stood in the sun, training hard with children that didn't look like him, who didn't even speak his language. A youth, tanned almost as dark as the other Gasts now, bowing his head to receive a necklace of pebble and bone, an inauguration.

Something pulled at Leiyn—no, someone. *Patli.* He was urging her to rise from the deep well of himself and return to her body. She knew she should, yet she struggled to do it. There was a sense of connection here that she hadn't realized she craved. This was the knowing of a person, a glimpse of true knowledge. It called to her like nectar to a bee.

The wardstones. Your mission. The lyshans hunting for you.

The last thought finally roused her. Leiyn pried herself apart from Patli and released his hand, catching her breath for a moment. When she could, she raised her gaze to meet the shaman's eyes and was relieved to find no reproach there, but only consideration.

"We will try again," he called to her. "Contain yourself to your body. Only sense what I do."

Leiyn nodded. As Patli extended his hand again, she took it with greater caution, holding her mahia tightly inside herself. They touched again, but this time she didn't dive through the connection, but kept at a distance, then sought after his actions as he'd bade.

Patli didn't feed the wardstone; instead, he reached into it, forging a connection with it as she'd done with him. Leiyn felt its draw as she felt the shaman's, though not as powerfully. Something in its inhumanity made her instinctively keep her distance.

Moments later, Leiyn sensed a pulse. She frowned. It had felt something like Patli, but also like the monolith. *A joined seeking?* She tried to follow the ripple, but it spread too far and fast to track. Moments later, the shaman broke his connection with the wardstone, and Leiyn released his hand, sighing as the strain evaporated.

Patli gestured back toward the others, and Leiyn followed him, fighting to walk straight as the tempest grew strong again. She raised her walls as she went, knowing they needed to hide once more. Reaching the rest of their party, she took Feral's reins from Batu, nodded her thanks, then mounted with the others.

They rode away from the monolith and the sandstorm. Only once the winds had died to a whisper did Patli turn his draconion back to keep pace beside Feral. Teya came up on her other side, while Batu hovered just behind. Leiyn looked at the shaman, then glanced away. Shame at her inadvertent prying kept her mouth glued shut.

"Where to next, Taht Patli?" the scout asked.

The shaman slumped in his saddle, but he spoke with energy as he pointed. "Two require our attention: Wolf and Eagle."

Teya's expression tightened. "On opposite sides. Very well. We will ride fast."

Leiyn pieced together all she'd experienced. "You connected with the wardstone. It showed you which need replenishment."

Patli nodded. "At Eagle, the next wardstone, I will show you how to do that. Then, at Wolf, you can try it yourself."

She nodded, though she wondered how either her or Patli's esse could fuel such an artifact. It had burned with a hundred-fold more life than they could supply, but she would just have to trust him. After all, the Gasts had survived this long by their methods.

With that, the patrol continued, heading toward where the sun reached for the horizon with as much speed as they dared.

Dust coated Leiyn's mouth and sunlight baked her like they rode through Legion's hells, yet she refused to request a stop. She knew the stakes. A seeking such as Patli had performed had to be felt for leagues in every direction by anyone with lifesense, and lyshans would have sensitive mahia indeed if they were anything like dryvans. Time grew short for their expedition.

While Feral carried her onward, Leiyn kept watch for any irksome rocks that might trip her mare and thought over what she'd witnessed while delving Patli's soul. The memories, she mostly understood; the first and last images of his lifemark, the drowning boy and the rising shadow, seemed plain to interpret as well. It was the middle one, the painting of the man, that absorbed her thoughts.

Who was he? What did he mean to Patli? He looked to be around her age, younger than the shaman by at least a decade.

Batu rode up next to her. "What happened back there?"

Leiyn told him in bursts of speech, the ride making it difficult to talk. When she finished, the former plainsrider shook his head.

"Wilds magic," was his only reply.

The wardstones came into view before they stopped to make camp. Leiyn's rump was bruised and battered, already unused to the saddle after days out of it, yet she wasn't ready to sleep. Her heart raced, and her mind invented dangers behind every rock pinnacle surrounding them. She'd never wished so desperately to be able to open her mahia.

She made up her bedroll next to Batu's but didn't lie down. Though the other scouts and Patli were settling, Teya still stood, staring off toward the northern horizon. Leiyn glanced at her friend and saw he was already curled onto his side, an arm cushioning his head. Moving as quietly as Tadeo had taught her to, she crossed the camp to stand next to the scout.

Teya's eyes slid over to her, unsurprised by Leiyn's stealthy approach. "You should rest."

"I've spent many nights without it before. No harm in one more."

A corner of the scout's lips curled. Leiyn's eyes lingered on those lips before she drew her gaze away to scan the surrounding land once more.

"Much as I appreciate the company," the scout said, "you will need your strength more than I tomorrow. Do you not mean to gift your *ilis* to the wardstone?"

Leiyn shrugged. "So Patli says."

"I must remain awake to mask our presence. Scouts do not see value in needless sacrifice."

Leiyn looked over to find the scout wearing an open smile. "Can't argue with that. But if there's any trouble—"

"—then your keen ranger senses will wake you before I can."

Leiyn flashed a rueful grin. "Don't fall asleep."

"A *situal* never does."

Even then, she found it hard to leave, but she managed it. As Leiyn slithered into the blankets, Batu turned toward her. His expression was serious, but there was a roguish light in his eyes.

"Stealing a goodnight kiss?"

Leiyn rolled her eyes. "You're lucky. Any other time and you'd pay for that."

He was still grinning as she turned her back on him. She didn't let him see her own smile as she ran the scene through her mind, again and again, until she slipped into slumber.

21

FEATHER AND FUR

Teya woke them before sunup. Their party was already mounted and headed toward the monoliths by the time light knifed into their eyes. Leiyn squinted at the wardstone obscured by the glare, which she judged to be a league away. Soon, Patli would reinforce the Eagle ward, then it would be Leiyn's turn to try.

If the lyshans don't find us first.

They broke their fasts in the saddle, their pace moderated from the day before. Teya looked haggard, her slouch atop her draconion grown more pronounced. Batu's shoulders were hunched, and Patli's head was bowed. Leiyn touched a hand often to her long knives, hoping a fight wouldn't be necessary, not with all of them worn down.

But if the lyshans meant to find them, they didn't yet succeed, for they reached the next wardstone without incident. The sandstorms weren't as strong there, and Leiyn didn't have to cover her face as they dismounted and approached. To her surprise, Patli summoned Taqel to join them, the burly scout consenting with a rumble.

They paused only a few dozen paces from the rest of the group, then Patli placed his hands on Taqel's outstretched forearms. Leiyn guessed he had opened his mahia before she felt the prickle against her walls. Taqel's jovial expression spasmed, and his smile slipped away. When the shaman drew back, the scout staggered, and Leiyn skirted forward to steady him. He grinned and drew himself upright again, only slightly swaying.

She looked between the two men. "You took lifeforce from him?" Though she'd practiced this with Xepi and done it to many enemies, the thought of stealing life from a friend made her stomach turn.

Patli stood straighter now and opened his mouth to speak, but Taqel beat him to it. "The gift is my honor, Ranger. I would give my life to protect my people; a crumb of it now will do no harm."

"I thank you, Scout Taqel, but there is no time. Come, Leiyn. We must move quickly."

Leiyn nodded at the big man before marching after the shaman. Patli was more animated than she'd yet seen him, his stride long and his eyes bright. His hands twitched at his sides as the monolith loomed out of the dust clouds above. She knew well the feeling of being overfilled with esse. The agitation. The need for action.

Reaching the wardstone, Leiyn detected only slight differences in it compared to the others she'd visited. It leaned away from them, and its top curled like the beak of the animal for which it was named.

Patli set his hands to the stone and looked sharply at her. "Come. Open your eyes and see what you must do."

Leiyn obeyed, lowering her mahia's walls and bracing herself for the onslaught. Yet the feel of the Eagle ward was different from the last. It was dimmed, containing more lifeforce than any in their party, but paling before Patli's glowing form.

Esse streamed from the shaman's hands, through the stone, and spiraled up the fiery tower. At once, it responded, blazing and amplifying beyond what the shaman gifted it. Leiyn sensed hidden workings, mechanisms of which she was only vaguely aware, that accepted and manipulated what Patli gave it in a way almost alive. Part of her longed to recoil; another part wanted to press closer, to understand how stone could be energized.

Patli cut off the stream and moved away. Opening her eyes, Leiyn saw the shaman staggering and dashed over to him. Just before she touched him, she remembered to close her walls. By his pallid essence, he couldn't afford to have her rummaging through his soul.

"Thank you," Patli murmured. With her help, he righted himself, then tried pulling away. Leiyn kept her grip.

"No time for pride," she told him. "Lean on me."

Reluctantly, the shaman complied. Together, they shambled back toward their party. Teya and Nahui met them halfway, Batu trailing just behind. He was hobbled by holding both of their horses, Feral proving far from compliant.

"Here, Taht Patli," the small scout blared. "It is my turn for the gift!"

Leiyn released Patli to her, and moments later sensed the glimmer of magic. Teya caught the woman when she staggered back, eyes rolling for a moment before she blinked to awareness.

"Always a pleasure," Nahui said with a sickly smile. When she could stand, Teya turned her around and they set back toward the mounts.

Leiyn looked at Patli to find him once more brimming with energy. His eyes flickered to hers, then he followed after the others. "We must go quickly to Wolf," he said, speech rapid, "and away from Eagle."

"Don't have to convince me."

Soon, Leiyn sat atop Feral again, the mare bearing her with the others south to the last wardstone. The bruises she'd gained the day before were battered afresh, the soreness in her muscles aching deeper. The sun had risen above the dust clouds, and she swam in sweat beneath her gear. She hardly minded. The thrill of the hunt and the chase filled her, drowning out all else.

An hour's ride and a wardstone later, Teya turned them toward Wolf. Just as the others had borne a passing resemblance to their name, so did this one, the top bifurcated so it resembled the jaws of a howling beast. Leiyn slid off Feral's back and threw the reins at Batu before hustling over to Patli, who already advanced on the monolith. A glance over her shoulder showed Teya and Coyoti trailing them. As Patli turned back, a pit formed in Leiyn's stomach. She knew what came next and wasn't sure she was ready to embrace it.

Too late to doubt now.

The shaman gestured, impatient once again. "You know how to draw out essence?"

Leiyn nodded and approached the strange scout. Despite the danger, Coyoti seemed bored, his mouth twisted up to one corner, his eyes wandering the top of the wardstone.

"Come on, Coyoti," Teya snapped as she held up the scout's arms for him. "We cannot waste time."

"Thanks," Leiyn mumbled as she gripped his arms. Drawing in a breath, she released her walls. Coyoti's essence burned against her hands, brighter than she would have expected, and she felt a slight pull from him to dive deeper, enough that she wondered if he also had a touch of magic.

There was no time to ponder. She kept her lessons with Xepi in mind as she gently drew on his lifeforce. The flames inside him flickered, resisting at first, then slowly coursed toward his hands and into hers. The intoxicating feeling began to buzz inside her at once. She fought the urge to suck it in faster and deeper, to drink the well of him dry, stopping short when she felt the boundaries of her body stretching to contain it all.

Leiyn stepped back, and Coyoti would have folded to the ground if Teya hadn't caught him. "Go," she said, waving Leiyn away as the scout leader took a step toward them. "Do your duty."

She only hesitated a moment longer. "I will," she said, then turned and jogged toward the wardstone.

Now she felt all Patli had before. The sense of invincibility. The need to act. She possessed power beyond what her body should have been capable of. Somehow, someway, she had to express it.

"Leiyn."

The wardstone towered above them, the base a few steps away. Closing the remaining distance, Leiyn placed her hands to a red stripe on the rock and pushed lifeforce into it. The flames had little trouble in settling in. As she had felt in the Eagle ward, hidden apparatuses began to churn, pulling and melding the energy into itself. It glowed brighter and brighter until it became difficult to behold.

"Enough. Enough, Leiyn!"

Patli's words registered belatedly in her mind. Leiyn tried pulling away from the swell of the wardstone, and for a moment, she couldn't separate herself. Fury flared within her. In it, she found the strength to sever the connection. Leiyn staggered back and blinked. Her senses reasserted themselves, though they seemed fuzzy at the edges, less acute than she was accustomed to.

"Veil your magic. Now, Leiyn. We must flee."

Part of her railed against the command, but Leiyn forced up her walls, then grimaced as the world around her went dark, the life fading from her senses. The discomforts from riding resurfaced with a vengeance, and her legs wobbled.

The shaman gripped her arm. "You did well. But we must be swift now."

He led her to the others, and three broke off from the group as they approached: Teya, a scout named Metzli, and Batu. Leiyn didn't know Metzli well, having only just met her on this mission, but she seemed a solid and dependable sort, stocky and with heavy braids falling halfway down her back. The scout stepped before the others, her arms outstretched in a silent invitation. Leiyn reached out and gripped them, apprehension gone. All she yearned for was the relief the fresh lifeforce would bring.

She lowered her walls, and the world lit up to her hidden sense again. But before she could draw the esse in, Leiyn hesitated. Something was different than before. Something was... off.

"Leiyn," Teya said, her voice low and urgent, "we must—"

A figure blazed to life among the scouts.

Leiyn released Metzli and stared at the newcomer. They shone like a full moon with the roiling force of their esse, so much that she could barely see with her eyes. Yet the voice was familiar.

"Run!" Foxfur screeched. "They come—"

Another appeared, and Metzli flew aside.

Leiyn staggered back, eyes wide, breath fast. The scout had been there only a moment before, but now, she sprawled across the sandy ground, a smear of blood trailing after her. Only the faint glow of life and her sluggish movements showed her to still be alive.

Leiyn reached for her knives, a snarl rising even as she hunted for their attacker. Her dulled senses barely took in what had occurred. Shouting filled the air; her companions blurred with movement, weapons drawn and striking. Foxfur was impossible to follow, only identifiable by the flash of her silver fur.

Then, as the dryvan enwrapped one attacker and threw it to the ground, Leiyn caught her first full glimpse.

It had a humanoid shape, yet she knew it wasn't human. Its head was like a knotted root, but gray in color, and interrupted with eyes that glared balefully around at the dryvan pinning it. Its mouth gaped wider, and it twisted, trying to bite at Foxfur like a rabid beast. Its body was much the same, limbs thin and corded, torso not quite straight, writhing like the body of a serpent.

Its lifeforce burned even brighter than Foxfur's, yet as it assailed the dryvan, Leiyn felt wrongness emanating from it, like the stench from a corpse-ridden pool. A moment later, she understood why.

It had not one soul, but many. Dozens. Perhaps even hundreds. They moved within it independently, all striving toward the same goal, yet interfering as much as helping. Layers upon layers of the souls had built up like callouses, but with the hardness of chitinous armor.

Leiyn could barely bring herself to look at it. Her stomach curdled; her limbs went weak. A single word filled her mind.

Lyshan.

22

WOLVES AMONG SHEEP

Staring at the lyshan, Leiyn's mind went quiet. She didn't know how to approach this enemy. Could her weapons hurt it? Could she strike fast enough to find out?

Yet her body still prepared itself to fight. Weariness was all but forgotten as the battle-thrill pumped through her blood. Her knives rose. Her legs tensed and braced. Her mahia expanded in a blaze through her limbs.

She formed herself into the weapon she'd trained to be and hoped it would be enough.

All the while, the two skin-walkers continued to wrestle. Though Foxfur maintained her advantage, it was clear by their esses that the contest was far from over. In a sudden twist, the lyshan loosed one arm, then whipped it around to drag sharp fingers across Foxfur's back. The dryvan loosed an inhuman roar, and her esse surged as she smashed her opponent back down to the ground. Her hand pressed on the lyshan's head, claws digging into hard flesh.

The lyshan screeched, then both it and Foxfur disappeared.

Leiyn strained to sense them but found no trace of the skin-walkers remaining. Her eyes flickered over to her companions to find their expressions just as confused. One moment, they'd been fighting, then the very air had sucked them away.

She spoke the answer aloud. "That other place. She took it there, I think."

Batu nodded, his jaw firm. He gripped his axe tightly with both hands. Gone was the uncertain youth he'd been before, replaced now by the bear that lay dormant within.

After another moment's hesitation, Teya moved. "Go," she ordered. "We leave while we can." She lowered her spear and jogged over to where Metzli had been tossed. The prospect of her rising seemed unlikely, but just as a ranger never left behind their fellows, Leiyn assumed the same was true for the *situali*.

Leiyn moved toward their horses, who had skirted back after Batu released them, but not fully fled. Feral had her teeth bared and hoofed the ground, ready to rear at any moment. Leiyn shushed her as she approached, though she only dared sheathe one of her weapons.

"*Fesht*, Feral," she cursed as the horse danced out of reach. "The sooner you calm, the sooner we—"

Shouting erupted from the main host of the scouting party. Leiyn left off her attempts to rein in Feral and spun around, drawing her second anelace again. The Gasts were fighting something in their midst; a moment after, a flying body confirmed what.

"Another lyshan!" Leiyn screamed as she charged, knives pumping by her sides.

The fight was quickly devolving. Two scouts were down, bloodied and moaning on the ground. Big Taqel was on his side, his arms clutched over his chest, gasping for air. Leiyn's rage rose higher as she saw the blood seeping out from around his limbs to stain the earth. He, too, was unlikely to survive.

Then the lyshan was before her, whirling and lashing out all around. Its esse was similar to the first's, ailing with the amount of souls stuffed into it, though its appearance differed. Only as she looked did she understand how it could attack in so many directions at once: it had not two arms, but six. Its legs had also thickened and burrowed into the ground, as if rooting itself in place. Its skin was ocher like the cliffs of Qasaar, the texture like stone. Its eyes, if they could be called such, were nothing more than dark pits, no sign of movement within them. Yet for all its lifeless appearance, it moved with a speed no human could hope to match.

Leiyn was silent as she struck, one blade leading, the other sweeping behind. Though its back was to her, the lyshan reacted at once, twisting its torso and sending out two arms against her blades. They ripped from Leiyn's grasp and were sent spinning across the landscape.

She stumbled back as a third arm barely missed her chest, then fumbled for her extra daggers. Out of the corner of her eye, she saw Patli leap atop his draconion and sprint off into the dust, as shamans were supposed to.

But she wouldn't abandon them. She wouldn't let the scouts die as the rangers had.

The element of surprise gone, Leiyn loosed a yell as she threw one short dagger forward, then the other. The three remaining scouts happened to attack at the same time, so though the lyshan blocked her first blade, the second won its way through. Leiyn stared at the knife lodged inside one of the holes where its eye should have been, rocking the head back. A killing blow, to any other creature.

Saints, let it die.

But her mahia told her otherwise. Its lifefire flickered, but barely dimmed. The lyshan hesitated only a moment before one arm swung fluidly around and pried it loose.

It whipped it toward her, the blade a blur, too quick to dodge.

Pain blossomed through her shoulder and spun her to the ground. Leiyn gasped, vision blurring, and used her other hand to lever herself back up. Her right arm hung useless. Her shoulder was aflame, and around it, the light of her esse had dimmed. She couldn't help but look. The hilt of the knife had struck, yet the blunt force had been enough to reduce her shoulder to a bloody ruin.

She channeled the pain into wrath as she turned back to her foe. The world reduced to the lyshan. She would bring him down, no matter the cost to herself. She'd kill him if it cost every drop of her blood.

Leiyn screamed and struck with all the power left to her. Her magic crashed against the lyshan, and she rocked backward, falling on her rump with the psychic force. If it was harmed, she couldn't tell, but the attack had caught its attention. The skin-walker spun toward her, and through dimmed vision, she saw its legs break apart from the earth.

Gathering herself for another assault, Leiyn tried sharpening her power to a point. The lyshan sped toward her, the Gasts forgotten. She struck blindly, a last desperate attempt, with no hope of succeeding.

A flash of silver crashed into the lyshan, sending it sprawling.

Foxfur shrieked again as her hands latched onto the lyshan's head. Its six arms beat against her, and her fur became stained with an amber ooze somewhere between sap and blood. But the dryvan didn't relent, wrenching at her enemy.

The head ripped free.

As the dryvan went stumbling off of it, Leiyn watched in disbelief as the lyshan rose again. Its lifeforce had sprung a leak, oozing out into the world around it, yet it stubbornly clung to life. Something began pressing out of the gap left by its head. She had a queasy feeling a new skull would soon form.

Leiyn lurched back to her feet, fighting pain and nausea to dash forward. She scooped up a fallen spear as she went, almost stumbling to the ground for it, then nearly blacking out as her bad arm swung against her chest. But there wasn't time for weakness. Leiyn gathered her last scraps of strength and closed the last of the distance before striking. Accompanying her speartip, she shot forward a javelin of esse, stabbing into the wounds both body and soul.

The lyshan shuddered, then collapsed, dark with death.

Leiyn staggered back, only barely keeping her feet. Dark spots flickered in her vision, but she fought to cling to conscious-ness. *More, there could be more. Fight for them, for Batu and Teya. You have to fight—*

Another lyshan blazed into existence before her.

Leiyn struck by instinct, but she was too weak and slow. The skin-walker turned the blow aside with a lazy parry, then reached forward and gripped her shoulder. Its reach extended deeper, and she cried out as talons rent into her spirit.

Her world peeled away in strips as Leiyn was dragged into a new one.

23

ACCORD

One moment, she existed, tethered to life by pain.

Then the lyshan cut her free.

Leiyn drifted, formless in a realm she couldn't understand. The pain was gone, but so were the limbs that had pained her. She couldn't move. She didn't even know if there was anything to move through.

Yet *something* was here. She could sense them, like seeing distant campfire glows. Leiyn tried seeking after them, hoping against hope they would help instead of hurt.

If I still can be harmed.

But before she could figure out how to reach them, something seized her. She tried resisting, but the pull upward was too strong a current to swim against.

She erupted back into her body.

Leiyn coughed, spat, and raised her head to stare blearily around. Her eyes alighted on a tall, unfamiliar figure and she lurched back, or tried to. On her knees, she only managed to sprawl back and provoke fresh spikes of pain from her shoulder. Ignoring it, Leiyn rolled back to her feet and stood, swaying as she fought to keep her balance.

The lyshan watched her from several paces afar. His features were more human than the others, with all the right elements in the right places, though longer in proportion than she was used to seeing. His skin was ashen-hued and looked as coarse as charcoal. His head was bare but for a circlet of what looked to be dried vines, yet they retained their verdant emerald. His eyes, like the other lyshan's, were dark as if hooded by a heavy brow, though his was shallow. Only through her mahia did she detect anything within them, two coals burning with furious depths of esse.

Though he seemed distinctive, she had difficulty focusing on his face. Somehow, the features shifted, like ripples on a pond's surface: the same shape, but a different formation from moment to moment.

His clothes stuck out in contrast. A robe hung to just above his bare feet, pale gold in color and ornamented intricately with silver lace and green stones. The patterns upon it shimmered as the sunlight caught them. A stole sprawled down his left shoulder to his right hip, dyed a deep cerulean and lined with large feathers she didn't recognize of a brighter blue. She didn't know if she was more surprised he wore clothes, or that they were of such a foreign and foppish style.

This one is different. She wondered how, and if she could find an advantage in it.

Still unmoving, the lyshan spoke. His voice was male, a baritone equal parts honey and poison, and accented in an unfamiliar way.

"You," he said softly, "are not what I expected."

Leiyn stared at the lyshan. A dozen questions shrieked through her head. *Why doesn't he attack? Why did he bring me here? Why am I still alive?*

She was in no condition to fight. If she stood any chance of survival, it was by delaying and figuring out just what the creature wanted. She wondered if she would die of blood loss before she had the chance. Weak as she was, lacking any ready sources of esse, she couldn't heal.

Working spit around her dry mouth, Leiyn managed to croak, "What do you want?"

The answer should have been obvious, but it no longer fit.

Lyshans had been stealing Gast shamans; what else could he want but to take her? But this was like a lion toying with its meat. A perverse indulgence, then?

Everyone needs a pastime, she thought grimly.

"Want..." The thin line of the lyshan's mouth curled upward, an approximation of a smile. "What is it I want? In some ways, I want for nothing. And so I crave everything."

Leiyn's patience was thinner than a thread, yet she didn't let it snap. "Who are you, then? What's your name?"

Even as she spoke, she searched with her mahia for Batu, Teya, Patli, and the scouts. Nothing. As far as she could sense, the most life around was cacti and various small critters. She'd expected nothing less. As soon as she reappeared alone with the skin-walker, she had suspected they were in that parallel world mirroring her own, where Glade and its dryvans hid.

The lyshan moved, a slow, fluid stalking, circling her. Leiyn shifted so she kept him in front of her, watching for an attack.

For all the good it will do.

He surprised her by answering. "Man'nah's Shadow, most would call me now. Those who know I exist. But once, to those who knew me best, I was... Sharo."

The lyshan paused, his pitted eyes rising to stare at the sky. She wondered what long-buried memories his name evoked. For all his outlandishness, he looked like a man lost to the past.

Moments later, Sharo looked back down at her. "I do not know you, but I sense I should. Your spirit... so small, yet so bright. Like ones I have known of yore."

Leiyn knew better than to trust any word from his mouth. She blinked rapidly to keep the black from her vision. "Why did you bring me here?"

Sharo continued his circle around her. "Time, Oldsoul. Is that not what every mortal desires most? Time for themselves, for those they care for. Time to labor, time to merrymake." His smile turned sly. "Time to procreate."

Leiyn ignored the gibe. *Oldsoul?* She couldn't help but wonder what he meant by it.

"But you don't desire time." It was a guess, but she was blind to his intentions. The best she could do was lash into the dark with a dull knife. "You have all the time you need."

"More than I need... if any need time." The lifeforce behind his eyes blazed a hint brighter. "Do you need time, Oldsoul?"

"Yes."

"So you have a need that I can supply." The words were slow, teasing. "But can you fill a need of mine?"

"You don't have any needs. You said so yourself."

The lyshan laughed. "The cleverness of the short-lived... your minds are sharp, your spirits rough-edged. One of the unrelenting pleasures of existence. Assume you are correct—that I have no needs, that freeing you bears no cost. Then should I simply let you walk free?"

There was a trap in the words, but Leiyn's wit had deadened too far to see it. Her eyelids kept drifting closed. She fought to snap them back open.

"Yes," she answered, her voice faint. "So long as the assumption is right."

"Just so... *if* it is correct. For your boldness, I will award you one secret: it is not."

As darkness edged in, Leiyn couldn't restrain any longer—she pulled on her esse. A rush of strength filled her body, and the wound in her shoulder screamed with fresh agony. Leiyn groaned, unable to repress it, and bowed forward. She only just kept her head raised to watch the skin-walker.

I bought a little time. A little longer. She doubted she could afford a second infusion.

"There is a cost?" she gasped. "Or you have a need?"

The lyshan stopped his revolution to turn toward her. So slowly and smoothly she thought she imagined it at first, he began to advance.

"Both." His murmur was soft as a summer wind. "But which shall fulfill it? Freeing you, or setting you upon him?"

She drifted in an ocean, the swell sucking her down. "Him? Who would you set me on?"

"Now you are coming closer to the crux, Oldsoul." The lyshan stopped a mere foot away, close enough she could have struck him, given the strength. He crouched, his golden robe sparkling. She saw that his skin flaked in places, like his very body was falling apart.

"Why are you here?" Sharo whispered. "You, one from the place called the Ancestral Lands, come to the edge of the world. What is your purpose?"

Leiyn met his depthless eyes. It seemed suicide to admit their true mission, yet how could he not know it? She'd killed a lyshan before he took her here. After decades of conflict with the Gasts, stealing their shamans and assaulting Qasaar, they must know how they were hated.

Only one answer to give. She drew herself up as straight as she could and spoke. "I came to kill you. You, and all your kind."

The smile was slow in coming. But as it spread, it claimed all of Sharo's ravaged face.

"Then an accord is reached. Fulfill my need, as I now fulfill yours."

His hand snapped forward. Leiyn grabbed at it, but only managed to grip his forearm, while his hand curled about her good shoulder. She just had time to register the sharp tips digging into her clothes before she saw nothing at all.

He lied. He killed me. Then... where am I?

No sooner did Leiyn begin to wonder than she saw again.

Life blossomed around her, dazzling to her lifesense. The sensations from her body, agony foremost among them, reasserted themselves, and she doubled over. Yet even then, barely clinging to awareness, Leiyn searched for threats. None of the esse surrounding her felt like lyshans.

Except one.

She startled, trying to come upright, before hands pressed on her, holding her steady. Voices spoke urgently around her, and she struggled to comprehend them.

"...listen to me, Leiyn."

Teya. Leiyn turned her face up to the scout, glad to see her still alive. But they weren't out of danger yet.

"Lyshan!" she cried. "There's a lyshan right—"

A familiar laugh cut her off. "Lyshan! She is head-hurt if that is what she thinks I am."

Relief flooded through her as she realized her mistake. Leiyn twisted around to stare at the speaker. "Rowan... I mean, Foxfur."

The dryvan still wore a grin, but her ghastly appearance soured it. Her fur was more golden sap than silver now, matted with what Leiyn assumed was her peculiar blood. Deep wounds carved themselves through every limb, and one scraped across one eye. Yet her esse burned strong and undiluted. She wasn't severely harmed by her people's standards.

As a wave of nausea nearly toppled Leiyn over, she realized the same couldn't be said for herself.

"Foxfur," she mumbled, reaching her uninjured arm toward her. She needed the dryvan, needed her esse at least, and perhaps her healing, too. The sky had gained a curious weight, pressing down her eyelids and making her body sag against the ground.

Her magic still saw. The dryvan approached and bent down next to her. A hand burning with latent power touched her head, talons gently caressing her hair. She didn't feel the same need to be swept up in the foreign soul, but instead reached for it like a flower to the sun, eager to soak in the light.

"*Drink,*" Foxfur's voice came, distant yet echoing in her skull. "*Mend, then rest.*"

Leiyn obeyed. She drank of the fire, and all else burned away.

PART IV

FIRE OF THE SOUL

24

THIRTEEN YEARS BEFORE

Onths passed at San Hugo's Sanctuary. The days grew bitterly cold, then warmer again. The leaves on the trees in the small courtyard out back began to sprout, almost the first glimpses of green since winter began.

Through it all, Leiyn survived.

It was as much as could be said of her experience at the children's shelter. Sister Alma was strict but fair, yet never warm toward the girls. She provided just as she had told Leiyn she would upon her arrival: the basic necessities of life. Leiyn came to understand that this was what she saw as her duty and nothing more. Affection or guidance was out of the question, a deviation from the faithful path rather than further down it.

Leiyn had grown up without a mother. She didn't need one now.

Life at the sanctuary demanded more of her than the simple existence at her burrow. She still didn't speak much, as most of the other girls were either wary or despised her, yet each affront straightened her spine a little more. Leiyn hadn't taken insults lying down back in Orille, but sorrow and caution had hollowed her out enough to blunt her anger still.

Instead of lashing out, she fed that inner fire until it grew so she almost felt like the person she'd been before the Blush. She shed the hardest of her protective layers like a nut sprouting and grew in height, girth, and hair, often in the most embarrassing places.

Isebel was foremost among her tormenters. The blonde-haired girl had gathered a close knot of the oldest girls about her, and together, they mercilessly oppressed the other children. Rare was the day that Leiyn didn't find some essential item missing, her food unspoiled, or her clothing untouched. Three times, she'd awoken with rotten food smeared down the front of her sole smock, Isebel's reminder of how she'd reeked when first entering the sanctuary.

Bide your time, Leiyn counseled herself as she confronted each fresh attack. *For now, just survive.*

Still, in her weaker moments alone on the hard, narrow cot she called her own, she wished the silver fox had never found her. That the frost had tucked her into a long, cold slumber.

But those moments were fleeting. Gone were the days when she survived for her father's sake alone. Though she still imagined his rough heavy hand gripping her shoulder or cupping her cheek, still saw his laughing face every time she closed her eyes, the guilt had given way to a deeper purpose.

Leiyn began living for herself.

She at once rejected the possible futures Sister Alma painted for her charges. "Remain faithful," she told them during meals, "and you may be blessed enough to join the Catedrál. That is where girls like yourselves can find a good life. Otherwise, you will end up in a brothel, or married to a fisherman, attending his every need." The crinkle in her nose betrayed that the priestess thought that fate worst of all.

Leiyn often had to loosen her clenched fists after such talks. When fetching food from a nearby temple, gifts of charity for their sanctuary, she'd seen the whores and how thinly they dressed, even in winter. Her stomach turned imagining that life for herself.

And though she wanted as little as possible in common with Sister Alma, she shared her distaste for having a husband. While the other girls pined over the handsome boys they saw on the streets, like the one with the white-toothed smile who called at them to buy his bangles and necklaces, Leiyn thought of some of the other girls. As much as Leiyn had grown to hate her, Isebel often rose foremost to her mind. Her breasts and hips had developed early, and she wasn't shy about reminding the others of that fact. Leiyn struggled not to stare when their baths coincided, though more from curiosity than anything else. The blonde girl was far too nasty to truly be attractive.

All the while, Leiyn clung to a core, unchanging belief, long instilled in her by her father: *We are who we are.* It had been the way he'd treated most everyone, judging them not for how he thought they should be but for who they were and how they acted. Only Gasts had been the exception, though there had been just reason for that.

She knew that her attraction to girls was unusual but refused to believe it wrong. It had to be better than her wilds-cursed mahia, at least.

So she cast aside the paths placed before her and searched beyond them.

Talk of the future often arose with the sole girl who was friendly toward her, Aracel. She was short, shy, and still losing her first teeth, so her smiles were all lip to hide the gaps. Her bushy brown hair and mousey features did fewer favors still for her looks. Leiyn found herself drawn to the girl at once, as Aracel reminded her of the friends she'd left behind in Orille.

"Where would you go?" the girl murmured as they scrubbed dishes that day. "Beyond Southport are wild lands, so my pada always said." Aracel tried to remain cheery, but a somber note fell in at recalling the loss of her father.

"I'm from those lands," Leiyn reminded her, anchoring her arm to pry at a stubborn layer of grime. Her arms were spotted gray and black up to her elbows with the burnt food she'd already scraped off. "They're not wild, they're *free*. Free of all this." She gestured with her head, sweeping it around.

Aracel gave her usual lippy smile. "Would you return to Folly?"

"Maybe."

"What's it like there? Suppose there aren't any sanctuaries if you came all the way here."

"No. No sanctuaries."

Leiyn avoided discussing the town she supposedly hailed from whenever possible, lest she betray her ignorance. None of the other girls knew of Folly either, but if word got back to Sister Alma of some misstep, the consequences could be dire.

"Southport doesn't fit me," she continued, pivoting to more comfortable topics. "It's too big, with too many people. I feel... crowded in all the time." Only after she'd spoken did she realize what she meant. Her mahia was under constant pressure, her walls always trembling at the sheer weight of life constantly milling about outside the sanctuary. She grimaced into her pot and tried to gather her thoughts. It felt as if she could never think clearly here.

"Then where would you go?" Aracel pressed.

Leiyn shrugged. "Maybe I'll claim a plot."

"Oh! Like the Caelrey allows along the frontier?"

Even in Orille, all knew of the Edicts and what was and wasn't allowed under World-King Baltesar's law. Foremost on many minds was what drove people into the dangerous Titan Wilds: the promise that anyone, man or woman, who could carve out a plot beyond the Gorge de Omn was welcome to call it their own. Land, for those brave and foolish enough to claim it.

But even as Leiyn nodded, she wondered if that would be enough. She knew some farming and was confident she could figure out the rest, provided she could acquire some seed and tools. But becoming a farmer... was that all she wanted? Or was that only a different kind of mere survival?

She knew the answer even as she questioned it. A different dream had been growing in her ever since Sister Alma's stray comment. It remained small and quiet under the blanket of winter but had grown and filled her as life returned to the Veiled Lands. It could only be a dream, for she knew too little to call it a plan. And it would be a long, dangerous trek, many times the length of the journey from Orille to Southport, with an uncertain end at its finish.

Yet dreams were like nuts: impossible to kill and always sprouting when she least expected.

"Or," Leiyn said, so softly she wouldn't have been surprised if Aracel couldn't hear her over the clatter, "maybe I'll join the rangers."

"The rangers?"

The protectors of the Titan Wilds seemed more legend than fact to the citizens of Southport, yet Leiyn knew from her father that they were real. It was said they could vie with titans, though she could scarcely think how, and that even Gasts feared where they walked.

She liked that last bit even more than the rest.

But darker things were also muttered about the rangers. That they became strange from living in such Saints-forsaken wilderness. That some were friends with *ferinos* rather than enemies. That they stole children in the night and used them to add to their ranks.

She dismissed the doubts as mere rumor. If they took in orphans and fought Gasts, as she'd always heard they did, that would be good enough for her.

Leiyn shushed her friend and darted a look over her shoulder. Her heart pounded at the thought of anyone overhearing, Isebel in particular. The torment would be endless.

Aracel winced and lowered her voice. "Sorry. I'm not saying you couldn't. If anyone here could, it's you, Leiyn. But why would you want to? They fight Gasts and titans, don't they?" The girl shivered. "I wonder how any survive."

Survive. That was one thing Leiyn knew she could do. And though she'd expected the resistance to her private dream to be crushing, it hardened her resolve instead.

"I will join the rangers. I'll fight Gasts, and titans if I have to." Her hands tightened over the pot and scrubbing brush, and she bared her teeth. *Fight Gasts.* That, at least, she could find some purpose in. She had a lot to repay them for. "I'll become a ranger."

Aracel gave her a tentative smile. "I don't like how crowded it is here, but I can't imagine living outside Southport. Maybe, though... maybe I could live in Folly, be a spinner there. My mada taught me something of it, before..." She shrugged one shoulder. Leiyn had never gathered exactly how her parents had died, but she hadn't told Aracel her story, either. Some things were best left unspoken.

"Then we'll see each other often." Leiyn pushed down her long-simmering resentments long enough to afford her fellow scrubber a smile. She hoped it would be true; Aracel was fast becoming the closest friend she'd ever had.

Leiyn had lost everyone else. She intended to cling to what she and Aracel had for as long as she could.

25

AWAKENING

*S*he opened her eyes to a familiar painted ceiling.
The barracks.

Leiyn groaned and sat up. A landslide might have hit her for how difficult it was to rise. Someone had changed her clothes and cleaned her before tucking her in, yet the fresh tunic felt rough against tender skin barely healed over.

"Leiyn."

She startled. She hadn't noticed the person next to her. But as she saw who it was, Leiyn relaxed.

"Isla."

Isla clasped Leiyn's hand in hers. Though her eyes were wide with alarm, her friend was a comforting sight. As Leiyn awoke and remembered, however, the feeling slipped away.

"What happened? How am I here? I fell in the Barren, and..." Her stomach churned at the memories. The scouts, bleeding and dying. *Taqel. Metzli.* Teya had still been alive—what of Batu? At least it was likely he'd survived; Isla didn't look as if she'd been crying. And there was Feral. As much of a pain in the arse as the mare could be, they were a team. It was difficult to imagine another horse suiting her as well, though she'd never admit it aloud.

"Foxfur carried you ahead. The others arrived earlier today. Batu's fine," she added at Leiyn's expression. "He took some hits, but nothing that Mother Xepi cannot put right. And he brought Feral back in one piece, too."

Leiyn breathed out in relief. "And the others?"

Isla's face crumpled. "Not many returned. The shaman, Father Patli, escaped unharmed. Teya is also well. I don't know the other scouts, but I saw only three of them. A short, loud woman—"

"That's Nahui." Hearing Teya had survived eased the tightness in her chest, as did each subsequent name. "Was there a thin, odd man, probably looking slightly dazed?"

Isla nodded. "Exactly how I would have described him."

Coyoti, too, still lived. Leiyn sighed. The news was welcome, but it was precious little to go by. Men and women had died, and what had they gained for it?

Don't dwell on what's behind you, Tadeo had often told the rangers. *Plot the path ahead.* She turned her mind to another of the many loose threads dangling before her.

"You said they arrived earlier today... How long have I been out?"

"Nearly a day."

"That long?"

Isla smiled in sympathy. "I was surprised, too. You didn't have any injuries that I could see when Foxfur appeared with you in the Whisperspire. But when I heard the condition your shoulder was in before, and what you did... Leiyn, it's a Saints-given miracle you're even alive."

"The Saints had nothing to do with it, believe me."

Memories of her shoulder resurfaced: the battered gore it had become, the bone peeking through... Leiyn gagged and swallowed. At Isla's movement toward her, she shook her head.

"I'm fine. Just picturing it."

"That bad? Batu said he couldn't look at it, and he doesn't have a weak stomach."

"At least I healed." Leiyn looked aside to stare at the wall, her mahia picking out the circle of lifeforce glowing faintly within it. "At least I survived."

"You did more than that, Leiyn. They say you killed a lyshan."

Leiyn couldn't help but laugh. "That's a bit of an exaggeration."

"So you didn't?"

"Well, I suppose I might have. But only because Foxfur tore off its head first."

Isla opened her mouth, then shook her head. "Fine. If that's the way you want to see it, that's up to you. But that's more than anyone in Qasaar can claim—or anywhere else, for that matter."

Leiyn shrugged, wondering if it mattered. She'd faced the corrupted skin-walkers, knew just how outmatched they'd been. If Foxfur hadn't intervened, they all would have been killed within moments.

I still should have been. For the first time since waking, she allowed herself to think of the strange scene before she fell unconscious.

As if Isla could peer inside her skull, she said, "There's something else. Batu says that partway through the battle, you disappeared, then came back half-dead... What happened, Leiyn? Where'd you go?"

She held her friend's gaze. "You wouldn't believe me if I told you."

"I've seen you awaken titans. I think I can handle this."

"We'll see..."

Leiyn told her of the conversation with the lyshan—as much as she could remember of it, anyway. With the condition she'd been in, the details blurred together. Yet a few parts stuck in her mind.

"Oldsoul," Isla mused. "What do you think it means?"

Leiyn shrugged. "Foxfur and the dryvans call me 'Awakener.' I'm guessing it has something to do with that."

"Maybe..." Her friend frowned out the window. "Though they don't quite seem the same."

"I'm more concerned with why a lyshan let me walk free, and why he wanted to converse in the first place."

"Sharo, you said his name was? Haven't heard of him. But Man'nah—that one, I know. The Tetrad has mentioned him."

Leiyn looked at her sharply. "What did they say?"

"He's supposed to be their leader. The lyshans haven't spoken much before this, only leaving the occasional scout alive to bear a message—usually to mock their resistance, more than anything else." Isla raised her eyebrows. "You look like you have a theory."

"A hunch, more like. Sharo asked what I intended to do, why I was out in the Barren. I said it was to kill him and the other lyshans. It seemed to please him, for he let me go." Leiyn hesitated. "Is it possible he wants us to kill this Man'nah for him? Maybe so he can take control? He called himself 'Man'nah's Shadow,' and though I can't tell skin-walker emotions easily, I'm guessing he resents that. He claimed not to want anything, but he was plainly after something. Ambition, maybe; amusement, at the very least."

The memory of how Sharo had toyed with her, smiling at her pain, laughing at her weakness, put some fire back into her. Before this was over, he'd regret letting her go; she'd make sure of it.

Her friend propped her elbows on her knees. "Maybe the title means he's Man'nah's second-in-command. But you're right —unless he's working against his leader, letting you go doesn't make much sense."

Leiyn opened her mouth to respond, then noticed someone moving through the hallway. She recognized Xepi's esse just before the stolid shaman walked slowly into the room.

"*Osat.* It is good to see you awake." Xepi paused. One glance proved sufficient to see Isla rising and backing away.

"I should check on Batu." With a sympathetic wince, Isla closed the curtain behind her.

Leiyn waited to speak until she felt her friend enter Batu's room. "Tell me of Man'nah and Sharo."

The shaman stared at her, unmoved. "You met with a lyshan."

Leiyn stiffened. There was something in her voice that hadn't been there in their previous conversations. As her muscles tensed, her mind scrambled for an explanation. She didn't have to reach far.

"He let me go, Xepi. I'm not under his influence." Leiyn forced a grin. "Besides, I doubt I'd pose you much harm just now."

The shaman hesitated a moment longer, then nodded and took the chair Isla had vacated. Still, Leiyn felt her mahia probing her. *Like checking for horse ticks.* Her smile soured, but she endured it.

"The lyshans?" Leiyn prompted. "Who are they?"

Xepi's gaze trailed along the stone wall behind her, as if following the stories painted there. "Sharo is unfamiliar to me. But I know of Man'nah, their leader, as far as they have one. He is... powerful."

Leiyn leaned against the wall, letting the silence draw the story out.

"After my..." The shaman trailed off, and Leiyn thought she detected a stirring of sorrow. A moment later, Xepi straightened. "After they stole a shaman a decade ago, Man'nah came to watch the assault on Qasaar. I sought him out, and for a moment, we... connected." Xepi's lips curled. "Lyshans, as you saw, have many-layered souls. This is from absorbing the *ilis* of those they conquer: shamans, others of their kind, perhaps even titans and similar beings. They are perverted by it, both in mind and spirit. I have felt this from other lyshans during previous sieges.

"But Man'nah's *ilis* was too distorted to even know which part of him ruled over the others. As I touched him, many parts shouted at once, each seeking to assert itself before the others. Too many lives were within him; hundreds, thousands."

Leiyn frowned. "Sharo didn't feel that way. His esse was layered—calloused and diseased, to my thinking—but he spoke with one mind."

"Not so with Man'nah." The shaman paused, her gaze growing sharp. "Of what did you speak with this Sharo?"

The suspicion was back. Though she sensed Xepi was avoiding something, for the moment, Leiyn thought it best to humor her.

"Little that I understood. It was like we were having two conversations at once. He wouldn't say what he wanted, but then seemed pleased when I told him I'd come to kill lyshans." She stared ahead, though she kept watch on Xepi from the corner of her eye. "Do you know why that would be?"

The shaman was silent a moment longer. "As I said, Man'nah appears to be their leader. But long have I suspected they are not united, not in the way humans often are. Each lyshan acts independent of the others. You can see that evinced in your battle: how they did not strike all at once. How Sharo took you aside even after you killed one of his comrades."

Someone's given a detailed report. She should have realized it as soon as Xepi knew of her conversation with Sharo. Besides, Teya and Patli had survived; either could have spoken with the shaman.

"Yet three attacked our company," Leiyn said. "They have a common purpose, and Sharo implied Man'nah was, in fact, their leader."

"As they are fractured among themselves, so Man'nah seems within himself. During these decades, the war he wages has been inconsistent. At times, he is aggressive, driving against the wardstones whenever he had a shaman to do so. Other stretches, the captured shaman is kept for seasons, even a year, before he makes any advance." Xepi shook her head. "Perhaps it is to keep us uncertain as to their intentions and tactics. But after touching his *ilis*, I believe there is a truer explanation."

Again, unspoken emotions simmered beneath her statements. But Leiyn felt whatever she hid wasn't something Xepi was ready to share. She pressed her lips together and kept her peace.

I'm not always rash, she thought to Tadeo, hand falling to her hip to touch his carved fox. For the moment, however, it wasn't there, removed with the rest of her clothing.

The shaman raised her gaze from the bed to hold Leiyn's. "You must help us win this war, *Osat*. You must draw upon Zuma's *ilis* within you. It is the only way."

Some things, she could leave be. But this wasn't one of them.

Leiyn leaned forward, ignoring the weakness of her limbs as she stared into Xepi's eyes. "Don't hold back from me, Xepi. We cannot afford to. I almost died out there. I need to know what Zuma took to his death, what secrets his *ilis* possesses that might save us."

The shaman's mouth became a harder line even than before. "You are not ready. You are only an initiate, not sage enough to even know your mark."

"Yet I killed a lyshan." *In part,* a voice whispered in the back of her mind, but Leiyn ignored it. "Every day that I remain in Qasaar, I'm risking my life. You have to take risks too, Xepi. So tell me: what did he know? It has something to do with titans, doesn't it?"

Creases deepened at the corners of her eyes as she narrowed her gaze. "How do you know this?"

"Acalan. So is it true? Can we somehow win this war with titans?"

Xepi was silent and still for a long moment. Then she nodded. "Yes. Titans are the key."

"How?" Her frustration was mounting, all the more for the hunger and aches plaguing her body. "By pitting them against the lyshans?"

The shaman shook her head. "That secret has long been known to us. This is a different sort of weapon. One that Zuma believed our ancestors wielded in their wars with the *sach'aan*."

"What is it?"

Her voice was a whisper. "Drawing in their esse. Taking on their power. The shaman can become, in some sense, like a titan."

Leiyn stared, sure she'd misunderstood. "Become like a titan? That's not possible."

All too well, she remembered how she'd felt before titans in the past. Humans were small and fragile next to their overwhelming power.

Yet they yield to our commands. A sea kraken spanning the length of Southport's bay had obeyed her, though it nearly cost her life. A hill tortoise had fought on Zuma's behalf before that.

To be like them... How powerful would she be then?

Leiyn's gaze fell. She raised it again. "I cannot imagine it, really. But Zuma was no fool." She sucked in a breath, then let it out slowly. "If he said it could be done, I have to trust that. And I swear to learn how he did it."

Xepi smiled, though it seemed a hard, brittle thing. "As I knew you would. You are impatient, rash; this I have seen in our short time together. But touching a spark of *ilis* cannot be rushed. You will make strides, *Osat*. Trust that it will be soon enough."

Rash. Perhaps what the Gasts needed now was just what she had in large supply. *If you only could have been alive to witness it, Tadeo.*

"I'll rest for now," Leiyn said. "Expect me tomorrow."

The shaman bowed her head and left Leiyn to her thoughts.

26

THE STEP FORWARD

Though she promised to rest, Leiyn only made it until that afternoon before she could no longer remain abed.

Stifling a groan, she stood and steadied herself against the wall. "Damn legs," she muttered as they wavered beneath her. Yet she remembered the extent of what she'd suffered. Touching her shoulder, she found only threads of scars remained; otherwise, the flesh was smooth and unblemished. Considering its ghastly state before, enduring a bit of weakness to heal was a bargain she would willingly accept.

Her ranger greens were crumpled in a pile in the corner of the room, bloodstained and torn. A cursory examination determined that this time, she wouldn't be able to mend them. She grimaced as she rose, staring down at the Gast clothes she wore. They felt garish and unfamiliar, but it was either that or going naked.

The clothes weren't her only loss: one of her anelaces had broken during the fight. That proved a more grievous blow. Tadeo had ordered them made especially for her at no minor inconvenience or expense. To lose one felt like losing a piece of her mentor.

They're only things, she reminded herself. *Nothing can take him from you.*

Belting on her remaining knife, Leiyn left the room as

quietly as she could so as not to wake Batu, who appeared to be sleeping in his room next door. Her shoes were gritty with sand from her trek through the Barren, but she didn't take the time to clean them out as she set down the stairs. Her growling belly, on the other hand, refused to be ignored, particularly when her nose caught scent of cooking meat. Her mahia and ears picked up someone busy in the kitchen.

"Tozi!" she said as she entered. "Where was this service before?"

The rangy man straightened from where he'd been bent over the stone oven and grinned. "A pleasure to see you awake, Ranger Leiyn! I trust you are recovered?"

"I will be once I get a taste of whatever you're cooking."

"And you will! I cook for you on order of Toa Acalan. But I would not grow used to it," he added with a faltering smile. "I have many other duties to be about after today."

Leiyn mock-scowled as she slumped into a chair. "If you insist. But about that food..."

Soon, Leiyn coaxed a plate out of the caretaker, receiving generous helpings of mutton and honey-drizzled squash and scarfing it down in short order. She didn't bother sitting at a table, instead hunching over a counter. Only as she neared the end of her meal did Tozi clear his throat and speak again.

"I must admit, I am also to pass on a message, Ranger Leiyn. Toa Acalan and the rest of the Tetrad wish you to attend them in the Whisperspire, if you are able."

Leiyn pushed her plate away and crossed her arms. "I wish you'd keep some things to yourself, Tozi. But I suppose there's nothing for it."

Feeling somewhat restored, if a bit drowsy, she exited the barracks and joined the line of people filtering down the cliff-side to the heart of Qasaar. She'd hoped to make other visits that afternoon, including checking in on Feral, Teya, and Patli to ensure they hadn't fared too poorly. She also needed to know which scouts had died and which had survived. The thought of Taqel gone made her chest ache, though she'd only known him for days. She could only imagine how Teya must be suffering.

So absorbed was she in her thoughts that she didn't notice the looks at first. As they multiplied, Leiyn could no longer deny them. Qasaar's residents had beheld her in a new light following her performance in the Spear Circle. Their deference now was different.

Before, it had been respect. This was closer to awe.

A sharp discomfort struck her middle. *Truth crawls, rumors fly, indeed.* She would have bet much that every person in the city knew she'd struck the final blow against a lyshan. Fables had a way of growing; before long, they would likely detail her killing the creature entirely on her own, if not taking on a group of them at once.

Leiyn smiled to herself and ignored the stares. With her gut roiling, she knew of no other way to cope.

Reaching the Whisperspire, she sensed the members of the Tetrad above. There were eight people, five of whom she could identify. Isla, Acalan, Xepi, and Teya she knew at once; Patli, she differentiated after a moment's study.

What are they doing here? Reports from the scouting mission should have already taken place. *Is another expedition already underway?*

Leiyn reached the top of the stairs and entered the room. Xepi and Patli's eyes found her at once, no doubt sensing her with their magic. The others looked around a moment later. Teya flashed her a smile, but it slipped away as soon as it appeared. Isla appeared even more anxious by the tells in her body language—a fluttering eyelid, a slight tilt to her head—that only those who knew her well could detect. Yet her eyes were wide with anticipation.

Leiyn stepped further into the room, trepidation rising.

"Envoy Leiyn." Acalan stood as he greeted her, nodding formally. "We are blessed by your presence."

"Likewise, Chief Acalan." She made her way to Isla's side,

wondering at the chieftains' stares. Acalan's deference put her even more on edge.

As Acalan sat, Zyanya shook her head, the beads in her braids clattering. "Yes, be welcome, Envoy. We are grateful for the assistance you provided to Father Patli and Spear Teya. Killing a lyshan... I did not think it possible."

Leiyn opened her mouth to point out that Foxfur ripping off its head helped a great deal, but paused as Acalan gave a small shake of his head. She grimaced and nodded. Trusting his judgment was her best option, though she wondered what path it was leading her down.

"The pleasure was mine," she settled on saying.

"Yes, very grateful." Ilaoti spoke with her usual brusqueness. "Now that they are both here, let us name our demands, or our city will fall before we can complete the negotiations."

Acalan's look at the chieftainess lacked its usual stoniness, as did his tone when he spoke. "We can, though an alliance requires concessions from both sides."

An alliance. Leiyn's heart beat faster. *Then it's happening.* She looked at Isla and understood her exuberance. Isla flashed her a smile before regaining her composure.

The Jaguar chieftain stared first at Leiyn, then Isla. "Baltesia's demands are that we aid in their war against Ilberia, their homeland. The form of assistance was left unsaid, though I assume the governor desired both soldiers and shamans. Is that correct, Envoy Isla?"

Isla nodded. "Allies in any form are needed. The Caelrey's capacities exceed our own, but with the help of the other colonies and your people, we will overcome them."

Ilaoti and Tinoch seemed to doubt that claim, but Zyanya at least looked considering. It showed hope for their mission's success, however marginal.

"In exchange," Acalan continued in his low rumble, "Baltesia aids in our war against the lyshans. He sent his envoys and rangers ahead to see what our needs would be with the promise of more.

Thus far, Envoy Leiyn has proven a greater resource than even I, having seen her in combat, would have anticipated. She killed a lyshan, a feat none of our *situali* or shamans have accomplished in the decades since our enemies came down from the north."

The truth burned on Leiyn's tongue, but she swallowed it down, hoping Foxfur wouldn't mind.

Zyanya spoke up now. "If Envoy Leiyn agrees to continue fighting on our behalf, no number of soldiers will be of further help. To my knowledge, Baltesia does not have shamans of their own."

"No," Isla said. "Ilberia has stolen any eligible. Most of them," she added with a raised eyebrow.

"Very well," the chieftainess replied. "Even one might turn the tide."

"But we have other demands." Ilaoti wore a tiger's smile. "We will have the land stolen from us back under our control."

Leiyn's breath caught. This was plainly what they'd desired all along: the return of their land. Her gaze flickered over the other chieftains and saw it confirmed in their expressions.

Of course they did; what else could they want?

Decades had passed, and most of them at the table hadn't been alive when the Titan War occurred, yet the consequences of it surrounded them in their daily lives. Qasaar and the Barren made for a hostile domain, even without having to contend with titans and lyshans.

They want to go home.

She knew that soul-deep ache. Most nights, she thought of her days at the Wilds Lodge, how they would never come again. Their return wouldn't be the same, even if she and Isla did rebuild the rangers, as they dreamed of doing. The world had moved on.

But the Gasts' dream was impossible. Lord Governor Mauricio wouldn't yield Baltesian land, not once he discovered how minimal the aid would be from the Gasts. Though she didn't doubt he was sympathetic to their cause, he couldn't afford to lose resources, nor give the appearance of weakness to the neighboring colonies or the Ancestral Lands.

Isla didn't look as baffled as Leiyn felt. Leiyn suspected the matter had been raised before, but her fellow ranger had neglected to mention it. Isla's nerves had disappeared, replaced by the confidence Leiyn was used to seeing from her.

"I cannot promise the Lord Governor will accede to these conditions," Isla said. "Giving up land would be a dear price—though I understand your perspective on the matter. But, as we have discussed, I will bear the proposal back to the Lord Governor. Until I return with his official reply, the agreement will have a conditional acceptance."

The implications of Isla's words sunk in a moment after. Leiyn stared at her friend. "*You* will bear it?"

Isla faced her, and suddenly Leiyn understood what was happening. She wasn't nervous about negotiating with the Tetrad. It was this moment her friend had been dreading.

She's leaving. Leaving me.

Cold curled around her bones. Only their evenings had been spent together of late, yet Leiyn knew she'd feel the lack of Isla every moment she was gone. They were comrades, friends. Family. They were the last of the rangers, the legacy of the Lodge.

But is she still a ranger? a part of her mocked. *Or only Mauricio's messenger?*

Even as she thought it, Leiyn couldn't truly believe that. Their lives had been formed too thoroughly by their training to ever be rid of its influence. But Isla didn't cling to being a ranger as Leiyn did. Her friend seemed content with her lot, even as it took her away from Leiyn's path. Away from the past they had shared.

Away from her.

Other eyes fell upon Leiyn. Silence swarmed the chamber. Were they waiting for her to speak? Drawing upright, she tried to regain her composure before looking at Isla.

She said the only words she could.

"While Isla goes south, I will stay here and fight with you."

A brief smile blossomed on her friend's face, full of relief. Beyond her, Teya frowned, seeming to catch the undercurrent of her words. Acalan's hard expression softened, so much so that Leiyn almost believed him sympathetic to her plight. One of the shamans might have probed her, but she put up her walls. The room felt cramped all of sudden, as much a cage as the one under the First Temple. She twitched with the need to escape.

But she couldn't flee yet. Leiyn stared at the opposite wall, trying to hold it together.

"Very well," Ilaoti still spoke with a sneer, though her bluster had lessened. "We will use your ranger while you fetch our refusal. If it is agreeable to my fellow chieftains?"

One by one, the others nodded. Tinoch let out a nervous laugh. "That settles it then, Envoy Leiyn. You are stuck with us."

She flashed a smile but could give no more.

The decision made, Isla excused herself and Leiyn. The chieftains and the others remained behind, no doubt judging how to best use their new lyshan-killer. Even the absurdity of the thought wasn't enough to wake Leiyn's smile.

She and Isla were silent as they descended the spiraling stairs, the voices from the room above slowly fading. Only as they stepped foot from the Whisperspire did Leiyn break it. Spinning toward her friend, she arrested her with a hand on her arm. She didn't care that Gasts milled about them fetching water from the nearby wells. She couldn't hold it in any longer.

"Why didn't you tell me?"

Isla winced. "Until it was settled, I didn't know if it would be necessary. They only came to the decision since your return, Leiyn. Now that they see what you're capable of, even Ilaoti is willing to negotiate."

"She's just using us. There's no chance Mauricio will accept their terms. Yielding land?" Leiyn shook her head. "But that's beside the point. You should have warned me. It's just you and me, Isla. The last of the Lodge."

"I know."

"And now you're leaving."

"Only until we return." But Isla's smile showed she knew how the days would weigh on Leiyn.

One of her words stuck out from the others. *We.* Leiyn felt breathless as she spoke.

"You're taking Batu, aren't you?"

Isla gripped Leiyn's arms in return. "I don't have to. I could travel alone—"

"No." Though it felt like prying an arrow from her flesh, Leiyn forced out the words. "He should go with you. It'll be a long journey, and it's dangerous besides, even for you. Suncoats are still out there, not to mention that the other two colonies, Altan Gaz and Ore-Ofe, might have sided with the Ancestral Lands."

"I know. But you... that'll leave you alone up here."

Leiyn tried for a smile and failed. "Don't worry. And if you do, well, you'll have Batu to comfort you."

Isla laughed, loud with relief. "Yes, I suppose I will."

"Be careful, though. Don't want to strain your fledgling love with the troubles of travel."

Her friend rolled her eyes. "It's survived this long. I think we'll last."

Their smiles faded. Leiyn pulled Isla into a tight embrace.

"Come back to me," she murmured in her ear. "Whatever it takes, make damn sure you come back."

"I will." Isla pulled away to look into her eyes. "But I'm more concerned about you. Who's going to tell you not to be rash?"

"Guess I'll have to tell myself."

"Promise me you'll not take any unnecessary risks, Leiyn. I know it's a war, but I... I need you to live."

Leiyn only hugged her again. "I'll survive. I promise, Isla. We'll see each other again."

She clung to her friend and hoped it was true.

27

FAREWELLS

With the decision made, there was little reason to delay. Leiyn rose early the next morning and saw her friends on their way.

The night before, they'd shared a last round of fiend's nectar and revelry. The laughter had been keen and the storytelling frantic. Leiyn cut off all of Isla's attempts to grow nostalgic.

"What will be will be," she said before pivoting to lighter topics.

Acalan even joined them briefly, and she saw him grin more than she'd thought he had in him. Spurred on by Leiyn, they teased the Gast chieftain for his apparent lack of romantic interests.

"You're not so bad looking," Isla noted, provoking a sidelong look from Batu and a snort from Leiyn. Acalan patiently bore it, never revealing anything of his private life.

Batu was still in high spirits the next morning. Aided by Xepi's healing, he'd made a quick recovery and seemed eager to be on their way. Leiyn's mood was considerably lower. Silence was easier than smiles.

Isla didn't try to coax her out of it, but only cast her the occasional look. Leiyn helped saddle Isla's horse, Mottle, the bags heavy with supplies. When all the gear was secured, Leiyn saddled Feral as well. She didn't need to; she didn't plan to go any farther than the top of the rise. Yet having the unruly mare next to her eased the encroaching loneliness, if ever so slightly.

"Any company's better than none, eh, Feral?" she muttered as she snuck in a quick scratch behind the horse's ear before having to dodge a bite.

They led their mounts from the cavernous stable up the slope. When the end of the city's gorge came to an end, Isla and Batu turned back, their expressions mirroring each other. Leiyn gave them a bracing smile, then held out her free arm.

"Come on, then. Best get you on your way."

She embraced them, one at a time. Words were unnecessary; all that needed to be said shone in their glistening eyes.

There was nothing left but for Isla and Batu to mount their steeds. Leiyn remained with her feet planted on the ground, staring up at them. With calls and pressed heels, they turned their horses around, then began to trot away. Before they'd gone a dozen feet, Isla twisted around and cried back.

"Don't be rash, Firebrand!"

Leiyn grinned through sudden tears. She raised a hand. "Give Mauricio my best!"

With final parting waves, they turned, then set on up the incline.

Leiyn watched as they grew smaller with every switchback. Feral pulled at her reins impatiently, but she remained at her vigil. The wind moaned, dry and rough against her skin. Her belt hung uncomfortably on her hips. Only as she adjusted it did she realize its cause: her missing knife.

"Isn't that an apt comparison?" she said to her horse. "One sheath's empty now."

Nothing felt quite right. This wasn't how her company was supposed to disassemble. How her little family broke apart. She stared up at the two people closest to her and watched them draw farther away. She tried not to wish she was going with them.

Shaking her head, Leiyn turned and mounted Feral,

surprising the horse. "Settle!" she barked at her. "We're going for a ride, just like you're always wanting."

She pressed her heels into the mare's flanks, then off they flew. Wind dragged fresh tears from her eyes and blew back her cloak. The cold pierced her Gast clothing. Yet she rode faster, Feral more than happy to gallop across the mesa.

They crossed terrain she hadn't yet visited, passed farmland and workers already setting about their daily labors. They looked up as she bolted past, no doubt wondering if there was cause for alarm. Leiyn only grinned. The things she'd been clinging to all morning began to shake loose.

When Feral was just beginning to lather, Leiyn dismounted at the edge of a cliff and stared toward the sunrise. The horizon smoldered in pastels of pink and orange. Light streaked across the desolate landscape, painting it like the colored bands on the cliffs spread around her. Shadows stretched from the stones, further striating the ground. The sand and stone that remained in the light glowed golden with the coming day.

The Barren's beauty was subtler than that of the Titan Wilds she knew best, but just as sure and present. It was a wellspring that ran deep and emerged with water clear and cool to drink.

Remember, she told herself. *Why I'm here. What my purpose is.* The Ranger's Oath hadn't changed, nor her duty to uphold it.

Perceive. Preserve. Protect.

But she had one more duty to add to the list: *Avenge.* She'd killed the conquerer Armando Pótecil, but he'd been a pawn of others. She meant to make the puppet masters pay for the destruction of her home and the killing of the rangers as well.

She'd tear them down, even if it was the Altacura and the Caelrey themselves she had to fight.

"But first," she muttered, "I have to kill death incarnate."

Shaking her head, Leiyn pulled herself into the saddle again, then turned Feral back toward Qasaar.

2 8

SUFFOCATION

She found Teya precisely where she expected to: back at the training yard.

After stabling Feral and gathering her longbow and quiver, Leiyn had been walking to the yard when she saw her. The scout was moving through a spear sequence with one of the dulled practice weapons. It involved both kicks and somersaults around the pell and was far more acrobatic than those she'd taught Batu.

"I'm impressed." Leiyn sauntered up. "You really showed that dummy."

Teya straightened, brushing the dust off with a grin. "Be glad I did not attempt that on you in the Spear Circle, Redlock. Else those lyshans would have killed the rest of the party."

At the reminder, their mood sobered. Leiyn blew out a breath and looked toward the Barren. She imagined she could see the place they'd been ambushed, a smudge in the distant orange and gray.

"How many came back?" she said at length. It was easier to ask after the survivors.

"Half." Teya's jaw tensed, then relaxed. "Taqel, Metzli, Yolot, and Tayanna fell, may *Tlalli* cradle their spirits."

Leiyn bowed her head, picturing each of the dead. Some she'd only known for the duration of the mission, but Teya's grief amplified her own.

"Your spirit touches mine," she murmured. "I'm sorry, Teya. I'm so sorry."

Teya's look drew Leiyn's gaze. "You have nothing to be sorry for. Without you, I would not be here to mourn, and we would have lost one of our last shamans. I thank you, Leiyn of Orille, Ranger of Baltesia, Envoy to Governor Mauricio. If need should arise, you have my spear."

The skin between her shoulder blades tingled. The words had the feel of an oath. Yet that look in her eyes, the warmth of her esse... she tried not to imagine it as something more.

Teya grinned and ground the butt of her spear into the dirt. "There is a time for mourning, but it is not on the yard. Show me how you slew a skin-walker."

Leiyn matched her smile, then went to fetch her wooden wasters.

⌇ ⌇

Afterward, sweaty and leaden-limbed, Leiyn made her way to Xepi's hut and was glad to sense the shaman inside.

"Show me how to access it," Leiyn said as soon as she strode through the door and sat at the table. "Zuma's spark. I'm ready to reach for it."

Xepi sat across from her. She looked up from the mortar and pestle in her hands and raised her eyebrows. "So you are still in Qasaar."

"Did you think I'd leave?"

"Your companions did."

When Leiyn didn't immediately respond, the shaman continued her grinding.

"I'm here, Xepi." Leiyn spoke with a low, measured tone. "I'm committed. Win or lose, live or die, I'm fighting this war. It's *our* war. And I'll do anything I must."

Xepi nodded, not looking up. "Good."

Leiyn tried not to feel annoyed as the shaman only

continued to mash away. She crossed her arms and waited but couldn't hold her tongue for long.

"So?"

The shaman set down the pestle, picked up a wooden cup, and tapped the contents of the bowl into it. Then she lifted a beaten copper kettle, which had been simmering behind her, and poured hot water in. She set the steaming cup on Leiyn's side of the table.

"It will steep for a few minutes, then you will drink it."

Leiyn drew the tumbler toward her and sniffed. "Smells savory. Like... mushrooms."

"It is, in part. Dried *nacatl*, a mushroom that grows only in the caves along the foothills of these mountains. There is also the crown of the *peyotl* cactus. Both of these affect the *ilis*, opening it. You will feel the borders of yourself fade and *Tlalli* meld with you. Be wary; do not drift too far. You must remain concentrated on your task."

She didn't like the sound of the toadstool tea's effect, but she didn't protest. *Just one more thing to grin and bear.*

"Accessing Zuma's memories. That's what this is for, isn't it?"

Xepi nodded. "If you succeed, you will feel a part of his presence. Do not fear this; it will bring you no harm."

"I never feared Zuma before. I don't plan on starting now."

It wasn't quite true. She'd feared Zuma a great deal before she came to know him. But once she'd opened herself to the aged shaman and recognized all he'd done for her, admiration had replaced any terror.

"You must not stop at sensing him but press into his memories. Identify his lifemark and follow it through his past. There, we will unlock the secrets you must know."

Doubts flitted through Leiyn's mind like crows over carrion. Xepi was no longer cautioning her, but urging her on, though she'd expressed doubts as to her readiness so recently.

Why doesn't she tell me these secrets?

Leiyn shook her head. She wouldn't let doubts stop her. They never had before.

After a few more moments, Xepi prompted her to drink the tea. Leiyn cradled the cup before her nose, steam pouring around her face. While musty from the mushrooms, the tea also had a scent bitter enough to nearly scald her nostrils. Hints of licorice root softened the stench. She looked up at her teacher.

"Don't suppose you have any honey to help this go down?"

That won her a small smile, but when Xepi didn't take her request seriously, Leiyn lifted the cup and sipped. The flavor proved worse than it smelled, so she poured it down her throat quickly. When she'd drained the tea, Leiyn slapped the cup back on the table and fought down a gag.

"What now?" she gasped.

"Soon, you will feel the tea's effects. Then you must reach for Zuma's *ilis*."

"Simple enough." Leiyn leaned back in her chair and crossed her arms. Her leg bounced, nerves making it impossible for her to sit still.

Xepi's steady gaze drew her own. "There is something I must warn you of, *Osat*."

Leiyn narrowed her eyes. "Isn't it a little late for that?"

"It is unavoidable. Yet you must be prepared for what you will find when you reach for Zuma." The shaman paused, then continued. "The memory of death is often the first to rise. Like oil on the surface of water, you must push through it to reach the knowledge that lies beneath."

The words froze Leiyn in place. Her own memory of Zuma's last breaths were bad enough. That rattling in his chest. The fading of his lifefire. The stiffening of his flesh. The guilt burning through her.

But she hadn't felt his torment. She'd toed the final threshold on many occasions, but never crossed over. This time, she'd have to truly experience San Inhoa's quietus.

Leiyn surprised herself with a grin. "Just another death to suffer through."

She laughed at Xepi's surprise but had no more time to enjoy it. Already, she felt a tingling on her skin, concentrated first at her fingertips, but quickly spreading through the rest of her body. Leiyn lifted her hands and stared at them, seeing them as if for the first time. How strange they were with their bendy appendages! She flexed her fingers, wondering how she'd never noticed it before.

Her awareness spread. Her attention was snagged by the light blossoming around her. Her mahia could always sense esse, but now it felt as if it had doubled in brightness. Leiyn stared with blind eyes at the world, only seeing with her lifesense. She noticed every bug crawling along the walls, the one drowning in the pitcher of water, the one rising up the leg of her chair. Some flew through the air outside, tossed in the Barren's incessant winds. They looked like sparks from a bonfire as they flitted through the sky. It fascinated her: how invisible they normally were, yet how bright they now seemed.

The hut's walls drew her focus next. In greater detail than ever before, she detected the intricate workings behind the windows that slid up and down on their own. *Like eyelids.* The thought made her giggle.

There was more there; in the very walls themselves, a network of life spread like veins through a body. They seemed to be drawing out the heat of the stone, slowly becoming brighter as their energy grew. *Cooling down the hut.* She'd always wondered how its interior remained so pleasant, even with the sun beating down on them.

"Leiyn, remember your task. Reach for Zuma."

As Xepi spoke, Leiyn looked at her, then through her. The images of her lifemark rose in stark detail: the eviscerated draconion; the dying hearth; the broken spear. Curiosity stoked, she reached in further, seeking after the meanings. Those images had the flavor of memory, and she meant to know them as her own.

A sudden rebuff drove her back.

Leiyn almost upended her chair in surprise. Smarting like she'd been cuffed on the back of the head, she stared dumbly at her teacher. Her mahia now asserted itself so strongly it was difficult to see her expressions.

"Do not seek into me," Xepi reprimanded. "Delve into yourself, Leiyn. Find Zuma within."

Zuma. Recovering, Leiyn tried to herd her scattered thoughts in a more productive direction. She looked down, and with her mahia, she touched upon the esse shining from her. There was still a layer of resistance, a hesitancy not entirely fallen. But it was like the first formation of ice on a lake: with a touch, she broke through.

And fell.

Leiyn was swept up, a branch in a river, tossed and turned around. She didn't try to fight it. Down, the current flowed, so down she went.

From the flames flashed images. She watched them flit by. Only after they'd passed did she recognize them.

A fox, prowling, hunting... or perhaps hiding. A taper, halfway melted—

Something roared from the inferno, soaring toward her. Leiyn cried out and threw up her arms, but the creature swept over her—no, *through* her—then dissipated in a cloud of smoke.

An ash dragon.

Leiyn didn't pause to consider what it meant. More of the images appeared, but they were vague and formless. She didn't attend to them, for something lay ahead: two points of light, burning like twin suns. She knew them in a way beyond words. Emotion rippled through her fiery surroundings.

Zuma. And... Mother.

She almost went to the second pulsing light. How long had she yearned to know her mother? To see her, touch her? It wouldn't be the same, perhaps, beholding her spark. But it would be more of her than she'd ever had.

No. Not yet. Later, she would seek her and come to know her as life had denied. For now, she had to mind her duty.

Leiyn approached Zuma's esse, then hesitated.

From the heart of the star rose his lifemark, rendered in sharper detail than any she'd seen before. First, a lone hawthorn atop a hill, its boughs heavy with leaves and moon-white blooms.

The branches stirred with a breeze, and sunlight warmed them. It was rooted, healthy. Content.

She looked to the second image, to the hands she recognized as Zuma's, calloused and stiffened from a long life. They were cupped as if to hold water, but in them was only ashes, a gray, pillowy pile that couldn't be contained. As ash streamed between the fingers, a gust caught it and swirled it into smoke. From these clouds, faces materialized for a moment, then were blown away. Leiyn didn't recognize the people in the smoke.

The last image froze her in place. It showed Zuma once more, his upper half distinct. Tucked in his arms was a babe fresh from the womb, filmed with blood and mucus, and with its life-cord still attached. At first, the child was as dark as night; then they lit up like a spark catching flame. She stared, transfixed, knowing what she looked upon, marveling that it could be so deeply embedded in him as to appear here.

My birth.

Battling her rising emotions, Leiyn advanced on the spark. It resisted her entrance, not as a guard wrestling an intruder, but with the pummeling force of a waterfall. She pressed forward, enduring the discomfort, and pushed inside.

She tumbled into darkness.

The next moment, she was lying down. She felt it more than saw it, for her vision had dimmed and muddied. Her body was weighed down as if filled with sand. Her heart beat as barely more than a patter, yet still continued, like an old hound that refused to leave off the hunt. But it was her throat, constricted and growing tighter, and her lungs, flattened and not opening, that spiked her terror.

Air. I need air!

Leiyn thrashed, or tried to, but neither her arms nor legs obeyed. She was trapped, cornered, with no escape in sight.

She was dying.

I won't go this way; I can't. Give me a bow and a battle—I'll fight to the end, I'll die on the field. Just don't let it end here!

She would have begged at the feet of the Saints, but they

were absent. She would have even pleaded to Legion, but the many-faced demon didn't witness her passing. She would slip into the night, unseen, unheard, unknown. Fading until she was forgotten.

NO!

Leiyn surged upward, and the hazy scene disappeared. She was rising, rising to the surface—then the hut burst into view again, Xepi's face before her, eyes wide, lips parted, hands grasping her shoulders, shaking her, her presence reaching in.

"Wake, *Osat*, wake!"

Leiyn grabbed her arms but didn't push her away. Xepi was solid, steady, a rock in a turbulent sea.

"I'm awake. I'm here."

The shaman released her but didn't pry her arms from Leiyn's clinging grasp. They remained there, locked in the pose, for several thudding heartbeats. Blood rushed to Leiyn's head. For a moment, she felt light-headed, then the feeling subsided.

"You did not succeed."

Leiyn shook her head. "I was choking, Xepi. I couldn't breathe. And the fear—" She bit the words off. Now that she'd surfaced, she knew them for what they were: plain and simple cowardice.

She warned you, a voice murmured in the back of her mind. *You had to pass through Zuma's death to reach beyond. Yet you fled instead.*

"I just couldn't." Her chin slumped to her chest. Though she'd come back to the world, her control over her body seemed to be slipping away.

Her teacher finally pulled back. "This task—it is difficult even for shamans who have trained all their lives. I would never usually put it before an initiate; never have I been forced to. It is too early for the attempt." Xepi paused, pursing her lips. "To falter does not make you weak. Only the strong can endure failure."

Her words offered comfort, but Leiyn found she couldn't accept them. "It's not about failing or weakness or doing things out of order. I have to do this. Doesn't matter how hard it is, I have to. It's the only way for me to fight the lyshans, isn't it, those secrets of Zuma's?"

She raised her head to see Xepi standing over her, eyes narrowed and considering.

"Yes," the shaman said at length. "It is."

"There you go." Leiyn gripped the seat of her chair, then forced out her next words. "I'll try again. I know what's coming. I can push through—"

"Not today," Xepi cut her off. "Another attempt would be foolish. I will give you a tonic to counteract the tea, then you are to rest. We will try again tomorrow."

The shaman gave her no choice but to relent. Leiyn watched her bustle about her herbs while her mind wandered. The esse surrounding her was still bright yet muted by her misery.

I will succeed, she told herself. *No matter how many tries it takes; no matter how miserable it makes me.*

No matter how many times I have to die.

PART V

BURIED SECRETS

29

THIRTEEN YEARS BEFORE

Leiyn's dream of becoming a ranger drifted to the back of her mind as spring took hold of Southport. The fruit trees lining the road outside the sanctuary first blossomed, then grew heavy with cherries, providing a welcome treat for any girl daring enough to steal them. Fortunately for Aracel, Leiyn had courage enough for both of them, and their bellies were often full at night, a welcome change after the winter.

But expeditions to steal cherries were bright spots among gloomy days. Most of their hours were spent on chores of which there seemed an endless amount. Sister Alma was merciless, driving them on day after day, the only exceptions made for holy days. Leiyn overheard Aracel praying fervently to the Saints for relief one evening and wondered if she should do the same.

Even more taxing was their daily instruction in letters. Leiyn dreaded these hours most of all, for determination and strength couldn't make up for her deficiencies. Her father had taught her little of reading and writing, as more practical skills had taken precedence. A welcome treat then, now she wished he'd shown her more. She was behind the rest of the orphans, and even after months, she had to speak the words aloud to understand them.

Isebel didn't miss the opportunity for further ridicule. The lessons were riddled with the girl's thinly veiled insults as she derided Leiyn's ignorance, her gaggle always giggling along.

Leiyn tried to ignore them but spent as much time fighting down her frustration as struggling to make her hand cooperate. Her lines never came out straight, and her curves had all the evenness of a river.

Despite these impediments, she slowly learned. Only when Aracel pointed out that Leiyn could now write her name, even compose a letter if she wished, or read all the books in the sanctuary's paltry library, did Leiyn begin to appreciate the worth of this hard-earned skill. Under the cover of darkness, she started sneaking into the library and burning tallow candles to read and practice, and so improved swifter still. Making it more thrilling were secret smiles with Aracel whenever Sister Alma demanded to know why all the candles were disappearing.

Yet the tedium of life made Leiyn itch for something else. Though she chafed at chores, she leaped at the chance to do any she hadn't before. So it was that she and Aracel found themselves pushing the sanctuary's small handcart over to the closest temple to fetch their allotment of food for the next several days.

The priestess had been hesitant to allow them the privilege of such an important job but relented under Leiyn's insistence. "I prefer the older girls do it," Sister Alma said with a frown. "Do not disappoint me."

The matron's hesitancy only made the prospect more enticing. Leiyn grinned as she pushed the rickety handcart onto the cobblestones outside. She fought it forward as it jarred her arms and tried to work free.

She knew the way to Fourth Temple, sometimes called Sacred Hand, just as all the girls did, for they visited it each week to bow before the Saints and give confession. Leiyn always skirted her sins during these sessions, suspecting collusion between Sister Alma and the faceless acolytes behind the wicker panels. Girls seemed to be caught at wrongdoing far more often after confession than other days, and she didn't mean to take that chance. *Omn will understand,* she told herself as she lied through her teeth. *Hopefully the Saints will, too.*

Now, as she headed for the temple, she and Aracel wove into

the stream of people walking and riding along the road. Their lifefires burned against her walls, quickly eroding them, yet Leiyn tried to ignore them and enjoy the sun caressing her skin, too rare a treat when stuck inside with duties. Soon, however, even that became uncomfortable.

"Why did we agree to this again?" she grunted as she pushed a sticky wheel over a large paver.

Aracel, who walked beside her, only hunched down further. She seemed to be folding in on herself to avoid touching anyone in the crowd around them, a task that proved impossible. "You insisted."

"Next time, insist I don't." Leiyn softened the words with a smile.

The gesture was lost on her friend. Aracel's eyes were wide as she stared at her feet. Leiyn frowned and pressed faster. She had to get her off the streets and as quickly as she could. Aracel had never seemed so miserable when they traveled to Sacred Hand with the others.

Must be different when she's among the other sanctuary girls.

Concern for her friend overrode her own discomfort. Leiyn hurried them on until the handcart's wheels bumped against the stone of the first stair up to the tabernacle. They dragged it up the stairs, receiving sharp words for their carelessness, which wilted Aracel and made Leiyn draw up straighter, then filled the cart with the weekly charity. Leiyn tried not to scowl at the food but couldn't entirely keep it off her face. It was always past fresh, usually closer to spoiled. She missed the days when most everything she ate came straight from the garden, freshly picked and deliciously ripe.

No. Can't think about that. The thought of her lost home hollowed out her chest, and she tried to push the memories away. Still, her responses sounded wooden as she thanked the priestess and wheeled the handcart back to the entrance.

"You alright?" Aracel muttered. She pushed the cart and seemed much better now that they'd been out of the crowd for a few minutes. "You look like you've seen a demon of Legion."

"Fine."

Yet her mind kept drifting back to those golden days when her father had been alive, when Orille had been her entire world, before the Blush swept through and changed everything for the worse. Though the plague had faltered, she still felt the pull of its tide, the ripples that washed over the rest of her life.

So withdrawn did she become that she didn't notice the stranger walking up the front steps until they were before her. She stuttered to a halt, her blood seeming to freeze in her veins.

Odiosa.

She'd seen the witch hunters occasionally throughout South-port and knew the look of their gray robes. More indicative of their order was how others avoided them, flowing around them like a stream around boulders. This one's head was bowed as if in prayer, a hood drooping over their face. She didn't think they had seen her.

Blood roaring in her ears, Leiyn edged to the side of the plat-form and glanced over it. A dozen-foot drop. Not an easy way down, but she doubted she could pass by the odiosa unnoticed.

"Leiyn?" Aracel watched her, brow knitted. Telling by her parted lips and her fluttering chest, her friend's anxiety was rearing again. But what could Leiyn do for her? She had to flee, flee before—

The odiosa looked up and startled, staring at Leiyn like she was a demon.

Leiyn tightened her walls. Something tingled against them.

He knows!

She could see it in his dead eyes, the flicker of surprise. The odiosa took another step up the stairs, one hand crooked into a claw as if to swipe at Leiyn. The sensation on her mahia grew to burning. She couldn't hold against it for long.

With a last look at her friend, Leiyn turned and scrambled down the temple platform.

Lowering herself from the edge made the drop just manageable. Her stomach flew until her feet crunched onto the dirt below, the impact jarring up her legs to rattle in her skull.

But she'd spent the spring leaping from trees and barely slowed, turning to run down the alley and away from the busy street.

The reek of urine and nightsoil was a small price to pay for escape. The greater cost was leaving Aracel behind, who still called Leiyn's name.

Three men stepped out of the shadows, barring the temple way.

Leiyn bared her teeth, every muscle gone rigid. The men reeked like spoiled fish and her old home's cellar, which was often filled with root vegetables and ale. The stench of depraved men. She feared them less than the gray-cloak close behind, but they could harm her in plenty of other ways.

"Look'ee here, lads," one breathed, voice husky from smoke. His pipe was lit and hung lazily from his thin fingers. "A pretty lass fell from the sky. A gift from the Saints themselves, I'd say!"

"And she came from the temple, too!" cackled the second, a man with beady, dark eyes and a tricorn hat that didn't match the rest of his rustic clothes.

Pipe scowled at Tricorn. "S'why I said that, you cock-headed knock-nut."

The third ignored the other two, his eyes never shifting from Leiyn. "Feisty, isn't she?" he murmured. His hair and patchy beard shone with oil, too neatly put in place. "I like feisty."

Leiyn raised her fists. "Move, or I'll make you."

Her threat had the opposite effect to what she'd intended. The three men laughed, and once again seemed bound in their purpose, their personal squabbles forgotten. They came a step closer.

"No need for that, girl," Grease said, his voice like a snake's hiss. "S'alright. Come quietly with us. We won't harm you."

Her legs trembled. Leiyn wondered if she could make it past them without being grabbed. Despite her fear, her voice was steady.

"Can't say the same if you don't let me go."

"Lass! Come, now." Pipe tucked his vice into his belt and

raised both hands, showing them to be empty. "We only want a good time."

"Better for us than you, though," Tricorn said thoughtfully.

"Shut it, you fat-headed, turd-brained—"

"Leiyn!"

Her hopes plummeted further. Leiyn snuck a glance back toward the alley's entrance, where Aracel stood. Despite all her hopes otherwise, her friend had followed.

"Oh-ho! Two flies in sap, now!" Once more, Pipe left off his insults to grin at the other scoundrels. "Legion's own luck's with us today, lads!"

"It might be," Grease droned, "if you stop talking and help." Ignoring Pipe's look of outrage, the oily man gestured toward Aracel and called to her. "Come 'ere, girl. We won't hurt you. Just want you and your friend together."

"Stay there!" Leiyn shouted, careful not to say Aracel's name in case these men could use it to track her down. She wondered how close behind the odiosa was. He knew Leiyn was a witch; he had tried breaking through her walls. She had to get them both out of this, and fast.

Grease lunged, but Leiyn had been expecting it. She twisted out of the way, her shoulder scraping against the stone terrace behind, then struck with a fist. The oily man lurched back, a smile twisting his thin lips.

"Feisty," he breathed. "Help me now, would you?"

"Leiyn—"

"Run!" Leiyn just eked out the command before all three men snatched at her. Tricorn got in Pipe's way, provoking another string of curses and a brief tussle. Grease, however, got a hand on Leiyn's throat, shoving her back against the wall. Pain blossomed through the back of her skull. Sparks flew through her vision.

Something inside her snapped.

Leiyn lashed out with all her strength. Her reach was short, so she punched at his arm. Though she couldn't get any momentum into the swing, the man still crumpled beneath her blow. Only as his grasp slipped away from her throat and she heaved in air did she realize why.

He was aflame; all of them were. The other two scoundrels, backing away. Aracel at the end of the alley. The odiosa strolling down the stairs. The priestesses and acolytes in Sacred Hand.

They burned with lifefire.

Her walls had fallen from around her lifesense, and her mahia flared open. The city flooded into her, the sheer amount of life rocking her back and stunning her as she became swept up in it.

"Fesht!" she heard Grease wheeze. Leiyn clawed her way back to reality and saw he was still on the filthy alley ground. Whatever she'd done to him seemed to have weakened him so much he could barely rise.

"What did you...?" He paused, then spoke the damning words in a whisper. "Witch. You're a little witch."

"No." Leiyn tried raising her walls, but the force was too great. "I'm not." She turned her head this way and that, but she could barely see through the forcefulness of her hidden sense. "Dammit, go away!" she muttered, backing against the wall. She tried grounding herself in feeling it solid against her back.

Grease laughed, low and mocking. "Gone mad already, haven't ya?"

"Leiyn, what's happening?"

Leiyn turned toward Aracel's voice, saw her lifefire still lingering in place. But she wasn't alone. Behind her loomed a greater fire, one that didn't stay contained in his body.

Odiosa.

"Go home!" Leiyn cried as she stumbled away. "Listen to me, please!" She could only hope her friend would heed her. All she could do now was run.

And so she did, even as the odiosa's tendrils trailed after her, teasing and touching no matter how hard she ran.

She sprinted blindly down the alleys, only seeking to be away. When the distance had opened between them, Leiyn leaned against a splintered wall, sucked in a breath, and finally managed to slam up her walls. The lifefires extinguished, and she was alone in her head once again. She might have smiled in relief but for the knowledge that seeped into the absence.

I cannot stay.

It would be too simple for the odiosa to track her down. He'd seen her leave the temple with a cartful of food. Inquire of the priestesses there, and he would have the name of the sanctuary, perhaps even their own names, if they bothered to remember them. Once he paid the shelter a visit, it would all be over. Leiyn couldn't evade him for long.

I have to run.

Part of her longed to dash through the north gate, but she knew that would be foolish. She wouldn't last a week without basic supplies: a knife, flint and a striking stone, things to trap or fish with.

No; she had to return to San Hugo's Sanctuary, at least for a moment. But she wouldn't stay long, not even to say goodbye to Aracel. It was best this way. Safer.

But where will I go?

An answer came at once. *To Folly. To the rangers.* How long had she dreamed of joining them? All knew Folly lay at the end of Frontier Road; she simply had to follow it north. So long as she set her will to it, she knew she could reach it.

Though could there be a place even there for a witch like her?

No. Don't doubt. Survive.

Leiyn pushed herself off the wall, steadying her wobbly legs. With her cursed magic blinded, she couldn't tell if anyone followed. Time was short either way. She had to move and hope her plan was good enough to keep her alive.

She followed the alley to its end to find a street she recognized. It was near the markets with the jeweler boy the other girls thought handsome. Leiyn pushed through the crowd thronging the street, drawing glares, curses, and shoves in return. She ignored them all, focused wholly on her task.

When she reached San Hugo's Sanctuary, Leiyn huddled at

the edge of a building and peered at it. She saw no sign of disturbance, be it from odiosas, Suncoats, or guards.

Time to go. Looking both ways, she crossed the street in an awkward skip, trying hard not to run and only halfway managing it.

Reaching the doors, she hauled one open and closed it as softly as she could. Yet before she could even turn around, footsteps clicked along the wooden floor, and Sister Alma appeared from the hall.

Fesht! Leiyn froze, unsure what to do.

"Leiyn! What happened to you?" Her eyes narrowed. "What have you done with Aracel and the cart?"

As the priestess spoke, Leiyn had an epiphany. *She cannot stop me.* It propelled her back into action, striding forward to get around her.

Sister Alma stepped in her way. "You will answer me, girl, or I'll—"

"Do nothing." Leiyn moved to step around her. "I'm leaving."

She expected the priestess to reach out and grab her arm. Part of her hoped she would. With her blood boiling and the power between them shifted, she was eager to prove she was her own woman.

But Alma only let her pass. As Leiyn strode down the hall, the priestess spoke to her back.

"You always were half-wild. Saints help me, I knew it would catch up to you in the end."

Leiyn barely heard her words. Her opinion didn't matter any longer.

If it ever did.

She focused on packing everything she could think of, ignoring all else. Any girl who spoke to her was met with silence. Not even Isebel could provoke her, and as Leiyn went about her tasks, the blonde girl finally fell quiet.

Once done, Leiyn wrapped up her blanket, tied it off at the top, and hefted the supplies onto her shoulder. She'd found more than she'd hoped for, including old wineskins for carrying water. The makeshift satchel was heavy, but manageable.

It had to be. She had a long way to walk to reach Folly.

She went to the front doors and noticed a procession gathering behind her. All the girls and Sister Alma followed, keeping their distance as they whispered anxiously to one another. Leiyn no longer cared what they said or thought. She reached out and opened the door.

Aracel stood behind it.

Her hand was raised as if she was just about to enter. Her mousy hair was even messier than usual, and her smock was smeared at the knees from a fall. Tears tracked down her cheeks, but her expression brightened as she saw Leiyn.

"Leiyn! You're alive! I thought you—"

"I have to leave," Leiyn cut her off. She felt her resolve cracking, her certainty breaking. It would have been easier to leave without having to say goodbye to her friend.

The friend you abandoned.

She couldn't deny it. When danger came, she'd saved herself rather than made sure Aracel came out alright.

Only to protect her, another part of her murmured. But she found it hard to believe.

Her friend's relief was morphing. "What? Why? But Leiyn, those men won't—"

"It's not them." Her throat closed up, and she forced the words out through it. "It's the odiosa."

"The odiosa? Why...?"

But Aracel never finished her question. Leiyn saw in her widening eyes that she understood. There was only one reason why odiosas would be after her.

"You're a... a witch?"

Leiyn fought hard not to cry. "Please, Aracel." She wanted to reach out, touch her, hug her, but couldn't make herself do it. Not now that her friend knew what she was. "Please, let me go."

Aracel stepped aside but didn't back away. "I-I understand. Should I... do you need me to come, too?"

Leiyn stared, uncomprehending, before the meaning of her words struck her. Tears finally leaked out.

"No," she managed to gasp. "Stay here. Become a weaver. Find a way to be happy." Leiyn smiled, and though it felt as limp as a dead fish, she hoped it showed she meant well.

"Alright." Aracel's voice was small. "Leiyn... I hope the same for you."

Leiyn stared into her eyes for a lingering moment. The last look she knew she would ever have of her friend.

Then, with a sharp nod, she turned aside and set down the stairs to the street below.

Leiyn didn't look back. Hefting the weighty bag, cuffing the tears from her eyes, she headed north.

30

LIFEMARK

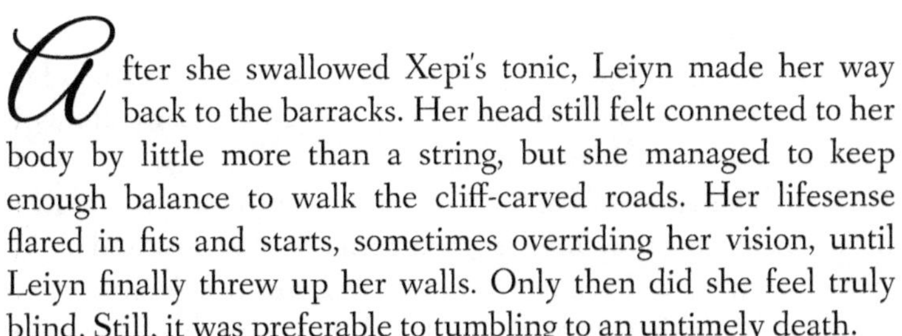

After she swallowed Xepi's tonic, Leiyn made her way back to the barracks. Her head still felt connected to her body by little more than a string, but she managed to keep enough balance to walk the cliff-carved roads. Her lifesense flared in fits and starts, sometimes overriding her vision, until Leiyn finally threw up her walls. Only then did she feel truly blind. Still, it was preferable to tumbling to an untimely death.

Ascending the final rise, slightly nauseous from the walk, she hesitated at the door to the old barracks. She didn't need her mahia to tell her it was empty within. Isla and Batu were headed south. The building had always seemed too big for the three of them. Now, it would be filled with heavy silence.

They're safe, as safe as anywhere in the Veiled Lands. Their leaving is a blessing.

She sighed and stepped through the doorway. No matter what she told herself, it didn't feel like a good thing.

Only as she entered did she hear the clatter within. She sniffed and caught a whiff of cooked meat and spices. Ears perked, Leiyn moved forward to peer into the kitchen, then straightened as she saw who it was.

"Tozi! What are you still doing here?"

The caretaker whirled around with a guilty grin. He stood before the stone oven once more, meat heartily cooking on the spit. "My apologies, Ranger Leiyn! But your companions departed today, did they not? I thought you might need assistance. Your training keeps you occupied, after all!"

Leiyn stared at him for a long moment, then a slow smile spread across her face. "You were worried about me."

"Me? Worry? I have nothing but worries!"

She strode across the kitchen to grip Tozi's arm. "Thank you. I needed this."

A hint of a blush touched his cheeks. "Please, Ranger, there is no need for thanks. I only do my duty."

"Just know I appreciate it." She released him, strafed around him, then bent forward to sniff the food. "Now, if you wanted to help, how about letting me slice off a strip?"

They made as merry a meal of all Tozi had cooked as she could have hoped for. It was simple fare, but Leiyn grunted her thanks as she wiped up the last of the grease from her plate with a crumbling slice of maize bread.

But the melancholy still simmered under the surface. Only a little while after they finished, she made her excuses and slunk away upstairs, the clatter of Tozi cleaning up coming from behind. She pushed away her guilt at letting him do all the work as she fell onto her bed. Wincing at its hardness, she reopened her mahia. The magic's volatility had subsided enough to be tolerable. With her walls down, the softness of the mattress returned, and she leaned back to stare at the ceiling.

The decorated stone seemed to subtly shift, the lingering effects of the tea confounding her senses. Her mind wandered, carrying her back to the afternoon. She remembered the experience she'd shared with Zuma: struggling to take a last breath, death pressing down hard. Her throat tightened. Leiyn had to breathe deeply for several moments before her heart slowed.

"He suffered," she whispered to the figures painted on the ceiling. "In the end, he suffered. Because of me."

Before, she'd convinced herself his had been a peaceful passing, though the awful sound of his final gasps was burned into her memory. Now, she had no more delusions about it. She shifted, trying and failing to find a comfortable position.

Can't squirm your way out of this one.

She wanted to escape, but where could she go to escape her mind? In the days at the Lodge, she would have sought out the range or the yard and lost herself in practice. But with her senses muddled, the yards far away, and darkness falling, she had no such luxury. She was trapped, as surely as she'd been trapped in Zuma's dying body.

Leiyn sat up and reached for her saddlebags, nestled in their usual corner. Their contents were still tucked away, as they had been every day since coming to Qasaar, but she'd never been the neatest person. Shuffling through them, she finally found what she sought. The smooth leather of the journal was welcome to her touch after so long without it. She ran her hand along it, then brought it and a graphite pen back to her bed and sat.

She opened the cover, breathed in the lingering must of the paper, ran a finger along the roughened edges. Flipping through her old drawings, she reached her most recent ones and paused. A thorned lion dominated the top-left corner of the page; tusked jackals were tucked in the opposite corner. She remembered that day again, hunting them with Tadeo.

Before all this began.

She would have to add the snow ape now, before its details faded. And there were so many other things she could detail.

The cacti of the Barren? The wardstones? Lyshans and dryvans?

She shook her head and flipped to a blank page. Setting the pen to it, she drew the first thing that came to mind.

Slowly, the illustration revealed itself. A perky ear; a curious eye; a short, whiskered snout. A fox's head emerged, sharpening with each reinforcing pass. Not just any fox, but her silver one.

Chispa.

The name rose from some unknown depths. She'd never named him before. He'd been a bright spark in some of the darkest moments of her past, yet he'd appeared so briefly and at times when she didn't have full command of her mind.

But now, as she looked back on him and how he still intersected with her life, it felt fitting.

Chispa. Spark.

She shaded in his fur, the subtle shifts in hue like shadows on snow. As she drew, she wondered why he'd merged with the dryvan. Jealousy tinged her thoughts. She'd always thought of him as her fox, in a way, though they'd interacted only a handful of times across the years. Yet when she'd needed him, he'd been there.

As he is now.

She finished off his face and set to work fleshing out his body. Chispa clarified something else for her; now she suspected she knew why Xepi called her *Osat,* or "fox." The shaman sensed something of him in her, his touch upon her life.

The thought led to another one. When she began drawing the fox, it hadn't been Chispa she thought of, but the things seen during her experience with Xepi. Her lifemark—the fox was imprinted on her very soul.

Why? Is he so important to me?

Her pen halted. Leiyn stared sightlessly at the lines as she strained to remember the rest of her lifemark. The melted taper —she remembered that, a candle halfway spent. It was simple to guess its meaning. Tadeo had once said to her: *Slow down, or your flame will burn out.* Long had it been since she hadn't pressed forward with all her strength, always reaching for the edge of it. The name "Firebrand" didn't only apply to her temper.

The last took the longest to remember. *A soaring ash dragon.* Could it be the same as had arisen from Nesilfo, the Clouded Fang? The encounter with Acalan's tribe had catalyzed the following tragedies, at least to her thinking. Perhaps his appearance was indicative of that. Or perhaps it was because she now embraced the magic she'd long reviled, and in turn accepted the titans.

This is who I am. My core. Me.

She set to sketching again, only pausing to fetch a lamp when the daylight faded. Her pen's tip was rounded by the time she lifted it and stared at the images of her lifemark. Despite the loneliness crowding the now-empty barracks, the weight of her responsibility, the impossibility of both wars—looking at these drawings, Leiyn found a small measure of comfort.

Enough to press on.

31

NECESSARY RISK

eya was a welcome sight the next morning. Leiyn didn't have to force a smile as the scout paused her routine to greet her. Though the sun had only just risen, she already glistened with sweat. Wiping a hand across her brow and flicking droplets away, Teya grinned at Leiyn.

"Come to cross spears?"

"I'll leave that to the men." Leiyn arched an eyebrow.

The scout snorted a laugh. "Some might be keen to, but there is no shame in it."

"No?"

"That is not our way, to shame the shape to which you are born. If it is love, if it is kind and good, who is to speak against it?"

Something in Teya's gaze made Leiyn look away. She swallowed, her throat even drier than the Barren usually made it.

"I have been thinking," the scout continued. "Perhaps I will pity you and come by your barracks some evening. You must be lonely without your companions. It would be cruel not to offer."

Turning back, Leiyn mustered a smirk. "If I happen to be in, you're welcome to visit. Just don't wait around."

A fresh grin spread across Teya's face. "Keep the candle lit in your window, then."

As the scout turned back to abusing her wooden pell, Leiyn set to her own morning practice. Once she was dripping with sweat herself, she waved farewell to the scout and set off for Xepi's hut.

All the while, her mind spun and her stomach fluttered with the implications of Teya's visit.

Don't get your hopes up, she counseled herself, to no avail.

The exercises the shaman assigned her soon wiped away any anticipation. Instead of repeating yesterday's experiment, Xepi returned to the lessons from before the ambushed scouting mission. Leiyn drew in esse from plants, careful not to kill them, then channeled the energy into herself. The result was an elation such as she'd rarely felt. She stood, feeling as if she could do the morning's exercise all over again, though she'd sagged with weariness only moments before.

Xepi guided her back to her chair. "You did well using it, but disciplining yourself afterward is more difficult. You must be the master of your body's whims."

Leiyn bobbed her head, though she was buzzing too much to sit still. "So I'm just going to feel like this the rest of the lesson?"

The shaman donned a small smile. "No. Now you will gift the *ilis* to me."

Though she suspected this task to be for more than instructive purposes, Leiyn complied, eager to be rid of her tremors. Gripping the shaman's hands, she closed her eyes, then touched her mahia to Xepi's. Again, she felt no compulsion to dive into the shaman as the energy flowed from her to the shaman. When she felt her weariness again, she cut it off and opened her eyes to her teacher's approving nod.

"Good. We will reinforce this with future practice. Now, let us touch on other areas."

They started with something that Leiyn knew herself capable of but hadn't consciously done: summoning living beings. Several times when she'd hovered at the precipice of life, she'd only survived by somehow gathering animals to her and sucking them dry of their essence. Now, Xepi showed her how to reach for an animal and, by gentle manipulation of their life-force, coax them closer.

"They can be compelled as well," her teacher said as she watched an ant crawling over her hand, eyes firm with concentration. "Humans, too, can be compelled by a strong enough mind. This requires a firm touch but acts on the same principles."

Leiyn tried not to think of the amoral applications as she struggled with the task. It wasn't long before she grasped the concept. At her commands, hosts of bugs began filling the hut. After watching them with equal parts fascination and revulsion, Leiyn released them and watched them slowly filter back outside, brushing off those that lingered overlong.

"Lastly," Xepi said, unfazed by her student's quick progress, "you must know how to heal."

Leiyn grimaced. Her failed healings of Isla were never far from mind. "You'll hear no argument from me."

Healing herself proved no great challenge. When Leiyn sliced her anelace across her palm, her mahia nearly mended the wound of its own will. After a few moments, Leiyn wiped her hand clean with a cloth and showed Xepi the thin seam on her skin, already looking as if it were weeks old.

"This will be more difficult," the shaman warned before cutting her own palm.

Yet Leiyn didn't struggle with this task, either. It took her a minute to navigate and probe her teacher's lifefire, but once she located the shade cast on it by the cut, it was simple enough to seal it shut.

She leaned back, smiling at Xepi's stony expression, but the pleasure was fleeting. "I've never had a problem with simple wounds. It's infection and disease that confound me."

At the promise of something she was ignorant of, the shaman perked up and set to showing her. Soon, it became apparent Leiyn's initial method of sawing through the black cords of corruption, while somewhat effective, was inefficient and incomplete.

"It must be burned out while keeping your ward alive," Xepi supplied. "Ignore this at their peril."

Though both of them were healthy—as shamans usually were, on account of their magic—Xepi still set Leiyn to practicing the techniques, flooding either her own body or the shaman's with esse, but containing the magic with sorcerous walls. In her own body, Leiyn accomplished this within a few attempts, but she couldn't yet find how to wall off entire sections within Xepi.

"Another day," the shaman finally said as the afternoon bled into evening.

"How about tomorrow?"

At Xepi's expression, she knew the answer even before the shaman spoke it.

"Tomorrow we must reach for Zuma again."

Leiyn sighed. "If we must."

She returned to the barracks and was disappointed to find it empty, hoping Tozi would once again be preparing her a warm supper, or that Teya had already come for her visit. Left to fend for herself, Leiyn soon took up her journal again, yet it couldn't hold her attention. Every time she went to draw, she found herself staring at the images of her lifemark instead, and her thoughts circled again over their meanings. They'd seemed a comfort the night before; now, they were stifling, limiting.

Is this all I am? All I'll ever be?

Setting the journal down, Leiyn stood and began pacing the length of the room. The sun had set, and blue dusklight filtered gently through the window. She let her eyes roam and her mind wander, but it found no place to settle. Too much was up in the air, uncertain or undecided. If they could fight the lyshans with any hope of winning. If her friends would survive their journey south. If the Gast alliance would succeed. If the Tricolonies would band together.

If Baltesia even remained standing.

Leiyn breathed through her frustration. On a countless revolution, she stopped and stared at the wall before her. Her lifesense detected the circle of glowing esse where the stone rippled outward. Though she'd ignored it until that point, now it demanded her attention. Slowly, almost cautiously, Leiyn approached it to stand a foot away. A realization unfolded in her mind.

That place beyond the wall—it was also a barracks. A secret barracks.

She reached a hand up to the stone protrusion but stopped short of touching it. A barracks might not house only soldiers. It could store their weapons as well. Weapons that might be able to kill lyshans, as the Gasts' ancestors once had.

I have to go back there.

She almost pressed her hand to the panel then and there, but vigilance stole back in. Leiyn stepped away and let her hand drop. She probed her resolution for flaws in its logic and found only risks.

"Necessary risks," she muttered under her breath.

She might never be able to get through Zuma's death to access his knowledge. Then how could she fight the *sach'aan?* It had taken him years to discover the secrets himself and master the use of titans. She'd nearly gotten herself killed trying to control the sea kraken off of Southport; she wouldn't rediscover Zuma's insights anytime soon.

Xepi had told her shamans didn't explore the ruins any longer, that too many had gone missing or mad to risk the few remaining. Lyshans might find her if she went in, but if she hid her mahia as Xepi had taught her, how would they ever know? She could find artifacts that would let them win this war.

Though her logic seemed sound, Leiyn still hesitated. *Not yet.* She'd only reached for Zuma's knowledge once. The fear of the second venture was what drove her toward desperate action now. She didn't want to be smothered by death again. She wanted to avoid it more than anything.

I have to try.

Letting out a long sigh, Leiyn slouched away from the wall and collapsed on her bed. She stared at the ceiling, despondent once more.

One more try, she promised herself. *Just one more. Then I'll go in.*

——— ◟◞ ———

Two nights later, Leiyn stood before the panel again.

The days had proceeded along the same lines as before. Training with Teya in the morning, Xepi in the afternoon. All the while she was with the scout, Leiyn wondered why she hadn't come to visit her yet. Her pride didn't allow her to ask. Instead, she cast furtive looks across the yard, watching the woman move nimbly through her deadly dance.

Pining, Isla would have called it. The thought of her friend made Leiyn smile.

As promised, Xepi set her to trying to access Zuma's esse. Once again, Leiyn failed. She rose from the trance gasping for air, the memories of death cutting through the haze of intoxication.

"That is enough. We will commence with your other exercises tomorrow." Leiyn heard the disappointment in Xepi's words. She didn't walk tall as she left the hut.

Her resolution to go into the ancestral halls beyond the wall hardened that night, and she spent much of the remaining daylight hours staring at the panel, her thoughts swirling with the residual effects of the tea. She was too muddled just then, but the next night, she knew nothing would keep her back.

Now, she stood before it, prepared to enter. Her remaining anelace was in hand, other small knives secured along her body. She wore Gast scout armor requisitioned at Teya's command, and it smelled like its last owner hadn't been particularly concerned with keeping it clean. Her other hand held a torch Tozi had fetched for her with surprisingly few questions. She'd already lit it in preparation for the darkness beyond.

She was as ready as she'd ever be. Leiyn sucked in a breath, raised the hand that held the knife, then pressed her knuckles against the panel.

At once, she felt the swell against her mahia, and the wall

tried pulling her in. Ready for it, Leiyn resisted, testing the strength of its enchantment. She found she could hold out against it, even step back, though the strain was painful.

But she was not trying to escape. Leiyn let go, and the world receded as she was swept into darkness.

32

SECRETS OF THE STONES

Leiyn stumbled as the ground firmed beneath her feet. As soon as she had her bearings, she slammed up her mahia's walls.

Blinking to clear her vision, she looked around. With her life-sense blind, the darkness pressed in closer, the torch barely suffi-cient to keep it at bay. Yet her eyes noticed details her mahia had not. The ceiling was arched, for one, and the walls painted.

Trying not to imagine shapes among the tall shadows, she held the light closer to the opposite wall. The murals were similar to the interiors of the other buildings of Qasaar but rendered in far more vivid color and detail. Almost, it seemed no time had passed since their creation. Greens, blues, and yellows dominated. Many things that should have been angular were curved: mountain peaks smoothed, ocean waves become ripples.

Some of the figures nearly looked human, though with longer proportions, while many bore the features of at least one animal. Here, the head of a bull; there, arms had become the wings of an eagle; even a rattlesnake's tail made an appearance. Gasts and the other natives of the Veiled Lands were known to depict humans partway intertwined with animal spirits in their art. These illustrations were a step closer to reality. Foxfur and her kin showed the truth of that.

Not wishing to linger, Leiyn pushed on, squinting into the

gloom ahead. The corridor continued for a short ways, then opened into a tall, broad chamber. Like the corridor, the edges had been smoothed so there were no corners to speak of. Her heart thumped faster as she saw silhouettes by the firelight, but she breathed a sigh of relief when she realized they weren't shaped like lyshans.

She saw what they were, and her hopes soared.

Weapons. Racks upon racks of them lined the walls, nearly two hundred at a glance. Leiyn circled the room, staring at their unfamiliar shapes. Even the materials of some looked strange. The axe-heads, their blades covered with hide sheaths, seemed made of some porous, yellow-white material that resembled bone. Other blades were made of wood and even amber.

These can't have been weapons. Perhaps they were ceremonial.

Yet another possible answer surrounded her: magic. The Gast ancestors might have imbued their weapons just as they did their homes across the city. How mahia could be used so defied her comprehension. She longed to examine them with her life-sense, if only to confirm her suspicions.

But there was another way. Stopping in front of a rack of short swords, Leiyn sheathed her knife to pull one loose. Yes— she felt something emanating from it, humming against her hand and her mahia's walls. Sorcery brimmed within the blade.

Peering at it, the sword itself captured her attention. It was shaped like a falchion: single-edged, slightly curved, and weighted toward the end of the blade. A sword made for slashing, primarily. About a foot and a half long, it was made of that same bone-like substance.

Turning it, she noticed intricate detail carved into the side, the same swirling patterns as occupied the walls, so shallow as to be invisible from some angles. The hilt, too, was lovingly detailed across the dark-lacquered wood. The cross guard extended a hand's width and curled up at the wings toward the blade. The grip was formed of corded leather. An orb of amber was set into the pommel. Its murky substance seemed to trap the light.

Too long. It was a fine blade, but she would sooner wield an anelace in a fight. She returned the sword to the rack, then turned to an archway opposite of her. Another darkness yawned beyond.

Steeling her nerves, Leiyn entered it. She passed through a short hallway that opened into a similar chamber as the prior, but here, an assortment of clothes took the place of weapons. Many were neatly sorted into cubbies in a specialized cabinet, while a few of the more notable designs were mounted for display.

Leiyn walked among them, marveling at the designs as well as the colors, which were deeply infused into the fabrics. The room seemed an armory, yet only the mounted sets resembled any armor she knew, and those just barely. The rest could have been ranger's greens, made of leather and cloth, with bone clasps and studs. A few pieces were hardened like boiled leather, but most were soft and supple.

She chose a tunic and held it up before her. The deep orange of the dawn sun, not a stitch on it was out of place, nor did it show any signs of wear. Magic tingled against her touch.

Could this have been the ancestors' armor?

Shaking her head, Leiyn replaced the shirt and moved before the first of the mounted armor sets. Bones like giant mandibles curved about the chest, and more bones formed pauldrons on the shoulders. She wondered what creature they came from to be so large; even a snow ape would struggle to supply them. Perhaps the bones of elephants. The rest of the set was leather and cloth that was dyed wine red, a sharp contrast to the rest of the colors.

Worn by a champion, perhaps, or during ritual combat.

Leiyn looked up and saw yet another chamber lay beyond. Time weighed on her as heavily as a prisoner's chains, but her curiosity pressed her toward the archway. She'd come this far, taken this much risk. If there was more to see and further tools they could use, she would brave the darkness to find them.

Her knife drawn again, she advanced on the doorway to find a slightly longer hall than before. At its end rested a smaller chamber. Cabinets crowded every wall, to the exclusion of all else.

A supply room?

She moved to one of the cabinets, then cautiously opened it, knife still in hand. What lay inside gave little cause for alarm. There were two wooden objects that were carved, planed, and glossed so they shone. Each wasn't much longer than her hand and were shaped like an hourglass. The etchings in them were every bit as ornate as those the falchion had borne but amplified with brushes of color. She couldn't imagine their use, yet she set down her knife to pick one up.

"Do mortals not caution against touching fire?"

Seizing her knife again, Leiyn whirled and faced the speaker. Only as she saw silver fur glittering in the torchlight did she lower the blade.

"Foxfur. Why do you always appear when I least expect it?"

The dryvan flashed her a wide smile. "Because I intend to do just that."

"And what are your intentions now?"

"To keep you safe from your curiosity."

Moving with her smooth, unnatural gait, Foxfur advanced toward her. Leiyn sheathed her knife, hoping no lyshans were waiting to appear out of empty air as she had. The skin-walker reached around her, and Leiyn caught a whiff of her scent: mammalian musk, interlaced with a deep earthiness like a healthy alder tree. She stepped back and watched as the dryvan took the wooden object in her clawed hand and held it before her, staring at it with emotions Leiyn could only guess at.

"These are *periaptu*," the dryvan murmured, her words resonating in the hushed room. "Talismans, the Gasts call them. As you would have felt, even closed off as you are, it contains great power, but of a specific and limited variety."

Leiyn eyed the object with fresh wariness. "What kind of power?"

Foxfur arched one eyebrow, where her fur was a deeper

shade than the rest of her face. "This one is designed to drain the life from your enemy."

Though she expected to be horrified, Leiyn found the answer strangely disappointing. "What would I need that for? I'm capable of that already."

"Yes, you are—but the common mortal is not."

"You mean anyone can use these talismans?"

Foxfur smiled broadly. "Yes. They were for those of my people weak or inept in Inheritance."

"Inheritance?"

"What we call our magic." She waved a hand lazily through the air. "Once, we Iritu believed it a sign of superiority to receive a strong Inheritance, as if it were any of our own doing. Some of my estranged kin still feel that way. They believe they are better than you mortals, and therefore your rightful rulers. Their memories are longer than your empires have existed."

We Iritu. Leiyn felt the need to pace again, but instead fidgeted in place, shifting from foot to foot. Foxfur had never revealed so much before, especially of her people and this place. Though every minute they spent in these halls was a risk, she had to know more. Had to know her enemy—and most importantly, how to kill them.

"These ruins, Qasaar—they weren't built by the Gasts' ancestors. They were built by you, the dryvans. The... Iritu."

Foxfur's smile lingered, but her eyes went flat. "So we call ourselves, though it is as dead a name as our empire. Those of us who remain are no longer united; we are divided into lyshans and dryvans."

Leiyn tried sifting through her spinning thoughts and the dazzling revelations. "Why did your civilization fade, Foxfur? What could have possibly overcome your kind?"

Her smile turned; her emerald eyes sharpened. "We doomed ourselves before anything else threatened us. In our arrogance, we ordered our society so that some stood atop the boughs of others, trampling their branches and shadowing their leaves.

Those of us strong in Inheritance were held up as the greatest of all, and our arrogance grew to match that renown."

Her expression grew distant, the twist of her wooden lips bitter. "But our power could not keep pace. We despised one another too much to stand together. Then came the spark that burned down the forest: the coming of the Gasts' ancestors."

Leiyn frowned. "So they conquered you?"

"Not at first!" The drvyan's laugh was brittle as a dead branch. "But when we turned them away, believing them to be lesser beings and unworthy of our attention, they quickly learned how to destroy us. And we allowed it, believing ourselves beyond their reach." She shook her head violently, her lips pulling back in a snarl. "We were ancient even then, and still, we were as foolish as saplings!"

Leiyn let the echoes fade before she ventured another question. "What happened?"

The skin-walker didn't answer for a long moment, only stared at the wall. *Perhaps reliving those days.* Leiyn knew how memory could slip up on the mind, even though she'd only lived a fraction of Foxfur's lifetime.

"Our Inheritance is powerful, but it has limits. We have control over our lifeforce, and thus can manipulate it in any way that suits us. As you have seen." She punctuated the statement with a sharp-toothed smile. "But there are realms in which we are as helpless as babes. The Vast Ones, the titans, are our greatest weakness."

"So I've been told. But why? I've felt your power, Foxfur. If I can do it, you should find it simple."

"That is not how it works, Awakener. You possess titan magic; I do not. It is as simple as that. Whatever it is that allows you to order them about as your pets, my species lacks it entirely."

Hope surged in her chest for a moment, but it quickly deflated. "Even with titans, I don't see how the Gasts could have overcome your people."

The dryvan cocked her head to one side. "There are many

secrets you have yet to uncover, I think. Titans are not only to be called; they are to be leashed, exploited. Harvested, even, for those who know how."

Leiyn furrowed her brow. Were these secrets she spoke of the same that Zuma had uncovered, that Leiyn suffered through remembered death to reclaim? If the dryvan knew them, perhaps it was possible to learn them from her instead.

But then again, Iritu mahia was different from humans'. Most likely, since Foxfur couldn't command titans, she would not be able to instruct Leiyn in how to do it.

Foxfur barreled on before Leiyn could decide if it was worth asking or not. "That same potential I faced then is in you, Awakener. I saw it from the first moment we crossed paths, and thus I gifted you your name."

"For which I'm grateful," Leiyn noted drily. "And what's your name, Foxfur? Your real name, not the ones you like making up."

The dryvan went entirely still, not showing even signs of breathing. Smile gone, lips pressed closed, she looked every bit as strange and foreign as her appearance alone should have made her.

"Do I frighten you?" Her voice was a low, whispering hiss. "Do you think I will harm you?"

"No."

Foxfur's lips parted slightly to reveal sharp teeth in the beginning of a snarl. Leiyn continued speaking, the words rushing to get out in front of one another.

"I know you could tear off my head, like you did that lyshan, before I could even blink. But do I think you will? No, Foxfur. I don't fear you. I trust you."

Leiyn waited, watching the skin-walker's reactions ripple across her face, too minute and quick to discern. This was a test of some sort, a question of worthiness. She doubted she'd like the results if she didn't pass.

The rigidness suddenly left the dryvan's body, and her wild smile returned. "Atastimina. That was my name. Atastimina," she repeated, working her mouth as if to taste the word. "Though I went by Ata."

"Atastimina. Ata. I'm pleased to finally meet you." Leiyn grinned, all the wider for how hard her heart thumped.

The dryvan let out a sudden laugh, throwing up her arms and roaring to the ceiling:

"*I am Ata!*"

A startled chuckle broke free of Leiyn. "Yes, you are. But should we still be here? Cannot the lyshans find us?"

For a moment, Ata ignored her. Then she lowered her arms and shrugged, acting as if her outburst had never occurred. "I suppose. The Veil does not touch here."

"The Veil that protects Qasaar, you mean."

"What else?" The dryvan strolled over to the cabinet and gently replaced the talisman, then closed the door on it. "We shall scurry away then, my mortal friend. Yes, we are friends now," she said at Leiyn's expression. "The sharing of names can mean nothing else."

Friends with a dryvan. Hardly the least expected turn her life could have taken, but it packed its own shock. She gathered her courage, then pushed her luck, as she usually did.

"Then call me by my name. Leiyn, not Awakener."

Ata laughed sharply. "They are both your names! But if you wish it so, I will, Leiyn."

They walked back through the chambers the way Leiyn had entered, a companionable silence falling. Leiyn's eyes wandered over the objects as the torchlight fell on them, a thought occurring to her.

"These weapons and armor... should we use them against the lyshans? Would they harm them more than ordinary steel? Protect us where no amount of plate armor could?"

"Harm them?" Ata shrugged, the silver fur on her shoulders rippling. "If you could hit them, yes. They are titanbone infused with heritage, after all."

Leiyn could guess that "heritage" referred to Iritu magic—

Inheritance, as Ata had called it. But the other comment gave her pause.

"Titanbone? You cannot mean what I think you do."

The dryvan's eyes gleamed as green as spring as she smiled. "So young," she purred. "So mortal. How is it that we became friends at all?"

Leiyn sighed. "Because you like strays, and I apparently like being demeaned."

"So it seems!" Ata swept an arm toward the cabinets, narrowly avoiding hitting Leiyn, then toward the entryways both before and behind them. "Take it, any and all of it! My people have abandoned this to dust. What use are artifacts to the Iritu now?"

Though there was an uncomfortable edge to the invitation, Leiyn nodded, then padded over to the clothes that had resembled a ranger's greens. She scooped them up under a free arm, then glanced at Ata to find her unblinking gaze on her.

"A fine choice," the dryvan murmured. "Comfortable, adaptable, light. Yet as long as heritage remains alive in the fabric, it cannot be penetrated."

Magic tingling against her side, Leiyn wondered how that could be true. But they were friends now; she doubted Ata would be lying to her just then.

Leiyn moved to the next room, returning to the falchion she'd drawn before. Four of them hung in a row from the rack. A perusal of the swords to either side yielded no better option, either too long or crafted so the weight would be close to the hilt, which didn't match her martial style. What knives were available were too short, most useful either for throwing or a last-ditch defense.

"These are the ones, I suppose."

Shifting the clothes to under the arm that held the torch, Leiyn extracted the scabbarded swords from the rack, then tucked them into her belt. The cross guards caught on leather, so they would hang there for the short journey back to her room.

Urgency biting deep, she hurriedly tucked one of the knives

into her sagging belt, then took up a quiver of arrows and slung them over her shoulder. She eyed the bows, but her own longbow was familiar and reliable enough that she saw little need to learn her way around a different one.

Leiyn turned back to her companion. "It's not too much?"

Ata smiled, but it lacked its usual ferocity. "If it will preserve your life, how could it be?"

It wasn't precisely an answer, but it seemed likely as good as she'd receive.

"I never thanked you. For saving my life."

"Why start now?"

Leiyn laughed. "Because I might need saving again. Thank you, Ata."

The dryvan cocked her head to one side. "That is not all you have to say. You have another question."

"I guess I do. How do you keep finding me? Out there in the Barren, you showed up just before the lyshans did. And now, here in these corridors, you found me minutes after I entered through the panel, even though my presence should be masked." She paused, wondering if she wanted to know the answer. "Do you always sense me? Always know where I am?"

Ata shrugged. "In a way. Not through my senses, but his."

"His?"

Her brow creased, fur pressing together. "The fox. Who else?"

The fox. Leiyn stared at Ata's silver fur, her mind delving back through the years. *Of course it's him.* How many times had Chispa found her in the middle of the wilderness to help her at pivotal moments? Ever since he rescued her from the winter and the loss of her father, she'd guessed he acted as her guardian, at least sometimes. But it had been so far out of her realm of under-standing she'd rarely thought about it directly. It didn't follow reason, but it didn't need to; it simply was.

He's still watching out for me.

"Thank you." She spoke the words without meaning to, then

grimaced as she realized what she'd done. "If you can hear me," she added gruffly.

Ata laughed and gestured to the archway. "Did you not say you should be leaving?"

"Right."

Leiyn entered the corridor she'd come from, then paused and looked back. The dryvan didn't follow.

"I suppose I'll see you again right before I'm about to die?"

Ata's smile returned. "I would hate to disappoint."

With a shake of her head, Leiyn set down the hallway, touched the panel, and left behind the Iritu ruins.

33

THE BROKEN SPEAR

$\mathcal{A}$t first light, Leiyn was up and palming through her newfound artifacts.

The emerald in the clothes was even more vibrant by day, though dark enough she wouldn't have difficulty blending into a forest. She ran her hands over them, wondering at the feel, both magical and otherwise. They were made from the softest wool she'd ever touched. The magic was just as integral to them as the fabric, woven through with an expertise she could never match.

The breeches seemed too tall and thin for her, and the tunic set to fall about her knees, but she tried them on anyway, figuring she could always hem them. As soon as the tunic settled over her shoulders and chest, a prickling spread throughout the fabric. Tensing, ready to tear it off again, Leiyn held her breath as the shirt rippled, then began to constrict. But it didn't try to choke her as she feared but stopped as soon as it molded to her shape, still leaving room for movement. She raised her arms and twisted around, but it didn't feel too tight anywhere.

"Those damned Iritu would," Leiyn muttered with a nervous laugh.

The rest of the outfit acted the same as the tunic had, even the belt, which had only a single clasp and tightened so it held around her hips. Leiyn flexed her hands, testing the hold of the armguards. She shrugged against the jerkin, lifted her legs, and moved about. All were a perfect fit, far better than the Gast clothing she'd been borrowing, and even better than her ranger greens, if she was honest. She wished she had a looking glass to see just how odd she looked, but mirrors were rare in Qasaar, and all the more so in an old barracks. She would have to find one of the rare fountains around the city to judge her reflection.

I could have asked Isla or Batu, if they were here.

She shook her head free of the thought. They were gone; that was that. Think on it too long and the melancholy would drag her into a pit from which she couldn't climb free.

Next, Leiyn took her new weapons down to the mess hall to feel them out. It would have been better to practice at the training yard, but she wasn't sure she should be seen wielding Iritu artifacts, much less wearing them, out among the Gasts. A gentler acclimation to the idea seemed prudent, and she was determined not to act rashly.

At least in this.

She drew first one sword, then the second, swinging them through a simple form. The two falchions were different in feel, apparently by intention; the one in her left hand was two fingers shorter and one finger narrower. If she were to employ them in battle, she'd have to adjust her rhythm to accommodate their designs. Even in the hour she spent slashing and whirling about the room, she began to feel it: like the gallop of a horse, a one-two rhythm of the shorter blade leading, and the longer following up with a powerful blow.

Having spent nearly the entire morning, Leiyn put away the Iritu weapons, and after a moment's consideration, the clothes as well. Instead, she pulled on her sweat-stiffened clothes from the day before, but not without a resolution to speak to Xepi about what she had seen and gained. The Gasts could no longer afford superstition, nor could she, if any were to survive.

As unlikely as that seems.

She left for the shaman. When she neared the hut, Leiyn sensed an unexpected, though not unwelcome, presence. Entering, she leaned against the doorway and gave the newcomer a grin.

"Miss me so much you had to seek me out, did you?"

Acalan, who stood behind the chair where Xepi sat, only crossed his arms. "I heard you were struggling. Perhaps I can help."

Leiyn's smile faded. "I don't see how," she said as she slouched into the unoccupied chair. "I have to do it on my own, don't I?"

"Yes," Xepi confirmed. "But Acalan carries something that might be of use."

"Alright, then. Let's see it." Though she doubted any object could help her suffer through death, the chieftain wasn't one to waste time. That, at least, was promising enough to raise her spirits ever so slightly.

Acalan extended an arm and opened his fist to reveal a small, wooden figurine shaped like a jaguar. At his nod, Leiyn took it and ran her fingers over it. The wood—black maple, by her estimation—had been sanded smooth, and there was little friction to the touch. She sensed no emanations of magic from it, though she explored it thoroughly with her mahia.

"It's just a carving." She looked at each of the others. "How is this supposed to be useful?"

"As a focus," Acalan rumbled. "Taht Zuma carried it for as long as I knew him. Once, I asked him about it. He said it was a reminder of his duty to his tribe. Now, it might serve as a reminder of who he was to you."

Leiyn let her hands fall to her lap. "If you say so. But as the one who has to die with him, I can tell you, I don't really want to identify any closer with Zuma."

The shaman and chieftain exchanged a look. Leiyn rolled her eyes.

"Fine, I'll try it. But don't tease me when I come back weeping."

Despite her light tone, her palms grew slick around the figurine.

I have to do this. I don't have a choice.

She'd made a promise to Zuma. She had a duty to fulfill. Even if it meant enduring death again and again.

Setting her jaw, Leiyn waited while Xepi prepared the tea. When it was ready, Leiyn ironed her will, then swallowed the musky concoction in a single gulp. She waited, allowing the effects to first seep in, then intensify. Only as the urge to plumb the esse around her became unbearable did she take the plunge.

The images of her lifemark flashed around her, but she'd performed this ritual enough times that she didn't lose herself in them but pushed through to Zuma's spark. Allowing no time for hesitation, Leiyn dove into the orb of esse.

Death gripped her tight in its claws, cold and choking.

The jaguar. Remember the jaguar! She tried to focus on the figurine, but the image seemed vague and distant. Her death was here, insistent and all-encompassing. What was a statuette when facing this?

She tried to draw in air once, twice. Each time, her collapsed chest defied her. The rattling came from her throat. She tried to claw at the faceless enemy smothering her, but no amount of willpower could overcome them.

Her vision was growing fainter by the moment, yet she saw something above, a distant smudge. *A face?* But it was no more substantial than the thought of the figurine.

Death dragged her down, and Leiyn fled before it.

As she rose from the memory, the world reasserted itself, as did her own body. Leiyn coughed and gasped for air, hands clawing at the table. The carved jaguar had fallen from her grip. From the corner of her eye, she saw Acalan bend over to retrieve it.

When she'd recovered enough presence of mind, Leiyn looked up. "Guess that didn't work."

Xepi sighed, and Acalan frowned. Leiyn turned her head aside, as much from her wandering attention catching on a fly careening in through a window as to avoid their gazes.

"We will try again in two days," the shaman said at length. "Thank you, Toa Acalan."

Acalan nodded, then turned to leave.

"I explored the ancestral ruins."

Only as the other two in the room stiffened did Leiyn realize she'd spoken aloud. *There you go again, Firebrand, always running off at the mouth.*

"When?" Acalan asked, his tone betraying nothing.

"Yesterday evening."

"Did I not warn you against it?" Xepi's words were softer than the chieftain's, yet somehow sharper. "Did I not forbid it?"

A smile won free of Leiyn before she could stifle it. "You did. But I'm not getting anywhere with Zuma's spark. Better to have some weapons than none at all."

"Weapons?" Acalan glanced at the shaman. "You took from the ruins?"

"I did." She shrugged. "At A—that is, Foxfur's invitation."

Feshtado fool! Was Ata's true name supposed to be a secret? She only hoped her revelations had them distracted from her slip of the tongue. *Damn these mushrooms...*

If the others noticed, they gave no sign of it. Xepi's esse burned brighter with each passing moment. A sliver of caution returned to Leiyn at the sight.

The shaman rose to stand over her.

"If you will not listen to me, I will not teach you. Leave and do not return."

Leiyn stared up at her, stunned into clarity. "What? You cannot... Xepi, what are you saying?"

"*Leave!*"

The shaman had never raised her voice within Leiyn's earshot, nor lost her temper. Now, it was like seeing a dormant mountain erupt, and she was speechless before it.

Acalan gripped her arm. She flinched as their souls brushed against each other.

"Come." Pulling her to her feet, he led Leiyn from the hut.

When they were out of earshot, she yanked her arm away. Still gripped by the tea, the world seemed to shift beneath her feet, like a thing alive and restless. The dry Barren winds were like a lover's caress on her skin, provoking uncomfortable shivers and gooseflesh. Leiyn wrapped her arms around her middle, trying to ignore the sensations.

"*Fesht,* Acalan, what just happened?"

The chieftain grimaced toward the desert. "Xepi values discipline," he said after a moment. "She prides herself in her dedication and is unflinching in it. You challenge that notion."

"I am disciplined. When I need to be," she added, thinking of certain riotous nights spent at the Lodge.

Acalan glanced at her, his face seeming made of stone. "That is not why she is upset."

"Then why?"

He did not answer for a long moment. Then he sighed and cast his gaze down to the sand and rock far below.

"We have lost many in our war with the *sach'aan.* Some grew up with one parent dead. Most have suffered the loss of a relation. And some... some have lost children."

Leiyn's throat tightened. "Who did she lose?"

"Her son. He was a shaman as well, newly initiated, and still full of the brashness of youth. Like others I know." He gave her a significant look.

She returned it with a tight smile. "I'm nothing if not brash. What happened to him?"

"He did what you did: explored the ancestral ruins. And, like you, he believed the items he found there could be used against our enemies. That with them, we could finally win this war, and not merely survive it."

A sigh worked free of the chieftain as he stared toward the wardstones on the horizon, dark smudges among the dust clouds. "He took one of these objects with him on a patrol. It proved his undoing. As if he carried a smoke signal, the lyshans found them before he'd even left sight of Qasaar. I watched as his draconion was torn apart and he was taken to become their slave."

The eviscerated draconion. The first image of Xepi's lifemark flashed into Leiyn's mind as she grasped its meaning.

"What did it look like?" she asked. "The object he took."

"It was made of wood, lacquered and smoothed, then painted over with strange patterns and bright colors. Not much bigger than a hand."

"A talisman." It sounded too similar to be otherwise, though who could truly know when it came to Ata's ancient people. "Did he say what he thought it did?"

Acalan cocked his head. "You have seen similar objects in the ruins."

"There's a chamber full of them. Foxfur implied that it allows those without magic to act as if they had it. Like stealing lifeforce from someone else." Leiyn shrugged. "I didn't see what use they'd be to me, but if they could make anyone like a shaman..."

The chieftain muttered what sounded like a curse under his breath.

"I do not like you entering these ruins," he said aloud. "But you are your own woman, and I am not your chieftain. So I will say as your companion—"

"As my friend, you mean?" She flashed him a grin.

His expression didn't shift. "Your friend, then. Be wary. Many shamans have failed to return from those depths. Some have even been stolen by our enemies. We need you to stay alive."

"I'd like that as well, as it turns out."

Despite the heady effect of the tea, his warning sobered her. Leiyn stared out over the Barren, the landscape sparking with sparse life against her heightened lifesense. She even imagined she could sense beyond the wardstones, where titans waited in uneasy slumber.

"I'll be careful," she said at length. "As careful as I can be. But we have to take risks, Acalan. Whatever your people's superstitions, I think we should use the weapons. They're not created by your ancestors. This whole city belonged to the Iritu, the dryvans and lyshans, when they were united."

She checked to see how the chieftain took this revelation if he even believed her. What she said countered generations of his people's assumptions. But Acalan, as usual, betrayed nothing of what he felt.

"How do you know this?" he asked quietly.

"Foxfur told me last night. She didn't say much more than that, only that they were their own undoing. More importantly, she said the artifacts from those ruins will be effective against lyshans. At this point, they're our only hope of survival."

If you could hit them, the dryvan had also said, but Leiyn saw no need to point out the obvious.

The chieftain was silent for a long moment. "You may be right."

She stared at him. "Did you just admit that?"

"Do not grow used to it. But to make this change will take time. There is no appetite for blood with so few shamans remaining."

"I hope they start hungering for it, then." Her vision was beginning to swim again, and Leiyn closed her eyes to ease the dizziness. "If they don't, there won't be any shamans left, myself included."

A gust whistled in her ears, bringing the dry scent of the Barren with it. Leiyn breathed in, trying to steady her tilting senses.

"What does a broken spear mean to your people?" she asked suddenly.

Acalan had grown so silent, it almost seemed he'd disappeared, but for his esse burning bright.

"An oath of vengeance," he said at last.

She is defined by the loss of her son. The loss of her people. The middle image had been of dying flames in a fireplace. The symbolism of it was simple enough to identify when shamans faded like sparks into the night. *She fears losing more.*

Leiyn opened her eyes and tried to will the world to stillness.

"We will lose more," she said, as much to Acalan as herself. "But when there's only two choices, it's better to fight than surrender."

Acalan shook his head and turned back to the mountain path. "This is why I call you huntress."

That won a small smile from her. It fled as she looked back and saw Xepi's hut, the shaman's esse shining within it.

"Will she change her mind?"

"Yes. If you beg her."

She snorted a laugh. "I'm in no rush to die again."

"We all must do tasks we would rather not."

The words echoed adages from both Tadeo and her father too closely to ignore. Leiyn sighed. "I'll give her the day to cool off first."

Acalan's look told her he knew better, but he didn't contradict her.

THE MURMURING CANYON

*E*ven after supper, Leiyn's head swam from Xepi's tea, so she went to lie down, hoping it would fade. No sooner had she done so, however, than she sensed someone stopping before the barracks and entering within.

Teya had finally decided to visit.

Leiyn sat back up, feeling her hair and scowling at its disarray. Teya gave her no time to better arrange herself, but came striding up the stairs, clearly sensing her with her own limited mahia. With Leiyn's curtain open, she leaned against the doorframe as her eyes traveled up and down her body. Leiyn endured her examination and subtly gave one of her own.

"For not visiting the yards today," the scout observed, "you look a mess."

"And you look one for having gone."

They grinned at each other. *Like girls over honeyrolls*, it seemed to Leiyn. She wasn't displeased with the thought.

Teya straightened. "If neither of us are too revolting to the other, I was thinking I might take you somewhere."

"You'll have to be more specific than that." Under her easy facade, Leiyn's pulse quickened.

"I am not sure I do." Eyes crinkling in the corners, the scout turned and loped off with that easy gait of hers.

Already, she knows me. Shaking her head, Leiyn eased

herself up with a groan, then fought for balance as she wove her way through the hall.

She caught up with Teya outside of the barracks, then walked by her side as they traveled up the incline. She wondered just how far the scout meant to take her, and if her dazed body would continue to comply, but Leiyn's pride wouldn't allow her to ask.

Instead, she indulged her curiosity by reading Teya's life-mark. It took a deal of concentration to gaze beyond the flames while walking, but with the help of the mushroom tea, images soon began to materialize.

First, a thundercloud formed then broke, crackling with lightning. Within it, the shadow of a tempest hawk appeared against the cloud's belly, silhouetted with each flash.

When the storm cleared, a different figure formed: a wolf, one standing before its pack. Its ears were down, and it led the others forward in a low crawl, hunting unseen prey.

The wolfpack passed, and a single object appeared, one familiar: the pendant Teya always wore around her neck. Having never looked at it closely, Leiyn was struck anew by its beauty. A turquoise stone, it was delicately imprinted with a crescent moon, stars surrounding it.

Teya touched her arm, and Leiyn returned abruptly to her surroundings.

"Stay the course, Redlock. You look a bit green. Are you sure you want to continue?"

She withdrew her mahia and tried for a smile. "How can I be sure when I don't know where we're going?"

"I am serious. You are well?"

"Yes. Just a little light-headed from Xepi's." Leiyn paused, considering if she should say more, then threw caution to the wind. "Truth be told, she dropped me as her initiate."

"Is that so?"

"You don't seem particularly concerned."

Teya laughed and released her grip. A great part of Leiyn wished she'd held on.

"She does not show her temper often, but when it flares, it is mighty indeed," Teya said. "Never fear. She will calm and see reason. She always does." After a pause, she asked in a quieter voice, mindful of those few passersby still on the street, "What did you say to provoke her?"

"I didn't provoke anyone."

As the scout raised her eyebrows, Leiyn relented.

"Fine. I may have slightly provoked her. I entered the ruins beyond the barracks wall."

Teya whirled toward her, stopping them in the middle of the road. "Not even you are so foolish."

Leiyn grinned. "Apparently, I am."

"I do not blame her for being angry." Teya paused, seeming to carefully consider her next words. "Her son—"

"I know," Leiyn interrupted. "Acalan told me."

"Acalan was present for this falling out?" Teya shook her head. "What an event to miss."

"Oh, I'm sure there will be plenty more to come."

They passed the stables without stopping, dismissing Leiyn's guess that Teya meant for them to go for a ride.

Not much farther to walk, then. I hope.

"What did you find?" the scout asked. "In the ruins?"

Leiyn laughed. "Where to begin?"

She told all she could, though she excluded Ata's confession of her name. After slipping up once, she didn't intend to do it again. Of her keeping artifacts in her room, Leiyn also said nothing, unsure yet how her companion would react to the news. Teya seemed to take most of it in stride. Apparently, she hadn't been overly attached to the idea that they lived in a city built by their ancestors, homing in on a different realization.

"Weapons created by the *sach'aan*, that can kill them as well." Teya narrowed her eyes as she stared at the ground. "You trust this dryvan?"

"With my life." Leiyn was surprised it was true. *Then again, we are friends.* Her lips quirked. How full of impossibilities her life had become of late.

"Then I must trust you." They took several more steps before the scout continued. "My people are forbidden to use the... Iritu artifacts."

"Yet you use the gate panels, and Xepi uses the windows. And the baths—how else do those draw water?"

They'd been a mystery when Leiyn first arrived, baths that filled at a touch from a panel. But like the furniture and whispering walls of the city, she'd quickly acclimated to them just as the Gasts had.

Teya waved a hand. "We know these to be safe. But weapons might harm the wielder as well as the enemy. How could we know until it came time to use them?"

"I don't think we need fear that." Leiyn hesitated, then decided she was tired of tiptoeing around Teya. After all they'd endured together, she trusted her as surely as she did Acalan.

"I took some weapons and practiced with them this morning in the mess hall. They didn't hurt me; in fact, they almost seemed to become part of me. Like how my old teacher used to say weapons should be. My mahia felt them and accepted them as extensions..."

Only then did Leiyn realize she'd started rambling. Cheeks warming, she glanced at Teya. The scout wore a small smile, but for once, it didn't seem mocking.

"You were a born warrior, Redlock. And mischief-maker. If the Tetrad discovers this transgression, you will regret stirring the scorpion."

Leiyn shrugged. "That seems to be my lot in life. I've come to accept it."

"As have I."

Leiyn wondered what that was supposed to mean as they ascended past the last of the cliff-carved dwellings and reached the top of the rise. Leiyn stuttered to a pause, but Teya pressed on, forcing her into a lurching jog to catch up.

"When are you going to tell me where we're headed?"

"Did I say I would?"

Leiyn lapsed into silence, seeing the futility in further questions. Teya led them around the edge of the canyon that contained Qasaar, heading for the backside of the derelict palace that lay farthest back. Leiyn stared at the edifice, cut from the rock like the rest of the city. It alone seemed to have been ravaged by time, its ceilings collapsed in places, the details worn to sand. She wondered what had caused the magic to fade.

Perhaps it suffered the same fate as the Iritu.

Now that she knew the truth of the city's origins, it seemed every worn building was a history waiting to be uncovered. Qasaar was as much a memorial to them as a refuge to the natives.

Teya broke into her thoughts. "It is not far now. Are you weary?"

"Takes more than a walk to put down a ranger," Leiyn lied. Truth was, her head had started to ache, a rhythmic pulse at the base of her skull. She wondered if she should attempt to heal, even in her present state; pain was the last thing she wanted just then. Not knowing how the tea might affect the process, however, she decided against it.

The scout only raised an eyebrow and faced forward again, not entirely hiding her growing smile.

By their path, Leiyn judged they were headed for the crevice before them. She wondered why, for to her eyes, it seemed nothing remarkable. But as she quested toward it with her mahia, she was startled to find the stone within was alive with esse.

Teya grinned at her, awakening a flutter in Leiyn's belly.

"I should have had you veil your magic," Teya said. "Now you have spoiled the surprise!"

"What am I looking at?"

"Come—you will see."

They reached the crevice, and Leiyn skirted as close to the edge as she dared. Pebbles kicked up from her shoes cascaded down into the depths. To her eyes, the ravine was dark; not so with her mahia. She stopped, not knowing what to make of it all.

The magic was like the dancing of reflected light from the surface of water. It moved across the cliffs, perpetually in motion. She'd perceived some color from afar, but now she saw the full spectrum: the deep red of a dying fire, the pale yellow of a noon sun, the blue of a night-shrouded pool. There wasn't only color; a wordless, rhythmless chorus channeled through her body, a happenstance harmony.

"Sit," Teya said from beside her, a smile in her voice. "I will explain as best I can."

Leiyn obeyed, dangling her legs off the cliff. Teya sat close, their thighs almost touching. The sensation drew her thoughts a little from the wonder in their surroundings.

"We call this place the Murmuring Canyon. It has been like this for as long as the Many Tribes have occupied Qasaar, or so my parents told me. The shamans say it is a place filled with the souls of the ancestors, like in the city." Teya paused, her head cocked. "Though I suppose they are not my ancestors, but the *sach'aan*, are they not?"

Leiyn shrugged. "Guess so."

"Still, the effect is the same: in such numbers, they become restless. Perhaps a great tragedy occurred here, the palace before it suffered an attack. Perhaps it was a burial place." She shrugged. "These skin-walkers do not seem regretful of their deaths to me. Why else would they sing for joy?"

"It's beautiful." The words left Leiyn's mouth before she could think better of them.

Teya didn't tease her, but only smiled. "It is."

They fell silent for a time, listening and watching. Leiyn leaned back on her hands, then realized Teya's hand lay only inches from hers. A debate awoke in her.

Reach for it. Just reach.

Leiyn had never lacked for courage. She could charge an armed enemy and throw herself into a melee without hesitation. But this required a different kind of courage, one she struggled to muster. This ventured into places she had scarcely explored.

Teya glanced at Leiyn. Wearing a small smile, she shifted her weight so that her hand was freed, then reached for her.

Their fingers touched.

Sparks shot across her skin, then dove deeper. Leiyn felt as breathless as if she'd run the wilderness training course she and Isla had frequented as apprentices. Teya's skin wasn't soft; she was roughened by sand and a spear's grip. It was just as Leiyn had imagined her touch to be.

Slowly, she met Teya's eyes. They were dark chasms to her sight, while to her mahia, her essence shone bright within them.

"Why did you come here?"

Leiyn blinked, Teya's question startling her from her trance. "What?"

"Why come to me and my people? Did you come to save us, Redlock?"

Teya's touch burned the same as before, yet Leiyn found her guard reawakening. She attempted to order her muddled thoughts.

"No," she said slowly. "Not to save you. I didn't even know what enemy you faced, much less that Isla, Batu, and I would be enough to fight it."

"Then why come?" Teya pressed. "Why travel all this way?"

Unsure what she dug for, Leiyn told the truth. "I made a promise. Besides, I have a talent for diplomacy, if you couldn't tell."

Teya snorted a laugh. "You have a talent for getting into trouble, though somehow you get out of it as well. Yes, I know you are dutiful and oathbound, but I do not think that is the true reason. Leiyn Redlock, I will ask you once more. Why cross the Silvertusks?"

Why... Leiyn looked up at the stars, which were just beginning to appear above them. She saw the constellations taught to her by Tadeo and her father. Many of the stories written across them were Gast in origin.

The Ancestors' Rage, the Forest Witch, the Titan Caller...

And there it was: an epiphany. One she'd glimpsed sidelong before, but never stared at directly. Like how she might watch a deer she stalked but didn't wish to alert. It felt too private to admit aloud. Too raw and tender. But something about the woman next to her lured it out.

"I want the truth. The truth of the Veiled Lands. The truth of my birth. I want to know what made Zuma who he was, and my old lodgemaster Tadeo, and even Acalan. I want..."

She trailed off. It was too much, opening these inner parts of herself, so long sealed behind callouses and thorns. Parts she hadn't dared breach, lest they expose how vulnerable she could be. That within, she was soft and weak, qualities she feared more than all the terrors of the Titan Wilds.

"Say it," Teya said quietly. "Not for me. Say it for you."

Like milk cut from a cactus, the words spilled forth.

"I want to know who I am."

Leiyn clamped her mouth shut, glad for the night to hide her flush, sure her soul was written across her face like the stories across the stars.

Teya tightened her hand over Leiyn's. Her chest tightened with it. Leiyn looked over and found Teya's eyes on hers, black in the night and all the more beautiful for it.

"I would like that as well," the scout murmured. "To know you."

Teya leaned close and pressed her lips to Leiyn's.

Fire and ice raced through her, burning and soothing at once. Her mahia lay bare to all she had barred from it before, and Teya's skin took on bright new meanings. Her earthy-sweet scent curled into Leiyn's nose and spread through her head, clouding her thoughts.

Tendrils of their esse touched, then embraced. For a moment, all separation fell away so they seemed not two people, but one. The heady sensation rushed through her like molten metal through her veins. She could scarcely tell where she left off and Teya began.

She wished it would stop. She hoped it would never end.

For a moment, she was too stunned to react. But as Teya pulled away, Leiyn roused. Her free hand snaked up to cup the nape of Teya's neck, and Leiyn stared at her as if she were prey that she stalked. To her lifesense, the night was set aflame, and they were the torches at its center.

"I wish that, too," Leiyn murmured. "To know you."

Teya blinked slowly. Her full lips curved upward.

"So you shall."

They leaned close like saplings in a storm, their branches tangling together.

PART VI

EMBER & ASH

35

THIRTEEN YEARS BEFORE

*L*eiyn made it past Saints' Crossing with no worse incident than many slips in the mud and a gnawing ache in her belly. The guards stationed at the bridge that spanned the Gorge de Omn eyed her strangely as she requested passage across.

"You know what's out there, don't you, girl?" one asked. A mole on his eyebrow kept attracting her eye, no matter how she resisted the urge to look.

"Trees," she answered flatly. "Plains. Game."

The two Baltesian guards laughed, while the Suncoats stared at her, stony-faced. Leiyn turned away from them, as nervous as she'd be if they were odiosas staring at her.

They cannot see my curse. They cannot know.

"Legion-sent demons, that's what," Molebrow said. "Titans! You seen a titan before?"

She hadn't, but Leiyn nodded, figuring she'd heard enough about them to fib her way through it.

The guard smirked. "Sure you have. Then you'll know how a hill tortoise can crush you with a single step, and a tempest hawk fry you with a stray bolt of lightning. Eh?"

Leiyn shrugged. "I'll dodge."

With another chuckle, the man waved her through. "You've got guts, kid. I hope you survive, wherever you're off to."

"Or running from," one Suncoat spoke up.

The words put a shiver down her back, but Leiyn refused to let it show. With unhurried steps, she moved past them to the bridge.

She'd been prepared to bandy words with the guard. She wasn't ready, however, for the bridge to whisper as she set foot on it.

The murmurs crept along her mahia's walls, crawled inside her ears and mind like ants toward unguarded food. Leiyn sealed her barriers as tightly as she could, but it was never enough. She couldn't keep out the voices of the bridge.

Yet though they harried her, the whispers didn't keep her from moving forward. When she reached the other side, the bridge abruptly fell silent. Heaving in what felt like her first breath since beginning the crossing, Leiyn glanced back and saw that she hadn't even noticed the severe drop below, hundreds of feet down.

"Afraid of heights, are you?"

Leiyn jerked around. A boy, clean and well-dressed in a smart green smock, sneered as he passed. The woman walking next to him, whom Leiyn assumed was his mother, only sighed.

"No," Leiyn said, her pride preventing her from saying anything else.

The boy only laughed and walked away.

Face burning, Leiyn shuffled past the guards on the other side and quickly walked through town. She only delayed to steal what food she could when vendors were looking away from their stalls, which was little enough in her filthy state, then continued on.

Beyond the town limits, she entered the true wilderness of the Veiled Lands.

The Titan Wilds. Leiyn stared around her, at the golden fields and the dark green tree line in the far distance. A place spoken of all her life; with fear, with longing, with awe. Where the titans that shaped this land still roamed in great numbers, not driven back by the old war.

Where I can be free.

She quickened her pace, her aches easing and the sack strapped across her chest lightening. There were many leagues yet to travel to reach Folly, but she'd already crossed half of Baltesia on foot. She would make it. She had to. Her oath to her father couldn't be broken; her promise to herself even less so.

I will survive. I'll reach the rangers.

Leiyn made it into the forest before the storm found her.

It whipped up from nowhere. One moment, the sky was clear; the next, a pregnant black cloud sagged into view, then poured its misery upon her. Leiyn scrambled to find shelter, but the aspens and thin pines provided little in the way of it.

Rain pelted her, with ever bigger droplets and more force than she'd yet endured. She staggered as a hundred blows pounded on her, barely able to see ahead. All the world had become gray and blue. Water rushed in ravines around her, sucked at her feet, seeking to drag her under.

Then she heard the thunder.

Or what she thought was thunder. Only as the sound became rhythmic did she understand this was something entirely different, a tempest unlike anything in her experience.

A monsoon? She'd heard they sometimes hit the coast in the summer, rain and waves so powerful they could wash away homes.

But this wasn't thunder.

It rumbled against her mahia's walls, crumbling them at their base, then shuddered through her being. Though this was a frighteningly new sensation, as her cursed magic peeked out from its cage, she knew instinctively what was coming.

Titan.

Its lifefire burned bright, a beacon to her unnatural sense. Through the trees and the storm, though it was still at a distance, she saw it. Its shape was unlike anything she'd seen before: four-legged like a mule, but broad-headed and thick-bodied, with tusks longer than a boar's. And it was *huge.* Just as the guard had said, this one looked as if it could crush her with one of its massive feet.

Only its feet didn't trample over ground, though leaves and branches shouldn't have been able to support such thunderous weight, somehow, it ran across the canopy.

She could sense no more as her mind scattered. Leiyn stood there, drenched to the bone, in the path of this behemoth. Yet she couldn't move. Part of her wanted to be blasted apart by this magnificent creature, then put back together, over and over.

Like rain becomes rivers, then lakes, then mist, then clouds.

She was tired of struggling to hold herself together. She wanted the freedom that the pounding footsteps of the titan promised to provide.

A flash of fire came from nowhere. Something tugged at Leiyn's leg, a sharp pain on her ankle.

Crying out, she came back to herself enough to lash at her small assailant. But as soon as she started to, she lurched to a stop. She saw who it was.

"Is it really you?" Leiyn shouted over the storm.

The silver fox stared at her. His coat hung miserably about him, the rain overcoming its natural buoyancy, but the fox didn't seem bothered. His body taut, his lifefire burning high, he darted in to tug at her leg again, this time his nip too light to hurt.

"Follow you?" she asked, but the creature had already darted off in the direction he'd pulled her.

Leiyn ran after him. As the rain titan neared, a trumpeting blare filled the air. She covered her ears, screwed up her eyes against the pain, and kept close on the silver fox's tail. She didn't know where they were going, but he had kept her safe before. Her only hope now was to trust him.

A rocky outcropping appeared before her, thrusting up from the forest. The silver fox nestled under the shallow alcove, and Leiyn joined him. At once, he nestled under her arm, and she felt the fraying parts of herself resolve back into themselves.

No sooner had she mended than she was battered apart.

The rain titan charged overhead, and Leiyn turned her head up against the blinding rain to catch a glimpse of its blue-gray body shimmering like water. *It is water*, she realized as its skin absorbed the raindrops and spray splattered with every step.

It threw back its head and trumpeted again, a sound that shook Leiyn to her bones. Lowering her gaze, she folded her body around the fox, whose lifefire burned hot enough to warm them both.

The titan passed.

Its footsteps soon faded into the distance. Minutes after, the rain eased to a drizzle, then stopped altogether. When Leiyn summoned the strength to lift her head, she found the sky clearing into patches of periwinkle.

The silver fox stood and walked a short distance away, then shook himself in a shower of droplets. Leiyn managed a small smile as she watched, but it flitted away as he looked back at her. His bright orange eyes seemed to burn with his inner fire. If he meant to convey something, she couldn't tell what it was.

"Thank you," Leiyn murmured. She slowly reached out a hand toward him.

The fox spun on the spot and darted away. Though she watched him go, he moved around a tree, and his lifefire disappeared.

He didn't reappear on the other side.

She stared after him, melancholy setting in. Once more, she was alone. But a thought brought her comfort a moment later.

I survived a titan.

The Saints' Crossing guard had doubted her, but she'd proven him wrong. She would prove them all wrong, those who doubted she could make it this far.

She would reach Folly and the rangers there. She would survive even the Titan Wilds. Even if it was with a bit of help.

Her legs were shaky, but Leiyn forced herself to stand. Her will the firmest thing in her body, she made back for the road and continued north.

36

THE BLOOD SIGNAL

After the moons had risen, they left the Murmuring Canyon.

Leiyn's face was still flushed, even as the Barren winds tried to rob the heat from her body. She no longer held Teya's hand, but their lifefires had inflamed each other's so that she almost felt feverish.

Just the tea's effects, she told herself. But she knew a lie when she heard one.

Teya remained close by her side, as if invisible strings kept either of them from straying too far. Often, their eyes caught, and smiles darted out like children sharing in mischief.

But as they reached the first of the domiciles along the cliff, Leiyn felt a shift in the mood. Hesitantly, she looked up to find Teya staring at her, her smile gone.

"I must leave tomorrow."

Leiyn's flush faded. "Why?"

The scout sighed and turned back to face her, hands propped on her hips. "You know why. One of the wardstones is faltering. If we let it fall, the titans beyond will have a way in."

"Maybe we should let them in, then."

Teya's eyes narrowed. "We cannot, Leiyn. We live in a city carved from cliffs. One *kainox* could kill hundreds, thousands even."

Leiyn had not known where her point led at the outset. Now, she unspooled it. "The Iritu fear titans. They're what allowed your ancestors to beat them long ago. And the *sach'aan* were the ones to put up the wardstones in the first place. If titans were around Qasaar, then maybe—"

"No. It cannot work." The scout crossed her arms. "Perhaps once, when we had shamans to spare, they could have kept the titans away. But now, we need the wardstones. Or will you remain here guarding our gate for the rest of your days?"

Remain here? Leiyn looked over the Barren, gloomy except for the few sparks her mahia detected. This was not home, not the Titan Wilds she knew and loved. No matter who was here, she could not stay.

"Fine. I'll go with."

"No."

She took a step closer. "You think you can stop me?"

"Only if you listen to reason."

Teya reached out to touch her arm. Fresh sparks traveled along her skin. Leiyn tried to ignore the feeling and hold onto her resolution.

"We cannot risk more than one shaman—or initiate—at a time, not anymore," the scout continued. "And Taht Patli will be faster than you, as he has done this many times before. Please, Leiyn. Stay, if only for my sake."

It was a hard plea to resist, yet she scrounged up the will for it. Yet as Leiyn shook her head, Teya continued, her tone softer, her words sharper.

"Do you not have another task you must be about?"

Leiyn winced. She wondered how far her failures had spread through Qasaar.

"I do." Part of her wanted to move her arm away from Teya, but good sense prevailed. With a sigh, her obstinacy drifted away. "Come back safe."

Teya grinned and reached up to brush Leiyn's cheek. Sparks seemed to burst through her belly.

"Now that we have shared this night," the scout murmured, "how could I not?"

Teya, Patli, and their party set off before dawn. Leiyn was there to see them off, though she had hardly slept that night. Xepi also came down and spoke with her fellow shaman while Leiyn bid the scouts farewell. Patli looked even wearier than Leiyn felt, dark circles heavy under his eyes and his shoulders bowed.

Yet he does his duty, she reminded herself. *As you must do yours.*

She and Xepi stood side by side as the stone gates opened and the draconions and their riders swayed through. After they'd passed, Teya twisted around in her saddle and raised her spear with a grin. Leiyn waved back, her smile limp.

As she lowered her arm, she glanced over to find Xepi watching her. The shaman's expression softened. Leiyn wondered how much she suspected of her and Teya's fledgling feelings. She certainly shared her worry from the creasing of her brow.

"Come," she said, turning toward the western cliffs. "We have work to do."

Relieved she wasn't ostracized from the shaman, Leiyn made no protest as she obeyed.

They set to their usual practices as if the disagreement the day before had never occurred. But with her mind elsewhere, her efforts were half-hearted, and even simple tasks like seeking felt a chore. It spoke to Xepi's own distraction that she did not criticize her, but only moved them through the motions. Noon had barely arrived before the shaman dismissed her, claiming she had other tasks to attend to. Leiyn didn't object, happy to let off the painful practice.

Yet, freed of obligation, she was at a loss for what to do next. *What can I do when Teya is out there risking her life?* Shooting a bow or swinging wooden weapons seemed fruitless wastes of time. Yet she knew she was likely good for nothing more so long as the patrol was out.

So she went to the range and loosed arrow after arrow. The sun beat down on her neck, the heat bludgeoned her, yet she didn't relent until long after the burn in her back and shoulders had progressed to a bone-deep ache. Where her mahia had suffered for her distraction, her marksmanship had improved. A few spectators gathered to watch her hit the targets from as far off as a hundred paces.

As she unstrung her longbow, one watcher approached. He looked to be a scout or a warrior, telling by the scar that cut through one mangled ear.

"You shoot well. Surely, one of my people taught you."

"Not me," she answered with a smile. "Seems like I have a few things to teach you."

That earned her a round of laughter.

"That could be," the man consented with a lopsided smile of his own. "Come back soon, and we shall see who has the better eye."

She shrugged. "I'll be here. Question is whether you'll show up."

Leiyn walked away to fresh laughs, a smile teasing her lips. She felt a bit better for the interaction, but it didn't even last her until the barracks. Stepping through the doorway, worry set in again.

Time to wait. She sighed and set to finding food, then distracting herself however she could.

Before late afternoon had even gone, Leiyn traversed back down into the heart of Qasaar. She wasn't alone in the early reception. Acalan already stood vigil, his shaved head shining with sweat, his green tattoos almost seeming to spark.

She stepped up next to him. "Haven't seen you at the training grounds. Too busy for us common warriors?"

He glanced sidelong at her, expression impassive. "Yes."

Leiyn rolled her eyes. "At least we'll have good conversation while we wait."

"Ask good questions and I will give good answers."

"That's how it is, then?"

The chieftain gave her the barest of smiles.

They waited largely in silence. Xepi joined them before evening set in, as did the other chieftains. A small crowd gathered behind them, commoners, scouts, and warriors intermingling. Leiyn wondered if this was how every patrol was welcomed home, or if the recent disaster brought it out.

She kept watch with her mahia, her reach expanding for leagues around, but she didn't sense any approaching party. Evening began to wane, then darkness fell. Her worries grew with each fading minute.

Where are you? she railed against Teya in her mind. *If you don't come back soon...* She had no way of finishing the threat. Would she ride out to find her?

Yes. I would.

Leiyn blinked, surprised at her certainty. She'd only known the scout for half a season, yet the woman captivated her.

To think I once hated Gasts. How times have changed.

"You find something amusing?"

She glanced over to see Acalan staring at her. Leiyn opened her mouth to respond, but before she could get the words out, something touched at the edge of her mahia's reach. She whirled back to the gate. From the corner of her eye, she saw Xepi stiffen as well, and knew she didn't imagine it.

A pair of creatures neared Qasaar, their lifeforce close to one another's. A moment's study brought them into focus: a human rode atop a draconion. And this was no stranger.

Teya.

Air threatened to strangle her as Leiyn saw the state of Teya's esse. Ordinarily burning with a brilliant blue, now the color was muted and the brightness dimmed. Darkness leaked in, twisting and mangling her spirit.

She was injured. Gravely so. It wouldn't be long before her fire faded entirely.

Before she knew what she was doing, Leiyn sprinted for the gates. Acalan shouted after her, but she ignored him.

"Open them!" she shouted at one of the guards. "Open the gates!"

The man stared at her before his eyes darted to the chieftains. But Teya didn't have time for delay. Tearing past him, Leiyn slapped her palm on the panel she'd seen Patli use before and felt the magic suck at her energy. She let it sap a little, then pulled back her hand as the gates flared to life.

With a shudder, they began to open.

"Give me your draconion!" she demanded of the guard next to her. When he, too, only stared blankly at the chieftains, Leiyn snarled and seized the reins to the beast from its peg. The giant lizard stared back at her with one yellow eye as she made her way to its side, its stink filling her nose. Clenching her teeth, she dragged herself on top of it, swinging a leg over to seat herself between the rows of spines along its back.

She had never ridden a draconion before, but during their long trek north, Acalan had run her through the basics of it. Whipping the reins slightly, just enough for the beast to feel it, she said in the Gast tongue, "Forward!"

The draconion obeyed at once, ambling at the usual slow pace that they could maintain for leagues. It didn't bump up and down like a horse, but swayed from side to side in a way that immediately affected her lower back. But she could deal with a little discomfort.

"Faster!" Leiyn whipped the reins twice in rapid succession. The giant lizard picked up momentum, then they flew across the ground.

Stomach sick, throat tight, Leiyn kept her focus on Teya. Before long, she could see her: a black speck against the gray background, the shape of the rider and mount distinct from the stone pillars around them. Only then did Leiyn wall off her mahia, though it had been a risk to keep them open so long among the Fingers. She would do the scout no good if she drew the lyshans now.

Faster! she urged the draconion, though they already were

going so fast she felt she could slip off and crash to the ground with one wrong step. Yet she couldn't help but wish it. Teya was hurt somehow, badly enough for her to sense it from so far off.

She cannot die. Not now.

The draconion began to slow, its exhaustion showing through the wobbliness of its limbs and its heavy panting. Yet its efforts had been enough. Teya was just before them, close enough Leiyn could see she didn't ride upright, but was slumped forward, one arm wrapped around the black spine before her like a saddle's pommel. Coming astride, Leiyn leaped from her draconion before it had even ceased moving, steadied herself on wobbling legs, then lurched toward the scout. The draconion, Bane, eyed her as she came up to it, but its eyelids drooped and its belly dragged. Gashes down its flanks oozed violet blood.

"Teya!" Leiyn was by her side, putting her hands on the scout, looking over her for injuries. At her name, Teya's head rose a fraction, then lolled to the side so she could see through the cascade of her braids.

"Leiyn..." she slurred, eyes rolling up. "Why are...?"

"Save your strength." Leiyn took in her wounds. *Shallow gash along left temple. Arm limp; possible shoulder dislocation. Claw wounds in upper right thigh; bleeding badly. Deep punctures in abdomen.*

None seemed immediately fatal, but combined, they might prove so. She ground her teeth, a scream building in her throat.

You cannot die. Not you. Not now.

Breathe. Just breathe.

Tadeo's voice spoke in the back of her head. Leiyn tried following the late lodgemaster's advice. Exhaling shakily, she set her mind on what she had to do.

A quick healing now, and for Bane, too. Then a sprint for the gates. It would exhaust her, make it difficult to fight if her magic drew enemies. But she saw no other way.

Leiyn drew in and released another breath, then lowered her walls.

She recoiled at the state of Teya's esse, but only for a

moment. Xepi's lessons in mind, Leiyn poured forth her own life-force, sealing off the wounds and containing the contamination that had poured in. Her work was sloppy and left behind numerous infections that would soon grow and spread, but for the moment, it was enough to keep the scout alive.

Drawing back, Leiyn blinked, the world tilting about her. She fought for balance and placed her hands on the head of Teya's draconion. The great lizard didn't pull away but opened itself to her mahia's touch. His wounds were deep, but his body seemed to naturally resist corruption. It was only a matter of sealing shut the cuts before she judged her work sufficient.

Leiyn closed her walls and staggered back. Her knees felt weak; her body dragged with weariness. To heal without taking in more lifeforce drained her to her core. There was nothing she could do about that, however. With labored breaths, Leiyn grabbed Bane's reins, then hauled him across the short distance to her own mount waiting patiently for her. It was difficult to drag herself atop the draconion's back, especially with one hand occupied, but with a last force of will, she managed it.

"Forward," she wheezed. At the whip of the reins, the mount obeyed.

Time bled together. Leiyn tried to keep a careful watch around her, but all awareness of her peripherals had faded. She felt drunk and sleep-deprived at once, unable to concentrate on any one thing. Her head swayed back and forth with the draconion's steps. A crick quickly formed in her neck.

Suddenly, others surrounded them: scouts on draconions, she registered belatedly. Leiyn let one pry the reins from her hands and leaned forward, nearly stabbing herself on one of the draconion's spines. Like Teya, she found herself clinging to it to remain on.

"Let go, Huntress. Release the *axolto*."

"Acalan," she muttered. Her eyes had drifted closed, but her mahia had opened. She knew the chieftain by his esse. Gently, he took her down from the draconion and carried her in his arms. Focusing on his burning core, images rose of their own volition.

A striped stone spire, towering high above, pulsating with life. *A wardstone.* A large cat, also midnight-black, prowling through thick foliage. *A jaguar.* A seashell, closed but opening, revealing the glimmer of a pearl within.

"Never thought you'd be a pearl."

"I did not know I am."

She only realized she'd spoken aloud when Acalan responded. With that jolt of recognition, a measure of her presence of mind returned.

"Put me down. I can walk."

"When you slur your words? I do not think so."

"Then I'll ride." Anger flaring, Leiyn pried open her eyes to stare blearily around. When her vision failed to become clearer, she felt around with her mahia, but there were too many people and beasts to sort through. "Where's Teya?"

"They are taking her to the scout barracks. Xepi will heal her there."

"Bring me to her."

"And let you rest on the floor? No."

Leiyn tightened her jaw, but it slackened a moment later. She let her head loll back against Acalan's arm.

"I'll pay you back for this once I'm standing," she mumbled.

The last thing she heard was Acalan's rumbling laugh.

37

OUR WAR

*L*eiyn awoke, then bolted upright. Only afterward did she realize why.

Life. It filled her to brimming, so full she felt compelled to move, to rise, lest it seep through her skin. She threw the covers off and moved her legs from the bed, then froze.

Someone sat next to her.

Her eyes focused. As she saw who it was, she exhaled a laugh.

"Xepi. You gave me a scare."

The shaman leaned back in her chair, hands resting on her knees. Her drawn face and pale esse told Leiyn all that her silence did not.

"You gave me your lifeforce, didn't you?"

Xepi nodded. "You are a fool," she said, her voice faint.

Leiyn raised an eyebrow. "Funny way of saying good morning."

Then she remembered what had happened and all good humor drained away.

"Teya," she said urgently. "You healed her?"

"Yes."

"So she'll survive?" Leiyn was on her feet before she'd finished speaking. "I have to see her."

The older woman breathed out a sigh. Only then did Leiyn realize how quickly she was speaking.

"Sorry," she said, only partly meaning it. "But I have to go to her. Will you be alright? Should I get you anything?"

Xepi drew in a labored breath. "Yes. Find me a prudent student."

Leiyn stared at her teacher, then burst out a laugh. "No chance of that!"

She looked around until her eyes rested on her gear, tucked into the corner next to her saddlebags. Though she didn't intend to leave Qasaar's limits just then, with enemies prowling the Barren and the latest patrol ambushed, it was anyone's guess what would happen next.

As Leiyn strapped on her weapons, she asked, "So Teya was the only one to return?"

Xepi mumbled something, and Leiyn paused to look at her. The shaman was more exhausted than she'd first thought. Stringing her longbow, she slung it over a shoulder and went to Xepi, then placed a hand on her shoulder. With a small force of will, Leiyn gifted her a bit of esse.

The woman jolted upright, then glared at her. "I came to heal you," her teacher noted.

"Who's the foolish one now? I had more than enough." Leiyn flashed a smile. The agitation of being overfilled with lifeforce already ebbed away. "Besides, I need information."

"Very well." The shaman's speech was clearer now, and she spoke almost normally. "Yes, Teya was the only survivor. At least, the only one to return."

Leiyn understood her meaning at once. "They have Patli."

Xepi sighed, her shoulders bowing forward. "He had only begun to reinforce the wardstone, by Spear Teya's report. Four lyshans ambushed them."

"How did she survive?"

"They let her leave to carry back a message. 'We are coming. Open the gates or we will break them down.' That is what the lyshan told her."

We are coming. She trembled like a tree in a sudden gust.

Something about the words reminded her of the lyshan that had taken her from the first ambush, Sharo. Though she had only intuition to go on, she was certain his hand was in this.

But what is your game?

"Have they left messengers alive before?"

Xepi shook her head. "The attacks most often come as a surprise, though soon after a shaman's capture. When it is later, we suspect the shaman held out against their methods of influence..." She trailed off, her expression pained.

Leiyn chewed her bottom lip and glared at the wall. The lyshans, whether it was Sharo, Man'nah, or another one behind this, wanted them to be prepared for the attack. Somehow, this played into their plans.

Perhaps it is mere arrogance. They could believe they cannot be opposed when so few shamans remain.

Her fists clenched, her muscles gone as rigid as a drawn bow. If *sach'aan* thought them easy prey, they were in for severe disappointment.

"I have to see Teya," Leiyn said. "Will you be alright now?"

Xepi waved a hand. "Go. But be ready for the pound of the drums.

She did not need to ask what that meant. *Battle.* It was the only possible answer.

Leiyn finished strapping on her knives, secured her quivers, then left without another word.

～

Qasaar was in an uproar.

Leiyn dodged around the people thronging the streets. Some seemed aimless in their wanderings, despair written across their faces. Most looked to be about specific tasks: hauling supplies from one to another, or gathering for a militia, weapons in hand and heavy clothes serving for armor. From warrior and commoner alike, she felt the same anxiety as pulsed through her veins.

But this isn't their first time. There was an efficiency to their actions that reminded her that siege was a part of a Gast's life now. War was known as often as peace. This time, however, they only had one shaman.

And me. Her lips twisted into a bitter smile.

Reaching the bottom of the cliff, Leiyn shoved her way across the plaza, heading past the wells where women and children filled buckets of water. The Whisperspire above them was, for once, devoid of life.

She pressed on until she reached the *situali* barracks which were nestled underneath the cliff atop which hers was set. At its entrance, she paused. While most of the rooms were empty, one was filled to overflowing. She could hear the commotion coming from it all the way downstairs.

Teya's room. She sensed the scout's esse and felt something in her relax. She'd believed Xepi when she said Teya was safe, yet witnessing it struck a deeper chord.

Leiyn hurried up the stairs and made for the crowded room midway down the corridor. The barracks looked much the same as hers, identical in design, but different in the illustrations upon the wall. The colors here showed more red and violet than the greens and blues she was used to.

Reaching the door, she muttered her pardons as she wove between the Tetrad attendants and made it inside. The bodies crowding the room made it uncomfortably warm, and her mahia felt stifled by the lifeforce radiating against it. Leiyn shoved down her discomfort and continued until she reached the ring of chieftains before the bed.

Acalan looked back as she reached his shoulder, acknowledging her with a nod. His arms were crossed over his broad chest, his expression grave.

She leaned toward him. "Don't think I forgot. You've still got one coming."

A smile lightened his face, but only for a moment. "She awoke a little while ago. We have been asking for further details about what occurred."

Leiyn gently pushed him aside so Teya finally came into view. She was sitting up, her back against the painted wall. Deep shadows ringed her eyes, and she bowed forward in a way that spoke of a deep exhaustion. Her eyes flickered up to Leiyn's, and she smiled, even as she continued speaking to whoever she was addressing.

Seeing the scout's distraction, the other chieftains looked over. Ilaoti scowled, while Zyanya and Tinoch were more respectful in their greetings.

"The Tetrad requires Spear Teya's testimony just now, Envoy," Teya's chieftain grated. "It would be best not to crowd her."

Leiyn glanced back at the press of people behind her. "Good thing she wasn't crowded before."

Teya chuckled aloud, while Ilaoti's expression grew blacker. Before the Red Hawk chieftain could speak again, Acalan intervened.

"We have heard all Spear Teya has to offer. Let us convene on our own and see to what can be done. We must defend Qasaar now."

Tinoch gave a nervous chuckle, and Zyanya's expression soured, but when they both murmured their assents, Ilaoti sighed.

"Very well. Remain here, Spear Teya, so we may speak more."

"Yes, Toa Ilaoti."

With that, the attendants filed out, and the chieftains followed after. Acalan paused at the doorway and looked back at Leiyn.

"Meet me at the Whisperspire," he said. "Xepi and I will find a place for you."

A lump appeared in Leiyn's throat. She contented herself with a nod.

After all others had vacated the room, she turned back to Teya. The scout stared at her, her smile fading.

"You should not have done that."

Leiyn flinched. "What?"

"Coming after me in the Barren was a great risk. The lyshans might have stolen you."

Leiyn started smiling before she realized the scout was serious. "Teya, I had to. You were dying out there, and Bane was gravely injured. I couldn't just stand by and watch." She pursed her lips. "Besides, if you'd escaped them, I saw no reason they should hunt you now."

It wasn't quite the truth. She'd had no rational thought when she charged out the gates. By her expression, Teya could tell.

But the scout only waved a hand. "Very well. I suppose that was a poor thanks for saving my life. Only... I wish you would not take such risks."

"Risks like you just took?"

Suddenly, both of them were smiling. Teya reached up and Leiyn took her hand and sat on the bed next to her. Warmth spread up her arm and filtered through the rest of her body, and not only from their intertwining esse.

"They are coming," Teya whispered. Her eyes flickered up to hers, then away to the opposite wall. "I do not know if we can stop them this time."

"We will." Leiyn tried to believe it was true. If she didn't believe it, how could she make it so?

"They could have killed me. You saw what a state I was in; I managed to drag myself onto Bane, but it would have been simple for them to hunt me down. Yet none did. Instead, one of them spoke and bade I bring back a message."

"I heard the words." Leiyn hesitated, then asked the question needling her. "What did this lyshan look like, the one you spoke with?"

Teya's brow knitted together. "More... human than the others. At least in his clothes. The details are fuzzy now, but he wore a robe, a gold one, and a blue sash over it."

Leiyn nodded. It was all the confirmation she needed. "Sharo."

The scout looked sharply over at her. "That was Sharo?"

"Sounds like it. His face was difficult to see? Like it was permanently in shadow?"

"Yes, I think so."

Leiyn stared at the floor for a moment. "He left us both alive. Can it really be for the reasons we think?"

"I do not know. But we have nothing else to believe." Teya moistened her lips, seeming to work up the courage to ask something. Her dark eyes found and held Leiyn's. "Have you unlocked Zuma's *ilis?*"

Leiyn winced and shook her head.

The scout pressed her hand. "It was too great a thing to expect. But do not forget—we still have Xepi, and she knows these same secrets. We will survive this attack. Though..." Teya drew a finger along her blankets. "They have never threatened so much before. Titans assaulted Qasaar in the past, not lyshans. If they come here themselves..."

"Then we'll have a chance to finally kill them." Leiyn punctuated the statement with a smile.

Teya raised an eyebrow. "I admire your courage, Leiyn. But how?"

How. The very question she'd been asking herself since arriving in Qasaar. Leiyn looked at the wall and mulled over it once more, as if now the answers would come to her.

As she stared, her mahia focused on the panel shimmering with life set in the middle of it. The realization struck her so suddenly she bolted to her feet, releasing Teya's hand as she did.

"The Iritu artifacts." She whirled back to Teya. "We just have to use the weapons in the ruins! We won't need shamans then. Even if it takes a hundred warriors, we can kill the lyshans, once and for all. End this *feshtado* war, here and now."

Teya stared at her, face drawn. "You *are* a fool, Redlock. Enter the ruins now? The enemy will be watching them. They will find you. It is a certainty."

"So what if they do?" Leiyn started to pace, mind turning as fast as a spinning wheel. "Sharo didn't kill me before; why would he now?"

"And if Sharo does not find you, but another lyshan does? What if it is Man'nah? He will not be inclined to let you kill him."

"Then I'll run one of his people's knives through him."

Despite her words, she shared Teya's doubts. She couldn't stand alone against even one lyshan, much less an army. But she had an ally she thought she could count upon, a friend who could find her no matter where she went.

Ata will fight with me if it comes to that. Chispa will lead her to me.

Teya leaned her head back against the wall and stared at the domed ceiling. "I cannot stop you, I know. But if I could, I would tie you to this bed and not release you until this was all over."

Leiyn looked over, an eyebrow raised. "That's not how I pictured our first sharing a bed."

They shared a brief smile. Teya sobered first.

"Be careful, Redlock. Leiyn."

The scout's eyes swam with buried emotions. Leiyn crossed the room and kneeled beside her, taking her hands in hers and holding her gaze.

"You risked everything for this war," Leiyn murmured. "How could I do any less?"

"But it is not your war."

Leiyn rose. "It is now."

38

LIGHTS IN THE DARK

She did not go to the Whisperspire, as Acalan had bade, but strode past. She sensed Xepi, Acalan, and the other chieftains in the chamber atop it. Leiyn pressed her lips tightly together as she paused to stare up at their shining essence.

When I have the artifacts, she promised herself, *then I can be of some use.*

Yet doubts assailed her as she strode up the slope to her barracks. If this was a foolish risk or a necessary one. If Ata would show up when she hadn't stopped the attack out in the Barren. If Leiyn wasn't running away, looking for any way to avoid the battle to come.

She could only grit her teeth and press forward. So long as she couldn't reach Zuma, this was her only path forward. She had to believe that, lest her courage falter.

Though she was ravenous, Leiyn didn't stop by the kitchens, instead striding to her room. There, she stared at the panel on the wall for a long moment, questioning herself again.

When a job needs doing, her father had often said, *use the right tool to do it.*

So she would.

Stripping off her patchwork clothes, she gathered the bundle of Iritu artifacts she'd already taken, then donned them. As before, each article of armor briefly glowed with esse as they molded to her shape.

The same happened with the weapons belt, somehow finding a balance that made the falchions hanging from her hips nearly weightless. She touched a hand to the hilts, then practiced drawing them, crossing her arms across her body to pull them loose. Her anelaces had always hung from her left hip; having a sword on either side felt awkward, and likely would for a long time.

Her longbow and the Iritu arrows, she left behind. With how cramped the corridors were in the ruins, it wouldn't do her much good in an ambush.

If any weapons will.

Leiyn straightened and faced the panel again. Taking up a torch, she lit it and held it aloft, heat buffeting her face. The cries from the city below wafted through the window, reminders of why she did this.

"Alright, Teya, Acalan, Xepi," she muttered. "Hope this doesn't get me killed."

She strode forward, raised her free hand, and touched the panel.

The world distorted, then reappeared in darkness.

Leiyn staggered, disoriented for a moment but quickly adjusting. Disguising her mahia, she didn't spare a look for the illustrated walls this time, but set down the corridor to the right, the direction she'd taken before.

Entering the weapons chamber, Leiyn wasted no time in gathering up all she could lay her hands on. Spears, long and short, and with every type of blade. Swords, axes, hammers, maces—anything she could drag to the panel, she took.

Hope your invitation applied to everything here, she thought to Ata with a grim smile.

After collecting enough weapons to arm a small company, she moved on to the next chamber. Leiyn focused on the clothes rather than the bulkier bone armor, opting to gather as many as she could. Soon, she had a pile mounded next to the weapons for more or less the same number of warriors.

Leiyn looked back down the hallway, the torchlight only illuminating just to the archway. She debated if she should go back for talismans. *Will the Gasts use them?* It seemed a step too far for them. Yet by Ata's report, talismans presented powerful tools for those without magic. If the fighting grew desperate enough, even their reticence might be broken.

Setting her jaw, she set out for the chamber.

The weapons and armor storerooms looked wrong with half their contents stripped away. Trying not to feel like the looter she was, Leiyn entered the talisman room. Turning to the first cabinet, she opened it to see more of the wooden objects like the ones the dryvan had shown her, though never quite of the same shape or size. Leiyn reached for one, but hesitated, hand hovering over it. Xepi's warnings of shamans gone missing or dying for tampering with Iritu artifacts played through her mind.

Maybe it's not worth it.

She had almost completely withdrawn her hand before mastering her fear. Baring her teeth, Leiyn grabbed the artifact, then tucked it under her arm to seize another.

Her only warning was a fluttering against her mahia's walls.

Something slammed into her side. Suddenly, she was flying. Leiyn crashed into a cabinet. Her torch went rolling away. With her ribs protesting and the back of her head aching, she squinted into the gloom, trying to see what had hit her. Almost, she hoped the talisman was responsible.

When sight failed her, her mahia's walls opened, and the room's lifefire came into bright display. Only then did she sense the three others standing in the room with her. Their esses, bubbled and layered as if with disease, betrayed their identities.

Lyshans.

Leiyn surged to her feet, hands scrabbling for a moment before drawing her swords. Her breathing was labored, but that she still breathed at all was a miracle. *The armor.* It shimmered where the skin-walker had struck her from behind. Though her flesh would bruise, it was far better than shattered ribs.

The lyshans slowly advanced. Their esses burned and bubbled, seething with barely contained power. She saw dozens of souls in each fighting for supremacy.

"Desecration!" the one on her left hissed, a female's voice. "She thinks to use our weapons against us?"

The one on the right laughed, a deep sound like stones grinding together. "The mortal shall die painfully for this."

The middle one didn't waste time with talk. Faster than Leiyn could follow, it sprinted forward and slammed a hand into Leiyn's sternum.

She retained just enough presence of mind to lash out as she soared once more. As she crashed into the cabinet behind her, it splintered. Something wet trickled down her neck. She was bleeding, and badly.

With a wheezing bellow, she flung herself forward, swords leading. The lyshan who had struck her backed out of range, so her blades found only air. Her tormenters laughed.

"Slow," the middle lyshan said, his voice male as well. "We shall tear her apart, limb from limb, when her time comes."

"But who will claim her soul?" the one on the right murmured. Neither he nor the one on the left had ceased their approach; they were nearly within reach of her swords.

She tried gasping a taunt, hoping to provoke one into a mistake, but her lungs wouldn't cooperate. For a panicked moment, she feared her chest had collapsed; the blow had been hard enough for it. Then air whooshed into her chest, and she bent over, coughing.

"Weak," the middle lyshan rumbled. "We shall take her as Man'nah wills."

Do something! she screamed at herself. But what could she do? They were too fast, too strong, and there were too many. Even if she managed to kill one, she would never get all three.

Make a stand. Don't let them take you. Don't make this war worse.

Leiyn coiled her esse tight, then drew on it to send energy coursing her body. Spitting the blood that filled her mouth, she bunched her muscles for a strike.

The air burst with a swirl of magic. A split moment later, one of the lyshans smashed into the wall, beset by a sudden assailant.

Ata!

As the lyshans shrieked and fell on the dryvan, Leiyn took her chance. Channeling esse into a burst of strength, she charged across the room and slashed at the back of the leftmost lyshan. Her blades swept through empty air, her quarry skirting away without even sparing her a glance.

Undeterred, Leiyn pursued, striking any time she saw an opening. The lyshan dodged again and again as she battered at Ata, who disappeared and appeared at will. The dryvan had mangled or killed one, but the remaining two lyshans were gaining the upper hand. Her lifefire sputtered; dark coils of corruption spiraled through her esse.

Help her!

Leiyn swallowed a scream. Instead of striking where the lyshan was, she aimed at the place where she thought he would be next.

The falchions hit, the impact jarring up her arms.

She saw the results by her mahia. Darkness sliced through the lyshan, cutting through the many layers of its soul and splitting open its core. A shriek filled the chamber, then her enemy was whirling and lashing back.

Stars exploded in her vision.

Moments later, Leiyn pried open her eyes, struggling to comprehend what had just happened. Pain threatened to drown her. Every breath came in wet. Half her face seemed consumed by fire.

Move, damn you, move!

Yet she couldn't, though she threw all her will into the attempt. Terror coursed through her. Was she paralyzed? Had the lyshan broken her neck? But no—she felt something in her limbs, a weak twitch in her fingers and toes.

Move! she tried to shout at her body, but it refused to comply.

Then she felt another sensation rushing through: her mahia seeking to mend her. She helped it along, directing it to the worst wounds. The areas around her face and neck felt purple-dark and almost devoid of light. She gagged on bile, her reflexes out of her control for the moment.

Don't suffocate now! She desperately healed. Agony throbbed through her head, worsening as her flesh repaired and pulled back together.

Her vision returned, then a little mobility in her neck. Leiyn sagged on her side and spat blood and bile until she could breathe again. Still unable to move much, she sought around her with her mahia, trying to see how the battle fared.

Someone surged into existence above her, and she jerked in response, trying to ward them away.

"Flee!" Ata roared.

The dryvan seized her, then Leiyn was soaring again. Only this time, there was no end to it.

Leiyn spun through a nameless existence, separate from the world, flotsam on a dark river, rushing toward the waterfall at the end. Soon, she would fall and be crushed on the rocks below. A scream welled up in her throat. Leiyn tried swimming against the current, but it was bearing her down, down—

She slammed into solid ground.

Where now? Sensations assaulted her. She was facedown, pebbles and grit jabbing at her skin. Heat beat down on her neck and back.

The sun. Outside, somewhere.

Leiyn groaned and tried to rise, but her magic was still working to repair her wounds. With each passing moment, exhaustion weighed heavier upon her as she drained her resources. The world dimmed at the edges of her mahia, her seeking losing range. Yet with desperate hope, she tried to sense any signs of life.

The most she found were cacti and tiny critters. Otherwise, she was alone.

Unconsciousness begged her submit, caressing her with smothering hands. Resisting, Leiyn sucked in a breath and heard something squelch in her lungs. Still, she suspected she'd survive. It was what came after that she feared more.

Ata sent me to a grotto.

She'd never visited a grotto without an Iritu before. She didn't know how to leave one on her own. And from the state Ata had been in when she last saw her, Leiyn doubted she would be fetching her anytime soon.

She was trapped.

The darkness pleaded once more. This time, Leiyn relented, grateful to finally let go.

39

SURRENDER

*L*eiyn awoke.

She tried opening her eyes, but something sealed them shut. Panic rose, but it was as weak and fluttering as a fledgling bird. Even for fear, it was hard to muster the energy.

The truth came rushing back.

Only dreamdust. She reached up a hand to rub it away. Only then did she realize that she could move her arms again.

I'm not paralyzed. I'm whole.

She moved each limb and digit, testing them. When they responded, she released a shaky breath.

Her relief was short-lived. Blinking open her eyes, she stared at her dun surroundings. The rest of the picture pieced itself together.

A grotto. I'm alone in a grotto.

Despair threatened to sap what little strength she had, so she pressed it away. Survive. That was what she had to do now. The rest of her troubles could wait.

But how? a craven part of her whispered.

Leiyn groaned and managed to rise to her hands and knees before she had to pause to recover. She looked around her. Beyond the two falchions, which had apparently come with her, she saw an unwelcome and familiar sight: the shriveled bodies of small desert animals. Lizards and mice and beetles, instinctively summoned by her mahia as her esse depleted, had died to sustain her. Farther afield, in a radius of a dozen paces, the small cacti that sprouted from the sandy ground were also shrunken and dead. Little enough lifeforce, but it had been enough to keep her alive.

For now.

Leiyn twisted around to sit on her rump, then hugged her legs close to her body. She stared toward the distant cliffs where she suspected Qasaar lay. It was as far out of reach as the Ancestral Lands on the other side of the sea. Even if she survived the walk, what good would it do her? Until Ata fetched her from this parallel realm, she was stuck. Strong as the dryvan was, that Ata would prevail against such odds was no certainty.

Leiyn was on her own.

She closed her eyes and tilted her head back. *Breathe, just breathe.* She calmed her racing heart and settled her spinning mind like Tadeo had taught her. Into the void, she let any idea that occurred to her waft to the top of her thoughts. When nothing arose, panic tried to set back in, but she stubbornly fought it back down.

Think. There must be something I can do. Some path I have yet to travel.

Her lips were raw and chapped. Her face still ached where the lyshan had struck her. She wondered if it would leave scars. Her esse burned low and sputtered at the edges.

None of that matters. Think!

One idea surfaced first. *Zuma.* Perhaps he had knowledge tucked in his spark that could help her. He had known many things; perhaps he'd even possessed mastery of grottos.

But she didn't leap to act on the notion. She had failed to reach him before under better conditions. Desperation might lend her the push she needed, but death loomed too close for her to want to leap into its embrace.

Feel with your lifesense. Maybe there's something you missed before.

Leiyn made the attempt, spreading her awareness out in a wide circle. There were other specks of life around, some even deep in the earth below, but she sensed nothing more. No, there *was* something, a shimmering in the air that was not usually present.

The grotto's walls.

But though she could perceive them, she had not the faintest idea of how they could be breached. Still, she tried. Leiyn clumsily manipulated her esse. She formed it like a spear, as she had against the lyshan she had slain, then thrust it at the air. It had as much effect as swinging a sword at the wind. There was nothing to strike, not that she could sense.

Sighing, Leiyn opened her eyes and squinted at Qasaar again. She could already imagine the destruction befalling it. Stone spiders like those from the Gorge de Omn ripping up buildings as they burst through the cliffs. Hill tortoises stomping down avalanches and charging through any people standing in their way. Who knew what other varieties existed out here, beyond the edge of the world. Titans of sand and wind, of rock and ruin.

She squeezed her eyes shut. *Don't think of that. Focus. Escape, then deal with what's next.*

"But how?" she whispered to the Barren.

Only two avenues remained before her. One, she could do nothing about. Either Ata would come for her, given enough time, or she never would. It wasn't a salvation Leiyn could rely on.

Which left her second option: finally reaching Zuma.

"One last time, then," Leiyn muttered under her breath. It seemed unlikely she would get a second chance.

Keeping her eyes closed, she breathed in and out, centering herself. When she'd calmed as much as she could, Leiyn used her mahia to focus inward on her lifefire. She went past the glaring outer layers, past her lifemark rising to greet her, deeper until she perceived the two pinpricks of light. Even without the mushroom tea's aid, she had practiced this enough to reach that far.

Temptation drifted her toward her mother's spark, but her present need proved stronger. As if from a distance, Leiyn felt her teeth grind and her hands clench as she steeled herself. But there was no putting it off.

She dove into Zuma's soul.

That suffocating darkness, so familiar now, swallowed her. Yet no matter how many times she felt the weight of death's hand, she always fought against it. Leiyn tried to breathe, to lift her chest and ease the pressure. It was no use.

I'm too little, too weak. I always will be.

She pushed away her fears just as she pushed against the impending death. This couldn't be the way she ended: out here, alone, lost in sand and memories. There had to be a way through.

But how?

As she'd been taught to do as a ranger, Leiyn reached out with her senses. Her hearing was muffled and nearly drowned out by the rattling in her throat, but the distant murmur of voices drummed against her ears. Her touch was either numb or fiery with pain. Bitter acid burned on her tongue.

But in her sight, something loomed above her. No, not something—someone.

Me.

Leiyn stared up through Zuma's rheumy eyes at herself. She had been present at Zuma's death, had witnessed his last breaths. And before they had happened, she had received a gift from him.

Death closed in swiftly, but somehow, her panic had lessened. Leiyn focused on her mahia, ignored in the rush, and found a little lifefire remaining to her. More important, she felt that of the other Leiyn touching hers, holding Zuma's hand, esse brimming at her fingers.

Then she understood.

Death could not be rushed or resisted. No amount of

strength could stop what was coming. It wasn't by force of will that it happened, but the lack of it.

Only through surrender could she conquer death.

The last of the air left her lungs. Her body stilled. All strength fled. Her senses dulled. But the pain sloughed off, too, those final agonies of living gone.

Leiyn kept her focus on the tiny flame, flickering its last. The little life remaining to her.

Be at peace.

Releasing it, she faded away.

———

Nothing.

Then—

Breath.

Leiyn jerked upright, wracked with coughing, hands scrambling across the rough rock. As she came back to herself, the knowledge of what had happened returned as well.

I did it. I survived.

She blinked and stared, her vision slowly resolving. Her senses reasserted themselves, to her immense relief. With living had returned the instinctive fear of its ending, and she hadn't been entirely sure she would return.

As she calmed, Leiyn noticed a new sensation, one only her mahia could feel. Before, she had been alone in the grotto of the Fingers. Now, another presence joined her.

Zuma?

He didn't communicate with words, nor was he wholly separate. She felt his individual spark inside her flaring, its boundaries open, feeding her as she fed it. Now, they weren't two separate beings, but one.

With cracked lips, she smiled, and felt the elderly shaman smile with her.

"What now?" Leiyn murmured. "How do I learn what you know?"

No sooner had she asked the question than she had the answer. As if by invitation, a gate in her mind opened, and behind it loomed staggering knowledge. Of Gast traditions: festivals and rituals, games and arts. Of faces she shouldn't have recognized, but now seemed familiar. On and on, all Zuma had experienced and learned continued, as vast and deep as Southport's bay. She sifted through it all, searching for the vital insight that could save her life. His mastery of mahia. The secrets of the titans.

As if it sought her as well, it surfaced before Leiyn. Hesitating only a moment, she touched it.

Epiphanies flooded her mind. She saw Zuma doing as she must, standing in the Barren just beyond a wardstone in much the same position as she was now. She felt his mahia delve deep into the world, searching, then finding. She witnessed as he grasped hold of another presence, and it seized hold of him in return.

She saw him be destroyed, then remade.

Leiyn gasped for breath and blinked away the images. *Surrender.* Her father had taught her to survive, to do anything she must to prevail. Tadeo had shown her how to adapt and had honed her fighting instincts to a razor edge.

Now, Zuma demonstrated a different lesson. Sometimes, strength wasn't enough. Cooperation could triumph over conflict.

Her shoulders were tight and her jaw clenched, but she exhaled long and hard. *I can do it. I can surrender. I've done it before.* After all, what else had she done with the kraken at Southport? When she found the sea titan, she hadn't fought for control, but given herself to it. The kraken had yielded to her will in turn.

And it would have killed you, but for Zuma.

But Zuma was with her now; a phantom presence, to be sure, but enough to be reassuring. She believed she could do this and survive, but only if she didn't cling to control.

Leiyn settled her mind, relaxed her body, closed her eyes.

Then, with Zuma's soul wrapped around hers, she dove into the earth.

Inhabiting her mahia, she could feel the forbidding palpitations from the wardstones. *Away*, they whispered, *away*. Not a command to her, but to the others whose realm she now traveled.

Leiyn dove deeper, deeper, until she felt the strain of the distance, the cracks in her magic. But with Zuma patching her flaws, she pressed on.

Finally, the wardstones faded, and all was silence around her. But the depths weren't devoid of life, as she'd thought they would be. Even here, leagues under the surface, there was life. Individually, they were specks, but together, they shone like a moonlit sea.

Deeper still, great bonfires blazed in the darkness.

Titans.

Leiyn called to them, pulsing like the wardstones, but with the opposite intent. *Come, come.* She beckoned, like a lighthouse on a cape bringing ships to a harbor. *Come to me.*

The magic rippled against the distant titans, and she felt them stir in response. They had been dormant, she saw now, for as they animated, their esse burned brighter. The familiar influence of titans pulled at her, and though it filled her with alarm, Leiyn didn't flinch from it. She waited as one titan drew upwards, quicker than the others. It grew in size and influence. She saw its soul take form, then hover before her, inspecting the one who had summoned it.

An ash dragon.

Leiyn's strength was frail, the strain greater with each moment, yet she knew she must hold on a little longer. Reaching with invisible hands, she stretched toward the titan, then touched it.

Merge, she said to it, an invitation not a command. *Join. Become one.*

The titan seemed to hesitate, making no more response than continuing to grow in brightness and force. Its winds scalded her being, threatening to burn away all attachment to her body.

Leiyn withstood it, accepting this as the necessary price, and calmed by Zuma's presence within her.

The ash dragon drew closer, then reached for her with flaming claws. She remained where she was, even as she thought terror would snuff her out before the titan could.

His claws closed around her.

For a moment, the world took on a new perspective. It wasn't the suffocating dark of solid ground, but the infinite black of a moonless night sky. She could see endlessly in every direction, and like stars in the void, she saw the other titans across the world. Hundreds, thousands, tens of thousands, in every land and in every form.

And all of them, united. One.

She couldn't linger on the moment, for the next she was rising, rising, then bursting free—

Leiyn opened her eyes to cutting daylight that darkened at once. Raising her chin, she stared at the form that settled clawed feet onto the parched ground, ripping its body free of the clinging stone. Smoke trailed down its figure. Cinders drifted down to carpet the ground around it. The scent of seared rocks filled her nose. Its wings, tipped with curved prongs, were folded against its long, sinuous back. Twin horns curled off its head, and a crown of spines adorned its brow. Scales covered it, some as large as shields, others as small as her hands, black but with a subtle sheen. Its long tail swayed behind, the tip just visible behind its bulk. Her heart tried cracking open her ribs as she raised her head to meet its eyes, eyes that burned like forge-fires, blue at the center, then cascading out to yellow at the edges.

This was no titan of ash and smoke. It was here, in flesh and scale and bone. It was *real*.

It wasn't the first time she'd seen it.

"I know you." She spoke aloud, though she doubted speech mattered. Their magics and minds were intertwined in a way she didn't understand, that sent a thrill shuddering through her. "You erupted from the mountain Nesilfo. Clouded Fang, we call it."

It didn't respond. Though it had no concept of conversation, their communication was instantaneous and disjointed, without beginning or end. And though gender, too, seemed a thing foreign to its nature, she began to think of it as a *him*. There seemed something masculine to his mind, to the deep rumble of his being, that she couldn't put words to.

As the ash dragon asserted himself in her, and she in him, Zuma began to fade, receding back to his spark. *Thank you*, she thought to him as his soul went back to sleep. She thought she felt a nudge in response, though with the titan thrumming through her, it was difficult to tell.

Leiyn rose to her feet. Her body's weakness was driven away by the ash dragon's strength. Through their connection, lifeforce flooded into her, repairing every pain and injury.

She faced him.

The titan stared at her, unblinking. Then he approached, the ground shaking with each ponderous step. She should have fled before him, mindless with fright. If he decided to kill her, she couldn't evade him, nor stop him with her mahia.

Yet she felt the currents of his fathomless mind lapping around the edges of herself. She waited: breathless, foolish, hopeful.

One stride away, the ash dragon paused, then bowed his head. When standing upright, his head loomed above hers, but now, one great smoldering eye came level with her.

So much for not being rash, she thought as she extended her hand to touch the bridge of his snout.

Sensations spiked across her awareness: the rough scaliness of his skin, the warmth seeping up through it, comforting like a hearthstone before a blazing fire in the dead of winter. The ash dragon's scent seeped into her deeper.

But her other senses perceived something occurring. A ripple spread out from where she touched the titan, one that obliterated his flesh and turned it back to black mist. Her ears filled with a rushing sound, like a gale fell from the sky to surround them. Her braid whipped over her shoulder, and stray hairs pulled from it to fall before her eyes, sticking where blood had congealed.

She sensed the moment she returned to the world.

Leiyn staggered, feeling as if the earth had shifted beneath her feet, though she knew the change happened in her mahia alone. Her hand fell away from the dragon's snout as it became immaterial. Sweeping a hand back over the loose hairs, she stared up at the titan and saw he had returned to the form she first knew him as. Smoke billowed out from him, and the great eyes were mere ember glows from deep within his being.

She smiled, feeling like she often did after a hard ride, breathless and exhilarated. "Thank you," she said to the titan. "For returning me to my world."

The connection that had formed between them remained, but it felt as if a gulf had emerged in it. She didn't know if he could understand her as he had before. A sense of sorrow, of something lost, threaded through her elation. It waxed as she saw the titan's smoky form was beginning to disintegrate.

Without shifting his gaze, the ash titan dispersed in the wind until not a wisp of smoke remained.

But it wasn't his end. Even as he disappeared, Leiyn felt him still. He was returning to his slumber deep within the ground, his home among the rivers of fire and molten rock. Where he belonged.

"Not entirely," she murmured as she felt him crawling into a magma cavern, curl into a smaller ball than seemed possible and fall sleep. "Part of you belongs to me now."

She didn't understand how she knew this, but she didn't question it. Zuma had guided them to this point, but what they had done, their merging—it had felt as natural as breathing. Leiyn had never yet been led astray by her instincts.

She exhaled the lingering emotions, then wiped at the dried blood on her face. Her wounds remained, reminders of her duty. Leiyn turned around to gaze at the cliffs and the distant mountains beyond them to find the canyon in highlands that marked her destination. Even re-emerging into the world she knew, the city was a long walk away.

Leiyn sighed and stooped to pick up the swords at her feet. Sheathing them, she began walking toward the mountains, then jogging.

To Qasaar, she thought, hoping she wasn't already too late.

PART VII

LEGION

THIRTEEN YEARS BEFORE

Leiyn shivered and pulled her ragged cloak tight around her. She still walked the Frontier Road—walking, ever walking. Summer had faded away, and with it, the green of the Titan Wilds had become yellow and brown. Soon, winter would grip the land once again.

Fear was her only constant companion. Fellow travelers were infrequent and had become more so since leaving Saints' Crossing. Those she didn't avoid, which were most, she asked how much farther Folly lay. All of them looked her over, and she tried not to lose courage at the skepticism in their eyes.

"Leagues north still," the final farmer said, bringing in the last of the harvest of the season. "Don't you have anywhere else to go?"

She only thanked him and kept walking.

Every part of her was cold. The darkness brought such fear she almost indulged in her mahia.

No. Keep it closed.

Magic was what had landed her in this mess. What might get her killed by the first snows if she couldn't reach the rangers in time.

Survive.

She'd promised her father. Promised herself. There was no other future for her.

Is there any future for you at all? a voice hissed in the back of her mind.

She tried to ignore the doubts as she walked. And walked. Her shoes became riddled with holes, then little more than thin padding beneath her soles. Her clothes were torn and caked with mud. Game had grown scarcer with the cold, as had farms to beg or steal from. Hunger bore its greedy claws into her, demanding more food than she could ever supply.

Still, she moved on.

Then, one day like any other, Leiyn looked up and saw something looming out of the morning fog. Squinting, she tried to make out the dark cliff extending before her. Was it a turn in the road, or an end to it?

She came closer and it became clear. Walls—they were log walls, uneven and sharp at the top. A town.

Folly. She had finally made it to Folly.

A smile spread across her face, and a relieved chuckle broke free. But as soon as they arose, they disappeared.

What if I heard wrong? What if the rangers aren't here? What if they don't want me?

Just the thought nearly buckled her knees and threw her to the hard dirt. Angrily, she thrust it away.

"I'll make them take me," she muttered under her breath. Straightening as tall as her gnawing hunger allowed, Leiyn approached the gate.

She expected the gateman to hail her as she came near, but no one appeared in the slot in the timber door. After a moment's hesitation, Leiyn called in, "Hello? I need to enter!"

No answer came. She pounded on the door until her fist ached, then called out again. Still, no one came.

Leiyn took a step back and stared at the door. It was set in a gateway that had the same foreboding top a dozen feet tall.

If I'm careful, I might slip through...

Recalling her days of climbing trees, Leiyn set her hands to the door, worked her fingers into crevices just deep enough to hold, then hauled herself up to place her feet on the door. She climbed, the effort exhausting her at once, but she didn't dare let go. Leaving the ground, she made it halfway up, then neared the top.

"Oy! What're you doing up there?"

Leiyn nearly fell as the shout came from the other side of the wall. Face flushing, she jumped from higher up than she should have. Wincing at her aching joints and splintered fingers, she straightened and looked into the door slot, now filled with the man's eyes.

"You weren't here," she answered, the excuse suddenly seeming flimsy and silly.

"I had to find a place to deposit last night's dinner. So you decided to climb?" The door guard's eyes darted around, clearly taking her in. "Why d'you want in so bad?"

Leiyn sucked in a breath, then let it out in a rush. "I'm joining the rangers."

A moment's silence—then the man burst out in uproarious laughter. She endured it, stewing, every muscle rigid, while her doubts hollowed out what insides remained to her.

"Join the rangers." The man wiped his eyes, a thick-fingered hand flashing into view. "Don't hear that often."

"They're here?" she asked.

"'Course they're not here! They live at the Wilds Lodge, don't they? Three days north, at least. But you'd have to know how to find it, and not many 'sides those strange folk know the trails."

Her hopes plummeted with each word until they dragged in the muddy ground, the same as her shoes. Leiyn only stared through the slot at the door guard's eyes, unable to believe it.

I failed. I still cannot reach them.

All her will and all her plans had been directed toward this one goal. Now, so close, the rangers were just out of reach. Unless...

"Are any rangers here?" she asked, fighting to keep a sob from her voice.

The door guard squinted off to the side. "Don't rightly know. They come through the north gate, see, and this south gate here is my post. Would have to ask Isai or Leonor, depending on who mighta seen something. Or," the man added, his eyes widening, "you could go to the mayor. She always knows what's what and who's who, if you catch my drift."

The mayor. Leiyn resisted the urge to glance at herself. Bedraggled and dirty, she doubted the mayor would allow her past the stoop any time soon.

"I'll try the guards. Where can I find them?"

The door guard was unbolting the gate as he spoke, and the great door swung in. She saw he was tall and thin and had been stooping to look through the slot. Curly gray hair framed his face, and a worn cap shaded it. He had a brown cloak, stained at the hem, wrapped around himself. He hardly looked imposing for someone who was supposed to be protecting the village.

"One'll be at the gate. The other you'll find at the Thirsty Giant come evening. Though, truth be told, either might be there now. Tell 'em Gaspar sent you."

She nodded as she passed in. "Thanks, Gaspar."

The door guard beamed. "Nah, it was nothing. What was your name?"

She thought about saying 'Aracel,' as she had called herself along the road north. But she hadn't come all this way to hide who she was.

"Leiyn. Of Orille."

"Orille?" Gaspar shook his head. "Never heard of it, which must mean it's far. And you look like you've walked a long ways." His eyes darted down to her feet.

Leiyn was already turning away. She didn't need him telling her what she already knew.

"Good luck finding the rangers!" he called after her. "I'm fearing you might need it!"

The guard at the north gate, Leonor, hadn't seen any rangers come in, so Leiyn tracked down the Thirsty Giant, but found no sign of Isai.

It was the tug that broke the fishing line. She didn't ask further after the guard, too demoralized to care. The tavern keeper looked glad to see her back; her nose hadn't stopped twitching since Leiyn entered her establishment.

Returning to the street, Leiyn discovered it had started to rain. Bowing her head, she wandered through the streets, progressively becoming wetter, yet finding it hard to care. So close to her goal, yet she had no way of going farther. She was tired, so tired, and hungry, and wanted nothing more than to lie down and sleep and never awaken.

"Are you lost?"

Leiyn startled at the voice behind her. She skirted away and spun around to see a man only a bit taller than her a few paces away. He looked to have just exited a shop, a tailor's by the swinging sign depicting a needle and thread. The man's hooded cloak was darkened by only a few droplets.

Her eyes darted over him, unsure if he posed a threat or not. His cloak seemed green at first glance yet looked brown at the next. His face was tanned and sun-roughened, and his eyes were shadowed by a prominent brow. A dark beard, thick but trimmed, spread across his chin and partially hid his upper lip.

Leiyn reached into her cloak to find her knife. He didn't seem unfriendly, yet there was something about him that screamed of danger. His stance spoke of vigilance and readiness.

Like a wolf, she realized. *Calm for the moment, but violence never far under the surface.*

The man's arms came out from his cloak, and she flinched, expecting a weapon. Instead, his hands were empty. Beneath the cloak, she glimpsed similar green-brown clothes and a longsword belted at his waist. The man's hands were covered in leather gloves that were trimmed to leave most of the fingers exposed. Only on the index and third fingers of his right hand were they still covered.

"You are safe with me," the man said. His voice was soft, and in another situation and from a different man, it would have been soothing. "What is your name?"

She didn't release her knife. No one else appeared up and down the street; they were alone.

"What's yours?" Leiyn retorted.

A smile broke out over his face, crow's feet at the corners of his eyes showing he smiled often. *Or squints*, she reminded herself, determined not to let her guard down.

"Tadeo of Lake's Edge," he replied. "Now will you give me yours?"

"Why do you care?"

The man lowered his arms. "I have not seen you in Folly before, and I am familiar with the people here. You are a newcomer. A stray."

Leiyn found her teeth baring in mockery of his smile. She almost pulled out her knife but thought better of it. If it came to conflict, it was better to keep it hidden until the last moment.

"I'm no stray," she lied.

"Then you're a newcomer." The cloaked man was almost unnatural in his stillness, betraying no hint of nervousness. She found it difficult to cling to her wariness, feeling the draw to believe he was as he appeared. Calm. Gentle. Concerned.

She shook her head. "What if I am? You going to try to take me? Think no one will miss me? I wouldn't try it if I were you. I'm not some toothless stray."

With her rising fear came the cracking of her cursed magic's walls. She had to fight to keep them up, but feared they would come crumbling down if it came to blows.

The man, Tadeo, watched her for a long moment. His eyes darted over her person, even settling for one moment at the place where she gripped her knife.

"I understand that you are afraid. Please, let me begin again. I am the Master of the Wilds Lodge, leader of the Frontier's rangers. My questions were not to prey on you, but to give you help, should you require it."

Leiyn stared at him, frozen in place. *Leader of the rangers.* The very man she searched for stood before her.

But how could she be sure he was telling the truth?

Yet all the facts slotted together like knots on a snare. His garb, ideal for blending into surrounding wilderness. His alertness and his sword. His keen skills of observation.

"You're a ranger."

"Yes." A smile flashed across his lips again. "But you should ask for our seal to know for sure."

She didn't ask to see the ranger's seal then, instead releasing her knife and straightening. Her face burned, yet she tried not to let her embarrassment show. She needed to show him who she really was, that she had what it took to be like him. That she wasn't a scared girl lashing out at every passerby.

"Master Tadeo, I wish to join you and the, uh, the Wilds Lodge. I wish to become a ranger."

She waited, not daring to move a muscle. The ranger looked placidly back at her. Did he look and find her wanting? Dismiss her for her dirty clothes and mangy appearance? Her jaw trembled, and she clenched it until her teeth ached.

Tadeo nodded and gave her a small smile. "The spirits must be awake to bring you to me. And so soon after another just arrived."

Leiyn blinked, unsure of how to answer.

"I believe I can teach you," he continued. "You made it to us from far south, judging by your accent and clothes. You have courage and determination." He paused, eyes creasing in thought. "But before I can accept you into the Lodge, you must do something for me."

A thrill of fear went through her. Would he deny her, after she had come so far? "What is it? Sir," she added as an afterthought.

Tadeo let out a soft chuckle. "Do not call me 'master' or 'sir.' I am the lodgemaster, but we are all equals at the Lodge—apprentice, staff, and ranger alike. What I require is simple. You must tell me your name so I have something to call you."

A fresh flush gathered as she realized she'd never told him.

"Leiyn. Leiyn of Orille."

"Orille." The ranger studied her. "You have come a long way from home."

She felt the urge to swallow. There was a glint of understanding in his eyes that was uncomfortable to endure.

"Yes," was all she could say.

Tadeo nodded, then made a small beckoning gesture. "Come. There are a few things I must attend to here in Folly today. As have you," he added with another of his small smiles.

Leiyn tried for a smile of her own and was surprised it came easily.

"But tomorrow, we will depart, for we must return to the Lodge before the first snows. The others will be waiting."

The others? She wondered just how many other rangers and rangers-in-training there were. For all her dreams, she'd neglected thinking of the details.

Tadeo didn't delay long enough for her to ask but strode down the street with the lope of a man long used to traveling for leagues without stop. He didn't turn back, simply expecting her to follow, or so she assumed. Leiyn found another smile creeping up on her, one born of relief and even a long-buried feeling she never thought to experience again.

Hope?

She trailed after the lodgemaster, holding her head high once more.

41

FIGHT OR FLEE

*L*eiyn ran.

Not long before, she'd been dying on the blighted sands of the Barren, half her face caved in from a lyshan's blow. Yet now, she raced across the desert, a well of vitality propelling her on. Though her legs began to burn and her lungs tightened, she didn't slow. She couldn't afford to—nor could Qasaar.

In the time since she'd begun running, she had covered almost a quarter of the distance to the city. The scabbards at her hips should have impeded her movements, but instead, they adapted to her stride, swinging in time with each step rather than thwacking at her legs, as ordinary scabbards would. Iritu magic had once again yielded a small miracle.

But even with her speed, she feared it wasn't fast enough. Her fears found fresh fodder when she looked to the east and saw a disturbance by the wardstones.

It was no ordinary dust cloud that rose there; even if she hadn't expected it, she would have known that. Towering hundreds of feet high, it rose from the Wolf ward, the one that Patli had failed to reinforce due to his capture. Even more than the sight, she felt its presence cascading over the lands, an outpouring of magic that could be triggered by only one thing.

A titan was awakening.

Infused with an ash dragon's essence and leagues away from where the great spirit rose, Leiyn was able to weather its storm on her mahia and keep running, though not without gritted teeth. This awakening felt different than any she'd experienced before. Her skin felt pelted with sharp pebbles and sand in a ceaseless wave.

What creature have you unearthed? she thought to the absent shaman.

She didn't slow to find out. All of Qasaar would see it soon enough.

Sprinting now, Leiyn tried to plan for the coming assault. Would it be this new titan alone they contended with, or would lyshans attack as well? Could she and Xepi alone turn back the titan? Unless her teacher—or Zuma's spark—had knowledge of contending with compelled titans, their defense would be improvised, a strategy that held scant hope of success.

She had too many questions and no way to find answers. Not before it was too late.

Leiyn had no other choice but to let the problem give way to the pounding of her feet, the searing of her lungs, and the lethargy of her limbs. She closed the leagues between her and the stone gate rising ahead, racing to beat the titan closing in with every heartbeat. Its storm dominated the sky, the sunny day turned a muted orange.

Somehow, she made it in time. Leiyn was wheezing as she came within shouting distance of the gate, while the titan remained some ways off. Wondering what held it back, Leiyn doubled over for a moment to catch her breath, then waved at the warriors atop the wall.

"Ho!" one cried in the Gast tongue. "It's the ranger!"

A moment later, one side of the gate began to rumble open. Leiyn coaxed herself into a limping jog. Wiping the sweat and blood from her face, she flashed a smile at the scout who appeared before her in the widening crack.

"Nahui."

The garrulous scout was in full warrior regalia now, a short spear in one hand and a buckler in the other. For a moment, she seemed so stunned by the sight of Leiyn that she couldn't speak. But her voice could never be dammed for long.

"Leiyn!" Nahui exclaimed. "Where did you go? And what happened to you? You look like you have been fighting. Is the blood yours?"

Leiyn waved a hand. "Can't explain now. Xepi, the chieftains —where are they?"

"The Whisperspire." Nahui frowned, seeming to puzzle through the mystery. "The attack is coming, no?"

"Yes. It's almost here."

Even as Leiyn answered, a drum pounded a warning from atop the cliff, Lualli. The scout looked toward it, as did many of the people beyond her. Warriors and citizens alike shuddered with the fear rippling through them.

"The titan drums sound." Nahui jerked her head toward the Tetrad's tower. "Quickly! I will bring you to them."

Though she felt as if she could barely move, much less run again, Leiyn set off after the scout. Those they passed stared, no doubt wondering at her as Nahui had. Leiyn ignored them all, tailing close behind the scout until they reached the base of the tower.

Ascending the staircase, the shouting came from above. She swiftly identified all in attendance with her mahia. Xepi and the chieftains were there, as Nahui had said they would be. Leiyn smiled with relief as she noticed Teya as well. With most of her friends safe, her thoughts flitted to Ata, hoping again the dryvan had made it out alive.

She and Nahui stepped into the chamber. For a moment, the room fell quiet as its occupants turned to stare at her. The moment didn't last long.

"Where have you been?" Ilaoti demanded.

"Bathing in blood, at a time like this?" Tinoch wore a desperate smile. "Not what I would advise!"

Xepi only stared. Leiyn avoided her gaze. The shaman saw too much for her liking.

Teya pushed through the others, Acalan close behind her. The scout gripped Leiyn by the shoulders. Looking her up and down, the tightening of Teya's brow loosened only slightly when she saw Leiyn was uninjured.

"You look like a hog after a spat, and smell like it, too." Despite the jest, Teya wore no smile as she released her. "What happened, Leiyn?"

Conscious of the others listening, Leiyn drew in a breath and projected her words. "I went to gather Iritu artifacts to help in the fight and was ambushed by lyshans. Three of them."

"And you survived?" Ilaoti snorted a laugh and turned away. "We do not have time for this. We must defend—"

"Foxfur came to my rescue," Leiyn interrupted. "She may be dead or too injured to help. We're on our own. But I can still retrieve the weapons."

"Iritu weapons." Zyanya shook her head, beads clacking together. "Even if you were not ambushed again, they cannot be relied upon."

"Ranger Leiyn is right."

At Xepi's words, all in the room turned to stare at her. The shaman had stood, but she had eyes only for Leiyn.

"I sense what is coming," she continued. "A sand stampede tramples across the Barren, set for Qasaar."

As the chieftains muttered curses, fear blazing in their eyes, Leiyn mulled over her teacher's words. *Sand stampede.* It didn't quite explain why the titan had felt so odd to her senses, but it provided some context. More than one titan was roused, and somehow, they were connected.

Xepi wasn't finished. "The ranger and I will rebuff them. But the *sach'aan* may attack as well. Man'nah knows we are weak. If the dryvan has been killed, he may wish to strike the final blow."

Ilaoti, Zyanya, and Tinoch erupted with objections, but Acalan's roar cut them off.

"*Listen to her!* We cannot argue any longer. Now, we must fight."

He turned his lowered brows upon Leiyn. She raised her

chin higher. His gaze felt like a challenge, but his words had a different feel.

"I trust this outlander ranger. She is rash but has sound judgment. If she believes the Iritu artifacts can help us, and Taht Xepi affirms this, then the time has come to break the taboo."

Ilaoti opened her mouth to object but shut it at a look from Zyanya. Tinoch still wore a smile, though it had turned queasy. At Acalan's continued stare, all three reluctantly nodded.

Leiyn nearly bolted then and there down the stairs to retrieve the artifacts, the risks be damned. She could feel the stampede coming nearer with every second, trembling through her mahia. But she hesitated a moment longer to look to Xepi.

"How are we to stop it?"

The shaman pursed her lips, white lines appearing around her mouth. "You have touched Zuma's *ilis.*"

"I did." Leiyn wondered how her teacher knew.

"He will know then." Xepi looked out the east-facing windows. "Take Lualli; I will cover Lakti. Keep the stampede as far from the gate as you can. Do not undermine anything I do. Understand?"

Leiyn nodded. All she could do was trust she would know what to do when the time came, with Zuma's help.

"Then go." Xepi waved her to the stairs.

Leiyn turned to leave but paused once more. She glanced at Acalan and exchanged a nod with him, then turned to Teya. The scout looked as close to afraid as Leiyn had ever seen her. It finally awoke terror of her own.

Stay safe, she wanted to say to her. *Run, don't fight.*

Instead, she said, "Come with me. You'll need to distribute the gear once I fetch it."

Teya flashed her a smile, a hint of relief creeping into her expression. She saluted the four chieftains, then strode after Leiyn down the stairs.

Once out of the Whisperspire, they set off at a jog again. Leiyn's legs screamed as they set up the slope, but she didn't allow herself to slow.

"So are you going to tell me what happened?" Teya turned to allow a small group of young warriors to pass them.

"You won't believe it."

"Let me decide that."

Between labored breaths, Leiyn did her best to explain. She held nothing back; not about her injuries and predicament, nor what it took to reach Zuma, nor even the ash dragon rising from the deep.

She finished just as they reached the barracks. Teya remained silent even as they crossed the hall and ran up the stairs. Only before Leiyn's room did she finally react. Leiyn pulled to a stop as the scout gripped her arm tightly. Chills ran up her skin at Teya's touch.

Leiyn turned back, protests on her lips, when Teya pressed her mouth to hers.

They lingered in the kiss before Teya pulled away. "Do not be stupid," she murmured, then pushed Leiyn into the room.

Dazed, Leiyn could only nod. She found a distraction in moving to the panel. Catching her breath for a moment, she focused on her mahia, then raised a hand to the circle of painted stone.

The wall sucked her into darkness, then spat her up in the Iritu hallway.

Leiyn had barely oriented to her surroundings before she bent over. By her lifesense, she detected that the stacks of artifacts she'd left by the panel were still there. She rushed to gather them at once; every moment she allowed her mahia to be open here would be like a beacon to her enemies.

Scooping up as much as she could hold, Leiyn hobbled back to the panel. Trying to keep everything in her arms, she reached up and touched the stone.

The world blurred, then reemerged. Leiyn stumbled into her room, spilling the objects from her arms onto the floor.

Teya was next to her a moment later, looking her over. "They did not find you?"

"Not this time." Leiyn flashed a smile, then gestured to the artifacts. "There's more in there, but there's no time to fetch them." The titan from the Barren thundered louder in her with every moment, like a herd of wild horses galloped in a circle around her.

"Then we will make these work." Teya bent to load her arms up with artifacts, then noticed Leiyn still standing there and waved a hand at her. "You have somewhere to be, do you not?"

Leiyn edged toward the door, pausing only to fetch her quiver of Iritu arrows and ranger longbow. She didn't know what use they would be against lyshans and titans, but a ranger always made sure to be prepared.

The need for urgency thundered in her chest, yet somehow, she couldn't make herself leave. When Teya looked up again with a raised eyebrow, Leiyn said the only thing filling her head.

"Stay alive, Teya. Whatever you do, please, make it through this."

The scout laughed, but Leiyn saw the promise she needed in Teya's eyes.

"Go, Redlock. I will survive if you do."

With a last lingering look, Leiyn nodded, then left to make her final stand.

42

SIEGE

As she reached the end of Lualli, Leiyn skidded to a halt and stared at the oncoming enemy.

The titan's tempest had spread across all the Fingers, hiding the black pillars from view under a layer of seething sand. Though it could be no later than midday, the haze made the day as dark as dusk. Even if she couldn't feel the esse pulsing from amidst the storm, she would have known it was sorcerous. There was a taste to the dust spiraling through the air, bitter and cloying as a week-rotten corpse. The turbulent winds at the storm's heart rose and fell like waves on the sea. Worst of all was the feel of its sorcery, a pounding thrum like a herd of horses on the run. Each moment she beheld it threatened to rattle her brain loose from her skull.

The sandstorm hadn't reached the Gast city, but it lingered a mere hundred strides from Leiyn's position atop the cliff. It wouldn't be long before the battle came. Then she and Xepi would be put to the test.

Leiyn reached her mahia across the Barren, ranging as far as she could in search of their enemies. Titans couldn't be commanded from too far afield, from what she understood. Certainly not from beyond the wardstones, not by a shaman of Patli's power. She squinted into the dust, scanning for the source she knew must be just before her.

There.

She sensed them close behind the bulk of the titan, mere embers next to the great spirit. There were three of them, one different from the other two, and familiar even at the distance.

Patli.

She couldn't know what had been done to him, but she doubted the lyshans flanking him offered protection. Would he stop short of destroying his home, or had resistance been so soon squashed out of him?

Leiyn grimaced and set her bow at her feet. *Better to be prepared and disappointed,* Tadeo had often said. Now, she took the words to heart, touching briefly on his carved fox, still secure in the pouch at her hip.

As she waited, Leiyn glanced at the opposite cliff. She could make out Xepi atop Lakti, a dark speck against the sorrel sky, while her esse burned bright. She was glad the shaman knew what she was doing, for Leiyn had only the faintest idea. She'd commanded a sea kraken and linked with an ash dragon, yet still felt as if she blundered through a fog of ignorance.

Zuma is with you. He'll guide you. You're not alone.

She thought of the others in the city, the defenders with an even more intractable problem. With only unfamiliar Iritu armor and weapons as aid, they were tasked with driving back lyshans. She could only hope Ata's estimation of the artifacts was warranted, or the city might be lost even if she and Xepi succeeded.

Her musings ended as something changed below.

Rearing from the front of the sandstorm, the titan took shape. As she had inferred from Xepi's description, the stampede didn't manifest as one giant beast, but many, rising nearly as high as where Leiyn stood. The creatures seemed like wild cattle, with strong, shaggy chests, curved horns, and spindly legs. The front halves formed, while their rears faded into the storm behind them.

With their emergence came a burst of lifeforce. Leiyn staggered as it swept over her, only just managing to keep her feet. Cursing under her breath, Leiyn glanced again at Xepi, then roused as she noticed the shaman's esse expanding.

Help me, Zuma, she pleaded inwardly as she reached for the stampede. From the recesses of her spirit, she felt the aged shaman reemerge.

With Zuma alive in her, she seized the titan. The titan resisted; holding it was like how she imagined it must be to ride one of the beasts, clinging to the horns while it bucked beneath her, always in danger of being thrown and trampled. Making matters worse was that this titan not only appeared as many but felt the same to her magic. Though she could hold the horns of one, the others still pressed past, dragging her toward their destination.

Just as she couldn't hold on any longer, the shaman's presence flared through her. Suddenly, she understood what she must do. Zuma guided her mahia like her father used to when she was a child and learning a skill for the first time, his hands over hers. Her magic spread, almost as if she sprouted a dozen more arms. From one soul, she grasped not just one of the great beasts, but many, wrestling them back by the horns. Her will flagged; she was losing ground. But she held.

She didn't work alone. Xepi clutched at the titan as well, and a strange confluence formed between them. There was a third contender for the titan, but his will seemed fractured, liable to break at the slightest press.

A thrill went through her. *We're winning.*

Xepi was doing something so magic pulsed in the sands. *Taking command.* Looking with her eyes, Leiyn saw that the line of beasts was turning, each fading from sight as they merged again with the dust cloud looming behind them. Leiyn felt the strain on her ease. She exhaled, letting down her guard.

Then the third presence surged into brilliance, and the titan threw off Leiyn's grasp.

"NO!"

She hurled her mahia at the titan again, scrabbling for a hold. The wild beasts had reformed, and despite all her efforts, they didn't slow as they charged for Qasaar's gates. She could see the warriors dotting its walls, feel their sparks of life. If it hit the city, all of them would perish.

Acalan was there. Teya.

The ground shook as the titan pushed toward the walls, their hooves stomping, smashing, shattering. Leiyn saw the red wall faltering, cracks spiderwebbing through it. Soon, it would break.

She couldn't let them die.

A scream ripped free of Leiyn as she threw herself against Patli. She felt the titan falter as she sliced into the link between the titan and the ensnared shaman. Patli had seemed so fragile before, but now, his will was as strong as stone. Distant magic between him and one of the lyshans told her why: they were infusing the shaman with their own lifeforce.

She'd be damned if she let that stop her.

Leiyn knew what she needed to do. Drawing on every bit of her strength, she sawed at Patli's command. It was like taking a dull blade to a ship's rope; though fibers frayed, it was too thick and strong to easily cut through.

She couldn't do it in time. She would be too late.

Then she realized her path. The only path forward.

Leiyn abandoned her course of attack and reforged her mahia. She didn't let herself think about the wall fracturing below her, the titan pushing into the city, the ancient buildings crumbling, the countless lives about to be lost. Like when she'd fought the infection in Isla, like when she'd set the kraken upon Lord Conqueror Armando Pótecil, she became nothing more than a tool—an arrow, hurtling toward her target.

Tears in her eyes, muscles clenched tight, Leiyn struck at Patli himself.

Even with lyshan magic coursing through him, he was too brittle to withstand the assault. She'd aimed to kill, and he folded under the blow. She saw his lifefire dim, his command of the titan faltering. The lyshans' mahia pulsed outward with all the violence of screams.

Leiyn didn't let herself think on what she'd done. Instead, she moved her awareness back to the sand titan to leash it. But her task was already done for her. Xepi had turned the stampede back again, sending it barreling back toward the lyshans.

Their enemy didn't wait for the sand titan to strike. In twin flares, they disappeared from sight, escaped to one of their grottos.

Leiyn blinked, looking again with her natural vision. Only then did she realize how smoggy the air had become. Dust covered the sky, and sand gritted in her teeth and stung her eyes. The ground still trembled with the stampede's passage, but it grew stiller with every passing moment. She waved a hand through the air, coughing and squinting, as she staggered over to the cliff's edge to peer at the city below.

The titan had made a ruin of the gate and walls. Where they had stood so proudly before, now they lay in a heap of rubble. Leiyn could no longer feel the magic instilled in the sliding stone doors; now, they lay as lifeless as the highlands around her.

Some of the buildings were in a similar shape, especially those nearest the canyon's entrance. The Whisperspire seemed to lean, but still glowed for all that. One of the wells had collapsed in on itself.

But the people were, by and large, alive. Xepi still stood atop the opposite cliff. Leiyn couldn't immediately find Teya and Acalan, but she had to hope they, too, had survived.

While Patli is dead.

She pushed the thought away, tried not to acknowledge her fault in it. This was war; people were bound to die. She hadn't known the shaman well, but she knew he would not have wished to harm the people who had adopted him as one of their own.

Still, as she turned to walk down the cliff to the city below, she couldn't quite push away the guilt.

Before she could take more than a few steps, something made her pause and turn back. Someone had appeared in the Fingers near the broken gate. She couldn't see them, but she knew by the strangeness of their esse that they were a lyshan.

A ringing shout sounded, just loud enough for her to hear. The words made her blood grow cold.

"Bring me Oldsoul! Bring her to me so we may determine your fate!"

43

THE BROKEN GATE

*S*haro had summoned her.

Leiyn made her way down the cliff toward the city below, head spinning, thoughts scattered. She was sure the lyshan who had called out was Sharo. Even if she didn't recognize his voice and esse, his name for her, Oldsoul, would have made it plain. What Sharo wanted with her, she hadn't the faintest idea, nor did she want to find out.

But he hadn't given her much of a choice.

Reaching the Spire Plaza, Leiyn found it in pandemonium. She had espied Teya and Acalan on the way down and sought them out where they stood before the ruined gate. They spoke with the three other chieftains. All were layered in red dust. Underneath the grime, Teya and Acalan bore Iritu artifacts. Though the bright colors clashed with the Jaguar chieftain's surly manner, they somehow seemed to suit Teya. Whether from the armor or their own prowess, neither seemed harmed.

Teya's eyes widened upon seeing her. The scout strode toward Leiyn, arms wide. But even for her, Leiyn couldn't summon a smile. Patli's fate and Sharo's call cast a pall on her mind. Still, she held tight to the scout for a long moment.

Teya pulled back and looked into her eyes, one at a time. "I can scarcely believe it, but you did it. You and Mother Xepi."

Leiyn looked aside. "Not without a price."

"A few were lost, true. But we fared better than in previous attacks."

Leiyn shook her head. "I meant Patli. I... I had to..." She couldn't say the final words, terrified of how Teya would take the news.

The scout drew back, yet her expression was soft rather than hard. "You did the right thing, Redlock. Patli was dead as soon as those devil *greshta* took him. He would not wish to be their puppet."

Leiyn nodded. She knew it to be true and yearned to be absolved of her guilt. Yet she still struggled to believe it.

The chieftains' approach cut the discussion short. Leiyn pushed it from her mind. How the victory had been won wasn't the most important matter just then.

"They want someone here," Acalan rumbled as he and the others fanned out before her. "Something tells me it is you."

Leiyn hesitated before relenting. "It is. 'Oldsoul' is what he called me before when he took me to his grotto."

"Grotto?" Ilaoti asked sharply but fell silent as Acalan held up a hand.

"Sharo, you said this lyshan's name was."

Leiyn nodded. She could sense him waiting in the settling sand beyond the canyon, his figure shining with malformed souls.

Acalan looked back toward the ruined gate. "And you claim Sharo wants you to kill Man'nah, though he serves him."

"That's the only conclusion that makes sense."

The Jaguar chieftain nodded as if to himself, then met her gaze. "You do not have to go, Leiyn. We have their weapons in our hands, their armor on our bodies. We know they can be slain. We will withstand their threat."

"Withstand them?" Ilaoti gestured back toward the gate. "We could barely stop the stampede! Our gate lies in ruin! How can we defend Qasaar now? The ranger must go. Better to sacrifice one outlander than our entire people!"

"And lose one of the last blessed?"

Their small party turned to Xepi as she slowly approached.

"She stopped the titan," the shaman continued, eyes resting on Leiyn for a long moment before looking back to the Red Hawk chieftainess. "It was not I, but she who struck the final blow."

Tinoch and Zyanya exchanged glances, while Acalan almost smiled. Teya nodded, her brow knit, knowing what that meant as well as Leiyn did. Her stomach churned as she remembered Patli as he had been in life. She wondered if his body still lay in the desert, slowly interred by sand and dust.

"I am grateful," Ilaoti grated, "but we must consider what is best moving forward—"

Xepi interrupted her. "For once, Toa Ilaoti, do not be an *egreshti* fool!"

The Red Hawk chieftainess was stunned into silence. Taking advantage of the moment, Leiyn cleared her throat.

"Thank you, Xepi, Acalan—I mean that. But I have to go."

Everyone stared at her. Only Teya spoke in a whisper.

"No, Leiyn. Please..."

Leiyn didn't dare look at her. Look too long and she might lose her resolve. She lifted her chin a little higher and straightened her spine, trying to appear as the ranger she ought to be. One that would make Isla proud, had she remained in Qasaar. One worthy of being raised by Tadeo.

"I don't think Sharo will harm me. I believe I still figure into his other plans."

"And if it turns out he is not alone?" Teya pressed. "If Man'nah himself appears?"

Leiyn made herself look at her. She forced a smile. "Then I'll have the chance to kill him."

Acalan rumbled with a short laugh. Xepi only stared at her. Tinoch's mouth hung open, while the chieftainesses looked unsure whether or not Leiyn was joking.

Teya stepped forward and took Leiyn's hand. She stood taller and broader than Leiyn, but something in her expression made her seem somehow smaller just then.

"Please, Leiyn. Do not."

It should have broken her resolve, that plea. But Leiyn found instead that it grew harder. She squeezed the scout's hand, this woman she had come to care for despite all the odds, and met her eyes.

"It could save Qasaar. Save you." She cocked a grin. "Besides, when have you ever been able to stop me?"

Teya opened her mouth to speak again, then closed it. She managed a small smile in return. "I have not found a way yet."

Leiyn tore her eyes from her to see a mixture of expressions among the others. Acalan's was most surprising, for she had rarely seen regret soften those stone-hard features. Before she could tease him about it, a voice echoed into the canyon from the wasteland beyond.

"Send out Oldsoul! I will not harm her, you have my word. But she and I must confer!"

Leiyn's chest tightened. She pried her hand away from Teya. "Looks like I'm needed elsewhere," she said lightly.

Sweeping her gaze over the others, Leiyn took in their faces. Each strengthened her resolve to do whatever she had to. Even Ilaoti deserved a better fate than what the lyshans could offer.

Not knowing what else to say, Leiyn spared one last smile for Teya, eyes lingering on the tears trailing through the dust on her cheeks, then set off toward the broken gate.

Acalan's grip on her arm arrested her. Turning back to look at him, she saw his prominent brow had drawn tight beneath the layer of red dust.

"Survive, Leiyn. It is what you rangers do, is it not?"

Survive. The same command given by her father long ago. Though she'd had to fight to do it, she'd always found a way.

Perhaps, even this time, she could survive.

Leiyn nodded, and the chieftain released her. The others parted before her. Leiyn shrugged her longbow into a better position on her shoulder, adjusted her quiver and falchions, then walked between them without a backward glance.

She held up her head as she strode past the Gast warriors

surrounding her in the rust-red air, staring, wondering. They raised no cheer as she passed. Perhaps none realized what she did. But she'd never needed accolades.

Leiyn picked her way over the broken gate, then set across the cracked wasteland toward the distant silhouette of the lyshan.

FINAL ACCORD

The wind wailed in her ears as Leiyn walked across the Fingers.

Once she set foot across the broken gate, she cast aside all the emotions that had burdened her. Teya's concern. Acalan's honoring. Xepi's consideration. Her own worry for Isla and Batu, wherever they were on their journey. She quieted her doubts, silenced her thoughts, and inhabited her senses, as a ranger should at the start of a hunt.

The huntress in her had lain dormant, but never gone away.

Repressing a cough, Leiyn quested out with the senses not stifled by the dust. She heard nothing beyond the gale left behind by the sand titan, and smell and taste were useless here. She kept watch with narrowed eyes and a keener vigil with her lifesense. So far, nothing beyond Sharo had appeared or shown any sign of doing so. Even the small creatures that usually inhabited the inner desert had fled before the stampede.

Her longbow was in hand, an Iritu arrow nocked, ready to draw and loose at the first sign of danger. Each stride was taken with caution, watching for the ambush that seemed too likely to occur.

Leiyn reached out with her mahia as Sharo came into view, ensuring the connection with the ash dragon remained intact. As she felt that gossamer thread, relief flushed through her. She might be walking to her death, but at least she wouldn't be alone.

And a hidden titan made for a distinct advantage.

At last, the lyshan became entirely visible. The wind had begun to die, making it easier to see and breathe. Leiyn wiped at the sweat, blood, and sand gumming her eyes to take him in. His eyes gaped as empty as before from his stone face, but his attire had changed. In place of the golden robe and blue stole, now he wore what she recognized as Iritu armor, an aqua tunic with a hauberk over it that was threaded through with titanbone. A sash was tied around his waist, hanging down as if to act as a fauld. He'd even replaced the vine circlet with a helmet, if of a strange sort: a fragment of bone, perhaps once belonging to a giant skull, painted and decorated with feathers and talons.

Sharo smiled as she stopped a dozen paces away. She liked it no better than she had on the first occasion. His eye sockets burned with esse as he stared at her. His face writhed with shadows.

For a long moment, she waited for the lyshan to breach the silence. A great part of her itched to raise the bow and be done with this. When Sharo failed to speak, however, she shot off words instead.

"Against all reason, I came. Now, what do you want?"

His smile widened a fraction. The unnatural look of it reminded her of Ata. Fresh worry for her friend washed through Leiyn, but she could do nothing more than press it down.

"Desire—it is the waterwheel of the world, is it not? What good is not done for want? What atrocity?"

"No more games." Anger flared, but Leiyn's words were cold, her mind focused. "No more sermons. Why are you here?"

Sharo's smile faded as he shook his head in a display of mournfulness. "Ah, the mortal impatience. But I suppose even the long-lived are subject to it. As your friend showed."

The hair on her nape stood on end. *Ata. He means Ata.*

"What have you done with her?" she demanded, raising her bow a fraction.

Sharo lifted a hand. What he meant by the gesture, she didn't know. "There is much you do not know, as potent as your soul appears. You come with arrow pulled, yet you do not even know where to direct it."

"Your heart would be a good start."

A grating laugh rose from the lyshan, and his magic rippled. She tensed, bracing for an attack, but none came. A moment later, his Inheritance subsided. He placed his raised hand to the side of his bone helm.

"Listen, Oldsoul, listen. Can you not hear the omens on the gale? They whisper of allegiances forged in shadow, of false service and hollow leadership. A marionette sits the throne, and another dances atop the altar. How far do the strings extend? How deep does Legion reach?"

She couldn't help but parse his words for meaning. *A puppet on a throne? Dancing on an altar?* With his unfathomable knowledge of the greater world, he could only mean World-King Baltesar and Gran Ayda, the Altacura. *And Legion?* Surprising enough that he knew that much of Catedrál theology, but what could he mean by evoking it now?

The truth struck with the force of a diving hawk.

Man'nah. Layer by layer, she peeled away the events that led to the Lodge's destruction. *How deep does Legion reach*—it all made sense now. She could follow the threads back all the way to the center. Now, she suspected she knew why all this had happened, and who was behind it.

Him, all along.

A puppetmaster had orchestrated these atrocities. Ilberia and the Catedrál were tethered to his strings. The Caelrey, the Altacura, Armando Pótecil—they danced to his whims, as did the Suncoats under their command. The deaths of her friends and Tadeo, the lives lost in Southport and Qasaar—all the blame lay at Man'nah's feet.

Fury blossomed then, a forest fire threatening to burn away all reason. Only the nearby threat let her push it back down. Sharo watched, fathomless eyes smoldering, a smile creasing his flaking lips. His manner was that of a satisfied cat after chasing down a mouse.

She would need her anger soon, but first, she had to be clever. All her moral outrage would do her no good if she couldn't survive to reach Man'nah.

Leiyn struggled for words for a moment, then managed, "Hard to trust someone who speaks in riddles. I'm listening, but I'm not hearing much."

With an unnatural fluidity, the lyshan turned the lower half of his body to begin strutting along the sand, maintaining the distance between them. His upper half remained facing toward her, level as he glided along.

"There it is once more: want. Propelling you toward a fate you do not comprehend."

"I know what you want. You told me power is your deepest desire. So you want me to kill Man'nah so you can take his place."

Sharo went still. Leiyn tensed her jaw, ready to draw her bow. The stillness was too similar to a predator's just before the pounce.

"Yes," he whispered, the word carrying to her ears. "It is a craving I have long possessed."

A weakness. Something to exploit. She readied her words like a knife, then jabbed forth. "There, we share something in common. So let's bring him down. Together."

She knew killing Man'nah would likely only raise Sharo to his place, but she found she didn't care. Justice had been too long denied. If this lyshan told the truth, Man'nah was the one who deserved her retribution. She was only too willing to oblige.

And there were other benefits. Any delay in the lyshan assault would improve the Gasts' chance of survival. This was a risk she had to take. As strange as Sharo was, she thought she might be beginning to understand him. Perhaps they could come to an agreement. Perhaps they could strike an uneasy truce, at least until Sharo saw them as impeding upon his aims.

The lyshan's legs shifted so his lower half faced her again, all without lifting a foot.

"An alignment of desire." He hummed for a long moment, reminding her of how the dryvan Eld used to do as he thought. Sharo's hum, however, sounded the buzzing of hornets. "An alliance of convenience. Shifting as want can be, it is like building a house upon sand."

"Do you have a different plan?"

"None that you would care for." The lyshan waved a hand through the air. Leiyn guessed it was a gesture of dismissal. "Man'nah wishes me to bring you before him, an offering by the Descendants in exchange for peace. But he will break it as soon as he has you. His want is too great to do otherwise."

Her pulse quickened, fluttering in her throat. *He summoned me.* But how could she have expected otherwise? By all accounts, she possessed mahia in abundance. If Man'nah was able to control her as he had Patli and countless others before, Qasaar would fall.

Again, she felt for her connection with the ash dragon. It remained, thrumming thread-thin, but ready to draw upon should need arise. Between that hidden advantage and her Iritu weaponry, perhaps it would be enough.

It has to be.

"Take me to him."

Sharo's eyebrows—or the impressions of them, at least—rose. "Mortals ever surprise me. The briefness of your lives makes your need to waste them all the greater."

Leiyn ignored his goading. "If you won't fight Man'nah yourself, help me indirectly. Keep away the other lyshans."

Evening the odds probably wouldn't improve her chances of survival by much. But she'd take every chance she had.

The skin-walker raised his hand in that peculiar gesture again. "You ask this like you think it possible."

"Is it?"

His smile spread wide. "It is. So we will strike another accord, Oldsoul. Be it the will of the world, you shall prevail."

She didn't wonder long over his choice of words; her mind

traveled to the battle ahead. What she could possibly do to kill the lyshan lord alone.

I could go back. Fetch allies for the fight. I could flee.

Leiyn bared her teeth. No; she would do this herself. She'd lost too many friends in the past year to risk more.

And if you fail? a part of her mocked. *How many more will you lose then?*

Conscious of Sharo watching her, Leiyn wove her fraying resolve back together. Meeting his eyes, repressing a wince at the sorcery surging from them, she nodded.

"I'm ready."

No sooner had she spoken than the landscape around her rippled. Like peeling away a page of a book, the terrain changed. The dying sandstorm faded, leaving a looming sky shadowed by mountains.

Leiyn turned, longbow raised and ready to draw, senses straining to take in the place Sharo had brought her to. The land here was as blighted as before, but in a different way. Though the Fingers had been sand and stone, they had possessed dots of life: cacti holding on in forbidding conditions, scorpions and lizards making their burrows.

Here, there was nothing. Not flies, nor trees, nor a single blade of grass. All lay lifeless and gray.

Sensing no immediate danger, Leiyn lowered her bow a fraction and eased the tension on the string. Her skin crawled at the stark emptiness, and all the more as she took in signs that life had once had a hold here. The path on which she stood was paved with what looked to be old planks, but had become something hard and calcified, leeched of all vestiges of life.

Around the plank path, what looked to have once been weeds sprouted from the ground. Now, they didn't shift in the breeze coming off of the mountains but stood as stiff and gray as the rest of her surroundings. It was the same with the other foliage: trees, bushes, vines, the flowers and fruits upon them—all had been frozen in time, like carefully carved statues, if a sculptor could be so skilled. Even the dirt had lost its vibrance.

As Leiyn shifted her feet to look around, it moved like ash, and felt about as substantial.

Eeriest of all was the fragrance of the place—or rather, the lack of one. She detected no whiff of decay, of decomposing bodies or plant matter. Instead, it was flat and scentless. As if even rot came to an end here.

Death, Acalan had once named his people's enemies. But this wasn't death. It was a fate worse than she could have imagined: the removal from all that was natural to the world.

More than plant life had once existed here. Buildings surrounded her, many blending into the foothills cascading down from the mountains. Branching off from the road were homes built into hills, signified by grand entryways and windows. These outcroppings were painted, and though faded, they seemed more vibrant for being the only colors but for the blue sky above. She recognized the patterns and shapes, and by them understood that this had been a place like Qasaar, an Iritu city lost to time and history.

Yet here, no sorcery sang in the stone. It was cold and dark in a way Qasaar never had been. A true ruin.

Leiyn turned to Sharo, who stood watching her. A sharp question sat on her tongue. But before she could speak, light burst from the darkness. It took her a moment to understand it wasn't light she saw, but lifeforce, burning bright against her mahia.

The city was full of lyshans.

Or so it first seemed. As her senses adjusted, Leiyn saw while they didn't number many, there were enough *sach'aan* to send her mind reeling. A dozen, then a score, appeared as they unveiled their magic. Had they been hiding, waiting for Sharo to lure her into a trap? Or sleeping like the dryvans did in Glade?

It scarcely mattered now. Leiyn raised her bow, aiming at the skin-walkers as they emerged around her, trying to pick a target. There were too many. She held her shot, hoping Sharo would be true to his word, suspecting he would not.

"You are looking in the wrong place," Sharo murmured,

drawing her gaze. The lyshan smiled as he waved a hand down the street.

Not knowing what else to do, Leiyn followed the gesture to see a gazebo she hadn't noticed before. Fifty paces ahead, it was set at the top of a wide set of stairs, the bottom of which was framed by two statues too worn to detect much in the way of detail but seemed to depict skin-walkers as they had been of old. Behind it loomed a cliff, worn smooth like a waterfall had once fallen there, now long dried up.

But it was the figure boiling with esse seated under the domed roof that held Leiyn's attention. A chair so large as to be considered a throne cradled him, curved in a way that reminded her of a large hand, the individual cupped in its palm. Gray, flowering vines stretched over its painted backrest. Though plainly a lyshan like the rest, this one oozed power in a way that eclipsed any of the others. She didn't have to look long to see his lifemark was perverted in a greater way as well. He brimmed with souls, too many to count, all vying for supremacy. A legion in one.

She didn't need Sharo to explain who this was. She knew him. This was her enemy, and the enemy of humankind for countless generations. The one who corrupted, who featured in their darkest nightmares.

Legion. Man'nah.

He frightened her, yet it was fury that ignited and spread through Leiyn. Her lips pulled back in a snarl. Her bow rose.

"Fair fortune, Oldsoul," Sharo whispered in a singsong tone. Then the world trembled again.

Leiyn blinked. Sharo disappeared. The other lyshans were gone.

Only Man'nah remained.

45

HUNTER AND HUNTED

*L*eiyn was alone with Man'nah. Just the two of them, as Sharo had promised. *His grotto.* That must have been how he isolated them.

The means didn't matter now. Only one thing did.

This was her chance.

Man'nah remained unmoving, so she took the opportunity to study him. His body was devoid of clothes, yet veiny roots acted as a replacement, layering over his skin as gray and stone-like as the throne on which he sat. Like Sharo, his shape and face held a human likeness, but there the resemblances ceased. Leiyn stared as one set of features dominated, then another, morphing in a constant flow. First appeared a middle-aged Gast man; then, an old woman of some tribe unknown to Leiyn; then, an Ilberian boy, a disturbing sight atop the man's body. On and on they went, unceasing, ever-changing, showing the true meaning of what it meant to be a skin-walker.

What lay inside him proved even more repulsive. He lacked a single lifemark; there were too many souls within him to detect just one. They muddled the inferno roaring within him, each straining to dominate the rest. She wondered if even he knew who he was.

Yet he was all of them, and he was none. He was the whole and each individual part. *Legion.* She knew the truth of this devil now. Of the madness that he possessed or possessed him.

For the moments she took him in, Man'nah still didn't move. She hesitated no longer.

Leiyn drew her bow.

When the hunter becomes the hunted, Tadeo once told her as they tracked down a particularly vicious wolf pack, *you must strike before they know.* He had shown the lesson then when they put down the wolves. It remained with her, long ago morphing into instinct.

She didn't hesitate now to loose the nocked arrow. Her aim didn't waver; her doubts didn't impede its passage. It flew across the span between them, arcing up through the air, the string and longbow thrumming, the arrow whispering.

It should have struck his chest, but the lyshan was no longer there.

With a speed faster than she could follow, Man'nah had risen and pivoted out of harm's way. His gaze lingered on the place where the arrowhead scored the throne, then looked up at her.

Leiyn was already loosing another arrow. Even as despair tried to claim her, she ignored it and pressed on. Maybe this venture was hopeless from the start. A futile fight.

But Man'nah was here, alone before her. The object of her vendetta. The target of her justice.

She couldn't just walk away.

Leiyn loosed again, hoping he wouldn't be ready this time, praying to the Saints to make it so. Her aim was true, and it flew toward his right eye.

An arm blurred. The shaft splintered and fell aside in two pieces, split by his raised hand.

"You." Man'nah spoke as slowly and calmly as if she hadn't just attacked him twice. "We do not know you." His words seemed to rise from all around her. Like Unera itself had been given voice.

Leiyn was losing hope that her shots would land, yet her

hand had already drawn a third arrow and nocked it. *All I need is one to land. Just one...*

She drew, loosed. Man'nah plucked it from the air, tossed it aside, and set one foot on the stairs leading down.

"Yet you are... familiar. A soul come again."

A fourth arrow flew, only to meet the same result. Fear threaded through her fury. She had known lyshans to be fast, but none of her attacks even fazed him. Sweat beaded down her face, tracking through the grime layering it. She didn't pause to wipe it away but took another arrow in hand.

Fifteen left. She had to make one of them count.

"Ah..." Man'nah's mouth stretched in a smile, like a ravine broke open in the flat slab of his face. "We understand. The raiders... So we did not cull all of you."

"Wrong," Leiyn grunted as she drew back the bowstring once more and sent an arrow soaring forth.

It hit.

Her hopes soared, but only for a moment. Though the arrow flew past the lyshan lord's deflection, it lodged in his shoulder instead of his neck.

Man'nah looked down at it, his stiff brow creased. Only as Leiyn perceived with her mahia did she see the arrow's true potency. Where the arrowhead stuck, darkness rippled through the skin-walker's esse. Layer by layer, it eroded at his seething souls. She feared to think what the weapon would do to her without such defenses.

The lyshan plucked the arrow out and snapped it in two, tossing the pieces to either side. He took another step down, then another. Each stride seemed to shed the rigidity that had claimed his body before.

"Yes, we remember you. And we remember, too, the pleasure of killing your kind."

Her shoulders screamed, having loosed so many shots so quickly, but Leiyn drew a seventh arrow.

Man'nah didn't give her another chance.

One moment, he was forty paces off; the next, he was beside her, his hand lashing out.

The world split apart.

She couldn't breathe, couldn't see. First flying through the air, then pummeled by the ground, Leiyn clawed at the gray grass, trying to rise and face her enemy. But there was something horribly wrong. Her chest wouldn't open; her lungs failed to expand.

Her sternum was caved in.

As the truth cracked through her shock, fresh waves of agony sapped her remaining strength. Cheek pressed to the ashy dirt, she saw through spotted vision Man'nah's bare, gray feet padding toward her, unhurried. To make an end of what was left of her.

No. Not like this. Not before I'm through.

Teya wasn't safe, nor were Acalan and Isla and Batu. She couldn't leave them to fight this thing on their own. She couldn't die.

Get up, Firebrand! GET UP!

Though it sapped the last of her willpower, she reached forth in the only way remaining to her: her mahia. She scrabbled against Man'nah's defenses, trying to confound his senses as Xepi had taught her. As quickly as she made the attempt, she abandoned it. It was futile; he showed no sign of relenting to her influence.

The world failed to yield any viable options. So she dove within it. Darting through the darkness, she reached for a bonfire buried deep below.

Ash dragon! she called. *Titan of Clouded Fang! Come, please, come... I need you!*

Even now, their frail attachment remained. She followed it down, past stone and sand, past the hidden lakes specked with infinitesimal life, to the rivers burning beneath.

Titan! Come to me, come...

She could feel him, close yet far. *Slumbering.* Would he rouse to her call? He didn't respond as she touched on his life-force, vastly dimmed from what it was when he was awake. And she was losing the drive to continue, her blood leaking out, her air-deprived body collapsing.

Titan... Clouded Fang...

She clawed weakly at his essence, scrabbling for any hold. Was it strong enough she could draw it into herself? She had no other choice but to try. She wouldn't last but seconds longer without it.

Using the mahia as had always been instinct for her, Leiyn sucked in the titan's lifeforce.

46

VENDETTA

She siphoned the esse into herself, just a trickle. Just enough to remain alive. It was all she had the strength for.

Yet, as if it were a tolling bell, the titan of Clouded Fang awoke. Surging to life, his form took shape. Then, like water breaking through a dam, the ash dragon flooded through her.

Leiyn soared on molten wings.

Returning to her body, flames spread through her limbs. But now, it was a cleansing fire: where it traveled, bones mended, and blood clotted, and flesh knitted back together. She blinked open gummy eyes, sucked in a breath. Though the air was agony, it was a pain she could embrace.

The pain of being alive.

The titan's esse churning inside her, she rose to her feet and cuffed her eyes clean. She lowered her hands to her swords' hilts. She faced her enemy once more.

Man'nah had halted several paces away, watching her, making no further advancement. His gaping eyes burned with more life than they had until that point.

He could have killed me. Why he didn't scarcely mattered now. It didn't change what she had to do.

Leiyn drew her falchions and stormed forward. As she closed the gap, she wielded the abundant lifeforce within her as

Xepi had taught her, channeling it into strength and speed beyond her normal capacity. She slashed, and her blade cut through the air so swiftly she could barely follow its movement.

Man'nah melted to the side, then struck back with viper quickness.

She went tumbling back, her right arm flailing, the sword falling from her now-numb hand. Leiyn spared a glance to see her shoulder in a bloody ruin, white bone sticking out from beneath torn flesh. Her stomach bucked, but already, the magic flowed toward the wound, repairing the connective tissue and closing the gaping hole. In moments, the pain turned from nauseating to a mere throb.

But there was a deeper ache settling inside her, one that had less to do with her body and more with her soul. Using the mahia so much in so short a span took its toll. Even with a titan's esse fueling her, she couldn't take many more hits.

"Yes," Man'nah murmured as he advanced, the ground whispering the word with him. "This... heat in our limbs, fire in our souls. The long, cold seasons have lacked for this. We must savor it."

It was a partial answer; he was enjoying the contest, enjoying her suffering. Leiyn bared her teeth and snarled as she stalked forward.

She didn't rush him this time, knowing any element of surprise was lost. Instead, she treated him as she would anyone in a bout at the Wilds Lodge, clearing her mind and settling into her training. Watching, waiting, keeping balanced and weapons at the ready. Evaluating strengths and weaknesses, weighing her opponent against herself. Knowing he would be faster than her, figuring out how to use that to her advantage.

The lyshan seemed content to circle her, appraising her just as she did him. Only he was a stalking predator, and she had to fight hard not to feel like prey.

It came to her then. *When he strikes, he commits. He doesn't second-guess.* It was the reason her arrow had landed. He'd misjudged the timing and didn't deviate from his course.

She held to that small insight and hoped it would be enough.

"You truly are one of them." Man'nah made a lazy gesture, his wrist folding unnaturally back, seeming to gesture to something beyond her shoulder. "Your beast betrays you."

She was so focused on the contest that only at the lyshan's words did Leiyn notice the presence looming behind her. The ash dragon had materialized, its blinding esse billowing out in a torrent. Only now, instead of the scathing winds eroding her inner fire, they fueled it. Even that only went so far to even the odds.

Focus. Let him make a mistake.

Man'nah moved. Ash swirled up in a cloud in the place where he'd stood. Leiyn tried to follow his movement, falchions raised and crossed in defense, but she was too slow. The lyshan slithered around the blades, arm snaking out under them, then—

She slammed to the ground, leg crooked, hip shattered.

Gasping, swimming to stay above the red flood threatening to drown her, Leiyn grasped at the ash dragon's esse. He yielded it willingly, pouring it into her quicker than she could use it.

Moments later, Leiyn rose again. The ache inside had expanded, like a migraine spreading throughout her body. The integrity of her Iritu armor had eroded as well. One or two more blows, and it would offer no protection at all.

Man'nah waited a dozen paces away while she recovered, his smile cruel and wide. She guessed that he sought to prolong the contest and its pleasures a little longer.

It came to her then. She was beginning to know him, even as foreign and mad as he was. She thought she knew how he would proceed, perhaps even where he would strike next. He thought he had her figured out.

This wasn't her fight to win; it was his to lose. At his first mistake, she had to be ready to take advantage.

Leiyn forced a rigid smile, then put on her best mocking tone. "I hope you're enjoying yourself, Man'nah, Legion, whatever you call yourself. That you don't tire quickly of your game.

Because I can keep going as long as you can. You can break me, again and again, and I will only—"

He struck before she finished speaking. But she was ready.

Her falchions started in defensive positions, long across her body to cover the widest amount of space. But as Man'nah moved, Leiyn shifted so the points extended outward.

Her body was exposed, vulnerable. Odds were, she wouldn't survive his next attack.

But neither would he.

The lyshan dodged around where her swords had been covering her, blurring forward to strike her left flank, which she had left slightly exposed. Her side exploded, and she began to collapse, but Leiyn forced her body into one last act.

A pressure on her arms, and the lyshan skewered himself on her falchions.

Leiyn collapsed to her knees. The magic had faded from her tunic and jerkin, and her body had taken the brunt of the blow. Her ribs were shattered, and from the roiling agony in her gut and the wetness to her breathing, her organs hadn't been spared.

But she clung to the falchions, driving them in deeper, and watched the artifacts spread their poison.

Man'nah froze before he tried twisting away. Her mahia showed the damage spreading through him, for where the titan-bone blades touched, his lifeforce died. The lyshan lord had accumulated hundreds of souls, thousands, yet in moments, they were eaten away by the creeping darkness.

This was his judgment, his reward.

Her revenge.

While her arms clung to the sword hilts, she seized him with her mahia. Even weakened as she was, the ash dragon still filled her. Together, they were more than a match for the shadow that remained of the lyshan. As he stilled under her grip, she rose. His face was a rictus of horror, almost human in its rawness. The truth of his fate had settled in.

Every moment he degraded, she mended: her ribs regrowing,

her innards repairing. The overuse of mahia sickened her, weakness whittling away her resolve.

But she had enough strength to see this through.

Leiyn leaned close, watching as the light faded in the cold eye sockets, as the body became as dark and stony as it appeared.

"That is enough, Oldsoul."

She jerked her head up to set eyes on the newcomer, though she already knew who it would be. Sharo stood only steps behind his old master, a slight curve to his fleshless lips. If the sight of her victory and the titan looming behind her intimidated him, he didn't show it.

"Sharo," she snarled. Even then, at the point of her victory and the height of power, his appearance struck fear through her. She wondered if he had come to finish the fight his lord had begun, though it seemed unlike him.

"You have done well," he crooned, "marvelously so. And with a *kainox* at your back." Sharo eyed the ash dragon for a moment, his smile never faltering. "Truly, you are our ancestral enemy reborn, the first in generations uncounted."

Leiyn had to fight to resist the confusion of his words, clinging instead to her purpose. "Leave me. Now. I need to finish your master."

The lyshan cocked his head. "But that would not suit my purposes."

They stared hard at each other while Leiyn tried to understand his intentions. *He doesn't want the thrill of the fight. He wants power, just like he's always said.*

The thought was like a key in a lock. Now, she knew what his machinations had been leading to. What it all meant.

Who was her true enemy.

"It wasn't Man'nah that did all you claimed he did," she said slowly. "He couldn't have. His mind was fragmented, his goals at odds. He was powerful, more powerful than you, but he wasn't cunning or subtle."

Rage grew in her again, and her voice trembled as the words ripped free.

"It's you. *You* are Ilberia's puppet master. The one who started the war. Who killed everyone at the Wilds Lodge."

The lyshan only raised his hand, palm facing the sky, in that unknown gesture that seemed like a shrug. "It was a ruse that could only continue until you faced Man'nah. If you survived, you were bound to uncover the truth."

"*Feshtado* bastard!"

She wanted to pull her blades free and run them through the deceitful skin-walker, the consequences be damned. But even if Man'nah wasn't her ultimate enemy, he would still try to kill her given half a chance. She had to see him to his grave first.

Sharo lowered his hand, his expression smoothing. "But you have served your purpose for now. Leave the rest of him to me—I have other plans for his essence."

Leiyn shook her head, her braid whipping over her shoulder. "I'm not doing a damned thing for you!"

The smile returned. "It was not a request."

The world rippled. The ash dragon roared. Her mahia's hold on Man'nah ripped away, and Leiyn hurtled backwards.

Then she came to a halt. She blinked furiously, orienting to the change. Her hands were still raised and gripping the swords, but the lyshan skewered upon them had disappeared.

Sharo had stolen Man'nah from her.

But even as she snarled in frustration, her surroundings seized her attention. She no longer stood alone in the Iritu ruin.

A battle raged around her.

47

AN END TO DEATH

For a moment, Leiyn could do no more than take in the chaotic scene.

It quickly became apparent that the lyshans were fighting for their lives—and losing. She could scarcely believe who it was that tore through their ranks.

Dryvans and Gasts fought against their enemies, side by side.

There were familiar faces among them. At the foot of the stairs leading up to Man'nah's throne, Ata wrestled with a lyshan, her silver-furred face twisted with wrath. No sooner had she pried back his arms than a Gast warrior leaped forward to stab a spear through its middle—an Iritu spear, by the darkness that ate at his esse. As the warrior stumbled back, Leiyn glimpsed their face. Her heart soared.

"Teya!" she shouted across the ruined city.

The scout whirled. Catching sight of Leiyn, Teya flashed a grin. But her expression hardened again as she hunted for her next victim, then ran off in pursuit.

They weren't the only ones she recognized. As Leiyn scanned the battle, she saw the other dryvans she knew. Mooneyes, the owl-faced dryvan, thrust a taloned hand into the chest of an enemy, ichor spraying up his arm. The wolf-shaped skin-walker tore at the same enemy's throat. On the other side of the ruins, Acalan fought with Nahui and Coyoti against a lyshan they had cornered, its body painted with amber blood.

Everywhere she looked, enemies were falling. Only a few remained alive, and these either fled or were swiftly being dispatched. Though the bodies littering the ground showed their gains had been dearly bought, the fray was all but won.

Closer at hand, Ata threw aside the dying lyshan she held and smiled wide at Leiyn. Her fur was matted and stained red and gold, yet her lifeforce still shone brightly.

"Killed him, did you, Awakener?" she called to her.

Leiyn could only shrug, abruptly reminded that she had left one adversary alive. It brought an idea to mind.

"Ata," she shouted back, "can you infiltrate a lyshan's grotto? I need to get to Sharo!"

The skin-walker strode smoothly over to her, angled eyes scanning for any signs of threat. Seeing none, her gaze settled back on Leiyn as she stopped several paces before her, a frown settling into her features.

"He is beyond our reach, Leiyn. For now." Seeing Leiyn's expression, the dryvan grimaced. "He dealt you a grievous wound, did he not?"

The words spilled forth. "It was him, Ata. It was Sharo all along! He's behind the Lodge burning, Ilberia's betrayal. Somehow, he's been directing the Caelrey and the Altacura. And I let him get away."

Ata seemed to consider this as she watched the last of the lyshans die to the Iritu axe Acalan wielded. "Him, and not Man'-nah." She nodded, the frown settling into some deeper emotion. A sorrow remembered, it seemed. "I should have known. He always was a clever one."

"You know him?"

"Yes, once. Long, long ago." The dryvan's expression smoothed. "You mortals must attend to your fallen. My kin and I will scour these dead lands for any who hide nearby. Perhaps Sharo will make a mistake."

With a final shake of her body, the *sach'aan* strode off toward the wolf dryvan, who was licking his paw and cleaning his muzzle. Nearby, Mooneyes preened his feathers, amber dripping from his beak.

The Gasts had slowly converged on her location, Teya and Acalan leading the group. Leiyn was surprised to see both Tinoch and Ilaoti among those fighting. Even more shocking was the Red Hawk chieftainess giving her a sharp nod, even if it remained reluctant.

Teya didn't seem harmed, wearing more of the enemies' blood than her own. Heedless of the ichor staining them both, she wrapped her arms tightly about Leiyn. She returned the embrace, breathing in the reek of battle upon the scout. Teya's esse soothed as it touched hers. When Leiyn stepped away, she scrubbed at her eyes and flashed the scout a quick smile before facing Acalan.

The chieftain had suffered more. Other than the deep scratches on his exposed skin, he limped, his Iritu armor showing where he'd received a blow to his thigh. His eyes were alive with battle-fire, but it was quickly receding as the conflict ended.

"You are rash as ever, Huntress," he rasped. "I am grateful."

"We struck a great blow today." Teya, too, looked filled with fire, hers still raging hot. "A dozen lyshans dead when we once thought they could not be killed!"

"And Man'nah as well," Leiyn added.

They stared at her, wonder and something darker filling their expressions. The Gast warriors behind muttered among themselves, and Ilaoti glared with narrowed eyes. Leiyn withstood it, waiting.

"You did that?" Teya asked in a hushed voice. "By yourself?"

"Not entirely. It's a long story."

For a moment, she touched upon the thread still connecting her to the ash dragon, who once again slumbered deep in the ground. She wasn't sure when he'd left, though he must have sensed the danger had passed.

"Then the telling will wait." Acalan looked around at the

others with them, a score of Gast warriors and scouts. "Gather the fallen. We will burn them with honor rites here.

Teya leaned close to Leiyn. "After this, all the tribes must follow Acalan. Through you and your dryvan allies, he has saved us."

And Baltesia will have its allies.

She should have felt happy. She'd slain the Gasts' tormentor and inadvertently led the charge against the lyshans. Yet the victory felt hollow, or at least incomplete.

"That's good," was all she said in response.

Teya frowned but said nothing more.

⌒ ⌒

The pyre burned high and hot with the Gasts' dead.

As many warriors had fallen as still stood, and the mood had turned solemn. Yet after the words of remembrance were spoken, and the flesh burned away to blackened bones, there seemed a lightness to the movements of those who remained.

Their war is won. Though Sharo and a few lyshans remained at large, Man'nah's reign of terror had been broken. She tried to feel their joy, to know the relief that must bring. But her own troubles and her sagging strength brought her spirits to the ashy dirt at their feet.

Still standing amid the Iritu ruin, she sought distraction by asking how the battle had come about. Teya explained it all.

"When you disappeared with that lyshan..." The scout paused, staring into the distance, emotions crossing her face. Leiyn smiled to see it. She took Teya's hand and pressed it.

"I went willingly," she offered, only realizing a moment after that possibly made matters worse.

Teya snorted a laugh and caught her eye. "I understand, Redlock. I saw your bravado as soon as I set eyes on you."

Not knowing what to say, Leiyn only shrugged.

The scout continued. "We set off to search the Fingers, but the drums called us back soon after we left. I did not want to go, but I could sense the strangers who had arrived at Qasaar. It was the only thing that made me return, for they stood a better chance of finding you than I."

"The dryvans," Leiyn murmured.

Teya nodded. "Your friend, Foxfur? She not only survived but brought all the other skin-walkers to fight with her—nine others, by my count. You should have seen Toa Ilaoti's expression! I thought she would fall dead on the spot."

A smile alighted on Leiyn's lips. "Wish I could have seen it."

"Foxfur was injured, but she seemed determined to follow you. I was not about to stay behind. Toa Acalan rallied two score more, and wearing the Iritu artifacts, the dryvans brought us... here." The scout swept her arm around, an eyebrow raised at the strange ruin.

"The lyshans were caught by surprise, but we lost many in that initial wave." Teya's expression darkened as she glanced at the smoldering pyre amidst the derelict city. "But the artifacts worked as promised, and the lyshans began to fall. Yet even with victory coming nearer, I think we would have faltered had we not seen you appear."

Leiyn stared at her. "Appear?"

The scout pressed her hand and grinned. "You and the *kainox*! Never in my days did I believe I would see such a thing. The titan awoke, rising from the ground in a cloud of black smoke—then you appeared in just the same way. I did not understand why then but thinking on what you and Xepi have been up to..." Teya gave her a shrewd look. "You called the dragon, did you not?"

Leiyn grimaced. "Yes."

"As I thought. So I knew, though you must be in a match of your own, one I could not assist in, that you were still alive and had allies to help. That gave me and the others the courage to fight on."

I appeared like an ash dragon. Leiyn shook her head free of the strange thought. "I only partially succeeded, Teya. Sharo... he's the one I should have killed."

The scout drew her close to clasp her hand to the back of Leiyn's neck, drawing her gaze up to hers. "You did a good thing, Redlock, a very good thing. You won my people's war, and I am grateful."

Even feeling as she did, Leiyn couldn't resist a smile. "Not alone," she reminded her softly.

"No," Teya agreed, then her lips found Leiyn's.

It was almost nightfall by the time Ata returned with Mooneyes. Judging by her dark expression, Leiyn guessed she hadn't found Sharo. The owl-faced dryvan appeared bored, returning to preening his feathers as his kin spoke to Leiyn and the Gast warriors.

"They have either fled or are hiding," Ata's eyes slid over to Leiyn. "We have done all we can. I do not expect they will have the will for fighting soon, though their threat is not entirely gone."

The cheer that had been welling up among the band faded to solemn nods. Acalan stepped forward and turned back.

"Do not mistake the *sach'aan*," he said. "We have won a great victory today. There are always more battles on the morrow. But for today, our war has ended."

The whoops burst forth from the warriors then. Tinoch burst out with a laugh, and Ilaoti softened to clasp arms with him. Leiyn smiled to see it, a bit more of the day's accomplishments seeping in.

For however long they last.

As the celebration died down, Ata spoke again. "Mooneyes and I will return you to your home when you are ready."

When everyone had gathered close, the dryvan called over her companion, who sighed and slowly complied. Leiyn stood near Teya's side, strangely nervous as she watched Ata. The dryvan, observant as always, smiled at her with a bit of her old mischief.

"You will barely notice," she said, just before the world shattered.

Leiyn groaned as reality stitched back together around her. Her soul felt as if it had stretched and snapped back together. Her legs trembled beneath her. Only pride and stubbornness kept her standing.

Their surroundings had changed, and they now stood in the middle of the Spire Plaza. A din rose around them as the people filling it crowded close. The stench of the war party, of blood and sweat and lyshan ichor, suddenly felt choking.

Teya clasped her hand, her aura reassuring. Leiyn sucked in a breath, then released it. She calmed by slow measures, the panic subsiding.

Damn the Saints, I hate crowds.

Slowly, she found the mood of the crowd infecting her. Ata and Mooneyes retreated, being given a wide berth by the Gasts, while Acalan stepped forth and roared, "We have prevailed!"

The Many Tribes answered with a roar of their own, the sound thundering down the streets. Teya grinned, and Leiyn smiled with her. She found herself clasping arms with those who had fought with them. The weakening sickness threading through her eased enough that she almost felt light again, like she hadn't nearly died several times just hours before.

This is why we fought. This is what we gained.

It wasn't the justice she craved, the justice Tadeo and the other fallen rangers deserved. It wouldn't stop the machinations from churning against Baltesia.

But in that moment, for that day, it was enough.

PART VIII

THE OTHER WAR

48

THIRTEEN YEARS BEFORE

As promised, Leiyn departed Folly with Tadeo the next day. He had ridden a horse there and brought a mule along to load down with the supplies he'd come to fetch before winter. She glimpsed some of the items as he packed them away: knives and tools, needles and spools of thread, even a few jugs of some sweet-smelling ale. Things far more suited to a farmhouse, she thought, but it only went to show how much she still had to learn of rangers.

Before they left, the lodgemaster attended to her needs as well. His influence seemed great enough in Folly that the mayor's house was opened to them. Mayor Itzel, as she came to know the short, pretty woman, first cast a critical eye over Leiyn, then had her bathed, clothed in new garments, and fed in short order. Leiyn was both impressed and intimidated by the mayor, and she wasn't sure which feeling was the stronger.

Her needs taken care of after months of neglect, Leiyn became suddenly sleepy, and she was escorted by the mayor's manservant to a bed in the loft. It was nothing remarkable, yet after sleeping in fields and tree hollows all summer and autumn, it felt like the most luxurious bed she'd ever occupied.

The morning after passed in a whirlwind of activity. Under Tadeo's instructions, Leiyn helped to pack the mule, then awkwardly climbed atop the ranger's horse and seated herself behind him. It was uncomfortable to be pressed against the back of a man she had only met the day before, her arms about his waist when she needed to steady herself, but not as much as she would have thought. Already, she started to trust him, even when she'd never expected to trust again.

Over the days of travel that followed, an easy rapport grew, and Leiyn was soon teasing the lodgemaster as she would have her father. Other times, they were quiet, and even the silence was comfortable and familiar.

The wilderness became thicker, the trails increasingly rugged, and their path led steadily upward, the land rising as it neared the northern mountains. Their peaks were often lost behind the trees, and Leiyn wondered how Tadeo knew where he was going, for the path they followed was not always readily apparent. Yet the ranger never seemed lost; to the contrary, he often wore a small smile as they rode.

He belongs here. She wondered if she would as well. When she breathed in the air, thick with foreign but wholesome scents, she thought she might.

In the afternoon of the fourth day, the forest opened into a field that rose to a hill. Tadeo stopped and glanced over his shoulder. Leiyn, looking around, didn't immediately see why he paused. Then her eyes found the dark shape above them, and her eyes widened.

"Is that it?" she asked, working hard to keep the eagerness from her voice. "The Wilds Lodge?"

Tadeo smiled. "Yes. Your new home."

Home. Leiyn let the word fill her, seeing if it fit, and was surprised it did. She took it, made it her own. A grin spread across her face. Warmth filled her chest.

The ranger led them up the hill, through the gently waving golden grass to the sprawling buildings above. The Silvertusk Sierra, its mountain tops tinged with snow already, rose into view. Staring around them, Leiyn could only think one thing to herself, over and over again.

I am home.

49

EXODUS

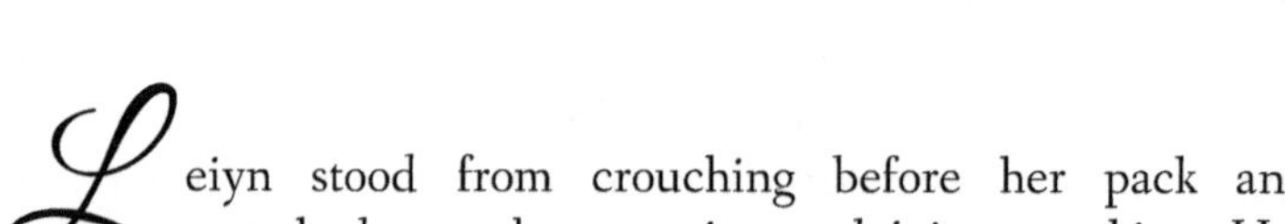

*L*eiyn stood from crouching before her pack and stretched, muscles groaning and joints creaking. Her wounds had healed, but the memories of them refused to fade. Somehow, the bruises seemed to go soul-deep, for there was blackness there where none had been before.

They will heal, she told herself, hoping it was true.

It had been a month since the battle with the lyshans. A month since she killed Man'nah and learned the truth about Sharo. A month since she'd summoned an ash dragon and merged with it.

She still struggled to believe any of it had truly happened, but her lingering connection with the titan was an insistent reminder. Enough time had passed to dull its novelty, and occasionally, she even forgot its presence. Yet whenever she used her mahia, there it remained, an awareness of the dragon slumbering in the fires deep below.

How she might use the titan to her advantage, she scarcely dared consider, yet she had been a ranger too long to do otherwise. A titan's power was a powerful weapon; of that, there was no doubt. Yet using it was like loosing an uncertain arrow in high wind. She didn't know the first thing about what it meant, much less how to use it. All she had accomplished thus far had been guided by Zuma's spark through memory and intuition, and those had their limits.

Too many questions still crowded her head. Would the connection remain indefinitely, or could it be severed? If she tried to command the dragon, would it turn on her, or obey? Was there a price to be paid for its allegiance, a debt she had little inkling of? What more power did it possess, and how could she wield it?

She had tried uncovering the answers, but to little success. Mother Xepi didn't know, and Zuma couldn't tell her. This was a task left solely to her. She prayed she was up to it.

I have to be.

Sooner or later, she would have need of the titan, for she meant to find and confront Sharo. As of yet, no one had seen any sign of the lyshan. She guessed they wouldn't until he chose to reveal himself. He was an enemy who preferred the shadows and to let others fight his battles. Only once she had cut off all avenues of escape could she hope to corner him.

Until then, she meant to ensure she had the means to kill him. Sharo knew her tricks, and he lacked Man'nah's death wish. To overcome him, she would need not only an ash dragon's alliance, but a mastery over mahia unknown by Gasts and colonists alike.

Is that all? a part of her mocked.

In the meantime, other concerns rose to the forefront of her mind. No matter how ill-suited the role felt, Leiyn remained the sole envoy of Baltesia. So it was that the day after the battle, Acalan had roped her into meetings with the Tetrad. She bore witness to their many discussions of their future course.

Despite the agreement earlier made, it was not as simple a decision as she'd hoped. Ilaoti had predictably tried to rescind her agreement to the terms Isla brought to Governor Mauricio. "If they do not yield the land rightfully ours," she challenged, "what then, Acalan? Should we fight and die in their war?"

Leiyn had no choice but to stand and speak out. "The Lord

Governor is an honorable man. He will uphold the agreement if you do."

Acalan rumbled after her. "Would you allow the outlanders to be more trustworthy than us? We need allies, Ilaoti, not more enemies. None will forget the blood spilled between our peoples, but I refuse to pass the burden onto a new generation. Fresh bonds can be formed, and old feuds be buried, if we let them."

His dark eyes found hers. Leiyn nodded, glad once more he was her ally as well as friend.

Eventually, the Red Hawk leader was ground down by argument and reason. The other two were all too happy to acquiesce to Acalan a new title: Toa'Yao, which translated to "war chieftain." He would lead the forces south to aid in the Baltesian war of independence, given full authority over all the warriors, no matter which tribe they hailed from.

When she was finally relieved of her duties, Leiyn all but collapsed into bed. *I didn't let you down,* she thought to Isla. *Though you could have done it better.* She wondered where her friends were on their journey, if they'd reached Southport yet. She wondered if Mauricio truly would give in to the demands.

He will. He must.

She put the thought from her mind. It was a matter for another day. And with the discussions at an end, a host of fresh concerns announced themselves, the first of which had come with Ata's departure.

Following her transfer of the Gast warriors and Leiyn back to Qasaar, the dryvan had disappeared for a time, only returning to bid a final farewell. Caught in the middle of the negotiations atop the Whisperspire, Leiyn had been all too happy to be pulled away after Ata appeared in the chamber. Amid the scowling chieftains and Teya fighting to keep a smile down, Leiyn went with her to a grotto, where they emerged atop Lualli. The city below was silent and empty, unsettlingly so. She wondered if this was its future. If the Many Tribes managed to gain back their ancestral lands, why would any remain behind in this forbidding land? Yet somehow, it seemed a shame to abandon it entirely.

The dryvan was strangely somber as she stared out over the Barren. The low howl of the incessant desert winds filled the air. Leiyn pursed her lips, waiting a few moments before asking one of the many questions needling her.

"You and Sharo—what's between you two?"

Ata's eyes slid to her, her form unnaturally still, but for the rustle of her silver fur in the breeze.

"We Iritu were a single people once, long ago," the dryvan said. "At the end, there were so few of us. Each of those I have killed, I knew well. I can name them still. Yav. Lilis. Seni." A sigh, like the groaning of an old oak in a storm, rose from within her. "But Sharo has been the only one I have missed."

"You were intimate?"

A shadow of Ata's fey smile appeared. "Something like that."

Leiyn let it lie, figuring the dryvan would tell her when and if she wanted to. Still, she couldn't help wondering what manner of intimacy it had been. A long-lost brother was a far cry from a jilted lover.

"I will keep watch for him," the dryvan said, her voice halfway to a growl. "The old barriers still stand. Should he be so foolish as to cross the mountains, Eld will know, and so shall I."

Hesitating a moment, Leiyn decided to risk another question. "So that's why they did all this? To build up their strength in order to cross the mountains?"

Ata's eyes gathered a fox-like slyness. "Motivations among my people are complicated. You must know this after spending time with me."

Leiyn grinned. "I suppose I do." Her thoughts turned back to Sharo, and the smile slipped away. "Can we not seek him out?"

The wind rose, a hundred mournful voices seeming to commiserate with Leiyn's plight.

Ata wore a hard expression, her emerald eyes gleaming. "No. He can evade me for as long as he likes, as he has always been able to do. But it will not be long, Leiyn. He will not wait until your short life is over."

"That's comforting," Leiyn muttered.

A smile touched the dryvan's lips, and a hint of sharp teeth showed behind them. "He feels the movements of the world, as do I. The restlessness of the Vast Ones." She turned and jabbed a clawed finger at Leiyn's chest. "That has much to do with you."

Leiyn frowned. "Why? What do I have to do with anything?"

"Did you not wonder at what Sharo called you? 'Oldsoul'?"

"Of course. But he said a lot I didn't understand." Leiyn hesitated, but she'd never been one to hold back for long. "I don't suppose you'd tell me. As a friend?"

Ata yipped a laugh and walked over to the edge of the cliff, so close that her talons hung off the edge. Pebbles scattered down the precipitous drop.

"Your power is like that of your ancestors, the ones who conquered my people, the Vast Ones, and the very land itself. In you, that magic comes alive again. It is a rebirth, or perhaps, an evolution."

Leiyn scowled off toward the distant wardstones, black against the hazy horizon. "That's a long way of saying little."

"I don't think this is a thing that can be explained, young one. You must discover it for yourself."

The dryvan suddenly pivoted and walked away from the cliff to the mountains at their backs. Leiyn hesitated, then sighed and followed.

No point in chasing lost prey. It was a lesson every ranger knew. Besides, no matter what others called her, she knew she would always be a ranger first.

"What now?" Leiyn asked after a dozen strides. "What will you do next?"

"Now. Next." Ata glanced at her sidelong. "Always caught up in the flow of time, mortals are, like flotsam in a river."

"So it's back to riddles, is it? Some friend you are."

"And I thought friends were fond of teasing." Ata didn't slow her walk, though where she meant to go was beyond Leiyn. As far as she could tell, all the dryvan needed to do to travel was will it.

Ata spoke again. "If it eases your time-worry, there will come a time when I find you again. Thanks to our little friend here." She tapped a claw to the eruption of fur at her breast and smiled.

Chispa. Leiyn wondered how the fox felt, nestled in the dryvan's esse as he was. Her lifesense felt after him, sifting through the skin-walker to find him. When Ata first appeared at the Whisperspire in her new form as Foxfur, Leiyn hadn't been able to distinguish him. It spoke much of how she'd progressed that it took mere moments to find him.

Ata must have felt her seeking, for she smiled. "He is another sign that *Rétori*, the World Beneath, is ill-satisfied. Not content to slumber any longer, nor let its children."

There was much in her words Leiyn didn't understand, as usual. She commented on the greater part.

"The world. Unera. You speak of it as if it's... alive."

The dryvan stopped and stared at her. For once, she looked astonished. Then a mischievous grin curled her lips.

"Is it not?"

The ground lurched, and Leiyn blinked. Once more, she was standing in the Whisperspire. Zyanya had been speaking, but she paused and stared at Leiyn as she appeared. After a moment's surprise, the chieftainess recovered, shaking her head with a clinking of blue beads before continuing with her point. Teya raised an eyebrow at Leiyn.

Leiyn smiled back, but only slightly. Ata was nowhere to be seen. As abruptly as she'd come, the dryvan had gone.

At least I'll have something to think about, she mused as she crossed her arms and waded through the rest of the meetings.

Ata's departure stuck like a burr in her mind, for it made Leiyn think of her own impending journey. The reminder was a pressure in her chest, growing with each passing day, an agitation that no amount of evening training could quiet, nor nightly activities with Teya. Even the clinging winter in the mountains couldn't deter her.

During the past week, Leiyn had begun making the final rounds for farewells. When she visited Xepi, she found the shaman wasn't alone in her hut. Three other small souls gathered around her. Leiyn smiled, anticipating the sight she would find.

She saw them as soon as she entered: three younglings, the oldest not more than ten summers and the youngest no older than seven. They sat cross-legged at Xepi's feet, looking up with listening obedience. Though Xepi was waxing poetic about the dangers of *semah*, the three turned back to stare at Leiyn. None were surprised by her presence. Likely, they'd always had their lifesense open, and it was as natural to rely upon as sight or smell. Their eyes were wide as they beheld her. Leiyn grinned at the blatant innocence, wondering what they'd been told about the outlander who slayed Man'nah.

Though Saints know that's enough.

Xepi frowned at their lack of discipline, then sighed and rose to her feet. "Practice looking upon each other's marks until I return."

As the children murmured their assent, the shaman ushered Leiyn back outside, then led her to the cliff's edge. For a time, they only gazed upon the sun-dazzled Barren, a sand-born haze casting it in an ethereal light.

When the silence grew long, Leiyn's curiosity drew her to the children's practice. As they attempted to view each other's lifemarks, their esses drifted from their bodies in a ghostly mist. The middle child had the most luck, seeming to use her magic with ease, while the oldest and youngest struggled.

Soon tiring of watching, Leiyn glanced at the shaman. After all her practice, Xepi's lifemark lay plain in view, and a change in its pattern drew her attention.

Where once the dying hearth had dominated, flames now blazed from the ashes.

Leiyn looked away, pretending to scrub at some grit in her eyes as she cuffed away a tear. By way of diversion, she said, "They seem willing students."

"At times. More willing than other acolytes I have had."

Turning back, Leiyn glimpsed the ghost of a smile touching the shaman's lips. She snorted a laugh, the tender feelings from before sloughing off.

"Stubbornness has its value," Leiyn retorted.

"As you have shown." As swiftly as good humor had appeared, it was gone, replaced by calm consideration. "To our good fortune and gratitude."

Leiyn looked away and shrugged. "It's all thanks to Zuma, really. Which brings me to something I wanted to ask you." She watched Xepi from the corner of her eye. "Why didn't he do as I did with the ash dragon? The titan in Southport's bay—it broke him instead of making him stronger."

The shaman nodded gravely. "I thought you might wonder this." The wind stirred through her short, wispy hair as she stared over the wasteland. "Taht Zuma was older than you knew, *Osat*. The greater portion of his *semah* was dedicated to maintaining his vitality."

Her chest tightened as she remembered the moments before the battle with Armando Pótecil's army. "Then if I hadn't taken the lifeforce he'd given me, he might have been strong enough."

"You could not have denied his gift if you were as weakened as you have said. And were you not near death when you first summoned the *kainox*? No; that alone is not the reason."

"Then what is it?"

"To have knowledge does not mean one can use it."

Leiyn turned back to the shaman. In those words was a more personal anguish than grief for a lost friend.

"Is that why you haven't done it?" she asked quietly. "Drawn upon a titan?"

"Yes."

Misery was furrowed into Xepi's brow. Like Leiyn, she hated to admit her shortcomings.

We're more alike than I'd thought.

Leiyn still searched for words to spare her pain when the shaman continued.

"I cannot submit. I have made many attempts, yet always..."

Xepi sighed, almost seeming to deflate. "In this, you are the braver."

"It's not bravery, really." Leiyn flashed her a smile. "I just don't know when to stop."

"Yes. Your strength and your weakness."

Leiyn considered that. The drive to accomplish her aim at any cost—as much grief as it had brought, it had enabled her to survive impossible trials. Yet it wasn't that understanding that made her uncomfortable, but the ability it had enabled.

In all the Veiled Lands, perhaps all of Unera, she alone wielded this titanic power.

No. Don't think of it like that. Especially when you don't know if you could do it again.

"Use it well, *Osat*. Knowledge without wisdom is a treacherous path."

A surprised laugh burst from Leiyn. "You calling me a fool, Shaman?"

Xepi only smiled.

"Probably not far wrong," Leiyn admitted, tucking her thumbs into her belt. "Much as I hate to admit you're right in anything."

"This, I know well."

Silence fell between them, interrupted by the sounds of the children's murmuring. A quick perusal with her lifesense showed they had strayed from their assigned task. Xepi evidently noticed as well, for she glanced back at them with a frown.

"I must return to the acolytes. Wait here a moment."

Her curiosity piqued, Leiyn watched the shaman shuffle inside the hut, then rifle among her possessions before returning. She guessed the identity of the ten small round objects nestled in Xepi's palm even before the shaman opened her hand.

"Amber beads," Leiyn murmured. The sunlight caught on them and made them glow as if with an inner light. The esse imbued in them made them shine brighter still.

"Take them and guard them. May they serve you as they have served me."

Leiyn held out her hand for Xepi to tip the beads into it. They were warm to the touch, each a small piece of coal. She closed her fingers around them and held them tight.

"Thank you, Xepi. For this and everything else."

The shaman nodded, then turned away. Leiyn watched her go, slightly bemused. It was as fine a goodbye as she could have expected from the woman.

With the decision of the Tetrad secured and her duties in the Gast city at an end, Leiyn had packed her belongings and made ready to head homeward.

Turning from her saddlebags, Leiyn moved to the window and leaned on the sill, peering out over Qasaar as the last of the day's light touched upon Lualli. Strange as it had seemed when she first arrived, the cliff-carved city had grown on her. Even its whispers held a certain comfort, like listening to the sighing of the wind. The Gasts' ways now felt familiar, a thing that would have been unimaginable to the young, angry woman she'd once been. Her lips twisted as she thought of the people she would leave behind, her mind latching onto one face in particular.

As if her thoughts had summoned her, Leiyn detected a woman striding up the slope toward the barracks' entrance.

Her expression lightening, she hurried downstairs to meet her at the entrance. Teya grinned and paused at the stoop.

"Ready to be rid of me?" Leiyn meant it to be a quip, but the words came out heavy.

Teya's smile faded. "You know the answer to that."

The scout entered, and Leiyn's nose was filled with her intoxicating scent. She could never get enough of it.

They embraced. Without thinking, Leiyn laid her head on her shoulder. Teya chuckled in her ear.

"I would almost think you are growing soft, Redlock. Relaxing your guard with a Gast."

"Times change," she murmured. "And some changes are good."

"Yes. Some."

They fell quiet. Leiyn was sure their thoughts had turned

toward the same thing. Hardly anything else occupied her mind of late.

Stepping away, she let her fingers glide down Teya's arms to grip her hands. Calloused and roughened from a hard life, just like hers, yet gentle when the moment called for it. Leiyn met the scout's gaze and held it.

"You're sure your warriors need a First Spear?" she ventured.

Teya smiled and squeezed her hands. "They might not, but Acalan does. Someone must balance out his surliness."

"I suppose you're the right woman for that."

Silence fell again, companionable but filled with unspoken words. Leiyn hadn't really tried to convince Teya to come with her, nor would she. They each had their duties, and neither would abandon them. It was something they held in common, and which Leiyn thought they both admired.

As much pain as it'll bring us.

"I could send someone with you," Teya offered. "Nahui would be willing."

Leiyn rolled her eyes. "And have her chatter in my ear for weeks on end? I'd rather ride one of those lizards you call mounts." She looked at her askance. "Besides, you know it's not the solitude that bothers me."

"I know."

As a third silence threatened to fall, a laugh suddenly bubbled up in Leiyn. Catching Teya's eye, she jerked her head back toward the stairs.

"I'd rather not spend our last night moping, though..."

The scout raised her eyebrows, but she grinned as Leiyn pulled her up the stairs.

50

THE WAY HOME

*L*eiyn rose before the sun and slipped into her gear.

It wasn't the right time to cross the mountains. Warm as it was down near the Barren, the snows would linger along the range for months to come, sometimes piled as high as she. Avalanches were a rising danger, particularly in the more navigable passes. Beasts starving from the long winter, like the snow ape she'd encountered before, would be roaming the foothills.

But she had to risk it. With spring's coming, the war would come alive in full, if it hadn't continued all through the season. Baltesia and her friends needed her tidings and her bow. Mauricio had to know that they didn't stand alone, and aid was on its way.

And, if she were honest, there were other reasons to go. As much as she enjoyed her time in Qasaar, Leiyn had long grown restless. She had learned more over the months than she thought possible and become closer to being the woman Tadeo had always believed she could be. But only in change could she continue to grow. A ranger never lay idle for long.

By the time Teya sat up in bed, Leiyn was clothed with her weapons belt on, falchions and quiver hanging from it along with a pouch that held Xepi's amber beads. Her ranger cloak, preserved from the worst of the damage the rest of the outfit had suffered, was secured at her collarbone, the familiar weight of it comforting. Her longbow leaned by the doorway.

All was ready, but for one thing.

Teya cuffed her eyes and blinked at her, knees curled up to her chest. She didn't wear clothes to bed, and Leiyn's eyes lingered long enough to provoke the scout's grin.

"Should have thought about that before you dressed," Teya pointed out.

Leiyn sighed and looked away. She didn't have to say how much she would miss Teya. The words hung heavy between them, a dark cloud promising rain.

The scout swung her legs off the bed and pulled on her smallclothes. "You are different, now. Than when you came."

Leiyn looked down. Her clothes were certainly different. Having felt the protection of Iritu garb, she'd gained permission to take a fresh set with her. Its colors were still too bright for her liking, the tunic dyed a deep aquamarine and gold, but the trousers were at least a simple tan. She figured she could go unnoticed if she covered up with her cloak. Two quivers of the Iritu arrows she also took with, as well as the falchions that had served her well in the fight against Man'nah.

But she knew that was not what Teya meant.

"Yes," Leiyn murmured. "I am."

Her smallclothes secured, Teya rose and padded across the stone to her. Leiyn liked the nervous tingling that seeing her approach put in her belly, and even more when she cupped the nape of Leiyn's neck.

"I like this form of you," Teya whispered, then brushed her lips.

Too soon, the scout pulled away with a teasing smile. She traced a finger down Leiyn's chest, and Leiyn had to fight to keep down a shiver.

"Something to remember me by," Teya said as she fetched the rest of her clothes.

Leiyn sighed, but knew it was best not to delay. Her journey wasn't the only thing she would be putting off. Downstairs, Tozi was bustling in the kitchen, the clamor evidence of his preparing more food for her departure. Outside, Acalan stood waiting, while Xepi slowly made her way up the cliff.

She smiled. She'd found more than a temporary home here. Teya wouldn't be the only friend she left behind.

Hefting her saddlebags and taking her longbow in hand, Leiyn followed Teya down the stairs. No sooner had they come in view of the kitchen than a voice cried out, "A moment, Ranger Leiyn!"

Turning, she saw Tozi had several sacks on a table, each beginning to spill over with the hardbread, salted meats, and dried fruit strips he'd filled them with.

"That's more than enough, Tozi." Leiyn wondered how she was going to transport them all. *At least it's Feral that has to carry them,* she thought as Teya hefted the sacks, grimacing at their weight.

The caretaker acquiesced, wiping his sheening brow with a sleeve. "You will be missed, Ranger. Thank you for all you have done for us. Truly, you are a blessing from *Tlalli!*"

Vaguely embarrassed, she set aside her bow to offer her arm. Tozi gripped it back with enthusiasm.

"Thanks, Tozi. I'll have to roll down the mountains with all this to feed me."

Leaving the caretaker beaming, Leiyn exchanged an amused glance with Teya, then took up her bow and followed the scout from the barracks. Xepi now stood with Acalan. Both turned at their appearance.

"We will see you off," Acalan rumbled. "To the edge of the city, at least."

Xepi nodded. Leiyn wondered what thoughts turned behind her eyes. The shaman's expression seemed stern even for her.

She didn't ask, however, but only led their small company up the rise to the stable. The stablehands had risen early to prepare Feral for her departure. Over the long stay, the grooms had worn down the unruly mare so she grudgingly allowed them to handle her. Even still, the girl who handed her off looked relieved to see the back of the horse.

With her bite, Leiyn mused, *who wouldn't?*

She ran a hand quickly over Feral's snout, grinning as the mare snapped at her. "Come on, old girl," she said. "Best get along. We have a long way ahead of us."

As Leiyn secured the numerous bags, Feral grew even more discontent. Leiyn was glad to stay on foot with the others and lead the mare. Once they reached the bend in the road, where it branched between the training yards and the path south, she turned back to her companions. They'd stopped as well, forming a small semi-circle around her, all glancing at one another.

Teya gestured at the shaman. "Taht Xepi, you had best start. Mine should wait for last."

Leiyn winced and held up her hand. "That's not necessary. Farewells were never my thing."

Xepi eyed her. "I will say only this. You have been blessed, Leiyn, and every blessing is given for a reason. Do not waste yours."

Cheery as always. But Leiyn held back the goad and nodded. In truth, she suspected there was more than a kernel of wisdom in the shaman's words.

Acalan drew her gaze with the intensity of his own. "There is a saying among our people," he said. "'One who returns never left.' I will bring our warriors south by the next autumn's end. We will meet your enemies together."

"Thank you, Acalan." She gave him a smile, and he returned a tight one of his own. A memory flashed in her mind of when she'd held him at arrowpoint, believing him and his people to be evil, the enemy responsible for her mother's death and many of the ills of Baltesians.

How far we've come. How far I have.

Teya stepped forward and took Leiyn's hands, drawing her back to the moment. She stared into the scout's nut-brown eyes and never wanted to look away.

"I will see you soon," Teya murmured. "Only have to last a season or two apart."

"Yes." It was all Leiyn could think to say. Her chest already ached.

Teya leaned forward, kissed her, then stepped back. Nothing more needed to be said. Leiyn let her touch linger before dropping her arms.

She paused a moment longer, looking between the three, the friends and allies she was leaving behind.

At least they're better off for my coming.

It made her proud to think that, to know it was true. That she'd brought a measure of peace to the world, and not just violence.

But as the farewell tarried, her discomfort grew too great to bear. Leiyn cleared her throat, then halfway turned. "Guess that's it," she spoke to the horizon, then glanced back at the three. "I'm off."

With that, she mounted Feral, the mare only sidestepping a little to try and confound her. Settling into the saddle, Leiyn pressed in her heels, starting the mare up the narrow path. Only when she'd gone several steps further did she look back. Teya raised a hand, and Leiyn raised hers in return. Her cheeks ached from smiling as she faced forward.

She continued up the mountain path.

Leiyn had long dreaded this moment, the departure. Yet as she settled into it, Qasaar growing distant behind her along with her friends, Leiyn felt an excitement buzz through her. The road had always called to her, with its yen for exploration of the unknown. Only in solitude did she know her own mind.

A ranger belongs on the road, Tadeo had once said. It had been one of the rare moments when he didn't seem to be teaching purposefully, but only confessing his own thoughts on a matter. *Walking a forest, a horse underneath, a bow in hand.*

As her ornery mare bore her up the switchbacks into the Silvertusks, Leiyn could not have agreed more.

Yet as she ascended, her thoughts turned toward what lay

ahead. War. Death. Justice to be seized or forsaken. All she didn't know of her remaining enemies. All she'd only glimpsed.

She shook her head free of the dark thoughts. For the present, she could do nothing about any of it. There was only the path, the fresh scent of the mountain terrain, and the stale pungency of Feral, cooped up as she'd been in the stable. Leiyn concentrated on the air in her lungs, the sun's heat at her back, the feeling of subtle life surrounding her. The world and the road that were her home.

Onward, she rode.

EPILOGUE

*H*e kneeled before the dying man and cupped his chin, tilting his head up to look into his eyes. There were only chasms there, darkness deepened by years of prolonged existence.

Overlong, Sharo thought, lips curling in a smile.

"This is the end, my dear, foolish master," he murmured, tightening his grip. "The rot will eat you away, soul by soul. You, who were once legion, will be no one. Nothing."

Though Sharo had slowed the contagion, too little of Man'nah remained to respond. Even in centuries of investigation, none had found how to stop the ancient malice. It would have its way, eventually.

But Sharo had never been one to let useful things go to waste.

"This way," he cooed to his dying kin, "I will preserve something of you. Though there is so little left, now."

The gloating satisfied him, filling a shallow want, but he wasted no more time on it. Seizing the bright essence inside the dying man, Sharo ripped it free of him and sucked it into himself.

The souls shrieked, then fought, then finally settled, joining the silent chorus already seething within him.

He lapped up every drop he could, then let the old leader of his people fall to the ground. Already, the world began to claim back his body, the edges of him crumbling into gray dust. No life burned in his eye sockets now.

Sharo rose and brushed off his robes, smiling as the brightness of the colors reappeared. "You were content to rule ashes," he said to the corpse. "To lapse into senescence. But we will rule far, far more."

Only after he spoke did Sharo realize his slip of the tongue. *We.* Where had it come from? Was he not the sole master of himself? He delved into his essence but found no sign of resistance.

"I," he whispered. "I will rule."

It was a momentary lapse, brought about by the transition, nothing more. Nodding, Sharo spared one last glance around him, sighed at its dreariness, then reached for his mahia.

The air shimmered, and he was gone.

AUTHOR'S NOTE

A hearty thanks from me to you, kind reader, for picking up *The First Ancestor*! I so hope you enjoyed it.

It's been a wild journey since I first started writing Ranger of the Titan Wilds. Like Legend of Tal before it, *The Last Ranger* was a turning point in my writing career. *The First Ancestor* continues that trajectory—for the better, we can only hope.

I'd love for you to be part of this series' story! One way you can pitch in is by leaving a review. Reviews, as I'm sure you know, help other readers take a chance on a new author and book.

You can leave reviews for *The First Ancestor* on Goodreads. In the summer of '23, it will be published to Amazon and Audible, where it's also very useful to receive reviews.

And if you haven't left a review for *The Last Ranger*, you can do so on Amazon and Goodreads.

If you're really loving this series, consider sharing it with a friend or two! Word of mouth is my favorite way of finding new books, and it's the strongest recommendation Ranger of the Titan Wilds could get.

The journey doesn't end here—not for Leiyn and her friends, and I hope not for you. The series will continue in the third book, *The Hidden Guardian*.

Keep an eye out for *The Hidden Guardian*'s Kickstarter near the end of '23 and for the retailer launch following that. To be sure not to miss it, follow me on Amazon or sign up for my newsletter on my website, *jdlrosell.com*.

Thanks again for reading this book. Until the next one, take care!

Josiah (J.D.L. Rosell)

APPENDIX A

THE CHARACTERS

Acalan Tikau - Chieftain of the Gast tribe the Tekuan, which translates to "Jaguars."

Adelina - A priestess at the First Temple of Baltesia in Southport.

Alma - The priestess in charge of San Hugo's Sanctuary in Southport.

Aracel - Leiyn's friend and fellow orphan at San Hugo's Sanctuary.

Arlo - The surgeon of the Wilds Lodge.

Armando Pótecil - A now-deceased conqueror, or general, of the Ilberian military.

Ata - Also known as "Hawkvine," "Rowanwalker," "Rowan," and "Foxfur." True name is "Atastmina." A dryvan whose appearance is humanoid with a blend of a hawk's features and knotted vines, and now the fur of a silver fox.

Ayda Santidad - The Altacura, or spiritual leader, of the Catedrál.

Baltesar Veda IV - The current Caelrey, or ruler, of Ilberia.

Bane - Teya's draconion.

Batu Khatas - An older plainsrider pupil of the Gazian Greathouse.

Camilo - A ranger apprentice of the Wilds Lodge.

Chispa - The silver fox who has tailed Leiyn after different points in her life. Presently merged with the dryvan, Ata.

Chuluun - A young plainsrider pupil of the Gazian Greathouse.

Coyoti - A Gast scout with an odd temperament.

Eld - A dryvan whose shape resembles a young elm tree.

Feral - The unruly, brown mare that once belonged to Lodgemaster Tadeo, and is now Leiyn's loyal steed.

Gan - A ranger of the Wilds Lodge. Originally from Altan Gaz.

Hugo - A ranger apprentice of the Wilds Lodge.

Ilaoti - A Gast chieftainess. One of the Tetrad.

Isebel - An orphan at San Hugo's Sanctuary who picks on Leiyn.

Isla Ogbi - A ranger of the Wilds Lodge. Leiyn's best friend.

Itzel of Folly - The mayor of Folly. It is a widely known secret that she has a long-standing romantic relationship with Lodgemaster Tadeo.

Joaquin - A ranger of the Wilds Lodge.

Kyaka Ndaye - The current Odisi, or ruler, of Eyi.

Leiyn of Orille - A ranger of the Wilds Lodge. Protagonist of the Ranger of the Titan Wilds series.

Man'nah - Leader of the lyshans. Said to be the strongest among them.

Marina - A ranger of the Wilds Lodge. A middle-aged, no-nonsense woman.

Mauricio di Siveña - Governor of Baltesia. Dresses like a genteel fop from Ilberia, but prides himself on his Baltesian heritage.

Mooneyes - A dryvan whose shape resembles a humanoid owl.

Naél - A ranger apprentice of the Wilds Lodge.

Nahui - A Gast scout who is small in size, but loud of voice.

Nathan - A curmudgeonly ranger of the Wilds Lodge. No one is sure how old he is, for he has been at the Lodge for as long as any remember.

Oktai of the Spears - The current Hesh Jin, or ruler, of Kalga.

Patro - A serving boy of the Wilds Lodge.

Sarnai - The surgeon of the Gazian Greathouse.

Sharo - A lyshan with uncertain aims.

Steadfast - Leiyn's black stallion. As loyal as his name implies, he barely makes any sound, not even a whicker.

Taban - A plainsrider of the Gazian Greathouse.

Tadeo of Lake's Edge - The lodgemaster of the Wilds Lodge.

Taqel - A Gast scout who has as big a personality as his size.

Teya of the Hunt - A Spear, or leader, of the *situali*, or Gast scouts.

Tinoch - An Uman chieftain. One of the Tetrad.

Tozi - A *tekip*, or caretaker, for visitors to Qasaar.

Xepi - A shaman of Qasaar who teaches Leiyn about magic.

Yolant - A ranger of the Wilds Lodge. Fond of singing for the Lodge and playing her stringed gourd.

Yul Khyan - Moorwarden of the Gazian Greathouse.

Zuma Apisi - A Gast shaman of the Tekuan tribe.

Zyanya - A Gast chieftainess. One of the Tetrad.

APPENDIX B

THE WORLD

An overview of the locations in the world of Unera.

THE VEILED LANDS
The three colonies of the Veiled Lands are also called "the Tricolonies."

Baltesia
Colony of Ilberia.

Southport - Capital of Baltesia.
Orille - Leiyn's home village.
Folly - A Titan Wilds town.
Saints' Crossing - The bridge town that spans the Gorge de Omn.
Lake's Edge - Lodgemaster Tadeo's hometown.
Breakbay - An abandoned city ringed by titans. Ruined during the Titan War.
The Wilds Lodge - The Titan Wilds stronghold of the rangers.

Altan Gaz
Colony of Kalga.

Orolt - Capital of Altan Gaz.
Helkist - Fur-trading town.
The Greathouse - Also called the *Baishin*. Stronghold of the plainsriders.

Ore-Ofe
Colony of Eyi.

Kunu - Capital of Ore-Ofe.
Lamayo - Fortified trading city; acts as a secondary capital of Ore-Ofe.
The Stormhold - Also called the *Izul*. Stronghold of the skystriders.

The Titan Wilds
Borderlands spanning the Tricolonies. In Baltesia, these lands extend beyond the Gorge de Omn.

The Barren - Arid wasteland beyond the Silvertusk Sierra.

Qasaar - Capital of the Gasts and other indigenous tribes.

THE ANCESTRAL LANDS
The continent is also called "Forye."

Ilberia
The Ilberian Union.

Vasara - Capital of Ilberia.
Refugio - Stronghold of the Catedrál; also considered a holy city.

Eyi
The Eyin Empire.

Mumsi - Capital of Eyi.
Kaiam - Important city of Eyi.

Kalga
The Kalgan Dominion.

Galkhir - Capital of Kalga.
Betgol - Important city of Kalga.

APPENDIX C

BESTIARY & BOTANICAL

BEASTS OF THE TITAN WILDS

Draconion - *Axolto* to the Gasts. A large lizard that resembles the monitor lizard of the Ancestral Lands, they have been domesticated over eons to be riding animals to the native peoples of the Veiled Lands. Docile unless threatened, they have spines along their backs except where a rider is seated. Draconions typically appear in four colors: orange, yellow, red, and black. They sometimes combine variations of these and have striped or mottled patterns.

Snow ape - A large ape with a shaggy white coat, a red snout, and blue around its eyes. An apex predator of the Silvertusk Sierra. It can be incredibly aggressive when provoked or when hungry.

Spirit animals - Little is known of the creatures that appear as animals, yet also seem to be more. Travelers through the Titan Wilds have reported being assisted by creatures who are often of silver or golden coloring. These have taken the forms of wolves, large cats, foxes, deer, and all other manner of beasts. Many believe them to be spirits from Omn, sent by the Saints to keep their followers safe. Others have reported the native peoples have stories of them as little gods taking forms that humans can understand, and that often their favors granted will someday need to be repaid.

Titans - Also called *"kainox"* by the native peoples of the Veiled Lands. Straddling the line between beasts and spirits, they appear as enormous animals or mythical creatures that ravage the land. Titans are not always present in the landscape; they "awaken" or materialize in cycles that can vary from months to years. Many appear to be tied to a certain feature in the terrain, but this does not appear to be accurate in all cases. Following is a list of the titans known thus far:

> **Ash dragon** - Volcano titan.
> **Gorge spider** - Rock titan.
> **Hill tortoise** - Earth titan.
> **Rain mammoth** - Rain titan in the shape of an elephant.
> **River serpent** - River titan.
> **Sand stampede** - Desert titan in the shape of stampeding wildebeest.
> **Sea kraken** - Ocean titan. Also called "The Wight on the Tide."
> **Tempest hawk** - Storm titan.

Thorned lion - One of the largest predators in the Titan Wilds, it typically poses little harm to humans unless starving. They have been known, however, to prey on livestock. The rangers of the Wilds Lodge have learned torches burning fennel are sufficient to drive it away from human populations. With a mane of spines, it is deadly to contend with. Aggression should be avoided whenever possible. Thorned lions typically travel alone, though females will care for their cubs until they are several years old.

Tusked jackal - An aggressive canine species known for their destruction of other animal habitats. Tusked jackals travel in packs of thirty or more and bring down their prey through numbers and ferocity. As they pose significant threats to humans and livestock, they are best driven away

Wolfdeer - A species of fanged deer that appear to be particularly aggressive. Unknown if they are carnivorous or not. Like other deer species, they travel in herds. Stags compete for the rights to mate with a herd's does. Fights have been known to be to the death. Mateless young stags often travel in a herd of their own.

PLANTS OF THE TITAN WILDS

Drybrush - A fern-like plant that shrivels upon a touch, then slowly stretches back out its leaves and limbs, regaining color and moisture and seeming to come back to life.

Echinacea - A pink flower whose extract is often used as a natural antibiotic.

Everscent - A flower that changes its aroma throughout the seasons, and sometimes over the span of a few moments. Usually, these scents are quite pleasant.

Firefruit - Aubergine berries that burn one's skin for hours. There are stories among the Gasts of using firefruit to incapacitate one's foes.

Hangman's vine - A carnivorous plant that strangles any creature unfortunate enough to be snared by it. Known by the red coloring of its vines and leaves. It is exclusively found wrapped around full-grown broad-leafed trees.Travelers are advised to be wary of which trees they rest against.

Nacatl - A mushroom found in the caves on the northern side of the Silvertusks. Has hallucinogenic qualities when ingested as a tea.

Peyotl - A cactus whose flower is used for a hallucinogenic tea by the Gast tribes.

APPENDIX D

GLOSSARY

Many of the terms not defined in previous appendices can be found here.

Akan'Oala - Translates to "Those Who Came Before." This is the name given by Gasts to their ancestors. Legend has it that they came long ago to the Veiled Lands and conquered them by benefit of their superior magic. In the eons since, time and war have robbed the Gasts and other indigenous peoples of many of these secrets, leaving their history shrouded in mystery.

The Altacura - The leader of the Catedrál. Addressed as "Gran" or "Her Sanctity." The Altacura has always been female. Many of those who reached Ascendance to become one of the five Saints have previously been the Altacura. Though officially a religious leader, by benefit of her station and the Catedrál's resources, the Altacura has traditionally wielded great power both in Ilberia and in the world at large.

Amente - Translates to "lover" in Ilberian, though usually intended in a derogatory sense; for example, a lover of Gasts, which would be seen by Ilberians and Baltesians as a negative label.

Ascendance - The process by which a person is made into a saint. Often, saints have arisen from a previous Altacura, though not exclusively. Holy miracles must be attributed to the person in order to achieve Ascendance, as do revelations of morality as divinely inspired by Omn. Only five individuals have thus far Ascended in the Catedrál's history.

The Caelrey - Also known as "the World King." The political leader of Ilberia. In practice, often has to share power with the Altacura and her Catedrál. Reigns from Vasara, the capital of Ilberia.

The Catedrál - Also called "the Holy Catedrál." A sprawling religious institution worshiping the prescience of Omn and the god's revelations. The Catedrál has largely acted as a matriarchy, with precedence given to women for positions of power. Though officially a religious institution, its significant resources and moral sway often translate to geopolitical power that its leaders are unafraid to wield.

Cloaking - The induction of a ranger apprentice into a full ranger by giving the apprentice a ranger cloak, a resilient and warm article dyed a forest green. Inducted rangers are also referred to as "cloaked rangers" by benefit of this ritual.

The Cloudholder - Leader of the Stormhold, the home of the skystriders of Ore-Ofe.

Conqueror - A general of the Ilberian military. In the colony of Baltesia, conquerors wield authority only surpassed by the Caelrey and, contentiously, the Altacura.

Dryvan - Also called "skin-walker" and "forest witch." Known as *"sach'aan"* to the Gasts. Among themselves, dryvans refer to themselves as "the Kin." Dryvans are shapeshifters. Though often possessing shapes approximately human, they are changed with attributes of animals and plants. Rarely seen, it is unknown what their disposition is toward humanity, for stories have been told of both boons and harms.

Epochs of Unera - According to the Catedrál, the first age of Unera was the Epoch of Sin, when all of humanity was mired in ignorance and transgressions. During that time, those with mahia were worshiped as gods, and all quailed at their power. Then, with the founding of the Catédral came the Epoch of Epiphany, the current age, which began with the miracles of the First Saint, Inhoa the Merciful. This is believed to be a time of civilization and virtue, when the truth of the Saints will be spread to the far corners of the world and all will be saved from their sins.

Esse - Also called "lifefire," "lifeforce," and "essence." Known as *"ilis"* to the Gasts. Esse is the vital life energy of a being. Invisible to most, those who possess mahia see it as bright life, often moving like flames throughout the body. Each individual possesses a unique esse, and those with an attuned enough lifesense may identify any being by it. Though mostly isolated to a being's body, mahia allows one to either draw it out of individuals or manipulate it to different effects.

Ferino - Translates literally to "feral" from Ilberian. A derogatory term used by Ilberians and Baltesians toward Gasts and other indigenous peoples.

Fesht - An expletive common in Baltesia referring to an aggressive sexual act. Thought to have originated from an indigenous tribe.

Gasts - Refer to themselves as "The Many Tribes." Though perceived by colonists as a cohesive group, Gasts entail various tribes bonded by cultural and spiritual beliefs held in common. During the colonization of the Veiled Lands, the Gasts resisted the Ancestral Lands, which led to the Titan War. Following their capitulation, the Gasts largely retreated to beyond the Silvertusk Sierra to the arid lands beyond the mountains called the Barren.

Ghosts - Called *"timili"* by Gasts. These ghosts are typically found in ancestral ruins and manifest as whispers and a lingering sense of esse.

Grotto - The Iritu term for a space outside of the ordinary world, created and sustained by magic.

The Hesh Jin - Also called "the Ocean Lord." Leader of Kalga.

Inheritance - The Iritu term for magic. Also "heritage," depending on the usage.

Lakti - The western cliff of Qasaar.

Legion - The force of evil to the Catedrál, opposing the good force of Omn and the Saints. Seen as a fragmented being with many faces on account of the tormented souls it has captured screaming for release. Some believe Legion manifests demons in Unera to serve his purposes. For some, titans and dryvans are a few of these demons, while others see them as natural manifestations akin to animals and plants.

The Lodgemaster - Leader of the Wilds Lodge, home to the rangers of Baltesia.

Lualli - The eastern cliff of Qasaar.

Mada - A familiar term meaning "mother" to Baltesians and Ilberians.

Mahia - Known as *"semah"* to the Gasts. Mahia is a magic of life and death, allowing its user to manipulate esse to various effects. These effects include healing, killing (by draining an individual of esse), and strengthening or energizing one's body. Mahia also seems to have something to do with titans, as the creatures appear to be at least partly magical in origin. While seen as having come from Omn by the Catedrál, it is also seen as a tool by which Legion could exploit human weakness and lead people into sin. The other Ancestral Lands have higher levels of tolerance, though most view it with distrust. Among the Tricolonies, these attitudes are often passed on, though more leniency has evolved.

Makayo - Translates to "Unity." The Gast afterlife, in which an individual merges with the world. The losing of oneself to the great whole of being is anticipated with eagerness.

The Moorwarden - Leader of the Greathouse, home to the plainsriders of Altan Gaz.

The Murmuring Canyon - A ravine near Qasaar where the stone is alive with spirits.

Odiosa - A witch hunter of the Catedrál. By virtue of possessing mahia, odiosas sense out those with magic and either recruit them to their cause or have them executed. It is unknown how people become indoctrinated as odiosas, though their odd temperaments allude to some sort of torturous process that addles the mind.

The Odisi - Also called "the Sky Queen." Leader of Eyi.

Omn - Also called "the Unknown" and "Omn Almighty." The god honored by the Catedrál. Most often depicted as a faceless, genderless orb of astral origin, similar to the sun and the moons, though distinct from both. Omn is believed to be the creator of all, including magic and titans.

Pada - A familiar term meaning "father" to Baltesians and Ilberians.

Plainsrider - A protector of the Tricolonies dwelling at the Greathouse in Altan Gaz. Akin to rangers and skystriders.

Ranger - A protector of the Tricolonies dwelling at the Wilds Lodge in Baltesia. Akin to plainsriders and skystriders.

The Ranger's Lament - An invocation spoken by a ranger after taking a life. Often spoken to alleviate guilt at the killing. The phrase is as follows: "Your spirit touches mine."

The Ranger's Oath - An oath taken by rangers at their cloaking ceremony, which they vow to uphold during their service. The oath is as follows: "Perceive. Preserve. Protect."

The Sacred Saints - The five individuals in Catedrál history who have Ascended from mortals into divine representatives of Omn. The Saints are seen as intermediaries between the faceless god and humanity, and interpret what is good and what is sinful. The Saints and their associated virtues are as follows:

San Hugo of Resolution and Equity
San Luciana of Sincerity and Candor
San Jadiel of Grace and Beauty
San Inhoa of Mercy and Quietus
San Carmen of Loyalty and Justice

Shaman - A magic wielder and religious leader of the Gasts. As those possessing mahia, shamans serve many vital functions within Gast society, including healing the sick and wounded, communing with the ancestors and the spirits of the world, and warding against titans. They are often highly educated and serve as advisors to chieftains. By benefit of magic, shamans have also historically been reservoirs of indigenous history. Unfortunately, if a shaman dies before they can pass this knowledge on, it is forever lost, a problem that became particularly difficult during the Titan War and was one factor that led to the Gasts' retreat.

Skystrider - A protector of the Tricolonies dwelling at the Stormhold in Ore-Ofe. Akin to plainsriders and rangers.

Taht - Meaning "father" or "mother," it is a respectful address for shamans.

Talisman - Also called *"periaptu"* by the Iritu. Items imbued with magic that produce various effects.

Tekuan - A Gast tribe with a reputation for being continued aggressors since the Titan War. Their name translates to "Jaguar" and their people are tattooed with this symbol.

The Ten Virtues - The ideals upheld by the Catedrál as being good and worthy of pursuit. All are associated with one of the Sacred Saints. The virtues are resolution, equity, sincerity, candor, grace, beauty, mercy, quietus, loyalty, and justice.

The Tetrad - The council of four chieftains that leads the Many Tribes of Qasaar.

Titan's awakening - The event when a titan first emerges from a natural body, such as a hill or river, and forms its body. It is believed titans may lie dormant in places for years before rising. Upon their awakening, those with magic perceived it as radiating very strongly from them, often so much so that it is impossible to resist their pull.

The Titan War - The war over the colonization of the Veiled Lands, fought between the Gasts and other indigenous peoples against those coming from the Ancestral Lands. After years of failed negotiations, the Gasts finally pushed back against the people invading their lands. Using magic, their shamans sent titans against the colonial settlements, devastating them and killing thousands. Though those possessing mahia from the Ancestral Lands did not know how to control titans, they used their magic against the shamans themselves, leading to the deaths of most of them. Following the loss of their shamans, the Gasts and other natives retreated beyond the Silvertusk Sierra to the lands known as the Barren. Only a few remained behind, and these were discriminated against, often to the point of violence.

Toa - Translates to "chief," the title given to a Gast chieftain.

The Uman - Another of the indigenous people of the Veiled Lands, and included in the Many Tribes.

Unera - Called *"Tlalli"* by the Gasts. Unera is the planet, the world at large.

The Veil - The misty boundary that separates the Veiled Lands from the Ancestral Lands. Once penetrated by a wisewoman from Kalga, it allowed for the conquest and colonization that followed.

Whisperspire - *Tepe'laka* in the Gast tongue; the tower where the Tetrad meets in Qasaar.

Wisewoman - A wielder of magic in Kalga and Altan Gaz.

BOOKS BY J.D.L. ROSELL

Sign up for future releases at jdlrosell.com.

RANGER OF THE TITAN WILDS

1. The Last Ranger

2. The First Ancestor

3. The Hidden Guardian

LEGEND OF TAL

1. A King's Bargain

2. A Queen's Command

3. An Emperor's Gamble

4. A God's Plea

THE RUNEWAR SAGA

1. The Throne of Ice & Ash

2. The Crown of Fire & Fury

3. The Stone of Iron & Omen

THE FAMINE CYCLE

1. Whispers of Ruin

2. Echoes of Chaos

3. Requiem of Silence

Secret Seller (Prequel)

The Phantom Heist (Novella)

<hr>

GODSLAYER RISING

1. Catalyst

2. Champion

3. Heretic

ACKNOWLEDGMENTS 5X8

A titanic round of thanks to the following people:

Kaitlyn, my wife and first reader, who prunes my bad ideas so readers aren't subjected to them!

Sarah Chorn, the eminent editor who always pushes my prose and stories further than I can do alone.

Félix Ortiz, the illustrious illustrator who creates such gorgeous covers and interior art.

Shawn T. King, the distinguished designer whose typography and framing elevates Félix's art to the next level.

Keir Scott-Schrueder, the monumental mapmaker who drew Unera by hand.

Shawn Sharrah, my paramount proofreader, for his keen-eyed catching of my errors.

My patrons on Patreon, for your above-and-beyond support: Debbie, Neil, Nick, Ben, Ruth & Tarris, Don, Tony, and Larry. That you care about my worlds so much means the world to me.

Julia, for always being a champion of this series.

And, of course, *all my beatific backers on Kickstarter*! Ranger of the Titan Wilds wouldn't be the same without your support. Thank you to all of the following people:

A. Buckner | AoeroZero | Alan Morgan | Alex G | Alex Luco
Alex Wrigglesworth | Alexander Bundt | Algie L. | AM
Amanda Dimmack | Amanda Trumpower | Amelia Armstrong
André Laude | Andrew Agnew | Andrew C | Andrew Claydon
Andrew Konicki | Andrew Wainwright | Andy F
Andy Peloquin | Angel Ocampo | Angelika | Anna Ostberg
Anthea Sharp | Anthony Briley | Ariane Sears | Arild Tvedt
Arthur Dixon | Ashley Brennan | Ashley Hagood | Astridd

Austin Hoffey | Austin S. Regan | B. Plaga | B. Zee | Bas de Beer
Benjamin Molina | Bentley Searing | Beowulf | Blake Strickland
Blumpsie | Boe Kelley | BoiledJellyfish | Boyd Atkinson
Bradley Hamm | Brandon J. Neal | Brandon Cleland | Brian H.
Brian Patton | Bridget C. | Bruce | C Taormina | C.Wilson
Caitlin Roberts | Calderon Medina family | Caleb Slama
Cameron Michaels | Carly W | Carol A. Park | Carson Brooks
Cassandra Baubie | Chad Bowden | Charli Maxwell
Chris Fisher | Chris Roeszler | Christa Rickard | Christian Bell
Christian Holt | Christian Kegley | Christian Meyer
Christiana Laudie | Christopher Boisvert | Christopher Colon
Christopher Froebe | CJ Skowronek | Clair Johnson | Clay Jones
CMT | Cody L. Allen | Collin Bartley | Connor Mayo
Connor Whiteley | Courtney Watkins | Crystal Palumbo
Cynthia M Coffman | Dan McLaughlin | Dan & Robert Zangari
Daniel Papke | Darren Fry | Dave Baughman
David Daughhetee | DBJ | Dead Fishie | Deborah Hedges
Debra Wilson | Dee Anna | Dexter Wilkinson | Diego H.
Dominik | Doug Erling | DramaDude1231D | Drew Gohmann
Duane Powell | Duncan Wilcox | Eduardo Soriano
Edward Maher | Elias Rondou | Elli Breakspear
Ellysa Hermanson | Em Sipprell | Emery Dueck
Ennead Comic | Eric Cotti | Eric G. | Eric Koenig | Eric Vilbert
Eron Wyngarde | Etienne C. | Fabian Way | Faelyn Curtis
Falk Gräpel | Floyd Weitzel | Gabriel Casillas
Gabrielle Duncan | Gage "oSpaceGhoat" Troy | Galen W Miller
Garret Castle | Gerald P. McDaniel | GhostCat
Giuseppe Centineo | Grace Bowes | Greg Tausch
Gregor PetekSLO | H. Deur | H.M. Clarke | Hank Nordic
Hayden Wilsey | Heather Harris | Heiko Koenig | Henry S.
Howard Blakeslee | Ian Rankine | J R Forst | J.A. Andrews
Jack Sayresmith | Jacob Battershell | Jacob H Joseph
James Kralik | James R McGinnis Jr | James Rao | Jamie Buckley
Jamie Dockendorff | Jamie Edmundson | Jan Birch
Jason Bowden | Jason D Martin | Jason Lovell | Jason R | Jason T
Java™ | Jay Johnson | Jeffrey M. Johnson | Jennifer Johnson

Jennings Family | Jeremiah Crouch | Jesse Trovato | Jessica Juby
Jezza | Joanna Davis | Joe Lee | Joe Rixman | Joel Kollander
Johannes Tuchscherer | John "AcesofDeath7" Mullens
John Gilligan | John Idlor | John Ladley | John Markley
John Shrek Walters | Johnny MacIsaac | Jon Auerbach
Jonathan Brown | Jonathan F | Joseph W. Aguiar | Josh Samples
Joshua Callahan | Joshua Oplinger | Judith Everett
Just David ¯_(ツ)_/¯ | Justin Greer | Justin Gross | K. C. Herbel
K. Hendrick | Kaleah Brewster | Karen M | Karis Rosell
Karl McGurty | Kars Reygent | Kate Kinley
Katherine Shipman | Katie Dresel | Katie Keith | Kaya
Keelyn Wright | Kendra Hooter | Kenneth Kauffman
Kerry Chorvat | Kim Garcia | Kindreth Silverwind
Kodie Caldwell | Kris Guthrie | Kris M | Krista Marx
Kristin Selzer | Kristopher Ecklof | Kurt Boulianne
Kyle G Wilkinson | Kyle Leubka | Kylie Wheatley | L. Haymond
Lahman Marcel | Lana @IndieAccords | Laura J | Lee Clark
Leniel Flores | Lia | Lia Casati | Lindsey Rubini | Lisa Maughan
Lord TBR | Lorenzo | Lorraine Bondi | M I
Maleesha Thompson | Malte Storm Boe | Margaret C. Beeler
Marie-Helene A. | Mark Espina | Mark Griffith | Mark H.
Mark Junk | Mary Satterfield | Matt King | Matt Knox
Matt Pfaff | Matthea W. Ross | Matthew Corbin
Matthew Mollo | Matthian | Max F. | Megyn MacDougall
Meredith Carstens | Michael B Mitchell | Michael DeCuypere
Michael Delaney | Michael Grovenburg | Michael H. Sugarman
Michael Hayes | Michael J. Sullivan, author | Michael Yeh
Michele Donahue | Michelle Cooper | Michelle S.
Miguel Fidalgo | Mike | Mike Welch | Mitchell McConnell
Monika Chmelková | Mustela | N. Scott Pearson | Nathan Jones
Nathan Klembara | Nathan Seaward | Nathan Turner | Neil
Nicholas Stodulski | Nick Becker | Nick Mandujano III
Nicola Wilkinson | Nicolas Lobotsky | Nicole Robinson
Niels Starfari | NightScribe | Officer Baby | Paden Cogswell
Paris Boschma | Paul B. | Peanut & Belle | Pedro Mendes
Pendleton Family | Peter Allen | Peter Younghusband

Pippin Took, the shire hobbit | PJK | polinchka | Ptahmet
Quinn G | Quintin W. | R. A. Morley | Raphael Bressel
RE Junker | Remington Cloutier | René Schultze | Rhona Santos
Rhianne R. | Richard Callanan | Richard Earl | Richard Fierce
Richard Libera | Richard Sayer | Robert A. DeFrank
Robert Barbour | Robert Brown | Robert C Flipse
Rochelle Moore | Rodriguez Saledor | RuinRuler | Russell Fisk
Ryan Buell | Ryan C. Reeves | Ryan Cahill | Ryan Hacala
Ryan Scott James | Samantha Landström
Samantha McClenaghan | Samantha Ranz | Samuel Barton
Sara Collins-Young | Sarah L. Stevenson | Sarah Nimmo
Sarah Phillips | Sarah S | Scott Casey | Scott Chisholm
Sean Conley | Señor Neo | Shane Heaton | Shannon Tusler
Shawn Sharrah | Stefke Leuhery | Stephen | Steve Locke
Steven "Waffles" Lane | Steven L Cowan | Steven Peiper
Sunny Side Up | T.Hise | T.L. Branson | ToM4H4WK_PR1ME
Tammy Dziuba | Tassilo | Taylor Haddock | Taylor Tudisco
The Frieling Family | Tiger Hebert | Tim Guyre | Tina Grim
Tom Dean | Ton Roongkham | Tonje Christoffersen | Tony
Tonya Henry | Tristan D. Morgan | Tyra Leann | Tyson Reyes
Vancil Thomas | Venita Pereira | Vickie Grider
Victoria Johnsen | Virgil Bower | Vulpecula | W.C. Austin
Walker Tuff | Will Rodd | William M. | Wizard Flight
Xiomara Reyes | Zeb Berryman

And, of course, thank you, dear reader. I appreciate you taking the time to read this book.

Josiah (J.D.L. Rosell)

ABOUT THE AUTHOR

J.D.L. Rosell is the author of Ranger of the Titan Wilds, Legend of Tal, The Runewar Saga, The Famine Cycle, and Godslayer Rising. He earned an MA in creative writing and dabbled in ghostwriting before committing full-time to creating his own worlds.

Always drawn to the outdoors, he often ventures out to indulge in hiking, archery, and photography. Most of the time, he can be found curled up with a delightful book at home with his wife and two cats, Zelda and Abenthy.

Follow along with his occasional author updates and serializations at www.jdlrosell.com or contact him at josiah@jdlrosell.com.

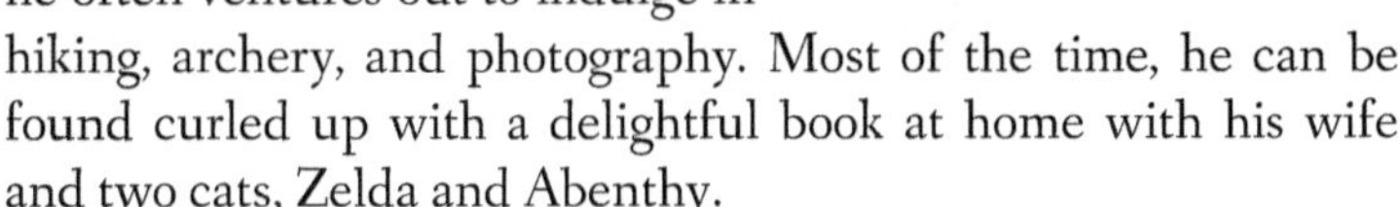